Praise for multiple award-winning author

CAROLYN HART
and
DEATH OF THE PARTY

"The queen of the traditional mystery in
America . . . Nobody does it better than Hart,
whose plotting skills rival those of Britain's
Agatha Christie."
Cleveland Plain Dealer

"Carolyn Hart's craftsmanship makes her
mystery's Queen of Cs—cozy, clever,
and chock full of charm."
Mary Daheim

"Hart provides plenty of suspects . . . then
plants intriguing clues, another murder, and
just enough red herrings to keep readers
guessing until the denouement. Those looking
for a change of pace from more street-smart
crime fiction will enjoy this cozy whodunit in
the Agatha Christie tradition."
Publishers Weekly

"Carolyn Hart is superb with
the amateur sleuth genre."
Green Bay Press-Gazette

"An expert at seamless storytelling."
Ft. Lauderdale Sun-Sentinel

"Carolyn Hart is a shining star
in the mystery galaxy."
Jackson Clarion-Ledger

Books by
Carolyn Hart

Death on Demand

DEAD DAYS OF SUMMER • DEATH OF THE PARTY
MURDER WALKS THE PLANK • ENGAGED TO DIE
APRIL FOOL DEAD • SUGARPLUM DEAD
WHITE ELEPHANT DEAD • YANKEE DOODLE DEAD
MINT JULEP MURDER • SOUTHERN GHOST
THE CHRISTIE CAPER • DEADLY VALENTINE
A LITTLE CLASS ON MURDER
HONEYMOON WITH MURDER • SOMETHING WICKED
DESIGN FOR MURDER • DEATH ON DEMAND

Henrie O

RESORT TO MURDER • DEATH ON THE RIVER WALK
DEATH IN PARADISE • DEATH IN LOVERS' LANE
SCANDAL IN FAIR HAVEN • DEAD MAN'S ISLAND

CAROLYN HART

DEATH
OF THE
PARTY

A DEATH ON DEMAND MYSTERY

AVON BOOKS
An Imprint of HarperCollinsPublishers

AVON BOOKS
An Imprint of HarperCollins*Publishers*
10 East 53rd Street
New York, New York 10022-5299

Copyright © 2005 by Carolyn Hart
Excerpt from *Dead Days of Summer* copyright © 2006 by Carolyn Hart
ISBN-13: 978-0-06-000477-4
ISBN-10: 0-06-000477-0
www.avonmystery.com

First Avon Books paperback printing: March 2006
First William Morrow hardcover printing: April 2005

Avon Trademark Reg. U.S. Pat. Off. and in Other Countries, Marca Registrada, Hecho en U.S.A.
HarperCollins ® is a registered trademark of HarperCollins Publishers Inc.

Printed in the U.S.A.

10 9 8 7 6 5 4 3

To my friends at the Library of Congress,
Dr. John Cole, Emily Howie, Dr. Stephen James, and
Abby Yochelson, in remembrance of a lovely day

DEATH
OF THE
PARTY

∿ *One* ∿

THE ROOM WASN'T MOVING. Britt Barlow held to that reality, no matter her dizziness. Yet the words in the letter blurred before her eyes.

Britt remembered a long-ago day in a small third-floor apartment in Mexico City, the rumble of wrenched walls, the swaying floor, the sweep of gut-sickening terror. She'd survived that earthquake, just as she'd survived divorce and loss and sadness and, once, a fury that had threatened to capsize her world.

Britt waited for that first shock to pass. She would survive. No matter what happened, she had always been a survivor. Earthquake, fire, flood, pestilence . . . Damn the world. She would fight this new threat as she'd always fought, with steely determination, with craft and guile, with a devil-be-damned smile.

The words in the letter came back into focus. ". . . I saw you that morning . . . understand the estate is settled . . . perhaps we could have a little talk about financial matters. . . ."

Britt felt hot and sick. She glanced at the mirror above the fireplace. Other than the bright flush on her narrow cheeks, she looked much as she had when she finished dressing this morning, the vermilion sweater a vivid contrast to cream wool slacks. She stared at her image as if appraising a stranger: glossy black curls, clover green eyes, a restless look of expectancy. With a twisting pang of incipient loss, she remembered Loomis's words to her just before he left the island last week. "I love your face, Britt. You have"—he'd paused, searched for his thought, brought it out with a triumphant grin—"the face of adventure. That's the kind of woman I've always written about. I made you up long before I met you. I didn't think you existed. Now I know you do. It has to be us, Britt. The two of us together." He'd kissed her, a kiss that held a promise of indescribable joy. "I'll be back. Count on it." Loomis was the late love of a life that had known so much loss. She'd never again expected to thrill when a man walked into her room. She loved the way he looked, the way he walked, the way he talked, his brilliance, his wry humor, his innate kindness.

She crumpled the letter, shoved it into the pocket of her slacks, folded her arms, began to pace. All right. The truth was going to come out. Jeremiah Addison had been murdered. Until now she'd pushed away all memory of that moment when she'd stood at the top of the staircase and looked down at the crumpled body lying at the base of the white marble steps, blood slowly pooling beneath his battered head. The downstairs hallway light had illumined death in a pool of brightness. She'd stared for a long moment, poised to hurry down if there was any sign of life. But death was obvious in the rag-doll limpness of his limbs, the awkward crook of his neck. Jeremiah Addison had not survived his plunge down the steep stone steps. It would have been a miracle had he survived that head-first fall. He'd always considered himself a miracle man, but his luck had finally run out.

She'd pulled her gaze away, knowing that no one could help Jeremiah now. She'd looked instead at the taut shiny wire stretched ankle high from the wall to a baluster. Why hadn't he glimpsed the wire? The answer was easy and such a commentary on the man. Jeremiah expected the world and everything in it to give way before him. He always strode forward at top speed, his long legs moving fast. He was Jeremiah Addison and the world waited on him. He didn't look down. He always looked ahead, focused on the next encounter, the next objective, the next triumph. He'd plunged fast down the steps and the wire had snagged him, flung him headfirst to his death.

Britt felt the wad of the crumpled letter in her pocket. Jeremiah had been dead for a year and a half. Now she had to remember everything that had happened and accept the fact that she'd been observed that silent summer morning. She continued to pace, though her breath came quickly and her chest ached.

She could have made a different choice when she stood there at the top of the stairs. If she'd screamed, some of the staff downstairs would have come running. The truth would have been there to see, Jeremiah dead and the means of his death apparent.

Murder. The word was harsh but no harsher than the reality. An investigation would have been launched. Everyone on the island, the very private and isolated South Carolina sea island of Golden Silk, would have been caught up in a homicide investigation. Oh, there were plenty of suspects, each with a burning reason to do away with rich, powerful, arrogant Jeremiah Addison.

Including herself, of course. Everyone knew she hated Jeremiah. He'd barely tolerated her presence on the island even though she was a great help with Cissy.

She could have screamed when she found him dead. She had not. Instead, with scarcely a moment's pause, she'd drawn a deep, steadying breath and whirled to run down the hallway to a bathroom. She'd grabbed a washcloth, raced lightly back to the stairway, listening all the while for a door to open, footsteps, a cry of horror, but the hallway remained silent.

Silent as a grave.

She'd worked fast in the early morning stillness, pulling out the nail from the wall, unfastening the thin but formidable strand from the baluster, checking to see if the telltale hole was obvious, grateful when the speck in the wall was easily covered by a fleck of lint from the carpet. She'd mashed the wire into a lump, put the coil and the nail in the pocket of her robe, and fled down the hall to her room. She'd waited there until a maid's shout brought them all tumbling from their rooms.

Everyone said, "What a terrible accident."

She'd been glad to leave it at that. Because she had to take care of Cissy. It wasn't until after Jeremiah's funeral that she'd truly believed the chapter finished. In fact, she'd rarely thought about Jeremiah's death through the next harrowing months as Cissy weakened, the cancer ferocious and unrelenting. Finally, Cissy slipped away, leaving Britt numb and exhausted. Cissy had inherited Golden Silk as part of her portion of Jeremiah's estate. That had been included in the prenuptial agreement when Cissy became his second wife. With Cissy's death, the island belonged to Britt. Golden Silk became Britt's haven and joy. She'd not spared an instant recalling Jeremiah and how he'd died.

Now she would have to remember every detail about Jeremiah and those who were there that fateful day. Thoughts fluttered through her mind. She walked more slowly, finally came to a stop, leaned her head against the cool white mantel.

Her fingers curled around the paper in her pocket.

Not much time passed, but time enough. Britt lifted her head. Her green eyes glinted. Her features molded into a mask of determination. It was always better to let sleeping dogs lie, but she had no choice. Oh, yes, she could make an arrangement with the letter writer— or to be clear about it, pay blackmail. If she paid off, that would be accepted as an admission of guilt and she would evermore be at the mercy of that silent observer. She had no intention of taking responsibility for Jeremiah's death. Behind her scheming and hoping and figuring, there was Loomis with his thin, kindly face, erudite, surprising, caring. He was worth fighting for. They could build a wonderful life together, but not if she had to look over her shoulder, and worry and wonder what might happen.

Abruptly, she laughed. She loved to take chances. She always bet on the red. Maybe her penchant for gambling had prepared her for this moment. Now she would take the biggest gamble of her life. The only way to save herself was to trap a murderer, serve the accused up on a silver platter to the police.

But how?

Dana Addison kept putting off the moment. But finally, the children were asleep. This was their time, hers and Jay's, the golden moment of peace at the end of the day. They usually relaxed against the softness of the tartan plaid sofa, his arm crooked comfortably around her shoulders, the chatter of the television a familiar accompaniment as they talked.

She stopped in the doorway of the family room. It was a haven of happiness against whatever happened in the world. She wanted to cling to the moment but she had no choice. She had to tell him.

Jay looked up, a smile lighting his sensitive face. She was swept by tenderness. She loved everything about him, his bigness, his gentleness, the way he impatiently brushed back the tangle of brown hair that stubbornly drooped into his face. He was doing so much better. It seemed to her that he was more confident every day, that he stood straighter, looked at the world more directly. He'd been so beaten down by his father. Jeremiah had been cruel and unrelenting in his disdain for his youngest son.

"Dana." Jay pushed up from the sofa, strode toward her, his face concerned. "What's wrong?"

She felt the hot burn of tears. He knew, of course. He always knew when she was upset.

"Teddy? Alice?" His eyes jerked toward the stairs.

"They're fine." She took a deep breath. "They're asleep. Oh, Jay, it's about your mother."

"Mama?" There was an echo of a little boy in his voice.

Dana reached out, gripped his hands. "I heard from Britt Barlow today."

He frowned, puzzled, uncertain. But not worried. Not defensive. Not yet.

Dana talked fast, wanting to get the words out, get past the pain she knew would come. "She's invited us to Heron House." His hands were suddenly rigid in hers. "She was doing some remodeling in the Meadowlark Room. You know she's turned the house into a bed-and-breakfast and named all the rooms. The Meadowlark Room—" She broke off at the terrible stillness of his face.

"Mother's room?" His voice was uneven.

Dana wanted to shout and cry, wrap her arms around him, push away the world and its awful weight. "Britt found some kind of note in that room. It has directions to a hidden spot. She doesn't know whether she should explore. She thinks the writing is your mother's. . . ."

The Honorable Millicent McRae did not have pleasant memories of Heron House, the exquisite South Carolina sea island plantation that had served as a showcase for Jeremiah Addison. Her last visit, hers and Nick's, had been in response to a summons from Jeremiah. There was no reason to sugarcoat the truth. She had received an invitation she could not refuse. Jeremiah had said only a few words in that telephone conversation, but enough for her to realize that she was in his power.

So she and Nick had come. Now she had another invitation. But this one . . .

Dear Representative McRae,

There have been hints in the newspapers in recent weeks that you are considering a run for governor. Since Heron House has often served as a backdrop in state history, I hope you will welcome an opportunity to meet with many who are excited about your future. Financial support can often make the difference between success and failure in politics.

As you may know, Heron House is now a resort with elegant rooms available in the main house as well as the accommodations in the private cottages. You and your husband, of course, will be honored guests.

This special weekend is planned for the second weekend in January. I will be pleased if you can accept. I've enclosed an envelope for your convenience.

Very truly yours,
Britt Barlow

Heron House
Golden Silk Island, South Carolina

Financial support . . . Millicent relished the delicacy. So there were some people—she wondered who they might be—who saw her as a winner and wanted to establish rapport. Money talked. Of course, it always demanded an answer. That was the reality of politics.

Give and take. If the well heeled took the most, who was she to fight the system? Because there was no other way to win. She was determined always to win.

Golden Silk. She'd hated the island. Jeremiah could have ruined her. But he couldn't hurt her now.

Millicent picked up her Mont Blanc pen, scrawled an acceptance, placed the card within the stamped envelope. She felt the same eagerness that suffuses a big-game hunter as the safari begins.

The office was enormous, stretching the width of the narrow building, with banks of windows all around. In a steady drizzle, downtown Atlanta was hazy and ill defined, a poorly done Impressionist painting sans color. Usually when he stepped into the room, Gerald Gamble saw his reflection in the panes and the movement would catch Craig's attention. Not today. There was nothing but dull grayness and Craig Addison hunched over the keyboard, powerful fingers thumping the keys.

Gerald loved watching Craig at work. It was not a pleasure he could voice or share. No one would understand. Or a listener would see what wasn't there instead of what was. Yes, Gerald was a company man. He'd worked for Jeremiah Addison for almost thirty years, and always kept his mouth shut. He'd seen the empire grow from a half dozen small newspapers in the South to almost forty across the nation as well as television stations and, lately, magazines and book publishers. Addison Media was a name known and feared by industrialists, brokers, politicians, and others in the business. Gerald had always done his best for the company. But he'd not realized how angry he'd been with Jeremiah until he was dead.

Craig Addison's blond hair shone in the light from the lamp. He wore his hair short but nothing tamped down the tight curls he deplored. His white shirt had begun the day crisp but now was wrinkled, with the sleeves rolled to his forearms. Even a back view spoke to Craig's strengths, his solid athletic appearance, his determination. His focus.

Gerald took an instant longer to savor the moment, Craig in his element, in charge, and likely lifting his lance to tilt at windmills that his father had ignored. Jeremiah had believed in no cause but his own. Craig was a foot soldier for the downtrodden.

Gerald marveled at the difference made by one man's death. Though he and Craig had joined in praise of Jeremiah Addison at the memorial service and on several occasions since, Gerald knew he would have been resentful had he been Craig. Enough, he would have said. It was almost as though Craig felt he owed a debt to his father, more than the fact of his inheritance. Gerald felt a quiver of uneasiness. But perhaps this time Craig would decline the opportunity to attend a dedication in Jeremiah's memory.

Isabel Addison impatiently pushed back a strand of silky dark hair. She'd made her bed. She must lie in it. Bed . . . Why had her mind tossed up those trite words, so trite, so terribly dreadfully true? That was the problem with platitudes. They sprang from a bedrock of reality. Yes, she'd made her bed and it was a cold and lonely place.

Craig. Oh, Craig . . .

There were no pictures of him in her apartment. She'd been determined to leave that life behind, start over. But she didn't need a picture to remember his short-cropped golden curls, his irrepressible gaiety, his quickness and enduring charm. The handsomest man she'd ever known. The only man she'd ever loved. She still loved him, wanted him, missed him, even though she was afraid that his temper, wild and hot and quick, had got the best of him, made him a murderer. She would have stood by him if he'd owned up. But he'd not said a word and yet he'd looked so terribly grim and shaken.

She'd left after Jeremiah's funeral. In her note she'd said only that she couldn't stay, not after the way he and his father's quarrel ended. She hadn't returned Craig's calls. They'd finally stopped.

Craig was sure to be at Heron House. He wouldn't turn down a ceremony in Jeremiah's honor.

If she went . . .

Kim Kennedy clicked off the television. She held the remote so tight her hand hurt. She wanted to fling it at the dull gray screen. Instead, using every ounce of will she possessed, which was considerable, she gently put down the remote. She picked up a pillow and punched it with her fist, every blow aimed at those bland, cosmetically enhanced faces on the news desk where once she'd been. She pounded until the fury lessened. She forced tight angry lines from her face and realized with another spurt of anger that she was rehearing in her mind the producer's snide comment: *She's just a pretty face.* She'd proved him wrong. She'd done a good job. A damn good job. At first they'd laughed at her in the newsroom, called her Jerry's babe. Not that they would have dared call Jeremiah Jerry to his face. They'd stopped laughing and started to treat her with care when the word got around that she was slated to be the next Mrs. Jeremiah Addison. You can't say they lack for brains in a newsroom. She'd made sure they got the picture damn quick. She'd had plans for that producer. If everything had worked out, she'd have gotten his ass fired. If everything had worked out the way she had planned . . .

But she did not become the next Mrs. Addison. And she'd been fired two weeks after Jeremiah's death. It was that producer. He didn't care that she'd done a good job. He was still furious he'd had to hire her because of Jeremiah. Now the best she could get was a podunk job on a podunk station downstate. Everybody knew you had to know somebody to get anywhere even if you had looks and brains. Maybe she should go back to school, get her degree. And pile up student loans like a mountain of boulders?

It was too bad she'd spent most of the money Jeremiah had given her. For a little while, she'd had plenty of money. For the first time in her life, she'd been able to buy anything she wanted—an Ecclissi watch, a Fendi purse, a Ruth Norman gown. The watch cost a thousand dollars and that damn pawnbroker only gave her seventy-five.

Now the money was almost gone. It had seemed a fortune at the time. Twenty thousand dollars. There'd been no reason to save. She had been confident he would marry her. She would have gotten round him, she was positive.

She glanced toward the coffee table, piled high with unpaid bills and fashion magazines. The letter from Britt Barlow inviting her to Golden Silk was lying atop a copy of *Elle*. Kim's lips closed into a thin tight line. The island should belong to her. She'd been certain he would marry her. If he had, she would be rich, rich, rich. Instead, Britt Barlow got the island when Cissy died. That would certainly have pissed Jeremiah. Now Britt was parceling out Jeremiah's things. She'd treated Kim like dirt that last week. Why now would she offer Kim anything?

Kim's eyes narrowed. The offer was there in black and white. Kim could come and pick whatever she chose from the drawing room as a remembrance of Jeremiah.

The letter didn't ring true.

She got up, began to walk up and down the shabby room. There was, certainly, no love lost between her and Britt Barlow. From what she recalled of Jeremiah's sister-in-law, Britt was one tough cookie. Not a lady to go all soft and fuzzy. Not someone to give a bloody damn about Kim Kennedy, now or ever.

Why did she want Kim to come to that godforsaken place?

Kim's eyes glowed. There had to be a reason. Britt wanted something, that was for sure. Kim twined a golden curl around one finger. Going back to Golden Silk had all the appeal of a bus ride to a pig farm. But sometimes one thing led to another. Britt was probably in contact with the Addison family. Maybe she could set it up for Kim to get a job on one of the California TV stations. And she'd damn sure hold Britt to the offer in the letter. Those silver candlesticks on the drawing room mantel had to be worth a minimum of ten thou.

Kim laughed aloud. Something big was going to happen. She felt it in her bones.

Everett Crenshaw marked off the January weekend on his calendar. His thin lips curled in a sardonic yet admiring smile. Since he was alone in his *study*—God, what a lovely, upper-class appellation and one he'd earned the damn hard way, not being brought up to riches—he could indulge himself. Ever since a long-ago editor had told him, "Everett, that cat-in-the-cream grin of yours is a tip-off even to a patsy that you're a swine," he'd learned to hide triumph. The better, he knew, to blindside a quarry. He'd charmed and cajoled and, when the time was ripe, cudgeled the information he needed to become a feared investigative reporter. But sometimes the stories lent themselves to discretion, which resulted in a hefty infusion into Everett's bank account. He always enjoyed making out his income tax. Those substantial sums were easily attributed to poker wins. He had no intention of getting crossways with the Feds.

The smile slid away as he remembered his last encounter with Jeremiah Addison. How the hell had Jeremiah learned about the Venture Inc. story? Or what should have been the Venture Inc. story, an exposé of the CFO of a shipping company who'd disguised contraband shipments to Liberia. Jeremiah had been supercilious and dismissive and, most galling, sanctimonious when everyone knew the man had the instincts and morals of a pirate. For an instant, Everett's narrow face had a look of animal cunning, a fox with head lifted, staring at a lamb. Jeremiah had made it clear that Everett was through at Addison Media. That was Friday night. On Saturday morning no one knew about that conversation but Everett and Jeremiah, and Jeremiah was dead.

"'Humpty Dumpty had a great fall . . .'" Everett quoted softly.

Everett laughed aloud, finished marking the calendar. He was looking forward to the weekend at Heron House. Britt Barlow had class. She definitely had class. Her letter had certainly surprised him. And amused him. Britt as Jeremiah's avenger was ironic indeed. Deliciously ironic. Whatever happened, he was sure to win and win big. Either a carload of cash or a big story. Sure, he'd show up. Hell, why not? He had nothing to lose.

"She just walked past again." Barb's hiss was right on a par with that of a perturbed cobra.

"Yeah, yeah, yeah." Max Darling's good-natured tone, somewhat muffled by the magazine draped over his face, robbed the retort of offense. Max pictured his secretary lurking—perhaps it wasn't a good thing for Barb to read the reissued Mary Stewart suspense novels—in his office doorway, her vivid imagination imbuing some apparently confused passerby on the boardwalk with who knew what romantic troubles.

Max wasn't tempted to lift the *Sports Weekly* from his face. Not that he was napping. Of course not. He was simply pondering fate. That's what he would tell Annie should she find him supine upon his lowered office chair. Annie was the world's best—and sexiest—wife, but she was all for encouraging work. Distracted, he envisioned the love of his life—flyaway blond hair, merry gray eyes, kissable lips. Very kissable lips. Oh yes, work. Annie believed in work. She insisted work was fun. She considered herself, as owner of the Death on Demand mystery bookstore on the idyllic sea island of Broward's Rock, South Carolina, to be the world's most fortunate entrepreneur. She encouraged Max to follow her example. Would she consider pondering fate to be work? He could ponder fate with the best of them. It was his duty, wasn't it? Especially since his mother was at the moment far afield. It was clearly his responsibility to uphold the family tradition of creative—how did Laurel put it?—imaging. But no matter how creative he felt, he doubted he could—with a straight face—envision a Mary Stewart–type heroine flinging herself into his office seeking help. Although he was sure that Confidential Commissions, his very original and unusual business, would surely have appealed to such a heroine had she the good fortune to come across the ad that appeared daily in the *Island Gazette:*

CONFIDENTIAL COMMISSIONS
17 Harbor Walk
Curious, troubled, problems?
Ask Max.
Call Today—321-HELP

Excitement lifted Barb's voice. "She's sidling up to the window again. She's cupped her hands to look inside. Black hair. Reminds me of an old Leslie Caron movie. Maybe thirty. Snazzy outfit. Ohmigod—" Barb went from a hiss to a yelp.

Max lifted the tabloid high enough to see his secretary plaster herself against the wall, crane to peer out into the anteroom. Barb was an unlikely figure for melodrama—blond bouffant hair, dangling turquoise earrings, pink wool sweater encrusted with fake pearls, too-tight black slacks, four-inch stiletto heels. Red stiletto heels. Annie always said Barb would have been a natural for one of Craig Rice's John J. Malone novels and likely would have distracted the portly detective from his bottle of rye. Max felt a stirring of concern. Obviously Barb was in need of a respite from Confidential Commissions. Maybe he should send her up the boardwalk to the bookstore. Annie could use some help unpacking boxes of new books. Barb, in fact, was losing it. Was this the natural consequence of nothing to do in the office compounded by reading thrillers? The woman at the window was probably looking inside to see if there were island maps. Clearly, she had lost her way. The likelihood that she was coming to see Max—

"Ohmigod. She's coming in. And you ought to see her face. She's scared to death!" There was a rat-a-tat of heels as Barb pelted into the anteroom toward her desk.

By the time Barb greeted their guest, Max was in place behind his desk, a massive Renaissance refectory table, studiously perusing a file. That the folder held only the *Sports Weekly* was neither here nor there. Max forgot about the upcoming Super Bowl as he stared in admiration at the woman following Barb into his office. Mmm and mmm and mmm. He was a happily married man but he wasn't dead, and he took a moment to enjoy an intriguing face beneath a mop of wind-stirred dark curls and a lithe and extremely attractive figure. Here came a woman guaranteed to catch the eye of any man under eighty. Make that ninety.

Max slapped shut the file, rose. It was easy to smile. He remembered Annie's injunction to pay attention to details as did all good detectives. A stylish mass of black curls, damp from the January mist. Clear green eyes with a look of uncertainty. Fear? Yes, it could be. A high forehead, thin nose, sharp cheekbones, dark red mouth, an intelligent, arresting, unusual face. A trim five foot seven. Her pale blue cardigan, matched pearls, and swirling gray wool skirt were attractive, new, and expensive. But she carried with her into the room a tenseness that drove the smile from his face.

Barb made the introductions. "Ms. Barlow to see you." Barb backed toward the door, absorbing every aspect of the visitor. Barb left the door ajar just a trifle. Max knew she stood on the other side with one ear pressed to the opening, hoping, of course, for a Real Case, stolen jewels or a missing lover or menacing calls in the still of the night. He made a mental note to bring Barb the new Jan Karon book. It was time to redirect Barb's thoughts. Father Tim was a perfect antidote for too many thrillers.

Max came around the desk. "Hello, Ms. Barlow. I'm Max Darling."

"I know. I looked you up on the Net. Your Web page says you'll find the answer to any question." Her eyes—worried, uncertain eyes—skimmed his face, glanced swiftly about the office. The ornately carved refectory table held the single file on its shining expanse along with a studio portrait of a smiling Annie, a green-shaded brass lamp, a silver letter opener, and a crystal bowl with a mound of foil-wrapped chocolate kisses. A red leather recliner, now upright, sat behind the desk. Two petit point chairs faced the desk. A collection of putters poked out of an oversized green pottery stand. The indoor putting green—a birthday gift from Annie—was innocent of balls. There were a half dozen in the silver chest atop the bookcase against the far wall.

His visitor's gaze settled on him with a gravely inquiring look.

Max folded his arms, raised an eyebrow. "Do I pass muster?"

"I don't know." Her voice was crisp, but her gaze was forlorn. "Oh, heavens. I'm terribly confused. I'm in trouble, but I don't know if you can help. I don't know if anyone can help. It's too late to change my plans. They're all coming back to the island. I'll have to tell you"—there was a wry pride in her voice—"how I tricked them. They're all coming, every last one of them. They arrive Friday. But I couldn't sleep last night. I woke up in a panic." Her gaze was wide and staring. "How would you feel if you knew you'd invited a murderer to your home?" There was a tremor in her voice.

For an instant, Max wondered if he'd entered an alternate universe. Or if this attractive woman was mentally disturbed. One look into steady green eyes and he knew he was dealing with intelligence, acuity, and scarcely controlled fear. "I'd be worried. What makes you think a prospective guest is a murderer?" He heard the reserve in his voice.

She gave a short, desperate laugh. "I'm not mad. It isn't a matter of supposition. I know one of them's a murderer. Please, will you let me tell you?"

Max gestured toward the nearer chair. "Of course." He could imagine Barb's intense excitement as she clung to the other side of the door. However, he wasn't in the habit of believing six impossible things before breakfast. Or after. But maybe he could be of some service. . . .

His visitor sat, face ridged with strain, back ramrod straight, and placed her handbag in her lap, fingers tight around the strap.

Max took the other chair, turned it to face her. They were so near, he could see the fine pencil line artfully used to enhance her truly remarkable eyes and the tiny hint of a mole at the corner of her carmine lips.

She took a deep breath. "Mr. Darling, I'm afraid I've been a fool. But I didn't know what else to do."

"You have guests coming. You believe one of them is a murderer?" The words sounded absurd and unreal, but he knew this woman believed it.

"I know one of them is a murderer." The words were measured, implacable.

Max reached over to his desk, picked up a legal pad and pen. "Who was killed?"

Those shadowed eyes met his gaze. "Jeremiah Addison." She looked at him, waited. "On Golden Silk."

Max felt a quiver of shock. He knew Addison's name. Addison had died more than a year ago. Wasn't it an accident of some sort? Some names are part of popular culture and that was true of Jeremiah Addison. His amazing wealth in newspapers, television stations, and magazines put him on a par with Ted Turner or Rupert Murdoch. And, of course, everyone along the coast was aware of Golden Silk, the private sea island owned by Addison. The interest was prompted as much by his selection of the name as the island itself. Private islands, many of them tiny and uninhabited, were not unusual. In fact, there was no firm accounting of the number of small islands along the coast of South Carolina, and a study was under way to list them all. Addison had named his island after the Golden Silk, an orb-weaving spider with a gold body and legs, which creates such a sturdy web in the woods that small birds can be trapped. Addison's remote island with its restored plantation house and newly built cabins, each in its own cluster of pines, had been featured in a glossy architectural magazine. A diesel-powered generator provided electricity. The article's title had been "Welcome to My Web, Said . . ."

"Golden Silk now belongs to me. I've turned it into a resort. The house is a B&B. There are eight cabins, each one quite separate and private. I'm getting established. Lots of people want to come somewhere and be cut off from the world. We're only forty-five minutes from the mainland, but once you arrive on the island, it's a world unto itself. Cell phones don't work. No fax.

No contact with the outside. There's a boat that brings everyone over on a Friday and it doesn't come back until the following Friday. People love it." There was a flash of pride and enthusiasm.

"You inherited Golden Silk from Jeremiah Addison?" Max was bland, keeping disappointment out of his voice. She didn't look like the kind of woman to be a rich man's mistress, but there were plenty of stories like that about Addison. And she'd given her name as Ms. Barlow. Not Mrs. Addison.

Her laughter was ragged. And unamused. "Not likely. He'd rather have seen me in hell, actually. Jeremiah and I—well, let's say we didn't care for each other. No, my sister Cissy was his wife. His second wife. Cissy . . ." There was an instant when her head bent and her lips were tight together. She took a breath, then looked at Max. "Cissy died last January. Six months after Jeremiah. The island and everything on it and a third of his entire estate came to her. And now, to me. That's not why I'm here. I'm here because Jeremiah fell down the main stairs that Saturday morning. I was up early. I heard a thump. I went out in the hall and listened. It was absolutely quiet. But I knew something was wrong. I went down the hall and that's when I saw him at the foot of the stairs. I could see from the way he was lying that his neck was broken. It was ugly. His head was battered from the fall. . . . I stood there and stared. I thought about going down to be certain he was dead. But I was sure. Then I saw why he'd fallen. There was a wire across the second step. Ankle high. It ran from a baluster to a nail in the wall." Her head lifted. Her gaze was determined. "Jeremiah had been murdered." She folded her arms across her chest, spoke dispassionately as if describing the actions of a stranger. "I got a cloth from the nearest bath, used it to loosen the wire. I put the wire and the nail in my pocket."

Max wrote quickly, all the while thinking that every word had a ring of truth. This was what she'd seen. This was what she'd done. His skepticism melted like snow in a hot sun. There was no disbelieving this grim recital of actions, culpable actions.

He looked at her hard face. "Why?" She was still an attractive woman, but he saw the coldness in her eyes, the set of her jaw.

"Cissy was sick. Terribly sick. Cancer. Treatments. She could barely cope. And now Jeremiah was dead. She adored him. His death was going to be a horrible shock. She couldn't handle anything more. Murder?" She shook her head with finality. "You know what?" Her tone was fierce. "I'm glad I did it. Cissy grieved but she didn't have to look at the people who were there—and she was fond of some of them—and wonder which face hid murder."

Max sketched a face with staring eyes. "You broke the law."

"Yes." She was decisive. "That's why I've come here."

Max's eyebrows rose. "I can't help you there, Ms. Barlow—"

"Please. Call me Britt. Everyone does." Her grave look was an appeal.

"Britt." He liked the sound of her name: crisp, fresh, different. "I suggest you contact an attorney."

"I'm not worried about that. Oh, I know." She shrugged. "I suppose I'll be in trouble. Maybe a lot of trouble. I guess"—her tone was thoughtful—"they could put me in jail. That doesn't matter. What matters is finding out who killed Jeremiah. I've thought and thought. I could go to the police, tell them what I've told you. Maybe they'd listen. Maybe they wouldn't. But what could they do?"

Max drew a massive question mark, decorated it with handcuffs. "If your report was taken seriously, a detective would interview everyone who was on the island at the time." But there was no physical evidence available now. Unless someone had seen something that would be meaningful once murder was suspected, the trail was cold. Still . . . "I recommend contacting the sheriff's department."

"No." It was a simple declaration. And final. "If someone—a detective—came to see them, they'd be warned. Oh, I've thought it all over. And here's what I want to do . . ." She leaned forward, her green eyes intent.

Annie Laurance Darling had the bookstore to herself. Well, she and Agatha and hundreds of her friends. That's how she thought of mystery authors. Her friends. After all, friends give to each other, and the wonderful writers had given her a lifetime of pleasure. Thanks to them, she'd detected from Atlanta to Zanzibar, all from the comfort of her easy chair.

Annie bent down, picked up the sleek black cat, draped her over one shoulder, sauntered down the central corridor toward the coffee bar. A fire crackled in the fireplace. The South Carolina sea island of Broward's Rock, home to the best mystery bookstore east of Atlanta, was never truly cold enough to need a wood fire. But there were nippy days in January when a fire was welcome and always cheerful.

Annie hesitated near the coffee bar. She should march straight back to the storeroom and open that latest box of Sister Carol Anne O'Marie titles. She had some returns to pack, orders to place. . . . She veered behind the coffee bar.

Agatha wriggled free, landing lightly atop the counter. The elegant black cat lifted a paw, licked, swiped at her cheek.

Annie smiled in contentment. Yes, Agatha should be removed at once from the countertop. But hey, she and her cat were alone in the store. So far as she knew, all health department officials were busy elsewhere. "Why not?" she demanded of Agatha.

Inscrutable golden eyes seemed to blink assent.

"Besides," Annie valued truth, "you'd bite me if I tried to move you."

Annie studied the mirrored wall behind the coffee bar, which held almost a hundred white pottery mugs, each inscribed in red script with the name of a famous mystery and the author. Annie started the cappuccino machine, took her time selecting a mug. She wanted the perfect one—the bon mot of titles. After all, this was a special day. There were no To Do lists in regard to the wedding because, of course, the wedding was over and a grand and happy success. Her father and his new bride were en route to Tahiti for several weeks. Pudge and Sylvia were now Mr. and Mrs. Laurance.

The wedding—last Saturday—had been blessed with a sparkling day, white clouds scudding in a robin's-egg-blue sky, the temperature a mild sixty. That was a bonus in the South. Even in January there were blessed days of warmth. After the reception, the assembled guests cheered and clapped as the bride threw her bouquet of pink and white carnations to the very surprised but pleased bachelor minister. The smiling faces included both Rachel Van Meer and Cole Crandall, who were now stepsister and stepbrother. At one time, the two teenagers had been anything but friendly. . . . But that was another story and well in the past. In fact, the two of them were now in Hawaii visiting Rachel's aunt. Pudge had insisted they too have a grand trip even if it meant missing a week of school. Last night Rachel and Cole had sent Annie and Max an e-mail detailing the excitement of their visit. Mmmm, Kauai.

The cappuccino machine bubbled. She yanked down a mug inscribed *Too Good to Be True,* shoved it beneath the spigot, admired the frothy milk. She carried the mug around the counter, perched on a tall stool. Oh, to be in Tahiti . . . That sounded especially glorious now because, of course, the capricious coastal weather had decided to remind everyone that, after all, it was January. Three days of rain had left the island sodden and the air colder than a wet sock. Golly, it would be nice to be on a fun trip.

"Where would you like to go?" she asked Agatha.

Agatha's green eyes slitted.

"We don't have anything planned," Annie said hastily. Agatha never approved of their travels.

Agatha rolled over onto her back, stretched.

"My goodness, even you are charming today. Not," Annie added hastily, "that I ever find you deficient in charm." It was Max who called Agatha the Lethal Lady, insisting the coal black feline must surely have been Lucretia Borgia in another incarnation. "You know what, Agatha," Annie confided, sipping the delicious coffee and milk, "things simply couldn't be better. Except for the weather." She smoothed a finger over the ridged red letters of the title. "Although it's kind of lonely with everybody gone." Everybody on the island wasn't gone, of course, though it almost seemed like it with Pudge and Sylvia in Tahiti, Rachel and Cole on Kauai, and Max's mother, Laurel, visiting Max's sister Jen in Monterey. Henny Brawley, who was by far the bookstore's best customer, was traveling with an old friend in England; Emma Clyde, redoubtable island author, was on a book tour in the Far West; and Ingrid Webb, Death on Demand's fine clerk, was in Chicago with her husband, Duane. "It's you and me, kid," Annie told Agatha. It was the slow time of the year. Damp January days weren't a tourist draw, so the occasional customers, almost sure to be locals, would receive a royal welcome.

Annie lifted the mug, turned a little to view the paintings above the fireplace. Every month she hung five watercolors. Each represented a scene from a superb mystery. The first person to identify all five books and authors received free coffee for a month.

In the first watercolor, two young men wearing dark wedding suits slashed with the long pig-butchering knives. Their strong wrists poked and thrust the knives into their victim, who was young and slim with curly dark hair. Blood spattered his white linen shirt and trousers. The dying man struggled to open the ornate front door. In the square behind him the almond trees were snowy in the light of dawn, colored wedding decorations hanging in their branches.

In the second watercolor, the body lay face up on the icy cold floor of a freezer, eyes wide in final surprise, his thin mustache frozen stiff, a dishcloth tucked into the string of his apron, a scrap of paper in one hand. Only the fingernails, which were crooked in a desperate scratching at the door, betrayed the panic of his final moments.

In the third watercolor, the light of the flashlight revealed a large crocodile edging through the night toward the cowering yellow dog tied to a stake near the river's edge. A plump black woman was calmly bracing a rifle against her shoulder and firing.

In the fourth watercolor, the blue of the sea looked far distant across the squelchy brown sand of the exposed tidal flat. Seaweed was strewn across the muck and dangled from spiky rocks. The man and woman near a particularly big rock were barefoot and muddy to their knees. The woman was in the midst of gesturing as she spoke. Her interesting, squashed-in face looked worried. The young man, dark haired and with a distinct pallor, was frowning as he listened.

In the fifth watercolor, a slender young woman with improbably red hair balanced on a window ledge. Light streaming from the window revealed the sharp-edged rocks in the gully below. She held desperately to the wooden window frame while stretching to search a gutter hidden beneath a mass of bougainvillea.

Annie sighed. Sometimes reading adventures set in faraway places seemed pretty tame. It would be fun to take a trip. Go somewhere exciting. She was already bored with the prospect of quiet days and little to do, though being with Max was always exciting. Still, here they were on the island, the wedding done, their family and friends away, the weather damp and chilly. She glared at the mug. *Too Good to Be True . . .* She needed a mug that predicted excitement. How about *Rainbow's End* by Ellis Peters? That had a cheerful ring to it. Maybe if she wished on a star . . . She glanced at the mugs. Yes, there it was: *Star Light, Star Bright* by Stanley Ellin. There was a star for wishing, if not the kind envisioned by the rhyme. "Star light, star bright," she murmured, "let me have this wish tonight." Of course, it was three o'clock in the afternoon but surely wishing afforded a little poetic license. "May adventure come through my door and lead me to a foreign shore."

She'd no more than finished her cappuccino and dropped from the tall stool, briskly heading for the shipping room and work, when the bell sang and the front door opened.

～ *Two* ～

"MAX!" ANNIE BEAMED WITH DELIGHT. Here he came, the man of her dreams, wiry blond hair, eyes blue as a northern sea. Tall and lithe, he strode toward her with easy grace, light tan corduroy sport coat unbuttoned over a navy turtleneck, khaki trousers crisp, cordovan loafers highly polished. She was thrilled to see him. Being by herself was fine. Certainly it was. But on a misty January day how wonderful for Max to come to the bookstore, though, of course, he should be at work. She glanced up at the clock.

Max stopped before her, shook his head. "Watched pots never boil. But, believe it or not, Confidential Commissions has a case." He didn't sound happy. "I guess I'll do it." He shoved a hand through his hair. His eyes glinted with irritation. He frowned. "Dammit, why are women so unreasonable?"

A smile pulled at the corners of her mouth. "Agatha and I assume that's a rhetorical question, rather on the order of 'Why can't a man ask for directions?'" She moved behind the coffee bar to the cappuccino machine.

He didn't smile in return. His tone dour, his body

language bristly as a porcupine's, he described Britt
Barlow and the death of Jeremiah Addison on his
private island—

Annie's eyes widened. She remembered the news
stories about Addison's death on Golden Silk. His ac-
cidental death.

—and the guests arriving on Friday. "One of them's
a murderer, according to Britt Barlow. Her idea is to
get them all together, challenge them to help her figure out who killed him. She spun a bunch of stories to
entice them back, and they swallowed them hook, line,
and sinker. But now that the stage is set, she's had second thoughts, started worrying. I should think so." His
tone was disparaging. "Talk about a half-baked idea—I
told her she was nuts."

The machine hissed and bubbled. Annie picked out
a mug for Max, *Unfinished Crime* by Helen McCloy,
filled it.

Max's blue eyes were disdainful. "She might as well
invite a tiger to the island and throw out raw meat." He
slapped a hand on the countertop. "I told her she was
toying with someone who'd already killed once and
wouldn't hesitate to kill again and if she strolled too
close the tiger would take her head off. I told her to get
on the phone, cancel those invitations, call the cops. I
couldn't have made it plainer."

Max settled on the stool, absently sprinkled chocolate flakes on the mound of frothed milk. But he didn't
pick up the mug. "I told her I wouldn't touch it with
a ten-foot pole. We were glaring at each other by that
point. She stood up and said she was going through
with it, one way or another. She said she should have

called the cops when she found Addison, but she
hadn't, and she had to make up for that. If I didn't want
to help, fine, she'd do it by herself."

Annie slipped her arm around his tight shoulders.
"She was walking out, wasn't she?" Annie leaned her
head against his, smelled the January mist in his hair
and a faint hint of aftershave.

"Yeah." An exasperated sigh. "I went after her. Told
her I'd come, do what I could." His voice was heavy
with resentment. And resignation. "Hell, you can't just
stand there and watch an express train bear down on
some fool who's spread-eagled on the tracks."

Annie understood. Max knew murder was the prov-
ince of the proper authorities. He saw the dangers Britt
Barlow refused to face. Or perhaps she was determined
to face them.

Golden Silk . . . Annie's eyes shone. It wasn't the
foreign shore she'd desired. But it was a shore and
foreign to her.

"I'll come too."

The wood fire crackled. It was a domestic scene, Annie
in a pink flannel gown and white terrycloth scuffies,
Max in navy flannel pajamas and soft brown leather
slippers. Dorothy L., the fluffy white cat, curled atop
her green tartan cushion in front of the fireplace, a
furred mound of contented somnolence. Cheerful
yellow ceramic mugs held hot chocolate topped by
a toasted marshmallow. As Annie was wont to insist,
What is night without a mug of good cheer? Max's
version of nightly good cheer varied somewhat.

It might have been any winter evening in the Darling household except for Annie's intense study of a legal pad. She finished reading, looked up. "Is that everyone?"

Max turned away from the fire, joined her on the couch. He slipped his arm around her shoulders, bent close to check the list and nuzzle his chin against the side of her face. After all, a man couldn't work all the time. "Yes. Let's see. One, two . . ."

Annie skimmed the names. Each was written in Max's bold back-slanting script with a brief statement:

> *Britt Barlow, 28. Owner of Heron House, now a B&B on the private sea island of Golden Silk. Heiress of her late sister, Cecilia Barlow Addison, widow of Jeremiah Addison.*
>
> *Jay (Jeremiah Thomas) Addison, 32, younger son of the late Jeremiah and his first wife, Lorraine. High school history teacher.*
>
> *Dana Addison, 29, wife of Jay. Former fourth-grade teacher, now a stay-at-home mom.*
>
> *Craig Addison, 36. Jeremiah's elder son. President of Addison Media.*
>
> *Isabel Addison, 34. Wife of Craig. Former news reporter, now working as a temp in a public relations firm. Living separately from Craig.*
>
> *Gerald Gamble, 53. Longtime Addison Media employee. Former executive assistant to Jeremiah. Now executive assistant to Craig.*
>
> *Rep. Millicent McRae, 52. Well known in state politics. Currently in Congress. Expected to announce candidacy for governor.*

Nicholas McRae, 70. Retired lawyer. Wealthy. Millicent's husband.

Kim Kennedy, 23. When an intern at Addison Media, she charmed Jeremiah. Within six months, she was on the news desk despite the producer's objections. Now employed in a small-market television station downstate, quite a comedown from Atlanta.

Everett Crenshaw, 40. Top investigative reporter for Addison Media. Host of a news feature patterned after The O'Reilly Factor *on Fox News.*

Lucinda Phillips, 54. Chief housekeeper at Heron House. Employed for 12 years.

Harry Lyle, 49. Caretaker, handyman. Employed for 9 years.

". . . Twelve. That's the lot."
Annie pointed at two more names.

Serena Gonzalez, I.
Juanita Garcia, I.

"What does 'I' mean?" Annie circled the letter.

"Irrelevant." He was brisk. "There's no invidious meaning, but the point is that Britt Barlow says the girls were the next thing to transients, didn't speak English, didn't know Jeremiah personally, had nothing to gain from his death, plus they are long gone from the island. She said there have been around nine maids between the time of his death and the present. Apparently she has a real struggle to keep the place staffed. You can imagine. Stuck out there on an island, no place to go, nothing to do. And those girls were definitely not trying to escape from the world, simply trying to survive. So, she invited everyone who was there at the time of his death excepting those two maids."

"Fair enough." Annie shook her head. "You'd think Britt Barlow could have been a little more forthcoming. She claims one of these people is a murderer, but she doesn't give any flavor of them. Who's bad tempered? Who's jealous? Who's greedy? That's a good question. I'll bet the family divvied up bundles of bucks. Who needed money? Why was there a politico on hand for what looked like a family gathering? And the intern on the make . . ." Annie ran her finger down the list. "Here she is, Kim Kennedy. She sticks out like a flamingo at an owl party. What's an intern doing there? Want to bet she's a knockout? Come on, Britt needs to tell us what's what. Who are these people and how did they feel about Jeremiah?"

"That's what I asked her. She said"—Max leaned back against the cushion, his face thoughtful—"she didn't want to prejudice me. She said she had pretty strong feelings about several of them, but she wanted me to see them fresh. Tabula rasa. I thought that was decent of her."

Annie raised an eyebrow. "Decent, maybe. Dumb, certainly. We need all the help we can get. We're going to meet them for the first time. Once they understand they're on a list of suspects, you can bet butter won't melt. And there's not time enough to investigate them." She glanced at the clock over the mantel. A quarter to eleven. They were scheduled to be picked up by a motor launch at the pier at eight in the morning.

Max stretched out his legs, yawned. "Not to worry.

Never underestimate Confidential Commissions." A less charitable observer might have described him as smug. "When I left the office, my trusty secretary—Barb murmured something about typing faster than Della Street—was finishing up dossiers of the twelve. We'll pick them up on our way to the harbor in the morning."

"Max," Annie said, her voice warm with admiration, "you are simply swell."

He twined a finger in a golden curl, tugged her face close to his. "Kudos welcome." His lips sought hers.

Who cared about tomorrow?

Sea legs. If they were for sale, she'd buy them even though the words evoked a mental image of a centipede clinging to a log. Logs. Logs—immovable and stationary—are found in the woods. Except, of course, when they bob as driftwood in the ocean. She wouldn't think of that. Instead she pictured a forest and scattered logs, evoking a serene vision of dry land. She thought longingly of dry land, preferably desert, and clung to the railing. In the front seat of the good-sized motorboat, the skipper—he'd introduced himself briefly as Joe and said, "You the folks for Golden Silk?"—hulked over the wheel, a formless mass in a yellow slicker damp from cold sea spray. He'd quickly settled them in the back after outfitting them with slickers.

Annie stared grimly and fixedly at the horizon as the boat plunged up and down over whitecaps and troughs. Keeping your gaze fastened on a stable point was supposed to help a queasy stomach. She ignored the tap on her arm.

"Hey, Annie?" Max lifted his voice above the thrumming of the motor and the rush of the wind.

Annie decided it was better not to speak.

"Oh." Max bent close, peered into her face. "I thought maybe you'd like to read some of the files."

"Looking at the horizon." She pushed out her answer, a syllable at a time. Although the horizon was hard to discern because of the lowering black clouds that turned the sky murky as a silted lagoon.

"Sit up straight. Breathe deeply." His voice was robust. "That's okay. I'll read the dossiers to you. Barb and I got lots of info. Personal stuff. It's amazing how people will answer questions over the phone when you spin the right story. My favorite ploy is the one where we say we're doing a company dinner that includes a 'This Is Your Life' tribute to the honoree. People can't wait to unload on a former friend or classmate or employee or renter. Anyway, you can concentrate on listening. Pretend you're at the store. You and Agatha at the coffee bar . . ."

Annie stared at the horizon—dammit, where was it?—and tried to imagine herself settled at one of the tables in the lovely heart-pine enclave at the back of Death on Demand, the cappuccino . . . No, she wouldn't think about the coffee bar. That brought up images of food and drink, images her queasy stomach abhorred. No. She was sitting at a table, a marvelously stationary table, with a book, maybe Tony Hillerman's latest, reading about bone-dry desert.

Beside her, relaxed, ebullient, and obviously pleased with the fact-studded dossiers, Max began to read:

"Britt Barlow. Grew up in Birmingham. One younger

sister, Cecilia. Mother Agnes, a single mom, worked two jobs to put them in a decent private school, pay for music and tap and tennis lessons. No contact with their father. Cecilia was a beauty, long blond hair, green eyes, sweet-natured, domestic, loved to cook and sew. Britt was a ranked tennis player in high school, straight As, ambitious, impatient. But the sisters got along famously. One old friend said, 'Britt adored Cissy. When Cissy got sick, I was afraid it would kill Britt, too.' Cissy dropped out of college to become a model. She was modeling at a charity benefit when she met Jeremiah Addison, who had recently separated from his first wife. Britt majored in English. After college, she went to New York. She held several jobs in advertising agencies but was laid off when the economy crashed. By this time Cissy was married to Jeremiah. They'd only been married three years when Cissy was diagnosed with ovarian cancer. Britt came to Golden Silk to be with Cissy during the treatments. Britt despised Jeremiah, thought he was an arrogant jerk, but she managed to be on pleasant terms with him because Cissy thought he was wonderful." Max lifted a sheaf of papers out from a pocket in the file. "Here are some pix of Britt and Cissy. Got a great one of them together. Barb found it in one of those house magazines. The article gave all the details of Jeremiah's renovations on Golden Silk." Max whistled. "He spent a fortune."

The launch veered out of the open ocean into the Sound, running with an island to starboard. In the more protected waters, the boat settled into a swift spank across the whitecaps. Annie's stomach slowly righted. She looked at the printout of photos, an ethereal Cissy in white satin, an aggressive Britt lunging for a forehand, the sisters arm-in-arm walking along a curving beach, a study in contrasts, blond Cissy in a softly swirling white cotton dress with a red sash, dark Britt in a vivid green jumper. Cissy looked sweet and appealing, her face turned with an inquiring, uncertain look. Britt's expression was forceful, determined. Annie had the same sense of sadness an old picture album evoked. The sisters together caught at her heart. Was there anything more poignant than photographs of careless happiness before storm clouds turned sunny days dark? Yes, she could imagine that Britt Barlow adored her younger and somehow, even in a photo, vulnerable sister.

Annie pushed back a strand of hair dampened by the spray. "What's the scoop on that intern?"

Max raised an eyebrow. "Annie, be fair. 'Intern' isn't synonymous with 'slut.'"

Annie waggled her hand. "Come on, come on. Six months' experience and she goes on air? She's on the magnate's private island? Some big news story breaking? I don't think so. What have you got on her?"

Max thumbed through the sheets. "Okay. Let's see, Kim Kennedy—" He handed her a photo.

Kim also wore all white—a crisp linen suit, and heels—but there was nothing bridal in her appearance. She held a microphone, leaned forward, blond hair smoothly coiffed, penetrating sapphire eyes, a rounded face with bright lips curved in a smile. She looked beautiful and predatory.

"—a junior in journalism at Georgia Tech. Hey,

you may have to eat crow." A quick glance at Annie. "Sorry. I'll rephrase that—"

Annie pulled in a deep, moisture-laden breath, welcomed the fine beads of sea water against her face. "Not to worry. I'm okay. I think."

"—you may have to make a mental apology. Outstanding student. Excellent reporter. Oh." He read, frowned. "You've got a point. She isn't a fluff but apparently she was on the make. She and Jeremiah were a definite twosome in Atlanta after Cissy got sick, and gossip had it that he planned to marry her."

Annie was pleased that two and two continued to make four, which was English for *cherchez la femme,* regretful that a woman ill with cancer was confronted with the living proof of her husband's unfaithfulness. "Had he asked Cissy for a divorce?"

"Britt didn't mention that." Max rubbed his cheek. "You'd think she would have if that's true."

Annie patted his knee.

He looked at her in surprise.

"You're nice." Her voice was kind and a shade patronizing.

"I am not." His rejoinder was swift and a shade offended. "Nobody's ever accused me of being nice." Then he grinned. "Except for Laurel and she's prejudiced. Anyway, why would Britt keep quiet about a divorce if it was in the works?"

Annie felt sad. She always felt sad when she knew a marriage was hollow, and nothing made a marriage more of a sham than an unfaithful partner. "Max, talk about a motive for murder . . ."

Max looked startled. "Cissy's dead."

Annie shook her head impatiently. "She wasn't dead when somebody strung wire at the top of the staircase. Sure, she was sick. But could she get up, move around? A cheating husband often comes to a bad end. Maybe Britt should look close to home for the murderer."

Max whistled. "She won't want to hear that. I'd say it's never occurred to her." He slipped the printout into the folder. "If Cissy killed him, we won't be able to prove it."

"We might." She took another deep breath. The moist cold air was a tonic. "We'll find out about Cissy. The housekeeper can probably tell us whether she was able to get around. Add Cissy to the suspect list." Annie was firm. "We aren't going to leave anyone out. Who's next?"

"Jay Addison, Jeremiah's younger son. Here's a picture—"

Annie looked at a tall weedy young man with shaggy brown hair, a handlebar mustache, and a shy expression. He cradled a silver loving cup in one arm. His untucked polo shirt was wrinkled and his cotton slacks baggy. A sweet-faced woman gazed at him with pride.

"—when he was named Teacher of the Year. Graduate of Clemson. Master's from University of Georgia. American history, specialty Franklin Roosevelt. Did a thesis on the public perceptions of Roosevelt and the successful efforts to minimize awareness of his paralysis. Scholarly. Diffident. He and his wife, Dana, have two children. Teddy is six and Alice three. Jay and his father had a strained relationship. Jeremiah divorced his first wife, Lorraine, the mother of Jay and Craig, to marry Cissy Barlow. Jay resented the divorce. The financial details of the divorce were never disclosed, but clearly Lorraine did not receive any money from Jeremiah. She went back to work as a nurse. A couple of years later, she was seriously injured in the crash of a medevac plane. She's in a nursing home and remains in a coma. Her sons were paying for her care, which caused a financial strain for Jay and forced his wife, Dana, back to work. She was an elementary school teacher. After Jeremiah's death, Jay's inheritance made it possible for her to quit and stay home with the children. Dana grew up in St. Petersburg, majored in education at the University of Georgia, where she met Jay. They married right after her graduation."

Annie glowered. "What kind of jerk was Jeremiah? I mean, he had millions, right?"

Max didn't need to check his files. "Right."

"So he couldn't pick up the nursing home tab for the mother of his children?" Her disdain distracted her from the bumpy ride. "If this was his typical behavior, no wonder somebody strung wire at the top of the stairs."

"Now, now." His tone was chiding. "We don't care if he was a double for Simon Legree, murder's not an option. And we don't know what his side to the story might have been."

Annie gave him a startled look. "Money out the kazoo and he refuses to pay for his ex-wife's care, puts the burden on his sons?"

"We don't know why." Max's look was stubborn though his voice was mild.

Annie knew Max was right. There were always at least two sides to every story. Jeremiah's reason might not be defensible, but they needed to understand why he had acted as he had. There was a haunting comment in *The Woman in White* by Wilkie Collins: "The best men are not consistent in good—why should the worst men be consistent in evil?" She made a mental vow to find out everything she could about Jeremiah Addison.

"We can take it for granted that Jeremiah irked the hell out of people." Max rattled the folder. "We'll know a lot more when we finish these. But our job is to focus on the people who hated him and do it damn fast." He bent forward, straining to see across the water. His impatience to get to the island rode with them, an impatience pushed by a dark current of uneasiness.

"It will be all right." She reached out, clutched his arm, wanting to reassure him, wanting to ease the pressure he felt.

His face was grim. "I'm worried, Annie. I'm afraid of what may happen." He almost managed a smile. "Okay, I'll admit it. I sound like one of your Gothic heroines." There was a flash of a quick lopsided grin that was gone in an instant, replaced by ridged jaws. "But it's the devil of a setup, an island with a very select group of guests—and one of them is a murderer."

Annie felt a soul-deep chill that had nothing to do with January wind or salty spray. The open boat was cold but not as cold as her foreboding. Right this minute she was en route to meet a murderer. She was going to walk into a room with the certain knowledge that a face she saw, a hand she shook, belonged to a person who had coldly, carefully, and cleverly arranged the death of a man.

Max made it clear. "One of the guests is very different from the rest. A murderer never accepts limits. Ordinary people think, 'That's wrong. I can't do that.' A murderer thinks, 'I will prevail. At any cost.'" He glanced at his watch. "We'll be there in about fifteen minutes. We've got to hurry." He checked the files. "Let's see who's left. Okay. Craig Addison." He paused and handed Annie another printout. "Prep school in Atlanta. Yale undergraduate, Columbia graduate. Golden boy. Excellent grades. Outstanding leadership qualities. Always did his best to please his father. Shot right up the ladder at Addison Media, but not just because he was the boss's son. Admired for his evenhanded treatment of news, though he ran afoul of his father because of his liberal politics. Craig did a series on hospital policies with residents, specifically the efforts of some hospitals to ignore changed federal regulations limiting hours on duty. Won a Pulitzer. Scuttlebutt at a Texas border newspaper in the chain said Jeremiah killed Craig's plans to do a story about a big-time Houston trucking company smuggling illegal immigrants. Latest word is the investigative series will run next month and it's expected to trigger a federal indictment. He married—"

Annie flipped the photographs of a handsome, well-built man in his thirties with a bush of tight blond curls, bright blue eyes, and an exuberant expression: A beaming Craig cut the groom's cake, Craig and his new wife embraced on the dance floor at their reception, Craig strode across a platform in an academic

robe with a bright hood, Craig tossed a red rubber ball
to a running black Lab, Craig stood beside a yawn-
ing grave. Annie frowned, held the sheet nearer. She
glanced back at the picture of the bride, a vivid young
woman with flashing eyes and dark hair and finely
boned face, high forehead, pointed cheekbones and
chin. Yes. The woman in black at the grave site, standing stiffly a few feet from Craig, was his wife. There
might as well have been a canyon between them, she
stood so pointedly more than an arm's length away.
Her face was strained, cheeks sunken, lips pursed. She
clasped her hands tightly together. Craig looked numb,
his face blank, perhaps from exhaustion, perhaps from
grief.

"—four years ago. Isabel Hernandez grew up in
Miami. Journalism graduate from University of Florida. Started out in an upstate small-market television
station. Excelled. Went to larger stations, ended up in
Atlanta. Met Craig when they were both covering the
trial of the guy who mailed live rattlesnakes to abortion
clinics. They got married three weeks later. She moved
out last year, quit her job on one of the Addison TV
stations, got a job in public relations."

"Wonder why they split." Isabel had accompanied
him to his father's funeral. "How long after the funeral
did she leave him?"

Max found Jeremiah's obituary, riffled through
notes, raised an eyebrow. "The next week." He made
another note, gave Annie an admiring glance. "What
made you wonder?"

She handed him the picture at the cemetery. "You
can tell they're poles apart."

Max studied the photograph. "Yeah." His tone was thoughtful. "She was obviously on the outs with Craig. But it might not have anything to do with his father's death."

"Timing is everything." Annie knew her pronouncement wasn't on a par with Charlie Chan's observations in the novels by Earl Derr Biggers. Her two favorites were "The deer should not play with the tiger," from *Charlie Chan Carries On,* and "The man who is about to cross a stream should not revile the crocodile's mother," from *The Black Camel.* But she felt a glimmer of excitement. Timing . . . Maybe her subconscious was clicking merrily ahead while she and Max were looking for trees in the forest. Or not seeing the forest for the trees. Whatever . . . "Timing!" she exclaimed. "Why did Jeremiah die that particular weekend?"

Once again Max favored her with a respectful glance. "That's a damn good point. Was it because someone had a chance to kill him who normally would not? Like the politician? Maybe we should focus on the people who usually weren't on the island. We can check that out with Britt as soon as we get there." Once again he leaned on the railing, staring toward the northeast.

Annie hated to rain on her own parade. "Timing is everything" deserved acclaim. But honesty compelled her to admit, "Of course, it could be that the murder occurred then because there *were* other people on the island. Or maybe the timing depended upon what one of them intended—or didn't intend—to do."

Max reached beneath the slicker, pulled out a small notebook. He opened it, began to write.

She bent close to read his neat printing:

1. Discover precise reason each person was on the island that weekend.
2. Were any guests unlikely to return anytime soon?

Annie counted with her fingers. "Okay, we've accounted for everyone in the family, right? Jeremiah, Cissy, Britt, Jay and Dana, Craig and Isabel. Also Kim Kennedy. Who were the other outsiders?"

Max pulled out several files, looked at the first. "Gerald Gamble. But he was certainly close to the family. He'd worked for Jeremiah for more than thirty years. Started off as a stringer for one of the small papers. Quick. Smart. Ruthless." He handed Annie a printout. "Gamble has a reputation as a—"

Annie knew she shouldn't judge a man simply from photos. But she already knew she didn't like Gerald Gamble—he was tall, thin with a cadaverous face and little squinty eyes. His dark suit hung from rounded shoulders. He stood with a closed face, arms folded.

"—hard-nosed guy, Jeremiah's hatchet man. Kept an eye on all aspects of the business. Jeremiah trusted him absolutely. Now he works for Craig." Max took the printout from Annie, replaced it in the file. "Absolute trust. That gives a lot of room for maneuvering. It certainly wasn't unusual for him to be on the island. That isn't true for the last three." He held up two files. "Millicent and Nick McRae and Everett Crenshaw. This was the first visit to the island by all three of them."

Annie looked at a photo of Millicent McRae at a posh campaign dinner. Her elderly husband was a step behind her. Millicent was a perfectly coiffed, fiftyish blonde with a big smile and cold eyes. Annie admired her lavishly embroidered silk shantung dress in a pale champagne color. Gorgeous. The dress, not Millicent. Millicent greeting donors was reminiscent of an alligator spotting a succulent duck. Nick McRae's bland expression and self-effacing posture were at odds with his sardonic, penetrating gaze.

"Millicent was a trial lawyer in Atlanta, married the widowed senior partner. They have a huge house in Buckhead. He has children from his first marriage, none with Millicent. She ran for Congress about ten years ago, riding the conservative wave, won easily. Of course, it helped that the Addison papers supported her." Max returned their file to his folder. He opened the last file. "Everett Crenshaw." Max's expression was a mingling of disgust and disdain.

She took the proffered printout, immediately recognized the unstylish pompadour, glassy smooth face, and thin lips curled in a supercilious lift. "I always turn him off."

"Lots of viewers don't." Max shrugged. "Numbers are all that count today. Millions tune in to see Crenshaw rip into his guests. You have to wonder at the mentality of people who agree to be on his show. I guess they think any attention is better than none."

She didn't state the obvious. Despite the best efforts of Miss Manners, civility wasn't fashionable. Of course, in a world where prime-time entertainment includes strangers dumped on an island and encouraged to seek sex, shouted exchanges masquerading as political commentary weren't remarkable. Plato would have been puzzled.

"Whatever the merits of Crenshaw's show"—
Max's tone left no doubt to his judgment—"he was
then and is now one of the top political commentators in the country and a definite star at Addison
Media. However"—he scanned the rest of the dos-
sier—"he wasn't a regular visitor to Golden Silk.
There's no suggestion he was on intimate terms
with Jeremiah." He raised an eyebrow. "Crenshaw
dropped out of college, got his start on a small
daily. Did an exposé of a crooked mayor. Went from
there to an Atlanta station. Two big series. One on
kickbacks in the nursing-home industry, another
on a crooked legislator on the take from a utility
company. On to D.C. and, as they say, the rest is history. Smart, brash, with all the charm of a blackjack
dealer." Max slapped the file back into the folder.

Annie clapped her hands together. "I like Everett
Crenshaw."

Max looked startled.

Annie grinned. Sea legs. It was just a matter of
time. "I like him as a suspect. He wasn't an intimate
of the family. Obviously nobody would ask him on
account of his charm. Why was he on the island that
weekend?"

"We'll find out." Max was suddenly ebullient.
"Annie, you have good instincts. We'll tackle the
Honorable Millicent first and then take on Crenshaw.
Now for the help . . ." He broke off. "That must be the
island." He lifted his hand, pointed.

Annie turned to look just as their skipper called out,
"Golden Silk to starboard." She felt the sudden grip of
Max's hand on hers, knew he too felt a jolt of appre-

hension, a sense of strangeness. And danger. The dark smudge on the horizon looked forbidding. Fog hung in dull gauzy swaths among the tall pines and live oak trees. As they bounced over the whitecaps, the sound of the motor raucous as the shriek of seagulls, the island suddenly darkened before their eyes.

Annie took a quick breath. "The sun's gone behind a cloud."

That was all it was, the abrupt shadowing of the land as a lowering cloud obscured the sun. Nothing more to it than that, nothing to cause breath to be hard to find, nothing to account for the racing thud of her heart.

In a moment—or a day—the sun would break through and Golden Silk would sparkle, a luxurious and welcoming retreat, once a rich man's piece of paradise.

But for now, the island lay in dense shade.

They sat in silence, hand in hand, as the boat plunged through the water. Gradually the terrain became more distinct, craggy headland bluffs of darkish red dirt topped by the maritime forest, seventy-foot-tall loblolly pines and live oaks. The boat swung east and ran the length of the island, once again struggling against larger waves in open ocean, before swinging around the southern tip of the island and curving toward shore. A long wooden pier jutted out into the Sound. Cloud-darkened water surged around the pilings, indicating a quick and forceful current.

The nearer the boat drew, the more remote and isolated Annie felt.

A flash of white moved at the far end of the pier and slowly took shape. A slender woman came forward, walking briskly. She stopped near the ladder and waited, hands in the pockets of her skirt. There was an aura of loneliness about that waiting figure. Annie thought of *Nighthawks,* the Edward Hopper painting of the diner and its occupants in the early morning hours. She felt the same sense of separation and anxiety. And doom?

When the boat bobbed alongside the pier, they shed their slickers. Max held Annie's elbow as she stepped to the bottom rung of the ladder. When she scrambled onto the pier, her eyes met Britt's. Annie held out her hand. "I'm Annie Darling."

Britt Barlow frowned. Her face, haggard in the morning light, reflected surprise and uncertainty. Her somber expression emphasized the image of a belea-guered sentinel alert for invaders.

Footsteps sounded on the wooden planks behind Annie. Max strode forward, Annie's carryall and a vinyl gym bag in one hand, a duffel slung over his shoulder, the folder tucked beneath his arm. "Britt, this is my wife, Annie. She often assists me on my cases." His voice was firm.

The ladder squeaked as Joe hefted his bulk up to the pier. "Anything more, Ms. Barlow?"

There was the tiniest of pauses. Annie prepared for battle. If this woman suggested Annie take the launch back to Broward's Rock, Annie intended to make it clear Max was leaving, too. It was all or nothing, the two of them together . . . No way would she leave Max on this remote island.

Britt turned to Max. "I expected you to come by yourself." There was no anger in her voice, simply thoughtfulness. Her eyes narrowed. Abruptly, she gave an impatient head shake, flung out her hands. "What am I thinking? I suppose"—her words were hurried— "I've kept everything secret for so long, it's hard for me to realize that time is past." She looked directly at Annie. "You're good to come. I will appreciate whatever help you both can give me." She managed a small smile. "Welcome to Golden Silk." She lifted a hand toward the waiting boatman. "Thank you, Joe."

Joe was already moving toward the ladder. "Back on Sunday. Five o'clock."

Five o'clock Sunday. Annie took comfort. That really wasn't such a long time. But she felt like a castaway as the roar of the engine lessened with distance, waned, was gone.

Britt Barlow looked toward the shore and a double avenue of live oaks and an antebellum house on the crest of the gentle rise. "We'll start where Jeremiah died. . . ."

∴ *Three* ∾

THE OVERCAST SKY AND INTERLOCKING BRANCHES of the live oaks created a cool purplish tunnel. Spanish moss hung in silvery swaths, haunting as a dimly remembered dream. Oyster shells crunched underfoot. Cawing crows fluttered skyward at the sound of their steps. At the end of the avenue, the house rose before them. Britt stopped and pointed. "This is my favorite view." There was pride of ownership in her gaze, a lift to her voice.

The two-story tabby house sat high on curved stucco foundations. Slender Ionic columns supported the double porticos across the front and on each side. The hipped roof with a central pediment and dormers at each end obscured much of—Annie counted—six tall brick chimneys. Smoke curled from two chimneys.

Britt followed her glance. "I love January. I have a fire downstairs in the dining room and in the room where you'll be staying."

A central stone stairway led to the bottom verandah. On the lower verandah white wicker furniture with bright cushions invited repose. The upper verandah was screened.

Annie could imagine settling into a rocker with a book and a frosted glass of lemonade. She'd brought a book bag, of course. She never traveled without a half dozen mysteries, most new, some from long ago. Her authors of choice for this journey were Charles Todd, Victoria Thompson, David Rosenfelt, Kathryn R. Wall, and two reissues by Eric Ambler.

The avenue ended in a wide paved walk to the front steps.

Avenue . . .

"No cars." Annie's voice rose in wonder. "Why, of course, there are no cars."

Britt smiled. Genuine pleasure softened her angular face. "Wonderful, isn't it? That's the first thing visitors notice and appreciate. No exhaust fumes, just the scent of the sea and wood smoke and"—she gestured toward a magnificent garden—"roses and magnolia blossoms and pittosporum in summer. No roar of engines or squeal of brakes." A shrug. "We have a big generator but it's around a bend and you don't hear it unless you walk there. Even the golf carts—there's one for each cabin and several for the house—are electric. The only gasoline-powered motor is the riding lawn mower."

Annie heard the sigh of pine trees, the rustle of magnolia leaves, the *chut chut* of squirrels, the chirp of winter birds. Underlying the mélange of sound was a profound stillness. This was what it must have been like a hundred years ago. Two hundred . . .

"If you stand very quietly," Britt's voice was soft, "it's almost as if you can hear laughter drifting from the upstairs ballroom. Sometimes late at night when the lamps flicker, you can see a woman in white. Our ghost, Caroline Louise. She's always glimpsed at the railing at the far end of the upper verandah." Her hand moved. "They say she's waiting for her lover to come, watching the sea for his ship. But"—a tone of regret—"he was killed during the siege of Battery Wagner on Morris Island. She grew old here, a recluse, walking and waiting and watching."

Annie stared at the shadowy upper verandah. The fascinating and touching truth about ghosts and faces glimpsed in yellowed photographs was that once all of them had been as alive as she. Each had felt a heartbeat and the gurgle of laughter and the heat of passion and the sting of tears. Ghosts and snapshots were a reminder that what is present will always and inevitably one day be past and what is past was once as real and vigorous and exciting as the present.

Britt nodded toward the windows to the west. "Your room—the Meadowlark Room—is the last one to the west. You can step out on the verandah where she walks. Perhaps you will see her." Britt glanced at her watch. "The others will be arriving after lunch. Every fifteen minutes on a staggered schedule." Her voice was brisk.

Max was impressed. "How'd you arrange that?"

She gave a wry laugh. "Money. I hired separate boats for each person or couple." There was a sardonic twist to her mouth. "Jeremiah's money, of course. I suppose Jeremiah would approve that expenditure, though he still must be whirling in his grave that I now own Heron House." She was clearly amused. Then her features toughened. "I'm not taking any chances. Do you think I want them to come face-to-face at the harbor in Savannah? What a reunion that would be! I can hear it now: 'Why, the last time we were all together . . .' It wouldn't take long to compare notes, figure out there was more to this gathering than they realized. No, I've got it figured to the minute—"

Annie was glad she and Max weren't this woman's opponents. Annie had a sense of inexorability. Britt Barlow had left nothing to chance.

Britt made an impatient gesture. "—but we don't have much time. There's so much you need to know. For starters"—she began to walk—"the house is always unlocked. That's important to remember." She moved quickly up the steps.

Annie wished there were time to savor the old house. The wide planks of the verandah dipped a trifle in front of the semi-elliptical front door with a lovely half-moon fanlight. But Britt was holding the door, impatient for them to enter.

When they stepped into the wide front hall, their guide nodded toward a love seat. "If you'll leave your bags, Harry will take them up later. I want to show you around now."

Max stowed the duffel near the small sofa, placed Annie's carryall and the gym bag on a cushion. He held on to his folder.

Britt kept moving, her steps clattering on the heart-pine planks of the hallway. "The house was built in 1795 by Robert Preston. He cultivated barley to brew beer, so the drawing room mantelpiece has stucco carvings of the grain. There are some ruins of the brewery on the grounds, a couple of partial chimneys, some vats. There was a fire in 1836. And later a flood from the hurricane of 1885. The house is a classic plantation home. It faces to the southwest for the prevailing breeze. There is a wide central hallway on the first two floors with rooms to both sides. Of course, the third floor is the ballroom. The stairway is toward the back, the drawing room on the right."

Annie admired the ornamental plasterwork on the ceiling and twin chandeliers. Two curved bays with magnificent Palladian windows overlooked the garden. Crimson damask curtains—Annie wondered if they were original to the house—offered a striking contrast to cool gray walls. A magnificent ormolu mirror hung above a Louis XV commode. The red of the drapes was echoed in an Aubusson rug. An antique French clock and matching silver candlesticks stood on the fireplace mantel.

"The dining room"—Britt turned toward it—"is all mahogany furniture, so I repainted the walls a faint cream. The rug is a gold-on-cream pattern. The walls had been painted green. A bilious green. I felt like I was trapped in Jonah's stomach. It looks much better now." She nodded approval. "That's a gilded Chippendale mirror above the Hepplewhite sideboard. I found it in an estate sale in Beaufort. You know, of course, that Heron House was a late acquisition by Jeremiah. It was during his Gentleman Jerry Period, as I call it. He grew up poor but smart"—there was grudging admiration in her voice—"and actually made his money. Gentility came later. He hired an antique dealer to find period pieces for the place. None of these antiques have any personal association with him. All it took to acquire the appurtenances of a landed Southern gentleman was money." She touched the shiny top of a Duncan Phyfe table. She gave it a considering look. "And, of course, lots of impoverished aristocrats. I like to think all those former owners—whoever they are, wherever they lived, however they lost their money— would rather see the things owned by someone like me. I love them because they are beautiful, and I'm nothing more or less than an innkeeper. Jeremiah, true to his cunning, had a premarital agreement with Cissy so her portion of his estate was this island and some money. Not enough to make me confuse myself with the gentry."

Annie thought she understood. If Heron House had been an Addison family home filled with Addison family heirlooms, the implication was clear that Britt would have had none of it. Since that wasn't the case, Britt obviously had no difficulty disassociating any memories of Jeremiah from the lovely old plantation home.

The long table was set for dinner, Blue Canton china, heavy silver, a shining damask cloth. Annie counted twelve places. Two painted china herons made a majestic centerpiece. Annie was enchanted by the bright colors and detail, the black cap, shoulders, and bill, white face and chest, gray tail feathers, pink legs. Again there were twin chandeliers, their crystal drops sparkling and lovely.

"The library is that way"—Britt stopped at the foot of the stairway and nodded down the hall—"and a study. The kitchen area is beyond that door. It's a later addition to the house, a huge kitchen and breakfast room and pantry. I serve a full breakfast." She spoke with satisfaction. "Apple and egg casserole, poached eggs on potato-and-bacon pancakes, sour cream crumb buns, ham with redeye gravy, grits." Abruptly, as if recalling the circumstances, she frowned. "But whatever happens this weekend, I'll offer the best possible meals to everyone. After all, the condemned are always offered a hearty breakfast." She shivered. "I'm sorry. Not in the best of taste, I suppose. Now, if you'll come this way . . ." With a deep breath, she gestured toward the stairway.

"Look at it closely." There was a wry tone in her voice.

Annie admired the glistening white steps, the delicacy of the balusters, the thin elegance of the handrail. Had the stairs been newly painted?

"The stairs are made of marble." Max stepped forward, touched the handrail. "Marble. Not wood."

"Right. Not exactly common in the interior of a plantation home. But Jeremiah met termites and he wasn't a man to be vanquished by an insect. The entire stairway was crumbling. You know termites, once there, always there. Or if not always there, likely to return. Jeremiah ordered marble. Marble he got. I call the stairs Jeremiah's Folly." Her lips twisted in amusement.

Annie gave her a sharp glance. The comment was cold and cruel. The man had worked to prepare a home for living. Instead, he had met death where and when he never expected it.

Britt returned her look with no sign of compunction. Finally, she shrugged. "You got it. I didn't like him alive. I don't like him dead. I'm sorry, but you might as well have the truth. It will be the oddest twist of fate if I'm the one to avenge him. Come with me . . ."

Britt clattered up the steps. Annie followed, Max close behind. On the second-floor landing, Britt turned to face them. Her flash of morbid pleasure when she spoke of Jeremiah's Folly might never have been. Her gaze was bleak.

Annie and Max stopped on the steps just below her. Annie felt the nub of his navy wool blazer against her arm. She gazed up at Britt, who looked much older and grimmer.

Britt made an impatient gesture upward. "The third floor doesn't matter. It's a ballroom. There are six bedrooms on this floor. The two largest rooms face the drive. The east room—Osprey Room—was Jeremiah's. Cissy was in the west bedroom, the Meadowlark Room. It had been turned into a sickroom for her. I spent the nights on a small bed in an adjoining dressing room." Her brows drew down in thought. "I guess that might have made a difference, the fact that I was in the dressing room. It is farthest from the stairs. Even if there had been something to hear—"

Annie pictured a figure kneeling on the stairs in darkness, heart pounding, hands sweaty, perhaps with a pencil-sized flashlight resting on a tread, illuminating a death trap.

"—I was too far away. Anyway, only the three of us were on this floor. Everyone else was in a cabin. I've put them in the same cabins. Except for Craig and Isabel. She's in Cabin 1 as they were that night. He's in Cabin 7. She's been living in Atlanta. I don't know why they separated. I doubt she would agree to stay with him. In fact, I was a little surprised she agreed to come. She may be upset when she sees him." Britt's tone was untroubled. A confrontation between Craig and Isabel Addison did not worry her. Her eyes settled on the pale green wall at an ankle-high level. "There's a hole there. I don't know if you can find it."

Annie bent, ran her fingers lightly across the wall, felt a prick on her skin. She turned to look at the thin marble baluster across the width of the step and wished for a flashlight. There might be a faint scratch remaining from the jerk when Jeremiah was caught by the wire.

"We know how he died." Max waved a hand, dismissing physical evidence. "You saw the wire, removed it. What matters is whether Jeremiah was actually the intended victim."

Britt looked startled. Her eyes widened. Her fingers closed on the ridges of the carved pineapple on the newel post.

Annie straightened. Max put his hand on her elbow, urging her up the final step. When they stood beside Britt, he looked up and down the wide hall. "As you said, there were three of you up here. What prevented you or your sister from being the victim?"

She shook her head firmly. "Jeremiah was the intended victim." She was confident. "I never went downstairs before he did. Cissy was too sick to walk. Her meals were brought up. Sometimes I'd help her into the wheelchair, roll her out onto the verandah. She hadn't been down the stairs for more than a month." A long-drawn breath. "She never went down them again. No, the murderer could count on catching Jeremiah. He jogged every morning. Rain or shine. He went downstairs for juice and he was outside as it grew light."

Annie knew the overcast day contributed in part to the present dimness in the hall, but the top of the stairway was likely always shadowy. "No wonder he didn't see the wire."

Max too looked down as if gauging the light. "What time was it when you found him?"

"Very early. Normally, I didn't get up until seven, but Cissy had awakened and I was getting ready to go downstairs, fix her an omelet. I heard a noise. An odd noise. I went to see. And I found him." Britt thumped the carved pineapple leaves decisively. "The wire wasn't meant for me. Or Cissy."

Max was stubborn. "If he'd skipped his jog, you might have been the victim."

Her smile was grim. "He never skipped a jog. Trust me, you can start with the premise that the right man died."

Annie nodded. "That's why you made the point about the front door never being locked."

"Yes." The single word was emphatic. "Anyone could come into or leave this house at any hour of the day or night. It made Cissy nervous. She always wanted the door to her bedroom locked. Jeremiah said locking doors was absurd. He said we were all on the island together and he didn't make it a practice to invite thieves or murderers. I asked him to install a lock and he refused. He did have inside bolts installed in the cabins. For privacy. But there are no locks on any outer door on Golden Silk. Anyone on the island could have slipped into the house that night and come up the stairs and strung that wire." She glanced at her watch. "Jay and Dana will be here soon. There's just enough time to show you the rest of the island. . . ."

A fine rain slanted across the lawn, turned the pines a dusky green, soft and smudged as a pointillist painting.

Britt paused at the door, reached into an umbrella stand. She handed umbrellas to Annie and Max. She opened her umbrella, started down the front steps. "The employee cabins and the generator and storage sheds are that way." She pointed west. "The guest cabins are beyond the garden, secluded in the woods." She pointed at the sloping terraces of the garden. "The azaleas are on a par with Magnolia Plantation. The gardens aren't as extensive, of course. But there are several acres of azaleas, camellias, roses, hibiscus, and lilies."

Annie imagined the gardens in springtime. The pink and rose and crimson and white and yellow blossoms would be startling in their beauty. The gardens were lovely even in January, misty in the rain with a sweet woody scent, pansies saucy in shades of pink and yellow and purple and even pumpkin orange.

They walked down the terraced slope to a rectangular rock pool. Water tumbled from simulated falls and spouted from a stone porpoise. Dense pine woods loomed behind the fountain. Britt nodded to her left. "That path leads to a gazebo near a lagoon. I love it there. The lagoon is rimmed by huge cypress. We stay on this path to reach the cabins." They curved around the fountain and into the woods. The path meandered through the pines. They followed it for about twenty yards to a turnaround. Britt waved her hand. "Pretend this is the hub of a wheel. The spokes are paths leading to the cabins. This path continues on through the pines to the beach. Cabin 1 is this way." Britt turned to her left. Although the undergrowth was trimmed back, there was a feeling of being in wilderness. Dollops of rain splattered onto their umbrellas from the canopy of branches. They reached a clearing and a gray wood cabin on posts. Steps led up to a screened-in porch. The cabin might have been a thousand miles from habitation. Rain pattered in a gentle song on the wood shingles.

Max looked at Britt. "Are all the cabins this remote?"

Her face was in shadow beneath the umbrella. "Oh, yes."

Max crooked the handle of his umbrella under his arm along with his folder. He flipped open a small notebook, rapidly sketched. When he finished, he held it out for Britt to see. "Is this how the cabins are arranged?"

Annie stepped nearer, studied Max's map. A rectangle represented the fountain. From it, Max had drawn a meandering line to a beach. Midway he'd marked the turnaround. Eight trails radiated from that circle. At the end of each intersecting trail, he'd placed an X.

"Yes. You can also draw an outer circle. The cabins are linked that way, too. But each cabin is totally private, a preserve of its own. 'Come to Golden Silk and leave the world behind.' That's what I'm going to put on the new brochures—if I can get all of this behind me." There was a bitter twist to her voice.

Max looked at her thoughtfully. He flipped shut the notepad. "It's time we talked about what you have in mind this weekend. I advised you to contact the sheriff. You wouldn't agree. Instead, you insisted on calling together everyone who was on the island when Jeremiah died. I agreed to come only because I felt a responsibility for your safety—"

Britt lifted a hand as if to ward off his words. "I'm not a fool. Contrary to what you may think. I can assure you I don't intend to take any risks."

Max was obdurate. "You have taken a terrible risk in bringing a murderer here." His face was grim, his voice stern.

Annie knew that voice. She'd only heard it once or twice in their years together. Easygoing, affable, charming Max had his limits and he'd reached them.

Britt stood still as a statue. There was only the sound of raindrops splatting gently against the cabin and the rustle of the pines, the top branches swaying. She met Max's gaze, her own equally unyielding.

"I came and brought my wife"—he nodded toward Annie—"because you may be in danger. You are determined to find out who killed Jeremiah Addison. You never told me how you intended to proceed. I'm warning you: Don't challenge a murderer."

Britt's lips trembled. For an instant, she swayed as if fighting a hard wind.

Annie wanted to step forward, slip an arm around the woman's thin shoulders. Britt had the troubled, uncertain look of an abandoned—yet angry and defiant—child. But Annie knew Max was right. They had to know what Britt had planned.

Max was decisive. "Here's what I suggest. Tell them you intend to turn Golden Silk into a memorial to Jeremiah. That's what you said in some of the letters you sent, isn't it? Introduce Annie and me as oral historians. You've hired us to interview each of them about Jeremiah. That gives us a reason to talk to them. We'll take it from there."

Britt's face squeezed in thought.

"As far as I'm concerned," Max said, "that's the only choice you have."

For an instant, Britt's green eyes glinted. She stared at Max, her face rigid.

Annie wondered if Britt and Max were going to quarrel. Max was determined to prevail. Britt bristled with anger and determination.

Finally, Britt brushed a hand through her dark hair, slowly nodded. With obvious effort, she softened her voice. "I suppose you can tell that I like to have my own way. But I hope I'm smart enough to admit when I'm in over my head. The fact is I've been scared to death. Every time I thought about standing up and telling them—" A swift head shake. "Now I don't have to do that." She stared at him intently. "All right. We'll do it your way. And it may be an advantage that no one will be on guard."

Max looked relieved. His stern look eased.

Hesitantly, Britt held out her hand. She looked like a waif hoping for a friend.

Max nodded and reached out to shake her hand. "We'll find out everything we can. We'll do it without putting anyone in danger."

Annie wondered if this agreement between Max

and Britt was more of an armed truce than a joining of forces. There was still a cold glint in Britt's eyes.

Britt gave a short nod. "You're the boss." She glanced at her watch. "I've got to get back to the house. I'll be busy this afternoon, greeting the others. I've arranged for Lucinda to bring lunch to your room. I thought you might want to see the guests as they arrive. I put a pair of binoculars on the wicker table on the verandah outside your room. Cocktails are at seven, dinner at seven-thirty." She brushed past them. At the edge of the clearing, she looked back. "Please, go wherever you wish. Make yourselves at home."

Annie hesitated at the top of the stairs, glancing down at the baluster where the wire had been strung. She wondered if Britt Barlow felt a similar quiver of shock every time she came upstairs, reliving her gruesome discovery, or if time had diminished that image.

Max squeezed her shoulder.

She reached up, touched his hand. He knew. Always. That made everything better. Always.

She took another step, grateful to reach the hallway. She was turning to the left when Max caught her arm.

"No one's up here. Let's look around." He gestured across the hall. "We'll start with Jeremiah's room."

The end bedroom was huge. An imposing sleigh bed sat against the north wall between bay windows. The burgundy spread matched the deep red of the drapes. Large windows overlooked the east verandah.

Annie turned on the overhead light but it did little to dispel an air of gloom and disuse. "I guess she hasn't rented this one lately."

Max walked alongside the bookcases that lined the interior wall. "Eclectic taste. Everything from Hawthorne to Kierkegaard. Volumes on Hearst and Bennett and Pulitzer." He opened the wardrobe, pulled out drawers in a chest. All were empty.

Annie stepped into the bathroom, admired the huge white claw-foot tub. "I hope our room has a tub like this. It's big enough for both of us."

Max didn't respond, a clear indication to Annie that his state of mind wasn't normal. Usually . . .

He stood in the middle of the room. "Except for the books, there's not a scrap to tell us anything about Addison. But we know he slept here"—Max glanced toward the bed—"the night before he died. Let's try an experiment. Go to the top of the stairs, take off your shoe and pound on the wall. Give it two quick, hard taps."

As she stepped into the hall, the bedroom door closed firmly behind her.

She hurried to the staircase, slipped off a black loafer, gripped the leather toe. She pretended she held a hammer and whacked twice on the wall with the sturdy heel. There was noise but not as much as she'd expected. Besides, if she'd been the murderer, she wouldn't have opted for a nail. A two-inch screw would work just fine. Bring along a screwdriver, fasten the screw in the wall, and leave a quarter inch exposed. Wind the wire firmly around the head of the screw, string it across the step, wind around the baluster. And presto . . .

She stepped into the loafer and crossed the hall. When she opened the door, Max popped up from the bed.

"I banged." She raised an eyebrow.

"Not a sound." He moved toward her. "As for the other main room, we know Cissy was medicated and Britt in her dressing room. So it was easy for the murderer to set the trap."

Annie explained her theory about a screw. "That wouldn't have made very much noise. Probably the murderer waited until the middle of the night to be sure Jeremiah was asleep."

Max gave a last look about the room. "We need to ask Britt where she put Jeremiah's belongings and find out whether he kept a diary or journal."

They stepped into the hall. Without hesitating, Max went from door to door, checking out the remaining rooms. None showed evidence of use except for the last, a small corner room with a ceiling that sloped on one side. There was just room for a single bed with a simple white cotton spread, a small chest, and a narrow table that served as a vanity. Pale pink walls, white woodwork. There was a studio portrait in an ebony frame on the table, another in a shell frame. Max crossed the room, looked at the photographs. "Cissy. And a man. His picture is signed 'Love, Loomis.'"

"Max, this must be Britt's room." Annie spoke in a warning tone, shot a worried glance behind her. "She'll be furious." *Love, Loomis.* Annie turned to catch a glimpse of the face of a man who must matter to their hostess. Dark hair, dark eyes, lips curved in an easy smile. Annie liked his face and was glad for Britt.

Max shrugged. "She's already furious. Didn't you pick up on that?" He moved to a bedside table, pulled out a drawer, looked inside, closed it. It took him only

a moment to circle the room, step into the closet and
a small bath.

Annie stood in the doorway. The bedroom was
simple, understated, tidy, and obviously not a place
where their hostess spent time. No books were stacked
by the bed. An afghan was folded and resting on the
seat of the rocker, the room's only chair. "Max, what
are you looking for?"

His brows drew into a tight frown. "I'm not sure.
But I want to find out more about Britt Barlow. For all
I know, everything she told me is a lie."

"About Addison's fall?" Annie considered the possibility.

"About everything." His tone was dour.

Annie said gently, "Max, ease up. Thing about it
is, she's made you mad. But she's upset and scared.
That's for sure. And it's crazy to think she'd admit
to being an accomplice after the fact to murder if it
weren't true."

Brisk footsteps sounded.

Annie whirled to look. Someone was coming up
the back stairs. "Max." Her whisper was sharp. She
gestured for him to come.

They were in the hall, Britt's door shut, and facing
the stairs when a heavy middle-aged woman reached
the top step, breathing deeply. "Those stairs are too
much for a mountain goat." She gave a quick cackle of
laughter. "And nobody'd confuse me with a billy goat."
She weighed well over two hundred pounds. Her round
face was cheerful, the plump cheeks reddened by exer-
tion. A red kerchief covered thick dark curls. "Hello,
hello." She stared at them with unabashed curiosity

out of inquiring blue eyes. She bustled toward them, carrying a tray.

"Lunch for two. You're the Darlings, right? Britt said you were in the Meadowlark Room. You've come too far. Here, I'll show you. A quick left at the top of the main stairs and that'll see you there. I'm Lucinda Phillips, cook and housekeeper." She didn't wait for them to reply, but plodded toward the front of the house, chattering all the while. "You'll find a small refrigerator in the dressing area. It was put there when Mrs. Addison was sick. I've stocked it with water, colas, cheese. You'll find a coffeemaker. Anytime you want a snack, you're welcome in the kitchen. Got hot oatmeal raisin cookies with cranberries today. Everybody gets treated like family. There's an assortment of snacks in the cabins. Breakfast at seven, lunch at noon, dinner at seven-thirty in the dining room, buffet style. Cocktails at seven in the drawing room." She propped the tray on her hip as she opened the door to the Meadowlark Room, held it for them to enter.

The room was serene, the walls pale blue, the woodwork ivory. Ornate gilt patterns decorated the French Empire furniture. Peacock blue upholstery looked bright and new on the sofa and chairs. A fire crackled in the grate. A chaise longue faced the fireplace. Annie was enchanted.

Lucinda moved past them, took the tray to a round table overlooking the verandah. It was set with bright yellow pottery. "Crab salad. Corn fritters. Ambrosia. Iced tea. Anything else you want, come down and tell me. I'll leave the tray and you can clear up and set it in the hall. Harry will attend to it later." She lumbered toward the door. "Enjoy your lunch," and she was gone.

Annie was first to the table. "Mmm, everything looks wonderful."

Max joined her. He propped open his small notebook next to his plate.

Annie ate a fritter first. "They're as good as Ben's!" Annie could give no higher praise. Her heart belonged to Parotti's, the down-home combination café and bait shop on Broward's Rock. "Don't you agree?"

Max speared a fritter, took a bite. "Yeah. Really good." He didn't look up from his study of the map he'd drawn of the cabins.

Annie found the salad delectable and the iced tea refreshing. Only in the South was iced tea a year-round beverage. She felt comfortable and cosseted. She admired the freshness of the blue walls and wondered if they had been painted recently. Or had Britt fixed the room this way for her ailing sister, trying to create cool and comforting surroundings? A door was open to a small adjoining room. That must be where Britt had slept.

Max flipped to a fresh page. As he ate, he made several sketches. He paused, thought, wrote rapidly.

"Scene of the crime?" Annie looked at him inquiringly. She finished the salad, was unable to resist a second fritter.

He turned the notebook, pushed it toward her.

Annie looked at a sketch of the house, the bedrooms labeled with the names of occupants. He'd also sketched the staircase, the wire at the top, a stick figure lying near the base. "The more I think about it, the more reckless it seems. There's absolutely no guarantee Jeremiah would be the victim." He held up a hand when Annie started to interrupt. "I know. Britt says he was always first downstairs. But how could that have been common knowledge?"

"That's easy." Annie sipped her tea. "I'll bet jogging came up at dinner the night before and he told everyone that's how he started the day. When we talk to people, we can find out."

Max looked skeptical. "Okay, let's say everyone knew he jogged early. That aside, consider the distance from the cabins to the house. How could anyone hope to get to the main trail, reach the garden, cross all those terraces, get into the house, creep up the stairs, set the trap, and get all the way back to a cabin without being seen by someone?"

"Who's up in the middle of the night? I don't think it was such a gamble. If I were going to do it, I'd slip out about two in the morning. And if the murderer had run into anyone, he'd have changed his plans. But he didn't." Annie considered a third fritter, reluctantly refrained. A wonderful lunch. But they hadn't come to Golden Silk for pleasure. She had a sense of time rushing ahead and danger coming.

Max looked hopeful. "For all we know, the murderer may have been seen. But the next morning there was no reason for that information to come out. Everyone was talking abut Jeremiah's 'accident.' We'll find out. Somebody may have been up, had insomnia, taken a walk. Though"—he was grave as he tapped the notebook—"these cabins are definitely isolated. Anyone can take a path, move without being seen."

Annie finished a sip of tea. Suddenly the pale blue room didn't seem as inviting, despite the fire and the succulent meal. She pictured the island after nightfall, populated with phantoms moving through shadows toward Heron House, where no door was ever locked.

Annie pulled on a windbreaker and stepped out onto the verandah. She leaned over the railing and watched as Max came down the front steps. He paused at the bottom, looked up, waved, then veered in the opposite direction of their earlier walk. Annie watched until he was out of sight. She sighed. The verandah was gloomy even though the gentle rain had ended. Wet branches glistened in pale sunlight. Annie paced impatiently, wished she'd gone with him. She looked down at the binoculars on the wicker table. Max's instructions had been clear. "You can get the first look at these people. They won't know anyone's watching. Pick up on their interaction with Britt. Get a sense of who they are." Annie knew she'd looked nonplussed. He'd paused at the door and grinned. "Come on, Annie. You can do it. Pretend you are Laurel." And he was gone.

She repeated the injunction aloud, though perhaps not in quite as encouraging a tone. "Pretend you are Laurel." A smile tugged at her lips. What a frightening thought. Max's mother . . . Well, truth to tell, Max's mother was delightful, delirious, unpredictable, mad-cap, and amazing. She was also empathetic. How often she'd known exactly how Annie felt and spoken the perfect words of encouragement or comfort.

Pretend she was Laurel . . .

Footsteps sounded on the front steps. Annie grabbed the binoculars and moved to a corner of the verandah to stand behind a tall potted fern. She had a clear view of the front drive and Britt striding toward the dock.

Pretend . . .

Annie knew that right this moment, hundreds of miles distant, Laurel's Nordic blue eyes widened with pleasure, her patrician beauty graced the day, her throaty laughter lifted everyone near. Laurel encouraged creativity, likening moods to the swirl of colored ribbons, divining auras as easily as an ornithologist identifying birds. If Laurel were here, she would form an instant opinion of those she viewed, and more often than not, her judgments would be sound.

An odd sensation suffused Annie's mind. She felt mellow as summer sunshine, liberated as a soaring eagle, joyous as an embrace. She lifted the binoculars. Three magnified faces moved into her eyes and mind, dramatic as visages on a theater screen, emotions easily discerned.

Britt Barlow—rather a hard face, but she was staking her future on what happened this weekend—no hint of fear—an impervious look—though that smile was forced—definitely a strong personality—welcoming gestures—quick jerky movements—hustling them toward the house—the lady was all business—an iron core—

Jay Addison—in a fog—a fog of sadness—his father?—doesn't care about Britt—oh, speaking nicely enough but he's looking toward the house—eyes like a hurt animal—pain down deep—likely always been on the outside looking in—not tough enough—mood swings—avoids confrontations—

Dana Addison—right at his elbow—defensive—worried—scared—pretty as a Persian cat, a soft round face, but there are claws even if they're sheathed at the moment—if anyone threatens Jay, she'll scratch their eyes out—buttons and bows, ruffles and calico, velveteen bunnies and teddy bears—

Annie watched Britt and her guests until they were out of sight, taking the path into the woods, then she dashed into the room, found Max's legal pad. She returned to the verandah and settled at the wicker table even though it was chilly. She didn't intend to miss a single arrival.

Now, to record her impressions. She chewed on the tip of the pen, then reminded herself she was simply pretending to be Laurel. The words spilled out on the page. . . .

Max stopped at the line of pines, looked back. It was a good view of the three-story house, the avenue of live oaks to the Sound, the long pier, the terraced gardens and, far distant, the rectangular rock pool against the backdrop of the maritime forest. Hidden in the forest were the eight cabins. He nodded, clear now on the geography.

He walked into the pines, following a wide and well-defined path, growth cut back, crushed shells underfoot. He'd gone about twenty yards when he stopped in surprise. Two metal stanchions on either side of the path supported a chain. From the chain hung a sign. Red letters proclaimed:

PRIVATE
EMPLOYEES ONLY
CLOSED TO PUBLIC
DANGER

Well, he was an employee. He stepped over the chain. The path was narrower here but still well covered with oyster shells. Wet ferns brushed him, occasional drops of water splatted down as the wind rustled the pines.

The path split. Max hesitated, then veered to his left. The forest looked almost impenetrable to either side, hospitable to foxes, raccoons, cougars, perhaps even wild boars. He'd gone another twenty yards before he reached a clearing. Three modest cabins rose on pilings. He strode to the nearest, gave a swift look around, and thudded up the steps. He knocked on the door. When there was no answer, he turned the knob, stepped inside.

His eyes widened. The chairs, sofa, walls, and lampshades were pink. Dolls of every age, type, and description filled two bookcases. Plump, skinny, large and small dolls sat, lay, and stood. Rag dolls, porcelain dolls, Barbies. Max stepped to a desk in one corner. He pulled out a drawer, found a checkbook. Lucinda Phillips. He poked his head into the bedroom. Pink ruffles on the bed. A pink satin chair. More dolls.

Max regained the clearing with a feeling of relief. The second cabin was empty. Each bedroom contained a single bed, nightstand, vanity, and small armchair. The living room decor was as impersonal and unadorned as a hotel room—a sofa, two chairs. There was no trace of occupancy, although one bedroom held a faint violet scent. Max's nose wriggled. His mother had always been fond of violet bath powder.

He paused at the front door for a final survey. At a guess, this cabin served as quarters for the maids, who, according to Britt, came and went. Apparently Golden Silk was presently without domestic staff.

In the living room of the third cabin, Max's nose wriggled again. Pipe smoke. A pipe rack, humidor, and heavy pottery ashtray in the shape of the state of Texas were the only items on top of a massive wooden desk. The furnishings were Spartan and clearly masculine, a brown leather sofa, a worn recliner, a rifle case, a boot-scarred pine coffee table. Hunting and fishing magazines were stacked atop a metal trunk beneath a front window.

Max's examination of the bedroom and its closet was cursory—work clothes, flannel shirts, a down jacket, a hunting vest, boots, boat shoes. Not a single suit. The chest held underclothing, sweaters, socks of all sorts.

Max was almost to the front door when he veered toward the desk. It had been easy enough to find the checkbook with Lucinda Phillips's name. He would do the same for Harry Lyle, though this was surely his cabin. Max pulled at the center drawer. The drawer didn't budge. The drawer was locked. He yanked at the side drawers. Locked, all three of them.

Max stared at the desk. Was Harry Lyle simply a very private man? Or did he have something in that desk that he couldn't afford for anyone to see?

Max looked again at the simple, spare furnishings of the living room. No photographs. No books. Nothing to tell about the man who lived here. Was Harry Lyle a man who made little impression on his surroundings or was he avoiding any revelations about his past? Max's gaze paused at the rifle case. He walked to it. Locked, of course, as it should be. The rifle case was near the metal trunk. The back of the trunk faced the room. In two strides, Max reached the trunk, bent to see. A closed padlock hung from the hasps. It took only an instant to remove the magazines, attempt to lift one end. The trunk wasn't merely serving as a window seat. The trunk—the locked trunk—was chock-full of something heavy. Max replaced the magazines.

Max frowned in thought when he regained the main path. Harry Lyle's penchant for locking up his belongings might have no relevance to the death of Jeremiah Addison. On the other hand, it might be of critical importance. It would be interesting to see what kind of information Barb had dredged up about Harry Lyle. What was it Annie had said? First she'd suggested they look hardest at the guests who were not ordinarily invited to the island. But she had made the point that if the murderer usually was on the island, it made sense to fix the trap when others were present.

Max followed the path perhaps a quarter mile to another clearing. There were three wooden structures—a good-sized generator with a deep, steady hum, a storage shed, and a garbage compactor. He circled the buildings, more out of thoroughness than expectation. On the far side of the generator station, he saw a faint opening into the pines. Another trail. He hesitated, shrugged, plunged into the woods. This path was much fainter and obviously less traveled.

A crackling noise sounded ahead of him. Max stopped to listen.

Annie held the binoculars steady. Here came money and power, sleek blond hair, a tan cashmere coat, alligator handbag and pumps. The man a step behind her wore a blue-and-gray checked cashmere sport coat, gray worsted wool trousers, black tasseled loafers. Head high, regal as a queen, the woman held out her hand to Britt Barlow. The cluster of diamonds in her wedding ring glittered even in the weak sunlight.

Pretend ...

Millicent McRae—ambitious as Cleopatra—lusty as Mae West—enigmatic as Marlene Dietrich—impervious as Margaret Thatcher—a nimble intelligence—humorless—clever—oozing charm to Britt—why?

Nick McRae—possessive—arrogant—proud of his wife—one of his possessions—disdainful of social inferiors—expects subservience—reluctant to be here—

Britt shepherded her guests through the garden. They rounded the fountain and were out of sight.

Annie returned to the legal pad, began to write though she fought a growing fatigue. In the future she must make more allowances for Laurel. Empathy was heavy work.

Brush crackled again, twigs crushed underfoot, a rustle of vegetation.

Max called out, "Hello?"

There was a silence, then a man answered. "Yo.

Hold up there." The command was brusque, the voice a deep growl.

Max waited. It was cool and dim in the pine forest. A cardinal flashed in a nearby tree.

A stocky man in a plaid flannel shirt, worn jeans, and brown leather boots laced to the knee plodded around a fern, stopped, folded his arms. A fringe of gray hair circled a round bald head. His sun-darkened face was as gnarled and tough as an alligator's back. Dark eyes peered from beneath grizzled brows. He stood with his legs spread apart. "This here's a private path, mister. Didn't you see the sign?" He looked as immovable as a granite boulder.

Max grinned, stuck out his hand. "Max Darling. I work for Britt. She told me I could go anywhere I wanted, look the place over." After all, Britt said he and Annie could make themselves at home. As far as Max was concerned, he had carte blanche.

The bunched shoulders relaxed. "She said that? Well, that's okay then." A strong hand gripped Max's.

Max was casual. "You're Harry Lyle." The man with a fancy for locks. "Britt said you keep everything shipshape."

"That's right. There's always something needs fixing. I was just stringing up a new aerial for the radio. Had a big wind last week with that storm." He gestured in the direction from which he'd come. "I'll show you." He turned and led the way.

Annie focused the binoculars on the long, dark, sour face of Gerald Gamble, Jeremiah's hatchet man, now

Craig Addison's executive secretary. If anyone ever looked the part of a villain, it was Gerald. Heavy-lidded dark eyes flickered from side to side, jutting cheekbones, thin lips, heavy chin.

Craig Addison smiled as he shook Britt's hand. There was no suggestion of strain in his greeting. He looked what he was, mid-thirties, handsome, success-ful, genial. His smile faded as he looked past his host-ess toward the house where his father had died.

Gerald—suspicious—deliberate—intuitive—spooked as a horse hearing a rattlesnake—

Craig—impatient—an underlying grimness—a hint of uncertainty—a determination to fulfill an obligation—

Britt seemed animated with these guests, pausing once to point toward the bottom of the garden. Gerald and Craig were both attentive, but there was no plea-sure in their faces.

Max estimated the yacht anchored in the cove to be fifty, maybe fifty-two feet in length. The pleasure boat glistened with care, the rails polished, the paint job fresh. "Good-looking." His admiration was genuine.

They stood at the end of a long pier. A motorboat was moored near a ladder. Harry rocked back on the heels of his boots. "I told Ms. Barlow she should use it for charter. I handle it by myself just for her, but I could pick up a crew in Savannah if need be. Lots of folks pay ten thousand a week to charter this kind of boat. But she keeps it for herself. And to herself. She says too many folks might think they want to come to an island and after they got here want to leave if they knew there was boats handy. As far as she's concerned, you pay for a week, you stay for a week. She tells them right off, once you come, you're here until the boat comes back to pick you up."

Max felt like making a fist and punching the sky. What a relief to know none of them were truly marooned on this island. His relief was immediately laced with a quick anger. His employer had been a little less than forthcoming. Britt Barlow hadn't said a word about a yacht or a motorboat. This cove explained why their skipper had gone out into open ocean and then swung around the southern tip of the island to the dock. He must have been instructed to avoid the lee side and this obvious harbor. Britt had said no one could depart until Sunday and the island was not in cell phone range of the mainland. What else had she neglected to mention?

But now he knew about the yacht. That knowledge might turn out to be an ace up his sleeve. And he would be as mum as Britt had been.

He looked at the handyman. "You were putting up an aerial?"

Annie adjusted the binoculars, brought the image into sharp focus. She murmured aloud, "What's an elegant woman like you doing in a place like this?"

Isabel Addison shaded her eyes, gazed at the house. Her face looked somber, haunted. The women were a study in contrast, Isabel a forlorn, uncertain guest, Britt the image of a woman in charge, crisp and brisk and forceful.

Isabel Addison—struggling with emotion—fear—despair—profound sadness—a troubled spirit—but brave, very brave—

Isabel had come to Golden Silk by herself. Craig had arrived with his employee. What had happened between Craig and Isabel? Why had she left her husband the week after his father was murdered? What were her thoughts as she returned to the island? Not pleasant, Annie decided. Definitely not pleasant.

Annie sighed as she added to her notes. So far, Millicent McRae was the only guest to evince any pleasure upon arrival, and Annie doubted Millicent's effort at charm was genuine. But lack of charm didn't equate to murderous impulses.

Annie tapped the legal pad with the pen. Odd. So far she'd picked up a plethora of emotions among the arriving guests, but not a hint of guilt. Perhaps there were limits to the depth of perception employed so routinely by Laurel. Perhaps Annie lacked her mother-in-law's skill. Perhaps—and the verandah seemed darker, chillier—the murderer felt no guilt.

Harry's boots thumped on the pier as he led the way to shore. A metal storage shed with its door ajar sat near a cabin on stilts. He scrambled up the ladder to the cabin, waited on a narrow porch for Max. He pointed to the roof and a crisscross of wires. "Got the aerial up." He opened the front door, stood aside for Max to enter.

The square room contained a worktable, several chairs, and, against the far wall, a built-in bench with a ham radio.

Max crossed the clean wooden floor, stood next to a swivel chair, studied the switches. Dials glowed green and gold. "Quite a setup."

"She's got the latest equipment. I'll say one thing for Ms. Barlow, she doesn't stint on upkeep. Or staff." Harry joined Max. "Now, what kind of work are you in, Mr. Darling?" There was a smile on his face but the eyes that watched Max had a cold, dark core.

Annie's lips pursed in a soundless whistle. Here came trouble. If not for her, surely for whoever stood in the path of Kim Kennedy. Britt Barlow looked wary. This might be an invitation she would rue.

Kim moved toward her hostess with the beauty of an enchantress, the stride of a Valkyrie, and the questing gaze of a smart, tough, ruthless reporter. She looked crisp and commanding in a soft wool jacket, black with a white windowpane pattern, black slacks, and black square-toed penny loafers. Kim greeted Britt with a brilliant smile, a brisk handshake.

Annie read the carmine lips in the magnified predatory face: *How kind of you to think of me.* And, Laurel-like, Annie honed in on Kim's thoughts—*No match for me—can't fool me, not now, not ever—what glorious fun—*

"Oh." Max's voice was casual. "I'm a consultant, Harry. People who are curious about things get in touch with me. I find answers for them. You can call me Max." His smile was sunny as he moved to the door. "Do you use the radio as well?"

Harry stood still for an instant, his craggy face unreadable, his cold eyes on Max. "Me? Oh, no. Not my job. Ms. Barlow takes care of emergencies, and that's what it's for. Like she said, you have to be prepared.

About a month ago, a guest got sick. Heart attack. Ms. Barlow called for help and medevac was here in a little over an hour."

He was still chatting, pointing out the storage shed, when they reached the ground. ". . . got ropes, extra life jackets, canned foods, flares, ship parts for minor repairs. Anything major we go into a marina in Savannah."

"You been a sailor for long?" Max picked up a stick, pitched it toward the water.

"Off and on." Harry folded his arms.

The stick splashed. Max picked up another, hefted it. "You from these parts?"

"Upstate." Harry's voice was laconic. "You?"

Max brushed pine straw from his fingers. "Broward's Rock. It's pretty quiet this time of year. No tourists. But not"—he glanced toward the pines—"as quiet as here. Is that what attracted you to the job?"

The question amused Harry. "Hell, no. I get paid big bucks. Mr. Addison paid me five times what I could get shoreside. Ms. Barlow does the same. Three weeks on, one week off. First week of the month, everybody leaves. Lucinda's got a sister in Aiken. I keep an apartment in Savannah. Britt puts the maids up at a seaside motel. Everybody does their own thing. Then we come back, work for three weeks. Best of all, I do my work on my own schedule. Nobody butts me around." His thin lips rippled in a satisfied smile. The smile wasn't reflected in his cold gaze. "Now, in your job, I bet you run into some funny setups. Though I don't know what Ms. Barlow would want you to do on Golden Silk. Everything here's pretty much aboveboard."

Max was bland. "You'd think so, wouldn't you? But sometimes it's a good idea to check things out. Thanks for showing me around." Max turned toward the pines. "I'll be back in touch."

Max didn't look back. But he knew Harry watched him all the way to the woods.

The face was familiar to millions. At home Annie would have clicked off the TV. Now she twiddled with the focus, and Everett Crenshaw's bleached mound of hair; pale eyes; long, thin nose; arrogant, patronizing smirk; and receding chin seemed close enough to touch and much too close for comfort. Why was it that media moguls often elevated to stardom talking heads with all the charm of rabid rats? Perhaps because political commentators now gloried in aggression and bloodlust, not qualities common to cultivated correspondents. Crenshaw wore his trademark floppy red shirt with a purple cravat, skintight black trousers, and desert boots.

Everett Crenshaw—excited—with a feline quickness—always out for number one—unscrupulous—a gambler—ready to fight but only on his terms—

"Britt, you look marvelous." He drew out the three syllables in a high mocking tone. "I'm looking forward to a most intriguing weekend." His carrying voice professed admiration while his magnified features exuded malice.

Britt Barlow appeared unfazed. She hooked an arm through Crenshaw's, turned him toward the gardens, bent her head and spoke rapidly.

His snickering whoop of laughter faded as they walked toward the fountain.

Annie wrote rapidly. She put the binoculars on the wicker table and hurried into the room with the legal pad. The warmth of the fire didn't ease the chill she carried with her. Soon she and Max would meet Britt's guests in the lovely drawing room of Heron House.

Along with Jeremiah's ghost, of course.

∾ *Four* ∾

MAX LEANED AGAINST THE OPEN DOORWAY of the bathroom, legal pad in hand. He finished reading, looked up. "Good stuff." He almost told Annie it was awesome how in tune her observations were with his mother's visionary thought processes. He opened his mouth, closed it. Least said . . .

"Yes?" Annie's gray eyes were alert even though her skin was shell pink from the warmth of the bath.

"Just thinking about my talk with Harry." Which was true in a sense. Mmm, very pink skin. What skin he could see. Which wasn't enough. Her arms and shoulders rose enticingly from a huge mound of billowy bubbles. Tendrils of blond curls peeped from beneath a shower cap. Max moved nearer the oversized claw-foot tub. "He strikes me as one tough dude. I'd be worried as hell if I thought we were stuck here with this weird mix of people. But there's a yacht, a motorboat, and a ham radio. None of which our hostess shared with us. So we won't let her know we know." His eyes glinted. He was clearly in a tit-for-tat mood. "And if anybody gets out of line, I'm sure I can count on Harry to give me a hand."

Annie sat up very straight. "If you need help, I'm here."

Rising from the bubbles . . . sexier than any mermaid . . . "Indeed you are. Right here." He tossed away the legal pad. It landed with a thud in the bedroom.

Annie's laughter was light and soft. "Hey, come on in. The water's fine . . . and so are you. . . ."

Ice tinkled in glasses. Sweet-scented hickory logs blazed in the fireplace. Twin chandeliers glistened, the teardrop crystals enchanting as limpid water in the summer sun, a glorious reminder of days when beauty was as important as function. The crimson drapes in the drawing room were closed against evening. It might have been any elegant party in a grand plantation home except for an underlying tension among the guests, reflected in oblique glances, a certain stiffness in conversation, occasional strained pauses.

Britt Barlow moved about the room, talking, gesturing, smiling. The easy drape of her blue tulip-print silk dress emphasized her slenderness. A midnight blue hair clip with rhinestones glittered in her dark hair. She was a thoughtful hostess, making sure her guests felt welcome.

Annie maintained a steady smile while resisting the impulse to tell Millicent McRae she had as much interest in politics as in astrology and thought the two had much in common.

Millicent's smile was steady, too, the practiced accoutrement of a woman always on stage. She was dramatic in a black woolen dress with printed white butterflies rising from the hem to one shoulder. Her ice blond hair was coiled to one side. ". . . expect a weekend such as this to be very instructive. I am always eager to learn more about my constituents. Britt assured me this gathering might form the core of a future support group. What prompts your enthusiasm for my programs?"

Annie recalled televised press conferences. Savvy politicos always avoided awkward queries by responding to a question that had not been asked. Her cheek muscles felt strained, but she continued to look—she hoped—eager and enthusiastic. "I believe in grassroots democracy." Even soulful. "Everyone here strikes me as utterly committed. Just as I'm sure Jeremiah"—Annie's tone suggested she and Jeremiah had often shared political insights—"was one of your staunchest admirers. What did you and he talk about that last weekend?"

"That last weekend?" Millicent's modulated voice repeated the words slowly. Pale blue eyes fastened on Annie as if seeing her for the first time. She stared at Annie, then slowly scanned the gathering, one person at a time. As her head moved, Everett Crenshaw walked through the open double doors into the drawing room, the last of the guests to arrive for cocktails. He looked speculatively at Britt. She gave him a pleasant smile. Everett strolled toward Isabel, sitting stiffly in an Empire chair near the fire, her face averted from the group. Tonight his floppy shirt was navy silk and the cravat a pale blue. It might be a dramatic costume on screen. In person he looked absurd. But there was nothing absurd in the questing glance that ranged the room, bright, quick, intelligent eyes that missed nothing.

When Millicent's survey was complete, her face hardened, making her look like an expensive parrot, with vivid feathers and a beaked face.

Annie wanted to exclaim, as Ann Landers always advised, *Wake up and smell the coffee.* And to ask, *Is this the first time you've really looked at your fellow guests? Oh, yes, sweetheart, it's a reunion, and everyone here except Max and me has a special bond.*

Millicent abruptly turned and walked away. Annie raised an eyebrow. It was as if—poof—Annie had disappeared. Obviously, she was no longer of interest to Millicent. The politician walked stiffly to the sideboard with the hors d'oeuvres. She stood with her back to the room, her shoulders rigid.

Annie sipped club soda, looked over the assemblage. Max was deep in conversation with Gerald Gamble. Craig Addison stood as far from Isabel as possible but his eyes never left her. Kim Kennedy, eyes intent, studied a pair of ornate silver candlesticks on the mantel. Jay and Dana Addison sat on the piano bench, Jay holding a mother-of-pearl picture frame. He stared at the photograph. Dana looked as broody as a mother hen with a threatened chick. Everett Crenshaw, head poked forward, prominent eyes pale as gooseberries, gestured to an aloof Isabel. Nick McRae fingered an ivory knight on a chessboard sitting atop the Louis XV commode. Hollow-cheeked Britt Barlow met Annie's gaze. Britt's smile was strained.

Balancing a tray with ease, Harry Lyle moved soft-footed across the room. He looked inquiringly at Britt. She shook her head. Harry nodded, began gathering up drink glasses.

Britt clapped her hands together. She looked solemn. "Everyone . . ."

Conversation fell away. Faces turned toward her.

"I want to thank each of you for coming to Golden Silk. I made some promises in the letters you received. Those promises will be kept." She took a deep breath. Now the words came fast. "I want to explain that this weekend also serves another purpose. As I'm sure most of you have realized"—her words fell into a pool of watchful silence—"everyone here with the exception of Max and Annie Darling"—there were several quick glances toward them—"was also here the weekend Jeremiah died." Her voice was uneven. "I suppose I should have broached my plan to everyone in advance, but I was afraid some of you might feel uncomfortable and decline to come." She made a helpless gesture. "That's why I couched the invitations as I did. But," she added hastily, "I have every intention of making sure everyone receives exactly what I promised. Anyway, now you are here and I can explain in person. I hope you'll agree this is the right thing to do and be willing to help."

Millicent McRae glared at Britt. "I understood this to be a gathering of politically astute individuals interested in taking part in my campaign. If that is not the case, I demand to return to the mainland. Immediately."

Britt was calm but determined. "I hope you will see fit to cooperate when I explain. Whether you do or don't, no one can depart until Sunday afternoon. I have arranged for everyone to be picked up at five o'clock. Until then"—her tone was decided—"you are my guests."

Annie exchanged a long look with Max. Only they—and Britt and her staff—knew transportation was within a stone's throw. But perhaps Britt's deception was necessary. Millicent was not the only restive guest.

Gerald Gamble's bony face flushed a dark red. "Sequestering guests against their will certainly amounts to a criminal act. If we are truly marooned here, I will hold you accountable to the law."

"Well, well," Everett Crenshaw drawled in malicious amusement. "We all should have known better." His voice was slightly thick. He took a gulp from his glass. "Golden Silk, those are spiders to watch out for. An orb weaver with a golden body and golden legs. High fashion in the arachnid world." He gave a high giggle. "Did you know Golden Silks spin huge webs between trees and that those webs are strong enough to trap a rider on a horse? Oh hey, I love knowing things like that. Little facts to titillate the masses. But Britt's outdoing even a Golden Silk. Damned if she hasn't trapped herself an island full of visitors. What a coup."

A frown hardened Craig Addison's customarily pleasant face. He strode to Britt, loomed over her. "What's going on?" It was the abrupt demand of a man now accustomed to being in charge.

Isabel Addison lifted a hand to her lips. Her face was grave, her dark eyes filled with foreboding.

Britt turned out her hands toward Craig in a plea. "I wrote you that I planned to create a memorial here on the island in your father's memory. That's what I want to do." Her voice was suddenly upbeat and her face alight with enthusiasm. She looked around the room at unreceptive, questioning faces. "All of us together. We can do it." She might have been a cheerleader urging a team to victory. "We were here the weekend he died. I want each one of us to think back to our last encounter with him, talk about the way he was. We can create a dramatic picture of a great man's final hours. And"—her smile was bright with pride—"I want it to be done right and that's why I invited Mr. and Mrs. Darling to join us." Her smile included them. "Max and Annie are oral historians, skilled in eliciting the kind of details that bring a narrative to life. I know you will enjoy talking to them."

Max's expression was genial. Annie ducked her head modestly while admiring their hostess's convincing demeanor. Annie was quite sure that Britt despised Jeremiah Addison. Yet now she recalled him as a great man with utter conviction in her voice. Annie was impressed. If she and Max carried off their roles as well, the investigation should be duck soup. Duck soup sounded rather greasy and not at all appetizing. Why should boiling a duck be synonymous with ease? Annie pictured the limp carcass of a duck in a cauldron then firmly reined in her mind. It was all right to emulate Laurel's thought processes to hone intuitiveness but it should not become a habit.

"And, of course," Britt added, looking hopefully at Everett and Kim, "I hope Everett and Kim will describe our efforts and create wonderfully compelling stories."

Kim's burst of laughter was abrupt and genuine. She flicked an impudent glance at Britt. "Honey, personal

recollections are way too tame for today's market unless you throw in some arson or incest or big-time lar-
ceny. That might add enough spice. Or you could bet
the island against the most interesting revelation about
Jeremiah. You know, up the stakes. Like the old-time
plantation owner wagering the home place on a throw
of the dice. I suspect"—her cool eyes moved around
the room—"some of those present might know some
dandy facts about Jeremiah." Kim was the epitome of
relaxed elegance, slim and complacent in a black col-
larless jacket and a sand-colored blouse that matched
her flared slacks. She reached out, picked up the
two-foot-tall candlestick, held it up until lights from
the chandelier were reflected in bright sharp flashes.
"I'll be glad to play your game. I have some interesting memories of Jeremiah. And I'll take these"—she
waggled the candlestick—"as a memento."

"Take them?" Isabel's voice was puzzled.

Kim pointed the silver piece at Britt. "I've got it
down in black and white. She said I can pick out something to remember Jeremiah by. Ask the lady. Maybe
she'll open it up for everyone. But first come, first
served. These candlesticks are mine."

A gong sounded. Harry stepped into the doorway
and announced, "Dinner is served."

Annie sipped fruity chardonnay and made occasional
admiring comments about the menu to Jay Addison,
who sat to her left. Jay's replies were monosyllabic. He
never looked toward her. Annie's enthusiasm was genuine. The buffet was extraordinary: Roquefort-stuffed
shrimp and chilled corn-and-crab flan, baked trout on

orange wild rice, tamale pie, oysters Florentine, acorn squash with raisins and walnuts, carrots with cognac, and asparagus with chopped egg and butter sauce. Annie knew Max would find time over the weekend for a chef-to-chef visit with Lucinda.

Despite Annie's enchantment with the delectable food, she paid attention to business. She ostensibly devoted her attention to Jay, but focused on the muttered exchanges between Craig Addison and Gerald Gamble. Every so often she snatched a quick look at the two men, who sat across from each other.

Gerald, his long face dour, squashed pieces of a cloverleaf roll into tiny pellets. "It's a damn fool idea. Oral history."

Craig scooped up a carrot. His ill humor in the drawing room was gone, but he looked weary. "I suppose it's well meant. In any event, it can't do any harm." His lips quirked in a wry smile. "It would have surprised the hell out of Dad to know Britt planned anything in his honor."

Gerald shot a glare at Britt. "Maybe she feels guilty."

"I wouldn't have thought so." Craig's answer was absentminded. He stared at his wife at the other end of the table. Their glances met. Isabel turned quickly to Everett Crenshaw. The reporter raised an eyebrow, looked from Isabel to her husband. Everett had carried a full tumbler of whisky to the table. He drank the last portion, held up the glass as Harry came into the dining room. Max gazed admiringly at Kim Kennedy, listened as if entranced. The former intern's lips curved in a seductive smile. The candlesticks were placed

prominently by her plate. She placed a possessive
hand on Max's arm, gave him a smile and a lingering
squeeze.

Annie's eyes narrowed.

Kim released Max and reached for the decanter of
wine, refilled her glass and Max's.

Max looked briefly toward Annie, winked. His expression suggested a man had to do what a man had
to do.

Annie glared and got a quick, wicked grin in response.

Gerald speared a crumb-and-cheese-topped oyster.
Sautéed spinach dangled from the fork. "What's so
special about Jeremiah's last couple of days? If she
wanted to round up memories, I could give her a list of
people who knew him well." He radiated disapproval.

Britt was locked into conversation with Nick McRae,
but her glance moved around the table. The way the
light fell from the chandelier, her face was partially in
shadow. Perhaps it was this obscurity that made her
look somber and fatigued. Millicent's husband gestured with one perfectly manicured hand. ". . . seems
essential to me that we continue to replenish the
beaches. Tourism is . . ."

Millicent was all charm with Craig, smiling attentively. "Of course, we can agree that deregulation is
the wave of the future. But in your opinion does this
mean . . ."

Annie finished her portion of tamale pie. This
wasn't the kind of evening to return to the buffet table.
Oh well. She brightened. Harry had just entered with a
trolley of desserts. Sherried fried bananas, lime sorbet,

almond cake. She debated whether it would be piggy to take a serving of both the fried bananas and the almond cake.

Harry began to clear the plates. He was deft and quick. Annie noted his powerful hands.

Britt's voice rose above the clink of dishes. "After dessert, we'll have coffee and drinks in the drawing room. I thought we might work out times tomorrow when Max and Annie can visit with each of you. And I hope everyone will enjoy walking on the beach and reading and relaxing. I want this to be a lovely Golden Silk holiday as well as an opportunity to remember Jeremiah."

"Remember Jeremiah." Everett drawled the words. His voice was ever so slightly but definitely slurred. His hand firmly gripped a tumbler once again filled with whisky. "Oh, come on, Britt. Stop the charade." He pushed back his chair, rose unsteadily to his feet, still holding the glass. "Tell everybody the truth. This is one hell of a party that's under way. Put everything on the table. Fill them in on the reason for their tête-à-têtes with our Darling duo tomorrow."

"Everett, come with me." Britt jumped up, hurried around the table, one hand outstretched. "I need to speak with you."

He backed away from her. "No, no, no." It was a tipsy parody of good-humored teasing. "You see, I've been thinking. My esteemed colleague"—he raised his glass to Kim—"or she'll be a colleague if she ever gets back to the big league. Maybe another media titan will be enchanted with her"—a lascivious smile—"abilities. In any event, my former colleague made a very good point. Nobody will give a damn about what anybody here remembers about Jeremiah. But everybody loves a juicy murder."

"Murder?" Millicent's cry was choked. She looked wildly about. "What does he mean?"

Craig pushed back his chair, stood, faced his employee. "Crenshaw, you'd better explain yourself." Craig's face was grim.

"Am I Everett Crenshaw, investigative journalist extraordinaire? Yes. Do I get the facts? Always." The slur in his speech became more pronounced. He wavered a little on his feet. "Come this way, ladies and gentlemen." He turned, walked with careful dignity toward the hall. In the doorway, he stopped, gestured impatiently. "Don't miss out. Come one, come all."

Britt was right behind him, her voice low and urgent. Crenshaw ignored her.

Max hesitated, then stood and moved toward the hallway. Annie popped up. As if on cue, chairs were pushed back and the other guests hesitantly followed.

Crenshaw smiled in drunken approval. "Showing is telling. That's my mantra. Show. Don't tell. Now let's visit the scene of the crime." He walked purposefully if a little unsteadily toward the staircase. He stopped, faced the straggling group, clamped his free hand on the newel post, raised his glass in salute. "Gather round, children, and you shall hear"—his voice dropped to a sepulchral tone—"a story all should fear."

Max came up beside him, took him firmly by the elbow, spoke quietly.

Annie close behind, heard, "How about a nightcap in your cabin? I'll walk there with you."

Crenshaw shook free. Whisky sloshed from his glass. "Now look what you made me do." Petulant, he squinted at the amber liquid, raised the tumbler to his lips, finished the drink. "Bug off, Darling. I won't shut up, go away, disappear, take a hike. I'm on a mission." He climbed two steps and turned to preen before his audience.

Harry Lyle strode down the hall, stopped beside Britt. The jerk of his head toward Crenshaw was a clear offer to remove him. Max, too, looked toward Britt. In the doorway to the kitchen, Lucinda was a somber figure, her smudged pink apron an odd domestic contrast to her watchful face.

Britt had lost her decisive look. She ran a hand through her dark hair and the resulting tangle made her appear young and stricken. "No. I don't want a struggle. If he wants to tell them, I can't stop him." Her voice faded to a defeated sigh.

Craig Addison stood like a bull, head jutting forward. His wife hung back, one hand braced against the dining room doorpost. A muscle fluttered in Isabel's throat. Kim Kennedy placed her hands on her hips. Her round face intent, she watched Crenshaw with narrowed eyes. Jay slipped a protective arm around Dana's shoulders. Gerald Gamble cleared his throat, took a step forward.

Millicent pointed at Crenshaw and said in a shrill voice, "You're drunk. All this talk about murder. That's absurd. I don't intend to spend a minute more in such an unpleasant situation." She turned to go, but her husband gripped her arm, brought her to a stop.

Crenshaw's reply was as quick as an adder's tongue.

"Murder. Oh, yes, it was murder. Jeremiah didn't fall, dear ones. Jeremiah crashed to his death over a strand of wire strung across the top of the staircase." Crenshaw clapped his hands over the babble of questions. His smile was full of malice. "Our dear hostess knows all about it." He made a formal bow toward Britt. "She found the great man and the wire that killed him and she removed every trace of the crime."

The silence was abrupt.

Annie looked into Everett Crenshaw's eyes. She expected to see the bleary softness of a drunk. Instead, his gaze was cold and calculating and pleased. When he realized Annie's appraisal, his eyes moved away. He blinked and gave a foolish smile.

Britt took a step back, came up against the wall. She looked lost and terribly alone.

Craig's feet were heavy on the heart-pine floor. He stopped a scant foot away from Britt. "What's he talking about?"

Britt clasped her hands together, tried to still their trembling. "Craig, please forgive me." She looked toward a stone-faced Jay. "You and Jay. I did the wrong thing but Cissy was so horribly sick."

Craig jerked his head toward Everett. "Is he telling the truth?"

Britt was a long time responding. Finally, she nodded. "Yes." Her answer was as faint as the sough of pines in a winter wind. "I heard a sound that morning . . ." Once begun, she didn't falter, the frightful words filling the stricken quiet of the hallway. "And when I looked down, I saw the wire. For an instant, it didn't make any sense and then I understood. Someone knew he was always first down to go jog and they came up the stairs in the night and fixed the wire to trip him."

"Dad murdered . . ." Craig stared at the stairway as if seeing a crumpled figure. His face hardened. "You found him and what then?" His voice was rough.

She met his gaze with a trace of defiance. "Cissy was dying. She adored him. I didn't want the police and questions"—she didn't look toward Kim, but there was something in the sudden movement of her shoulders that jerked Annie's eyes toward the young blond woman—"and all the nastiness that was sure to come out. I didn't want Cissy to be hurt. I thought—if nobody knew—if everyone thought he had fallen, it would be all right. I took the wire and got rid of it."

"Goddamn." Kim's cry was harsh. "Somebody—oh, if I ever figure it out, somebody's going to pay."

"So that was all a lie, about a tribute to Dad, and these people"—Jay flapped a big hand toward Max and Annie—"aren't here to find out about him?"

"Duh," Crenshaw drawled. "No wonder Papa made you sit in the corner with a dunce cap."

Jay's face flushed. He took a step toward his tormentor. Dana grabbed his arm, held tight.

Craig wasn't distracted. His eyes never left Britt. "You aided and abetted a murderer. What's your game now?"

"No game." Her voice was uneven. "I got a letter from Everett. He told me he'd been at the house early that morning. He'd wanted to have a private talk with Jeremiah. He came in the back door. When he walked into the hall, he saw Jeremiah and then he saw me at the top of the stairs. I was on my knees . . ." Again she brushed a hand through her hair, her face bemused. "I was shocked by his letter. It never occurred to me anyone would think I was responsible. I knew then that I had to find out the truth."

Craig swung toward the stairs. His scowl was ferocious. "Do I get the picture, you sorry piece of shit, that you kept quiet and then decided to try your hand at blackmail?"

For an instant, Crenshaw's composure wavered. He finally managed a cocky smile. "Not me. But I kept remembering how Jeremiah looked. Like a broken puppet. Hell, I dreamed about him. I decided I should call the cops. I wrote Britt to let her know what had happened and how I was having second thoughts. That seemed the only fair thing to do."

Kim hooted. "If you believe that, ladies and gentlemen, have I got a deal for you on a beachfront house in Arizona."

Everett ignored her though his ears burned a dull red. "Anyway, Britt wrote right back and explained what had happened but said it was time to clear everything up. And she was going to hire a detective." He glanced toward Max.

Gerald Gamble's long face was unamused. "Are we to understand that the Darlings"—he gestured toward Max and Annie—"are detectives?" He might have said "maggots" with the same intonation.

Max was pleasant but firm. "My wife and I specialize in obtaining information. With the cooperation of everyone here, we will be able to present authorities with a summary of the events leading up to Jeremiah Addison's death."

Annie felt like cheering. No one could handle the turmoil and hostility among the guests better than Max. He was now the focus of every eye, dominating the hallway with easy confidence, his pleasant voice devoid of bombast and arrogance, his gaze inquiring yet respectful.

"That is our objective." Max looked at each in turn. "Of course, I advised Ms. Barlow to contact the police."

Britt moved swiftly to Max's side. "Please, I want everyone to understand. Max urged me to notify the police. But everyone was scattered . . . I didn't see how that could work. I know the police have to be involved, but I thought it would be better if I gathered everyone here. I definitely intend to see this through to an answer. Everett's letter only made me do what I know I should have done long before. It wasn't right to hide murder." She shivered. "Murder. I still find it hard to believe. That someone here—"

Again there was silence in the hallway, but this quiet was dark and ominous, heavy as a purple sky before the storm breaks.

"—but I know it's true. All right." There was an echo of her usual briskness. "Now you know the situation. I felt it would be easier for Max and Annie to talk about that weekend if the murderer wasn't on guard. But maybe this way is best. Now everyone knows how important it is to remember everything as accurately as possible. And the great thing about it"—her voice lightened—"only one person should be reluctant to cooperate. Only one person is guilty. Everyone else is innocent and should be glad to help trap a murderer. I feel sure I can count on all of you—except one—doing your best for Jeremiah. In the morning, Max and Annie will find an opportunity to speak to each of you. Tonight everyone can try to remember details that may help." She gave a huge sigh of relief. "I didn't know how wonderful it would be to have this out in the open. I feel better than I have in a long time. Confession really is good for the soul." Her look was diffident toward Craig and Jay. "I understand if you are angry, but I hope you can find it in your hearts to forgive me. Now, let's go into the drawing room for coffee. Harry can bring the desserts—"

"Everybody can be *sooo* charming." Crenshaw gave a drunken laugh. He stood in the archway to the drawing room, holding up a tumbler. The glass was full again.

Annie wondered if he'd filled it from one of the decanters in the drawing room. Surely Harry hadn't served him another drink. No, there was Harry, still a foot or so from Britt, his face thoughtful, his stance pugnacious.

Crenshaw held up the tumbler. "Here's my dessert. It's been a great party, but I like to leave on a high note. I'm sure all of you will enjoy an opportunity to explain how you weren't the one who strung the wire. And tonight, just like Britt suggested, you can plumb your memories, get primed for a heart-to-heart with the sleuths tomorrow. In fact, you'd better be clear about that weekend, where you were, what you did, what you and Jeremiah said to each other. Because"—he gave a little hiccup—"I've been doing some more thinking. And damned if I didn't remember some other intriguing facts, like who Jeremiah was pissed at. It won't do"—he wagged an admonitory finger—"to pretend you were great pals with him if you weren't. I've got a deal with Britt. I get first crack at what the Darlings discover and *I* get to write the first story. So don't fudge even a teensy bit or old Uncle Everett will know you're a liar. And if I tell Britt, why, the game will be up, won't it?"

It was a dramatic exit line.

When the front door closed behind him, Kim Kennedy wrinkled her nose in distaste. "There goes nothing." She strolled toward Britt. "We'd better get one thing straight. He doesn't get an exclusive. I've got my own ideas and I intend to nose around. I'd think the more people looking, the better. We'll see who gets a scoop. And, thanks for the candlesticks." She had them cradled in her arms. "Good night, all."

With her departure, the others streamed toward the door.

Millicent McRae's smile was brittle. "Of course, Nick and I are simply appalled at this turn of events. Jeremiah murdered! Obviously we will do everything we can to help apprehend the perpetrator." Nick followed her, but with a sharp backward glance at Britt.

Craig Addison was blunt, his glance at Britt icy. "I expect to be kept apprised of everything. You've taken quite a bit on yourself." He looked around, "Isabel, I'll walk you to your cabin."

His wife's lips parted, then closed. "Thank you, Craig."

She darted a glance past him. "Gerald, would you like to come with us?"

Craig frowned, but Gerald was moving past him, his lugubrious face suddenly eager. "Isabel, it's good to see you even in such difficult circumstances. Have you . . ." And they were outside, their words lost. Craig drew a sharp irritated breath and followed.

The door closed. Britt looked resolutely toward Jay and Dana. From the dining room there was the sound of dishes and cutlery as Harry cleared the table.

Jay still stood near the base of the stairs, looking up toward the landing, face locked in a scowl, shoulders hunched, hands jammed in his pockets. "I thought he'd tripped himself, going fast the way he always ran over everybody. Instead . . ."

Dana tugged at his elbow. "Honey, please."

He massaged his temple with the heel of his hand. "So he finally pushed someone too far. Who had the guts to do it?" He sounded amazed.

Watching him, Annie was afraid there was also a hint of admiration in his voice.

Dana spoke loudly, overriding his words. "Jay, I'm tired. Let's go now. In the morning everything"—he pulled away from her—"will be clearer . . ." She broke off, knowing he wasn't listening, knowing she could do nothing to protect him.

He walked directly to Britt. His demeanor changed abruptly. The anger and bitterness were gone. Instead, his voice was eager, hopeful. "Did you really find something Mother wrote?"

"I'll show you in the morning. It's just a scrap. I think it's directions to a spot near the gazebo. It may not be important. I'll bring it to breakfast." She gave him a kind look.

"The gazebo." A smile lighted his face. The transformation was amazing. When he'd glared at the staircase where his father had died, there had been a scarcely leashed and frightening malevolence. Now he looked diffident and gentle. "She loved the gazebo. I can always see her in my mind, an old straw hat shading her face, her gloves all stained with dirt, her favorite trowel. She had wonderful roses there. 'And all rare blossoms from every clime / Grew in that garden in perfect prime.'" He brushed back a drooping lock of brown hair. "She loved Shelley, too." His voice was soft. "Whatever you found, I'd like to have it. We'll see you at breakfast."

Dana slipped her arm through his, clearly determined to maneuver him away. "Yes. We'll see you then."

As the door closed behind them, Annie turned from a study of the stairway. "Cops look at the responses of suspects in a murder case. For example, hubby claims to be devastated at the news that his wife's been shot in the library, but his color is good, his appetite hearty, and he can't wait to use his cell to call a bimbo named Tootsie. What's wrong with this picture? So who acted inappropriately tonight? Hands down, Jay Addison is off the chart. Everybody's talking about the murder of his father and what does he do? He stands here"—she patted the newel post—"and all but says, 'Hooray, somebody got him.' When he walks over to Britt, you'd think he'd ream her out for covering up a murder. But no, he goes all dewy-eyed about his mother and roses."

Britt shrugged. "Everybody knows Jay and Jeremiah were at odds. I'd say he responded exactly as anyone might have expected. Now"—her smile was uneven—"since everyone's left—and I don't suppose I blame them—we can have coffee and work out a plan for tomorrow."

"That can sort itself out in the morning. First we've got to talk to Crenshaw." Max took a step toward the door.

Britt shook her head. "Oh, Max, let it go. I should have expected something of the sort. He's incapable of playing a subordinate role. He was just being the life of the party. He has to be the center of attention. I knew he was drinking too much but I don't know what I could have done about it. Anyway"—she spread out her hands—"he may have done us a favor. I hadn't thought about it that way, but everyone will want to find out the truth except the murderer. That will surely make things easier. There's no point in scolding him."

Max's face was somber. "It's too late to worry about what he's done. But we have to find out what else he knows."

Britt looked puzzled. "I don't know what you mean. He told everything I did."

"His farewell zinger. He said he knew who Jeremiah was mad at." Max's tone was grave.

Annie quoted, " 'So don't fudge even a teensy bit or old Uncle Everett will know you're a liar. And if I tell Britt, why, the game will be up, won't it?' "

Britt considered for a long moment, then gave a tired laugh. "That was just Everett being Everett. He'd lost the spotlight and he wanted it back. We can't take that seriously."

Max reached for the doorknob. "What if the murderer takes it seriously?"

∴ *Five* ∴

ZIPPING HER WINDBREAKER AGAINST the damp chill of the January night, Annie scrambled to keep up. Max's flashlight beam bounced along the path through the garden. The banks of azaleas were dark mounds on either side. Annie wondered if their hurried progress was under observation, perhaps by an alert gray fox or a bobcat with glistening golden eyes or a curious raccoon. The crunch of oyster shells underfoot overrode the night sounds except for a ghostly *whoooo* of a nearby owl. Though the sky was overcast, there was a hint of moon glow until they skirted the fountain and plunged into the woods. The darkness was as thick and enveloping as pulling up a cover at midnight.

"Everett's not going to tell us anything." Annie's irritation was evident.

"I know. He's a jerk. And Britt may be right. His whole performance may be nothing more than bravado. Or too much bourbon." Max paused, flashed the light at a wooden sign. A reflective numeral 5 glowed. An arrow pointed to the right. He turned the light that way. "We can't take a chance. If I were the murderer, I'd be wondering exactly what Everett knew. I'd look for a chance for a private chat with him. Maybe a final chat."

Annie scarcely heard the last muttered comment. Max was pounding along the trail in front of her. It was harder going on the narrow, offshoot path. She hooked her fingers to the back of Max's waistband. They came around a curve to a blaze of light spilling from the cabin windows.

Max thudded up the front steps, pounded on the door. Annie followed at a more relaxed pace. She doubted Everett would cooperate. He didn't, to put it nicely, have a cooperative nature. Everett was the kind of person who always caused trouble, one way or another. If he knew anything, he'd refuse to share simply to be contrary. If he didn't know anything, he'd pretend he did with gleeful malice.

There was no response to Max's knock. The cabin lay silent. They waited. Sound surrounded them, the rustle of tree limbs, the cackle, hoot, and chortle of courting barred owls. But the brightly lit cabin was as quiet as a small town at midnight.

Max didn't hesitate. "Stay back." He grabbed the knob, flung open the door, stepped warily inside. "Everett?" His shout was urgent.

Annie swallowed hard and followed. The living room was impersonal but lovely—rattan furniture, a shell motif, the colors of sea and sand. It was meant for easy island days, a haven for gracious living.

Every light blazed.

"Everett?" Max turned to look beyond the breakfast bar toward the small kitchen.

No answer. No movement.

His face intent, Max circled the room. He walked with his shoulders bunched, hands hanging loosely by his sides. He glanced behind the sofa, headed toward the open door to the bedroom. His voice drifted from the bedroom. "Not here." Relief was evident in his voice. "Looks like he has one suitcase. It's open on a luggage rack. No sign of any disturbance."

Annie surveyed the living room. There was a book spread open on an end table. She knew the cover, J. A. Jance's *Exit Wounds*. It was one of Annie's favorites, with appealing characters, charming dogs, and a fascinating puzzle. A green leather folder lay on the breakfast bar. Annie moved swiftly to the counter.

Max's voice was muffled. "Shaving kit's in the bath, strewn all over. Left his shaving can with a wet bottom sitting on the tile. Clothes are wadded up, dropped on the floor beside the bed. Not a hostess's delight. Three hundred and sixty dollars in twenties in his billfold. Alligator billfold. Four credit cards. Frequent-flier cards. Hmm, what looks like a little black book. Women's first names and phone numbers and—" Max broke off, cleared his throat.

Annie looked around the room. Clearly Everett wasn't in the cabin. It would be interesting to check out the folder. She slid the contents onto the blond wood. On top was an envelope addressed to Everett Crenshaw. Her eyes widened. The return address: Britt Barlow, Heron House, Golden Silk Island, South Carolina 29928.

"Hey, Max, here's Britt's letter to Everett." Annie plucked the enclosure from the envelope.

Max came to the bedroom door. "Her letter? We

know what she said." Clearly he wasn't interested. "You stay here and I'll scout around for him."

Annie held up a hand. "Here's what she wrote." She read aloud: " 'Dear Everett, Your letter came as a surprise. I had no idea I was observed that morning. Clever of you to be so quiet. I confess I did something I should not have done. I removed all traces of the trap which someone set for Jeremiah. That was wrong and I am willing to accept responsibility for tampering with evidence of a crime. However, I want to be clear that I knew nothing about the wire until I found it in place and saw Jeremiah dead at the foot of the stairs. I'm surprised you didn't speak up at the time.' " Annie paused in her recitation. "That's a bland way of implying she's certainly wise to a blackmail attempt." Annie cleared her throat, continued to read. " 'But your letter encourages me to ask your assistance in discovering the identity of Jeremiah's murderer. I am inviting everyone present on the island that weekend to return. I have hired a detective to investigate. I promise you access to everything we find out. It could be a sensational story for you. Best Regards, Britt.' "

"Okay." Max's tone was impatient. He waved a hand. "It's nice to have some confirmation of what she told us, but right now we need to focus on finding Everett. The damn fool." Max strode across the living room.

Annie replaced the letter, picked up a folded sheet torn from a legal pad.

Max was at the front door, hand on the knob. "I'll scout around."

Annie opened the sheet. Her eyes widened as she scanned the handwritten notes. "Max, wait. You've got to see this. He's—"

Max stopped in the doorway. "Hey, Everett." Max's shout was loud.

"Yo." The stairs rattled.

Annie drew in a quick breath. Here he came and here she was, right in the middle of his private papers. She started to replace the sheet in the folder, then shook her head. She folded the paper twice, tucked it in the pocket of her jacket. She shoved everything else into the folder and tried to remember how the folder had appeared on the breakfast bar. It had been a little askew. She gave it a push, then dashed across the room to stand near the sofa.

Everett Crenshaw stopped on the front porch, looked curiously into his cabin. His supercilious face was sharp and hostile. "I don't remember inviting you in, buddy. Oh yeah, I guess I couldn't have. I wasn't even here and yet there you are." He peered past Max at Annie. "Ah, not one sleuth, but two." He glared at them. "What are you two doing in my cabin?" He pushed past Max, moved to the center of the living room, and swung around to face them, arms folded. His blue shirt was covered by a gray sweater that hung loose over khaki pants. He was barefoot in leather loafers.

Max struggled to hold his temper in check. "You make it damn hard to care, Crenshaw, but we're here to protect you. Your smart-ass exit from the house sets you up to be as dead as Jeremiah. Didn't it occur to you that the murderer might wonder if you have some incriminating knowledge? What would be easier than slipping in here late tonight with a steak knife? Or the murderer might hold a pillow over your face. You acted pretty damn drunk up at the house. Funny how sober you look right now." Max's stare was hard. "The murderer may expect you to be too soused to wake up."

Everett looked startled. "A knife? For me?" His voice was thoughtful.

"I think you're damn lucky you're standing here alive right this minute. I don't know where you've been—" Max's eyes narrowed.

Everett's face smoothed into blankness.

"—but the fact you made it back is pretty good proof whoever you went to see is innocent."

Everett's grin was sudden and almost disarming. "A nice lady. She's innocent of everything but lousy taste in men. She's . . . But I'll let you do your own detecting. You're getting paid for it. Me, I'm holding on to my cards until the pot gets sweetened."

Max shook his head. He spoke with easy certainty. "Dead men have a hard time spending cash."

Everett smoothed his thick bush of hair, walked toward the kitchen, but a quick frown pulled at his face.

Annie carefully didn't look toward the green leather folder. She felt as if neon letters glowed above her: SNEAK THIEF HERE.

Everett yanked open the refrigerator. "Beer, anybody? Amstel. Dos Equis."

Annie slipped a hand into the pocket of her jacket, curled her fingers around the square of paper.

"So you can sleep better?" Max strolled to the breakfast bar, leaned against it. "Make an even easier target?"

Everett slammed the refrigerator door. He held the beer bottle in a tight grasp, glared at Max. "Nobody's going to kill me." But his eyes were uneasy.

"There's one way to be sure." Max slid onto the barstool. "Tell us what you know, then come to the house with us. Britt can put you up. There's plenty of room. No one will know where you are. Tomorrow at breakfast we'll announce you've made a full report to us. That should protect you."

Everett wasn't listening. He flipped off the cap of the beer, took a big swallow. Face furrowed, he leaned against the breakfast bar. Abruptly, he slammed a palm against the counter. "Wait a minute. I've got an idea. Let's say you're right." Bright eyes glistened with satisfaction. "Let's say I've poked a tiger and tonight he'll prowl. Well, ducking into a hidey-hole doesn't get us anywhere. Here's what we'll do. You and"—his glance appraised Annie—"your good-lookin' lady stomp out of here, yell around that I'm a damn fool and you'll be back in the morning and maybe I'll have come to my senses and be ready to spill the beans. I'll act drunk—"

Annie couldn't resist. "Like you did at dinner?"

His glance was sharp. "What the hell. We're on the same side. Yeah, just like I did at dinner and everybody fell for it. I was getting bored and I wasn't about to let Britt get away with that phony tribute to Jeremiah. I decided to have some fun, but"—he flicked away beads of moisture from the beer bottle—"I'm not going to be anybody's sacrificial lamb. So, we'll put on a little show in case anybody's watching. You two split. I'll bang around like I'm getting ready for bed, turn out the lights. Give it twenty minutes, then you"—he jerked his head at Max—"play Indian scout and get down here in the dark. When you come up the steps, knock like this." He made a fist, knocked on the counter twice, paused, twice again. "Whisper, 'Max, the knife,' and I'll open the door. You can bunk on the couch. Maybe we'll get lucky and the evildoer will try to get in. If we catch him, I get the story, you get the glory."

Max paused by the bedroom door. His frown was heavy. "Damned if I like leaving you here by yourself." He wore a navy sweatshirt and sweatpants and dark jogging shoes. He'd tucked his sports bag under one arm.

Frowning in return, she stood with her hands on her hips. "Damned if I like your serving as cheese in a trap."

Suddenly they both grinned.

She rushed across the room, flung her arms around him. "I've got an idea. I'll go with you and—"

Max said gently, "That sofa looked like a tight fit for one. You stay here and I'll bring him up to breakfast by the scruff of his neck if necessary."

Annie almost insisted, but Max was quite capable of taking care of both himself and the unlovely Everett. The sofa had not looked comfortable. She smothered a yawn. The pillow-laden bed with its soft white spread beckoned to her. But she held tight to Max's hand for a moment. "What if the murderer has a gun?"

Max shook his head. "Not likely. Most of the guests flew to Savannah, so they had to clear security. Besides, there's no reason why the murderer should be armed. Only Everett knew there was going to be an investigation. I'll be careful." He patted the vinyl bag. "A fully loaded forty-five and an oversized flashlight. Actually, we don't need to capture an intruder. My plan, should someone try to break in, is to shine the flashlight, get a good look. If I have to, if the visitor's armed, I'll be prepared to shoot. If not, all we need is an ID. Once we know who it is, then we can worry about proving a case."

It sounded reasonable until the door closed behind him.

Annie wandered over to the fire. Of course Max was going to be all right. But what if the murderer had a gun? Startled by a flashlight beam, would the murderer shoot toward the light? Okay, she was worried. Funny, she was always exhorting Max to work hard, hew to the course, embrace the Protestant ethic. Now he was working hard and she wished he were back in his office lining up a ball on the putting green. Still, murder had to be reckoned with. No matter what happened, she was confident Max would come out on top. He was capable, savvy, and, if necessary, tough as a Tony Lama boot. She smiled as she put a small log on the grate, carefully closed the fire screen. The warmth was cheering. She'd better get to bed. Whatever happened tonight, tomorrow was going to be challenging. If an attack was made on Everett, they would have a murder suspect. If not, the questioning of Britt's guests was sure to be difficult.

Abruptly, Annie jammed a hand into the pocket of

her windbreaker, pulled out the folded square of yellow paper she'd filched from Everett's leather folder. She opened it, dropped onto the small sofa in front of the fire, and scanned the sheet. Everett had scribbled a series of question marks across the top of the sheet. Those on the island the weekend Jeremiah was murdered were listed in no apparent order. Notes were jotted after each name.

Annie read with growing excitement. Everett might have a lousy pompadour and all the charm of a palmetto bug, but he knew how to find facts. Or, if not facts, he was a whiz at unearthing innuendos and suppositions, leading to tawdry conclusions. What a treasure trove. She popped up, retrieved the legal pad that contained her observations of the guests as they arrived. Humming to herself—wouldn't Max be amazed when she showed him in the morning?—she began to expand Everett's cryptic comments into a narrative entitled:

Everett's Dirty Digs

Everett's sources may not be impeccable but he has no qualms about imputing unsavory appetites and/or aims to our hostess and her guests.

Britt Barlow—Sometimes a lucky lady, sometimes not. Twice a year she goes to Vegas, ten-hour stretches playing roulette. The lady loves Red 7. A couple of years ago she'd racked up big gambling debts at a private club in Manhattan. She couldn't pay the rent on her apartment on the Upper East Side and came to Golden Silk. Cissy slipped her money on the side to pay off what she owed. Jeremiah

ordered Cissy to cut off the funds. Cissy was dying
of cancer but she inherited a bundle from Jeremiah.
Now the money and the island belong to Britt.

Annie raised an eyebrow. Britt obviously hadn't
told Max everything that might be pertinent. She had
admitted to disliking her brother-in-law but she hadn't
explained that gambling debts had anything to do
with her arrival on Golden Silk. The revelation didn't
surprise Annie. Britt approached life with a devil-may-
care attitude. Otherwise she would never have set up
a murder hunt.

Craig Addison—Craig and Papa had engaged in a
shouting match that Friday in Jeremiah's office.
The intercom was on and a secretary heard the
whole thing. A double whammy for Craig. Not only
did Jeremiah kill the story on smuggling of illegal
immigrants, he vetoed Craig's plan for charity
10Ks to raise money for cancer research in Addi-
son Media cities. Craig slammed out of the office.

Annie placed the legal pad on the side table.
Whew. Just writing the facts made her feel the anger
and turmoil. What had been Jeremiah's problem?
Had he begun to feel old, sense his own mortality,
been jealous of his son's youth and vigor? There had
to have been a dark coil of reasons behind his deci-
sions. What kind of history was there between this
father and son?

Annie opened the small refrigerator, found a bottle
of chocolate milk. A cloth-covered platter atop the

refrigerator held a half-dozen oatmeal cookies. Annie picked one. Her hand hovered. She selected a second and returned to the sofa with her snack. The chocolate milk was dark velvet, the cookies divine, studded with tart nuggets of cranberry. Refreshed, she bent again to her task.

> *Gerald Gamble—After Craig's angry departure, Gerald had urged Jeremiah not to cancel the charity event, warning it would be a PR nightmare. Jeremiah refused to budge. Gerald told him the cancellation would embarrass Craig, undermine his authority in the company. Jeremiah replied that he was the company and no one could authorize major events except him. Gerald lost his temper and told Jeremiah he didn't deserve a son like Craig, and in today's TV climate he'd better be ready for some nasty attacks: Big boss refuses to support cancer drive even though wife dying of the disease. Jeremiah exploded. He told Gerald he'd better remember he worked for Jeremiah, not Craig. And why was he spending so much time with Craig? Was it Craig's boyish charm that attracted him? Gerald hadn't uttered another word. He came out of the office, closed the door behind him, and muttered, "One of these days, somebody's going to kill you."*

Somebody had. Annie wondered about Gerald's sexual persuasion. Was Jeremiah's perception correct? Or was he seeing affection and admiration as something more? She rustled through the bios in Max's folder. Hmm. No mention of a wife or family for Gerald. How much did Jeremiah's cruelty to Craig matter to Gerald?

> *Isabel Addison—Happy as a lark in her marriage until Jeremiah was murdered. She split with Craig immediately after the funeral. What does she know? She's lost weight this year, avoided old friends. There's not another man or the word would be getting around.*

Not even the rich chocolate milk lifted Annie's spirits as she recalled Isabel's haunted face when she'd looked toward Heron House upon her arrival. There was a depth of despair in Isabel's gaze that could only result from an anguished heart. Or a guilty heart. If Isabel had rigged the wire, would the enormity of having killed the father of her husband have driven her away from Craig's embraces? Annie shivered. Either prospect was possible.

> *Jay Addison—Was desperately short of money until his father died. Turned down for a loan. Hadn't seen his father for several months. He and Dana came to Golden Silk without an invitation. Jay resented Cissy, was rude to Britt. When they arrived, he told Britt he had to talk to his father. Britt said they quarreled that last night.*
>
> *Dana Addison—Will do anything to protect Jay. Bitter at having had to return to work. On a day-care excursion, son Teddy wandered away in a park. After a two-hour search, he was found a half-mile distant. He was safe and uninjured though sobbing.*

Dana was hysterical, said if anything had happened to him it would have been Jeremiah's fault.

Annie pushed away the last of her cookie. She couldn't push away an image of a terrified toddler's tear-streaked face. If she felt stricken reading of Teddy's hours of fear, how had Dana felt? Angry enough to make certain there would be money enough for her to stay home? Because that's what she had done. As soon as Jeremiah died, Dana quit her job.

Millicent McRae—There have been rumors about her secretaries, all handsome young men. Jeremiah had some pix of Millicent and Bobby Baker, her current secretary, that wouldn't have looked good in the family scrapbook. Rumor has it that M.M. was supporting a bill in the House that Jeremiah wanted to see defeated (trucking regulations onerous to major transport lines).

Nick McRae—Some people think he knows all about his wife's pastimes. But his knowing and public disclosure are entirely different kettles of smut. A proud man. He would be furious at a news story revealing that his wife was cheating on him.

Annie recalled Nick McRae's arrogance. He had a patina of social superiority. That didn't mean that he was immune to feelings of anger and sorrow and despair. Did he love Millicent? If so, knowledge of an affair would devastate him. Even if he no longer cared for her or had never cared for her and was well aware of her proclivities, public disclosure would be humiliating. He was not a man accustomed to humiliation. As for Millicent, she depended upon her husband for her social eminence and the ability to mix with wealthy business leaders and industrialists. A nasty scandal would likely have dried up campaign contributions. Scandal was averted because Jeremiah died.

Speaking of scandal—Annie tapped her pen on the pad. Everett's notes about Kim Kennedy were as revealing about him as about her. Apparently, he'd made it a point to keep close tabs that weekend on Kim and Jeremiah. Did he have the temerity to try to blackmail the big boss? It seemed foolhardy but why else had he skulked along behind them trying to eavesdrop? She shook her head, began to write.

> *Kim Kennedy—Everett was lurking behind a crape myrtle in the garden when Kim rushed up to find Jeremiah. The conversation, according to Everett:*
>
> *Kim: "Jeremiah, I couldn't find you anywhere. I thought we were going out on the yacht."*
>
> *Jeremiah: "I understand you've been telling people I'm going to marry you. I suggest you clear up any misunderstandings before you leave."*
>
> *Kim: "Leave?"*
>
> *Jeremiah: "The boat will take you back to Savannah at eight in the morning."*
>
> *According to Everett, Jeremiah turned and walked away, left her standing in the garden. Her face wasn't pretty.*

Annie doubted Kim Kennedy had been willing to accept dismissal. Had she hoped to charm Jeremiah

out of his ill humor? Or did she know him well enough
to recognize defeat? Had he lived, she likely would
have lost her job as well as her hopes for marriage to
a rich and powerful man. What had been her reaction?
Had she felt confident her charms would prevail? Had
she decided to cut her losses? Or was her ego such that
she would see him dead rather than be discarded? As
it turned out, she had lost her job. But no one—except
Everett and now Annie—knew that her last encounter
with Jeremiah had ended in rejection.

Annie put down the legal pad, pushed up from the
sofa. She carried her milk bottle and cookie plate
to the dressing room, rinsed them in the sink. She
felt jumpy and restless. She wished Max were with
her. Everett's cabin might as well be on the moon. It
seemed very last century to be totally out of touch.
This was the world of cell phones, but not on a
remote island. Was Max asleep? And, please God,
safe? Surely he and Everett had slid the bolt shut, se-
curing the door, and perhaps wedged a chair beneath
the handle. How far was the couch from a window?
Would an intruder try the windows on the porch?
Probably. That would make noise, enough noise to
awaken Max. He could roll out onto the floor, use the
couch for cover, wait for a dark form to slip over the
sill, then flick on the light.

Annie found herself at the door to the verandah,
looking out at darkness. She pulled on the knob,
stepped out into the moist chill of the night. It was hard
to estimate the distance from the house to Everett's
cabin. The path into the woods behind the fountain
curved and turned and switched. Likely it wasn't far in

a direct line, but it seemed a long way on foot. Would she hear gunshots? She'd leave the door open when she went to bed. Just in case. She walked slowly up and down the verandah. She needed to get to sleep. She was turning to go inside when she saw a flicker of light deep in the garden.

Max bunched a pillow behind his head, twisted uncomfortably. The lumpy sofa cushions were unyielding. An extra blanket from the bedroom closet offered plenty of warmth. Gradually he relaxed, though thoughts tumbled in his mind. There was much to do tomorrow. He would try again to get Everett to share whatever he knew. There were the other guests to interview. He'd start with Gerald Gamble, the likeliest to know why each person had been invited that particular weekend.

As Max slid into a light sleep, attuned to the night sounds and the windows that opened on the porch, the flashlight and gun on the coffee table within easy reach, he tried to remember what it was that wriggled deep within his mind, something he needed to know, something he must ask about, something he'd missed . . .

Annie leaned over the verandah railing. She strained to see. The sky was overcast, hiding the stars. The garden was a series of black shadows, except for an occasional flash of light. Just like connecting dots, Annie followed the progress of the light—and someone who held it—toward the house. Whoever moved in the garden was making every effort not to be seen, only using the flashlight often enough to keep to the path.

Annie whirled, dashed across the verandah. She hurried through the bedroom, opened the door to the hallway. Heron House was never locked . . . never locked . . . never locked . . . That openness no doubt usually charmed visitors, who might revel in the sense of security afforded by a remote island. But not now, not when everyone knew a murderer was a fellow guest. The flash of light in the garden marked a covert progress. What was the reason for stealth? Annie wanted to know who slipped through the night, but she definitely wasn't disposed to enter the gardens by herself. It took only a moment to run lightly down the hall to Britt's room.

Annie knocked, called out, "Britt, it's Annie. Someone's in the garden." Her words fell into silence. Annie knocked again, then turned the knob, pushed open the door. "Britt?"

Darkness. Silence.

Annie took a deep breath, turned on the light. The room was empty. The bed wasn't turned down. Britt's lovely blue dress was tossed across a chaise longue. There was no sign of disarray.

Annie turned, moving fast. She stopped at the stairway, flipped on the upstairs hall light, and checked the top step. She didn't expect to find a wire stretched in place, but nonetheless she didn't intend to be careless as long as she was on Golden Silk. Reassured, she clattered down the hard steps. The rose-shaded lamp on the hall table cast a soft glow, though the hall and rooms beyond were in inky darkness. Annie found the panel of switches and switched on all the lights, welcomed the flood of brightness. She was standing in the entry hall, the chandeliers blazing, when the massive front door opened.

Britt stopped in the doorway, lifted a hand to shield her eyes. In a black turtleneck and jeans, she looked athletic and purposeful. And startled. "Annie?"

Annie gestured at the flashlight in Britt's left hand. "Was that you in the garden just now? Turning your light off and on?"

"Yes." Britt placed the flashlight on the side table, brushed back a lock of curly dark hair. Her chiseled features were somber. "I think someone was out in the garden." She sounded puzzled. "I came down to get a book from the library and I happened to look out the window. The drapes hadn't been drawn. I thought I saw a light near the fountain." She pressed fingers against her temple. "There's no reason for anyone to be out this late. I thought it was odd."

Annie's voice was sharp. "You went down there by yourself?"

Britt's was equally sharp. "I had to go. I've brought everyone to the island. I can't ignore anything that seems out of the way. Actually, I went upstairs to see if you and Max were back, but you weren't. So"—she lifted her chin—"I went out to see."

Annie understood. Britt felt responsible for the safety of her guests. But to go out alone in the darkness, knowing there was a murderer on the island, ranked between foolhardy and extremely courageous.

"I got a flashlight from the kitchen. I know the paths so well, I only used the flashlight a little bit." She looked uneasy. "It may have been my imagination, but I felt as if"—the words came slowly, as if dredged from deep inside—"there was something wrong. Something bad. It was incredibly dark, like trying to walk blindfolded. I kept stopping and listening, but the owls make so much noise, I couldn't hear if anyone was moving around. I had this feeling . . ." She shook her head, her dark hair flying. "Anyway, I crept around on tiptoe." A sudden smile lighted her face, made her look younger. "I suppose I looked like an idiot." The smile seeped away, and once again she was weary and somber. "I almost called out. Then I didn't. I was scared. I started to go around the fountain and somehow I couldn't make myself do it. That's when I came back to the house. I slipped from shadow to shadow."

Annie had watched those pinpricks of light, recognized stealth. Now she knew why. "You shouldn't have gone out by yourself. You should have waited. We got back a little while ago, then Max left." Quickly she explained Max's decision to stay at Everett's cabin. And why. "Max has a gun. If you'd waited—"

Britt's gesture was impatient, imperious. "If I'd waited, there would have been no chance to find out what was going on. And here I am, safe and sound. Nothing happened to me. Maybe I imagined the whole thing. I'm at the point where I see danger in every shadow."

Annie never dismissed intuition. "A policeman once told me to run like hell if I ever felt in danger. If you had that sense, the murderer may have only been a few feet from you. Don't go out alone again."

Britt suddenly looked amused. "I'm not a complete fool." She reached into her pocket, pulled out a blue-black handgun, held it loosely on her palm. "It belonged to Jeremiah. I suppose I should have sent it to Craig or Jay. I didn't even think about it when I boxed up Jeremiah's papers. It's kept in the desk in the library. Now I'm going to put it back and get a drink. Why don't you join me?" She turned, headed down the hall, still talking. "You know, I'm not sure I really saw a light. The moonlight comes and goes. Maybe—"

Annie followed. Britt wanted to be reassured that everything was all right. Or as all right as it could be under the circumstances.

Britt turned on the lights in the library. "—that's all it was. Anyway, come on in." Britt moved behind the desk, bent to her right and reached for a drawer. The bottom drawer rolled out smoothly. Britt placed the handgun inside, pushed the drawer shut, then took a key from her pocket and twisted it in the lock. She stuck the key back in her jeans, made a moue of relief. "There's something hideous about a gun." She swung toward Annie. "Don't you feel that way?"

"Yes." They looked at each other with complete understanding.

Disposing of the gun seemed to lift the cloud of worry from Britt. Her entire demeanor changed. She gave Annie a wistful smile. "I wish you and Max could be here for fun. The island's so beautiful. Maybe, once everything's cleared up, you'll come and stay and tramp on the beach at low tide and look for shells. Let me show you what I found recently. Come see."

Britt moved eagerly to a side table. Annie followed. Three decanters sat on a lacquered tray. Shelving behind the table held an assortment of glasses. Britt pulled out a central drawer. Shells rested on green velvet. She reached down and handed a kitten's paw to Annie. "I found it just last week. Isn't it glorious?" The shell was about an inch and a half long with six wavy ribs on the outside. The red-brown markings on the ridges were in soft contrast to the white shell. "And here's a perfect auger shell." Britt held up the long, narrow shell.

Annie replaced the kitten's paw, admired the whorls on the auger shell. Yes, it would be fun to come to Golden Silk and hunt for shells and knobbed whelks and sand dollars. But there was a small matter of murder.

Britt fingered the ridges of the auger. She gently returned it to the velvet, ran her fingers lightly over a calico scallop, a Scotch bonnet, and a banded tulip. She stared at the collection for a moment, then closed the drawer. Her pleased look faded. She picked up a decanter, her face once again drawn in tired lines. "Sherry? Brandy?"

"Sherry, please." Annie strolled to a Brittany sofa, admiring the bright splash of a peony pattern on the yellow fabric. She settled onto a cloud-soft cushion.

Britt half filled a sherry glass. She poured herself a generous amount of brandy. She brought the sherry to Annie. She didn't sit down. Her movements impatient, she paced toward the fireplace, turned to face Annie. She stared into the golden liquor, took a sip, and gave Annie a curiously intent look. "I thought we might relax for a little while, visit and have a drink and talk about the island. But it's no good, is it?"

The shadow of murder leached ease from the comfortable room, made Britt's eyes pools of fear, drew

Annie's gaze to the dark windowpanes. Britt followed her glance. She placed the snifter on the mantel, and hurried across the room to draw the drapes. "I can shut out the night." Her lips trembled. "I can't shut out the fear. I don't think anybody's out there. But, there could be. Dammit"—her voice was ragged—"I hate being afraid. Maybe it will be over soon. It has to be over."

Annie hated to take advantage of Britt's distress. But the more Max knew, the more likely he could find a solution, free Britt from the burden of Jeremiah's death, restore the island to serenity. "Britt, you know these people." Annie flung out her hand toward the garden and the forest and the secluded cabins. "You must have some idea who killed Jeremiah." How much did Britt know about her guests? Enough certainly to have an estimate of character. Did she know as much about them as Everett did?

Britt was once again at the fireplace. She stood stiffly, her face thoughtful. She drank down half the glass of brandy.

Annie sipped the sherry. Mmm, cream sherry, sweet as nectar. Usually, she adored a glass of excellent sherry. Tonight her pleasure was diminished by the atmosphere of gloom. Britt's tension permeated the room.

Britt placed the glass on the mantel, clasped her slender hands tightly together. "I don't *know*." She emphasized the verb.

Annie's eyes widened. Britt might not know, she might have no proof, but she suspected someone. She had in mind a particular person, and that possibility upset her.

Britt ran fingers through her hair, disarranging her dark curls. The turmoil in her mind was reflected in the wildness of her eyes, in her tousled hair, in the jerkiness of her movements as she turned, paced, turned again. She spoke fast, the words tumbling over each other, breathless, stricken. "In a perfect world, it would be Gerald. No one likes him. I don't think Jeremiah liked him. Gerald is useful. He can always be counted on to do the dirty work. I guess that's why Craig keeps him on." Her eyes swept unseeingly over Annie. "I'd think Craig would be sick of that adoring look. Gerald's like a dog."

Annie scarcely breathed, she sat so still. She didn't want Britt to notice her. She especially didn't want Britt to realize how much her disjointed, emotional speech revealed.

Britt's tone curdled with disdain. "The master and his dog. But if it can't be Gerald, I'd pick Kim. I wish it could be Kim. I hated Jeremiah for bringing her here. Cissy was too weak to get up and she couldn't eat and that blond bitch paraded around the island like it belonged to her, talking about changes she'd make when she lived here. Or Everett. He's slimy enough. If only it were Everett. It would be just like Everett to have done it himself, then try to blackmail me." Britt drew a quick breath. The flush in her cheeks subsided. Gradually her breathing slowed. "I'm sorry. I'm not fit company. If you don't mind, let's go up. Though I don't know how well any of us will sleep. Please take your sherry with you, if you like." Her hand darted out, clutched the snifter. She downed the rest of the brandy in a single gulp. "Tomorrow everything will be better." A broken laugh. "Okay. Maybe not better. But we'll get things organized. You'll help, won't you?"

"Of course I will. I'll do everything I can." Annie rose, leaving the glass of sherry on the end table.

Britt was already moving toward the door, reaching toward the light switch. As Annie came even with her, Britt hesitated, then swung toward the desk. She darted behind it, bent, rattled the bottom drawer. When she joined Annie in the doorway, she looked embarrassed. "Just making sure."

Annie followed her silently down the broad hall and up the stairs. She wished the front and back doors were as securely locked as the desk drawer holding the gun.

On the landing, Britt glanced down the hall toward Annie's room and said abruptly, "Jam a chair under your doorknob."

✌ Six ✌

"HEY, BUDDY." A FOOT THUDDED into the back of the couch. "Nobody messes with my papers and rips me off. Where the hell did you put it?"

Max flailed awake. He landed on his feet in a crouch, hands bunched. Weak sunlight filtered through partially open wooden blinds, casting striped shadows on the wooden floor. Birds chittered morning warbles. The smell of strong coffee mingled with the minty scent of aftershave.

Everett Crenshaw, his freshly shaven face twisted in a scowl, stood behind the couch in a floppy sweatshirt and glen plaid boxer shorts. He held Max's opened sports bag in one hand. Abruptly he flipped it over and the contents tumbled out—shaving kit, T-shirt, shorts. Everett held the bag up, rattled it.

"Put it down." Eyes steely, Max took a step forward, fists high.

Everett backed up one pace, two, abruptly tossed the bag to the floor. "Hold up, Darling. I've got every right. You got into my folder." He jerked his head toward the breakfast bar and the green leather envelope. "You stole a private paper."

"No." Max's face creased in a frown. He came out of his combative crouch and glanced toward the folder. "Something missing?"

"Damn sure is. I want it back. Pronto." Everett kicked the vinyl bag out of his way, strode to the counter. He thrust his hand into the folder, pulled out a letter and a notebook, held the folder wide open. "Empty as a bum's wallet and there should be another couple of sheets from a legal pad."

"Whatever it is, I didn't take it." Truth gave weight to Max's words.

Everett's glare changed to a puzzled frown.

Max stepped behind the couch, picked up his belongings and dropped them into the bag. He placed it on the coffee table by the gun and flashlight. "You're sure the paper was there last night?"

"Positive." Everett slapped the folder on the counter. "I looked it over right before I went up to the house for dinner."

Max strolled into the kitchen. Everett had apparently loaded the coffeemaker, then reached for his folder. The last drops of coffee cascaded into the glass pot. Max poured the fresh brew into two mugs, pushed one toward Everett. "Somebody must have come into the cabin before Annie and I got here. You were gone. The door was unlocked."

Everett ripped open a packet of sugar, dumped it into his mug. "Yeah. I guess that's what happened." He glanced toward Max's sports bag. "You don't have it. It's gone. That means somebody else got it." He drank from the mug, his eyes thoughtful.

"What's missing?" Max drank the hot, strong coffee, welcomed the swift rush from caffeine.

"Oh, this and that." Everett's tone was vague. "Maybe that's why nobody fell into our trap last night. If it was the murderer who got the sheet, well, any fool—and I don't think we're dealing with a fool—would realize that if I dug up this stuff, other people could too. So, there was no reason to come after me." His relief was apparent. "Looks like we can go up for breakfast without expecting an ambush. And"—he glanced at the clock—"it's almost seven. The feast will be spread. I tell you, Darling, a Heron House breakfast is to die for. I'm damn near there." He headed for the bedroom.

Max carried his shaving kit into the bathroom. In the bedroom, Everett pulled on sweatpants and stepped barefoot into worn loafers. "I'll leave you a sausage." He paused long enough to brush his pompadour to perfection, then banged out the front door.

Max was midway through shaving when he stopped and stared into the mirror. A missing paper that contained unpalatable facts about other guests might not assuage the murderer's unease over Everett's farewell taunt last night. If Everett knew facts the murderer wanted hidden, Everett might still be in danger. The fact that no one had tried to attack Everett last night was no guarantee he was safe today.

Annie spread her hand across the sheet, felt nothing but clammy coolness. Max . . . Her eyes opened. The room was grayish but there was enough light to make out the furniture. She stared at the straight chair she'd wedged beneath the doorknob, as per Britt's instruction. She pushed upright, came to her feet. She had a sense of urgency, an unsettling feeling that she was late, that she must hurry to prevent something dreadful. She was in the bathroom and out, hair quickly combed, face damp, pulling on a sweater and slacks and loafers, and on her way downstairs in less than five minutes. Midway down the stairs, she heard voices below, including—oh happy moment, relief exquisite, exuberant joy—Max's clear tenor. ". . . not down yet? I'll run up and get her. And hey, Everett"—as he came out of the dining room, his words were louder—"stick close to Britt. We'll talk in a minute."

"Max!" Annie flew down the steps and into his arms, his wonderful, welcoming, strong arms. The bleak morning suddenly pulsed with cheer. "I missed you."

He held her tight, pressed his face into her curls. "Me too, honey. Tonight we'll stay together if I have to hog-tie Everett to get him up here."

Abruptly, she pulled away, looked up. "Everett's okay? What happened?"

Max's shoulders rose and fell. "Nothing. Slept like babies." He remembered twisting and turning. Something he'd tried to remember . . . "Well, sort of. Anyway, nobody came near the cabin."

"Somebody was out and about." She told him of Britt's adventure.

Max's frown was quick. "She went out alone?"

Annie slipped her arm through his, spoke softly as they crossed the hall. "She took a gun with her. And, Max"—this was a whisper—"I think she has an idea who killed Jeremiah. I'll tell you later."

In the dining room, the table was set with bright yellow pottery and woven cherry place mats. The centerpiece of herons had been moved to the Louis XV commode. In its place was a tall translucent blue vase. Stalks of yaupon with bright red berries added winter cheer. The chandeliers dissipated the early morning gloom. Britt adjusted the Bunsen flame beneath a serving dish. Everett stood at the end of the buffet, his plate piled high. "Apple egg casserole. Poached eggs on potato pancakes. Cheese biscuits. Salmon and cheese." His sigh of satisfaction brought a smile to Britt's face.

She stepped toward Annie and Max. "Lucinda's outdone herself. Come and see." She might have been any hostess greeting guests except for the paleness of her face and the shadows beneath her eyes.

Annie caught Max's hand, tugged. The buffet was a magnet. She was ravenous. Apple egg casserole was one of Max's specialities. He used sharp cheddar cheese and a full pound of sweet Tennessee bacon slow-cooked to perfection and then crumbled.

Everett walked toward the table, filled plate in one hand and a goblet of foaming orange juice in the other. "How amazing no one else is here." He glanced toward the china clock on the mantel. "A quarter after seven and our captain of industry has yet to arrive and his major minion apparently still slumbers. I suppose the Honorable Millicent has decided there aren't any pockets to be picked. So here I am, the early bird. We all know what that means. I can pick my spot. First come, first served." He cut his eyes toward Britt. "What say I get Jeremiah's throne?" He nodded toward the massive mahogany chair at the far end of the table, the only one with arms, clearly the seat for the host.

Britt's gaze was measuring. "You don't believe in ghosts?"

"As in, such a blasphemous desecration might evoke Jeremiah's petulant spirit?" Everett laughed aloud, plunked his plate on the cherry mat at the head of the table. The yellow plate was brilliant against the vivid red cloth. "I'm willing to take that chance." Seated, he raised the goblet of orange juice. "How about a toast. Here's to crime."

Britt's eyes flared. "Everett, that's tasteless even for you. Remember, you're talking about Jay and Craig's father."

He scooped a forkful of casserole, poked it in his mouth, chewed. His reply was indistinct. "Yeah. Yeah. And Cissy's philandering spouse and Kim's boyfriend and the Honorable Millicent's nemesis—"

"I beg your pardon." The icy voice would have reduced most people to shamed silence. In a periwinkle blue cotton cardigan with ottoman stitching and white wool slacks, Millicent was immaculately groomed and haughty. Her stare equated Everett with something nasty pulled into the drawing room by an ill-bred dog.

Unfazed, Everett scooted back the big chair, half rose, bowed to Millicent and her husband. "Good eats, folks." His blue eyes glinted. "Maybe not quite on a par with a certain hotel in Boca Raton. Quite a favorite of a young fellow named Bobby. You and I can visit about that another time, Representative McRae. I don't want to keep you and hubby from the victuals."

"Boca Raton?" Nick was disdainful. "I doubt you've spent much time there." He touched Millicent's elbow. "I believe the buffet is ready."

His wife moved ahead of him. Her face was suddenly pinched, the flesh tight against sharp bones. She looked old and stricken. She moved past Annie and Max with a mumbled "Good morning." The hand that reached for a plate trembled.

"You never know who you're going to see at fancy resorts." Everett's loud voice followed the McRaes. "Or be seen by." Everett's smile was malicious. "Bobby's been there several times. Looked like he was having fun."

Annie was suddenly angry. She hadn't liked Millicent McRae, but Everett's feline cruelty appalled her. Had Nick heard rumors about his wife and Bobby? If not, Millicent would obviously be terrified at what might be revealed. If Nick was aware, the moment's ugliness would be excruciating for both Millicent and her husband. Annie said loudly, "Boca Raton. The last time we were there—"

Max looked puzzled. They'd never stayed in Boca Raton. They had visited charming Stuart on the East Coast and shell-rich Sanibel on the West. "Annie—"

She gave his arm a tiny pinch "—all it did was rain. You know, it was that summer Florida had buckets of rain. Mmm, the casserole looks perfect. Millicent, did you see the potato pancakes? Let me hold the lid for you."

Suddenly the dining room seemed warm and hospitable. Britt picked up a silver coffee carafe, followed them to the table.

Millicent and Nick took seats as far as possible from

Everett. He wiped away a dollop of marmalade and grinned. "Hey, there's plenty of room down this way."

Britt held up the carafe. "More coffee?"

Annie headed straight for the chair next to Nick. A short nod to Max indicated he should join Everett. "Have you read the new biography of Franklin?" she asked Nick. Thankfully, there was always a new biography of Franklin.

"Franklin remains an enigma." Nick's tone was judicious. "He was a fascinating man. Was he a patriot or a clever dissembler . . ."

Max glanced from Millicent's set face to the dull patches of red in Nick's thin cheeks to Everett's sly smile. Max slid into the chair nearest Everett. "I've been thinking about last night—"

A door near the buffet opened. Lucinda, her face red and cross, stepped into the dining room. Her yellow calico apron was smudged with flour. "Britt"—she jerked her head—"you got a minute?"

Britt looked surprised. Still carrying the carafe, she walked swiftly to Lucinda and followed her through the door.

"—and the kind of information you had collected—"

Everett's sly eyes darted down the table.

"—and I think the safest thing for you to do is sketch out that material and give it to me."

There was a curious flicker in Everett's bright green eyes. "And be cut out of the loop? No way, Darling." Everett spread butter atop the poached egg on the potato pancake. "Nope, here's the deal. I get first look at everybody's report. If anybody's left out something important, you'll be the first to know."

Max folded smoked salmon over cream cheese. "I wouldn't take that gamble if I were you."

"I didn't get where I am without taking chances. I'm not going to miss out on this story." His pale eyes gleamed with pleasure. "Besides, no bogeyman came after me last night."

Max looked grim. "I'd advise you to be on guard. Nothing happened last night, but that doesn't mean you are safe."

The door from the kitchen opened. Britt poked her head out. She looked irritated, flustered, and puzzled. "Max. Will you come, please?" She withdrew and the door closed.

Max put his plate on the table. "Excuse me."

Annie pushed back her chair. She sailed a vague smile toward Millicent, who was talking steadily to her husband. ". . . believe I will accept that invitation . . ." Clearly Millicent intended to ignore Everett and confine conversation with her husband to mundane topics. Everett paused in eating, his curious eyes following Max. From the central hallway came the sound of voices and footsteps. More guests were arriving for breakfast.

Annie followed Max into the kitchen. The long, bright, sparkling-clean room was gloriously homey with the mingled fragrances of baking and frying, the stove laden with pots and pans, starched red-checked curtains at the windows, old-fashioned white wooden cabinets and woodwork, and a calico cat slumbering on the hearth. The cheerful surroundings were marred only by Lucinda's evident displeasure and Britt's harried expression.

Lucinda clanged a lid on a pot. "It's bad enough we don't have any girls right now. I said I could manage this weekend if Harry helped. But I can't do all the cooking and cleaning and serving and clean the cabins as well. I don't care if he was up and flitting around in the middle of the night and getting no sleep and making himself tired, that's his lookout. It wouldn't be the first time, but he's always made it up to the house in time to serve. What that man finds to do when Christian folk should be asleep is a puzzle to me. I saw his lights on till all hours and heard him slamming in and out to boot. Kept me awake and I need my rest. He's picked the wrong morning to sleep in, what with a dozen to feed and care for." Cheeks flaming, she grabbed a pot holder and yanked open the oven. "Got to get the cheese grits out."

"I'll serve, Lucinda. And clear up." Britt was conciliatory. "I'll take care of the cabins, too." She looked uncertainly at Max and Annie. "I didn't hire you to help with staff problems, but I really need to stay here and help Lucinda. Max, would you mind rounding up Harry? It isn't far to his cabin."

Max looked thoughtful. "I don't mind at all. Is he often late?"

Britt shook her head. "He's always been dependable. Tell him I sent you. He can be gruff sometimes." She pointed to the back door. "Take the path to the left. It goes behind some pines. You'll see a sign indicating the path is off limits. Continue on until you see a path branching to the left."

"Won't take a minute." Max was casual. He turned toward the door.

Annie looked from Britt to Lucinda. She didn't see anything to indicate either was worried. Annie wondered if she was the only one who felt a sweep of foreboding. In any event, she didn't want Max to go down that path by himself.

"I'll go with you." She dashed after her husband.

With the door closed behind them, Max stopped, put his hand on Annie's arm. "Maybe you'd better stay here."

"You're worried, too." She held his gaze.

"About Harry?" Max frowned. "No, he's probably fine. Punched off the alarm, rolled over, went back to sleep. From what I saw of him yesterday, he's no pushover. He can handle anybody on the island. There's no reason to think anything's happened to him. But I don't like the feel of this place."

Annie understood. The damp gray morning seemed inimical, the leaden skies dulling the landscape. The thick green forest, dark and primeval, was choked with ferns and shrubs, impenetrable except for the narrow opening of the path.

"All I know for sure"—Max sounded grim—"is that I wish you hadn't come to this damn island."

Annie loved him for that quick instinct of protectiveness. But she was a big girl. "Not to worry. We'll see it through." She moved ahead of him toward the pines, determined to appear at ease.

Max caught up. "Stay close." He walked ahead of her.

The misty cool tunnel beneath the trees had the glowing green quality of an aquarium. There was no wind and the forest seemed unnaturally silent, leaves and branches and undergrowth utterly still. The occasional trill of a bird seemed raucous, as out of place as a whistle at a funeral. Oyster shells crunched underfoot, announcing their progress. Annie fought growing uneasiness. "I don't believe he overslept. What if something's happened to him?"

Max pushed back a huge frond of a Resurrection fern, gave her a quick glance. "Why Harry?" He walked faster. "No, it's more likely he overslept. But I agree with Lucinda. I'd like to know what he finds to do in the middle of the night. From what she said, last night's not the first time he's been out and about late. Okay, here's the turnoff."

Annie rushed to keep pace. This path was narrower. "Maybe he's the one who was in the garden last night."

"Britt didn't get a glimpse of anyone?" Max swiped a damp hand on his trousers.

"No. She tried to blow it off, said maybe there hadn't been anyone prowling around. I told her she shouldn't have gone out by herself, not even with a gun. I think she realized she'd made a mistake." Annie sidestepped a dangling swath of Spanish moss. "She was pretty upset last night. She tried to put a good face on it, but when I asked her who she suspected—and, Max, I'm sure she has someone in mind—she lost her cool. She went on and on about who she wished it was, like Gerald or Kim or Everett. Well, that's a pretty good indication she doesn't think it's one of them. That narrows the list to Jeremiah's family, the McRaes, or her employees. There's no reason why she should be distressed if either McRae was guilty. I doubt she feels any attachment to the Addisons. That leaves Lucinda or Harry. They've stayed on the island, helped her make a go of it as a resort. She has to feel pretty close to both of them."

The path opened to the clearing. All three cabins were dark. Max pointed. "The middle one is for the maids when they have them. The nearest is Lucinda's. You ought to see it. Doll heaven." They walked swiftly to the third cabin. Max moved ahead of Annie to climb the stairs. On the porch, he paused. "The door's ajar." He knocked. The crisp tattoo startled a flock of crows, who lifted skyward, cawing. "Harry?" Max bellowed. "Max Darling here."

Birds chittered. A gray squirrel near a live oak held an acorn, peered at them. Gray clouds with the texture of fissured granite layered above the clearing.

Max glanced back at Annie. "I'll take a look." His tone was calm; his eyes were wary. He pushed the door open, stepped inside. He muttered an exclamation and strode across the room.

Annie, heart thudding, came right behind him. She stopped in the middle of the room and frowned. No one was here. There was an aura of disarray, cushions awry, empty drawers tumbled to one side of the desk.

Max banged around in the bedroom. In a moment, he came to the doorway, spread out his hands. "He's gone. He's taken everything with him—his clothes, all his stuff. Hey—" He dashed around her, came to a stop near the desk, staring at the emptied drawers. "Yesterday the desk was all locked up. And look—" He pointed at scored wood and a large rectangle bare of dust beneath a front window. "There was a trunk there.

Locked with a padlock. And a rifle case. Everything's gone."

Annie was bewildered. "Where could he have taken everything?"

Max gripped her elbow. "I told you yesterday about the boat. A big cabin cruiser. Harry had urged Britt to hire it out for charter. Come on . . ."

Max ran ahead of Annie. She loped after him though she doubted there was any reason now for haste. He burst out of the woods, skidded to a stop, stared grimly at the empty cove. "The yacht was anchored out there." Max pointed to the deeper water. "He's gone. And he's made damn sure no one can follow him. There was a motorboat, too. He must have attached it to the stern with a line, pulled it with him."

Annie came up beside him. A raft of herring gulls bobbed near the point. There was nothing else to see but a vast, empty expanse of gray water and gray sky. "Why?"

Max slammed a fist into his palm. "If we knew that, we might know everything. Okay"—he paced, head down—"what happened? Last night Everett told everybody Jeremiah was murdered. Harry was standing in the hall. He heard all of it. Harry knew that whatever happened this weekend, Britt promised to take the results of her investigation to the police. Now"—Max tipped his head, looked at Annie—"what do we conclude when Harry packs up and leaves, stealing a quarter-million-dollar yacht to make his getaway?"

"He killed Jeremiah?" It was a question, not a statement. Annie bent down, scooped up a handful of crushed oyster shells. She threw a big one as hard as she could. It skipped across the murky water, then disappeared. Just like Harry. It looked as though Harry was guilty. Innocent men do not steal a yacht and sail away. But still . . . "Nobody's said anything, Britt included, to suggest why Harry would murder Jeremiah."

Max was ahead of her. "If Jeremiah discovered Harry was involved in criminal activity and threatened to inform the police, Harry might have had a very good reason for murder. Dammit, I should have been smarter yesterday."

Annie looked at him quickly. "Short of reading Harry's mind, I don't see what you could have done."

"I could have insisted on knowing what he kept in that locked trunk." Max jammed his hands in his pockets. "Last night I had trouble sleeping. I knew there was something important I needed to remember. I kept trying to think what I'd forgotten, what worried me. It was the trunk. What was the point in locking it? His cabin was in an area off limits to guests. There was no reason for anyone to be in his cabin except by invitation. That wasn't good enough. He had a padlock on the trunk. The only possible reason was to hide something dangerous or illegal. Lucinda said he was in and out of his cabin last night and now we know why. He was hauling everything he owned to the yacht. But he'd come and gone late at night before. That sounds like drugs to me. He probably met another yacht out of sight of the island, transshipped cocaine. Then he delivered it to Savannah at his leisure, maybe even a few bricks at a time. Come on, we've got to tell Britt. She can radio the Coast Guard, get a search under way, although I expect he's already landed in some out-of-the-way place. She can arrange for a charter to come to the island."

On the way back to the house, he quizzed Annie. "Did Britt say where she saw the light in the garden?"

"Not specifically." Annie frowned in thought. "Then she dismissed the idea, said she may have seen something glint when the clouds parted and there was a glimmer of moonlight."

"If it was Harry, there may be some trace of what he did. We'll check to see if there's been any fresh digging. He may have had more stuff hidden." Max rubbed knuckles against his cheek. "Damn, if only I'd remembered about the trunk last night. It almost came to me when I was drifting off to sleep." He was irritated with himself.

Annie was quick to reassure him. "It wouldn't have mattered. You were convinced Everett needed protection. You wouldn't have left him alone. You'd have thought there would be plenty of time to check out the trunk this morning."

They came out of the pines into the backyard. Britt was waiting on the kitchen steps. As they hurried toward her, she looked past them with a frown. She didn't give them a chance to speak. Her voice sharp, she demanded, "Where's Harry?"

Max was blunt. "Harry's cleared out. He took everything he owned. And the yacht. And the motorboat. He made sure no one could follow him or get to the mainland before the charter comes tomorrow."

"Harry's gone? The yacht's gone? And the motorboat?" Fury hardened her face, made her look older.

A lifetime of combativeness was reflected in the jut of her chin. "He's marooned us here? He'll pay for this." Abruptly she stiffened, looked warily at Max. "How did you know about the boats?"

Max's level stare challenged her. "I don't like being kept in the dark when I take on a job. I took a look around while you were greeting your guests. I went up the off-limits path and found the employee cabins. I talked to Harry, told him I was working for you. He was delighted to give me a tour—the inlet with the yacht in deep water, the pier with the motorboat tied to a piling, the office with the ham radio."

"You didn't mention that to me." The distance between them seemed to grow.

Max was unruffled. "I'd say that makes us even. Maybe now we can work together. You can use that radio to get some help for us, start a search for Harry, have him picked up for questioning."

"Questioning? If he took the yacht, he's a thief. I'll have him arrested." She plunged her fingers through her hair. "I can't believe it. Maybe there's some explanation. Perhaps he left a note. Did you check the office?"

Max shook his head. "There's no mistake. His cabin's empty. He took everything he owned—clothes, shoes, pipes, everything in his desk, as well as a locked trunk and a rifle case. There's nothing left but old magazines and trash. Harry is gone. He probably has"—Max glanced at his watch—"five or six hours' head start. The sooner you get in touch with the sheriff, the better."

"Yes. I'll do that." She bit off the words. She started to turn away.

Max called after her. "Tell the sheriff Harry's armed and dangerous."

Britt stopped, faced Max. "Dangerous?"

Max's face was grim. "I said he took everything with him. That includes a rifle case. A man doesn't steal a quarter-million-dollar yacht on a whim. Last night Harry was in the hallway when Everett dug up the bones. You made it clear there would be an investigation into Jeremiah's murder and whatever we learned would be presented to the authorities. Harry didn't wait around. You need to lay it out for the sheriff from start to finish. That will give him enough to put out an APB for a murder suspect."

For an instant, Annie thought Britt was going to refuse. Or, at the least, disagree. Her expressions changed with the rapidity of cards flipped by a dealer, but Annie was certain she saw surprise, assessment, calculation, and decision.

Then she nodded. "I'll do that." Still she made no move to go, an air of abstraction still evident.

Annie was afraid Britt had dealt with one crisis too many. Perhaps she'd always taken great comfort in the knowledge that she had a boat at her command and was never marooned. Annie understood island fever. Even though she and Max lived on an island, Annie's sense of security was based on the knowledge that Ben Parotti's ferry was always available as well as Max's motorboat. Moreover, Broward's Rock was not Hawaii or Bermuda. On visiting those far-distant outposts, Annie had never been able to shed the persistent uneasiness engendered by the knowledge that hundreds of miles of ocean separated her from the mainland.

And here was Britt looking as if she'd taken a step and found the floor missing.

Annie said quickly, "Do you want us to come with you?"

Britt gave her a grateful look but shook her head. "There isn't anything you can do. I'll take care of everything. Why don't you and Max finish breakfast?" She frowned. "Don't say anything to the others. I'll explain when I get back." She gave a short laugh. "Explain! That won't be easy since I don't understand myself. Harry gone. And"—she glanced toward Max—"you think he killed Jeremiah. I don't know. I suppose it makes as much sense as anything else." She swung away, moving fast toward the pines.

At the back door, Annie hesitated. "What do we tell Lucinda?"

Max shrugged. "Whatever we tell her, she's going to be mad."

Annie reached for the door. "Let me handle it."

When they stepped inside, Lucinda paused in lifting a slotted spoon holding a poached egg. "Well?"

Annie hurried across the room, smiling. "Harry won't be up. Britt is going to explain in a little while. I'll help you with everything as soon as I finish breakfast."

Lucinda eased the poached egg atop a steaming potato pancake. She gave Annie a harried glance. "If you could refill the serving dishes, I'd appreciate it."

Pushing through the door, Annie carried a plate of sausages and bacon. Max followed with an apple egg casserole. As they moved toward the buffet, conversation in the dining room fell away.

"Look who's back!" Slouching at ease in Jeremiah's chair, Everett looked as replete as a cat with a mouse tail dangling from its chops. His pale eyes gleamed with amusement. And intelligence. "Talk about suspense. Clearly disturbed, our hostess summons the detective-in-chief. He is followed by his lovely wife and helpmeet"—Everett inclined his shining pompadour toward Annie—"and we"—his gesture encompassed the long table—"are left to wonder what further misdeed has been discovered. As if the weekend weren't exciting enough with an announced murder, assorted suspects, and incipient investigation, now we await—with bated breath—elucidation. What the hell is going on? Has Britt misplaced a pet cobra? Found a map to a buried treasure? Another body?"

Max slid into his place, reached for his coffee. "Sorry to disappoint you, Everett." He drank the remainder of his coffee. "You and the others"—Max looked up and down the table—"can address all questions to Britt. She'll be here shortly with some information. All of you might want to relax with coffee and stay to hear her."

Annie settled into her place and returned to her breakfast with enthusiasm. Though the food had cooled, it was still delicious, especially the apple egg casserole. The coffee was magnificent. She wondered at Max's easy assurance that Britt would be with them shortly. That didn't seem likely. Annie thought the sheriff might have a good many questions when apprised out of the blue about a murder unreported for more than a year and a missing yacht. And the sheriff had yet to hear Max's theory about drugs. But if Max's reply staved off Everett's snide queries, so much the better.

As she ate, she darted interested looks at her companions. Sitting opposite her were Millicent McRae, Gerald Gamble, Craig Addison, Kim Kennedy, and Max. Nick McRae was at Annie's left. To her right were Isabel Addison and Dana and Jay Addison. The brilliant light of the chandeliers was unflattering to most. Nick's angry color had subsided, but his thin nose looked pinched. He hunched over his plate, stiff as a man marching through a snowstorm. Gerald ate as if the food were a problem to be solved. Craig made monosyllabic replies to Kim's enthusiastic description of the latest Falcons game. Kim looked young and vivid and eager, and was clearly making every effort to charm the CEO of Addison Media. Millicent twisted in her seat, her glance irritable. "When will we get more coffee?"

Annie smiled and said, "I'll see to it." She hurried to the kitchen, refilled the coffee carafe.

Lucinda turned from the sink. "Do I need to come?"

Annie shook her head. "Everything's fine. I'll clear the plates when they finish." In the dining room, Annie moved around the table, offering coffee, filling most of the cups.

Millicent held the steaming cup in both hands, lifted it to her mouth. She no longer had the aura of a successful, powerful woman. She drank, avoiding her husband's gaze.

Isabel had put very little food on her plate and eaten only a bit. Her dark beauty was somber. "Yes, I'd like coffee." She looked across the table at her husband, sighed, looked away.

Dana bent toward Jay. "You haven't eaten a bite. The pancakes are wonderful. Would you like some, honey?"

Ignoring his wife, Jay frowned at Max. "Where did Britt go? She said she'd show me that note Mom may have written."

Max buttered a croissant. "Britt should be here soon." He spread the pastry with marmalade.

Annie returned to her place, refilled her own cup. She finished the rest of her breakfast, drank the excellent coffee, welcomed the ever amazing surge of energy from caffeine.

Lucinda bustled into the dining room, moved toward the buffet. Annie started to rise. Lucinda waved a hand, indicating she would clear the dishes.

Everett rubbed his nose. "What well-bred guests, patiently awaiting their hostess." His disdain was evident. "Come on, people. Show a little life. Being well bred is a sure ticket to boredom. Let's get a pool going. After all, Britt's known as a gambler. She'll be pleased. This is a well-heeled crowd. Everybody throws in fifty bucks. I'll round up paper and pencils. Make a guess as to what new disaster has occurred and whoever's guess comes closest wins the pot. If all the guests play, the total will be four hundred and fifty bucks. If our sleuths join us, the pot goes up to five fifty. If nobody wins, we'll draw straws. At the very least, we can read the entries aloud and avoid keeling over from ennui as we wait for Britt's return." He pushed back his chair. "I'll nose around, find some pencils and paper."

"Take your time." Gerald's tone was sardonic.

Craig's blue eyes followed Everett. His gaze was not admiring.

Annie studied Craig. He had the look of a bulldog ready to snap. He was not a man to trifle with and he had ultimate power over Everett's future at Addison Media. Annie was puzzled. Everett might be obnoxious but he certainly wasn't stupid. Why was he willing to aggravate the boss?

As Everett strolled into the hall, Millicent hissed, "He's disgusting." Despite delicately applied makeup, her face was splotchy. Harsh lines flared from her mouth.

Isabel smoothed back a lock of raven black hair. Her dark eyes worried, she turned to her sister-in-law. "Do you think something has happened?"

Dana's round, gentle face squeezed in uncertainty. "It can't be anything major." She glanced up and down the table. "Everyone's here."

Lucinda returned from the kitchen, moved toward the buffet.

Quick footsteps thudded in the hall. Everett stopped in the doorway, his face alert and suspicious. "I've been gone from the dining room a minute and a half. You can all swear to it. You haven't heard any crashes and bangs, right?"

Craig slammed down his cup. Coffee splashed on his hand. "Crenshaw, I'm getting damn sick of your performance. I suggest you—"

Everett was gruff. "Not a performance." His voice had lost its mocking undertone. "Simple self-preservation. I don't intend to get the blame for smashing into Britt's desk."

Annie came to her feet. "Are you talking about the desk in the library?" She didn't wait for an answer. She ran across the room, passing an openmouthed Everett. She skidded into the hall, her shoes slapping on the heart-pine floor. Max called out her name. There was the sound of voices and clatter of movement behind her.

She dashed into the library, skirted a chair near the desk, jolted to a stop with a clear view of the bottom drawer, which dangled from the gouged and chipped right side. The front of the drawer had been prized loose. The drawer was empty.

Max came up beside her. "Annie, what's . . ." He saw the vandalized desk.

She pointed and somehow managed to keep her hand steady. "Britt put the gun there last night. She locked the drawer."

Behind her a murmur rose . . . *gun . . . gun . . . gun . . .*

Annie glanced at the doorway. Anxious faces peered at her. Dana held tight to Jay's arm. Nick and Millicent moved uneasily, restless as thoroughbred horses scenting a snake. Isabel pressed her hand to her lips. Eyes bright and eager, Kim called out, "What gun? Who does it belong to? Is it loaded?" Gerald, cadaverous face even longer than usual, muttered, "Did somebody get Jeremiah's gun? Why?" Craig bulled his way through the throng. Lucinda, holding a casserole, peered worriedly into the library.

Everett tried to push past Annie to reach the desk, but Max held out an arm to bar him. "Keep back. We don't want to mess up evidence."

The others edged into the room, straining to see.

"All right, everybody. Quiet." Craig stood in the middle of the library, both hands held up. He gave a short, peremptory nod at Annie. "You said Britt put a gun in that drawer last night. Why did she have a gun? What was going on?"

Dana murmured, "I don't understand. Why would anybody break into the desk and take the gun?" Her round face was frightened.

Her husband tugged nervously at a thick tangle of untidy hair. "I don't know. I don't like it."

Craig shot his brother an irritated glance. "Shut up and let's find out what's happened."

Jay's face flushed. He glared at Craig. "I'll talk to my wife if and when I want to. If there was any way to get her off this damned island, I'd take her out of here right now."

From the hallway, Britt cried out, her voice sharp and tense, "What's going on here?"

The onlookers in the doorway made way for her. Britt looked as harried as she had earlier in the kitchen, her eyes shadowed, her slender face drawn into a tight frown. She moved swiftly into the library, looking from face to face.

Annie gestured toward the desk. "The gun's gone. Somebody broke into the drawer. Everett found the desk this way just a few minutes ago."

Britt reached Annie, looked past her at the smashed drawer. "Oh my God . . ."

Annie was crisp and to the point. "I told them you locked the gun in there last night. The gun's been stolen."

Craig strode toward Britt. "What gun? Why did

you have a gun out last night?" His tone was demanding, his stare imperious. He may have been head of a media empire for only a year, but clearly he was a man now accustomed to deference and obedience.

A nerve pulsed in Britt's throat. She reached up, touched it with a shaking hand. "I was downstairs late. I saw a light in the garden. I took the gun with me when I went out to see." Her stare at him was defiant. "After everything that's happened, I was frightened. But I didn't find anything out of the way. When I came back, I put the gun away. Annie was here. And now "—she looked in disbelief at the shattered desk—"it's gone." Britt's murmur was low and shaken. "I thought it was perfectly safe there." She looked around the library, a peaceful room with the deep rich walls of cypress, bookshelves filled with many old leather-bound volumes, heart-pine floor, an ornate Chippendale clock hanging above the Adam mantel, a faded Aubusson rug. The room's elegance and grace were in sharp contrast to its uneasy occupants. "I suppose it's all part and parcel—"

Everett was strident. He might have been confronting a guest on his news show. "Part and parcel of what? What the hell is going on here? First you summon the supersleuths to the kitchen. Anybody would figure something's happened. They were gone at least twenty minutes. When they got back, Darling"—he jerked his head at Max—"said you'd explain everything on your return. Where did you go? Now it looks like somebody's busted into your desk, filched a gun. Why?"

Kim chimed in. "Something's upset you, Britt. Usu-

ally you're cool and collected. Tell us what's happened."
Her tone was encouraging, almost kindly.

Annie had a feeling Kim ached to have a microphone in her hand. She saw Craig's quick glance at the ex–TV reporter. There was a flicker of admiration in his eyes.

Britt swiped the back of one hand across her eyes. "I'm sorry. Yes, I'm upset. I've discovered that Harry Lyle has disappeared. First, I want to explain that I wasn't frank yesterday. I told you there was no way to leave the island until the charter arrives tomorrow at five. Actually, Golden Silk has a yacht—"

"Dad's yacht. *The Yellow Kid.*" Jay looked excited. "Sure, we should have thought of that. It was part of Cissy's inheritance. I assumed you'd sold it. Oh, hey"—his sigh of relief was huge—"that's great. We can leave now."

"I wish that were so." Britt's words were clipped as though she was trying to maintain her composure. "The boat's gone. Harry Lyle took the yacht and the motorboat as well. This morning when he didn't show up, I asked Max and Annie to go get him." She described their discoveries. "He took all his possessions."

Max nodded in confirmation. "That includes a locked trunk I saw in his place yesterday. Lucinda told us he was up and around late last night. Now we know he was clearing out his belongings. Apparently he often was up and around late at night. Here's my take on it . . ." Max sketched out his theory that Harry was a conduit for drugs coming from Latin America.

"There had to be something illegal in that trunk. Why else would he run?"

Kim clapped her hands together. "Drugs! That explains everything. Jeremiah must have figured out Harry was involved in smuggling, so Harry rigged that wire. Last night Harry heard Britt promise to report everything to the police. That meant a thorough investigation of everyone who was on the island when Jeremiah died. If there was a shipment of cocaine in that trunk, Harry had to get away."

Gerald, his expression judicious, cleared his throat. "Or there might be some reason we don't know about that will come to light when the police investigate. Since there's no doubt the yacht was taken by Harry Lyle, it follows that he must have broken into the desk, absconded with Jeremiah's pistol."

Britt fingered the collar of her blouse, a blue silk with white banding. She looked doubtfully at the splintered wood. "I suppose so."

Dana was puzzled. "Don't you think that's what happened?"

"Yes." There was an uncertain note in Britt's voice. "But I would have thought he'd have a key. Or use some tool and open it more neatly. It seems so messy for Harry. He was—oh, it sounds silly—but he was always so neat and careful. There's something savage about the way that drawer was pried out."

Annie looked at the battered desk. There was a reckless viciousness in the gashed and nicked wood. The fact that she and Britt had slept through the assault demonstrated the thickness of the walls and floors of the old house.

"But it's wonderful." Dana's light voice was a peal of thanksgiving. "Don't you see? Now we know that everyone here is innocent. Innocent." She sang the word like a declaration of joy.

There were murmurs and movement. The ease of tension was as palpable as the ripple of grass in the salt marsh from a gusty sea breeze.

Max cut through the flurry of comments. "What's the upshot, Britt? Did you contact the sheriff? Is a search under way? Have you arranged for a boat to come and pick us up?"

"A boat coming!" Millicent turned the ceramic bracelet on her wrist. "When will it get here?"

"No boat." Britt's face was grim. "No sheriff. No search. Harry was thorough. He took *The Yellow Kid* and the motorboat and the ham radio. We're stranded and there's no way to call for help."

∴ *Seven* ∾

"A HAM RADIO? YOU SAID there was no contact with the mainland. You lied to us." Craig's tone was scathing.

Anger blazed in Britt's green eyes, spotted her cheeks fiery red. "It wasn't anybody's business." She was defiant. "I had a ham radio and a computer in case there was an emergency and we needed help immediately. The Coast Guard has helicopters for evacuation purposes."

Millicent stalked across the floor. "I hold you personally responsible for this fiasco." Much the taller woman, she stopped, folded her arms, stared down at Britt.

Antagonism bubbled between them.

Millicent's voice quivered. "Everything you told me was a falsehood from start to finish. I came expecting to meet with supporters. Instead, I have been subjected to verbal abuse, accused of criminal conduct, and placed in jeopardy. Now the hired man absconds with our only means of escape from this hellish place. It is your duty to your guests to employ trustworthy people. Who was this man? What did you know about him?"

Craig jangled coins in his pocket. "Ease up, Millicent. You're going after the wrong person." His tone was conciliatory. "Dad met Harry at a skeet shoot in Savannah. They had a few drinks, hit it off. Harry told Dad he was between jobs. Dad hired him on the spot. I don't know if Dad ever got references. Now it looks as though that may have been a mistake that cost him his life. We can't fault Britt. For Harry." His look at Britt was cold. "But there is no excuse for covering up Dad's murder."

Britt pressed her hands against her flushed cheeks.

Craig was unrelenting. He took a step toward her, his voice rough. "You claim you were trying to make amends by getting us all here, doing an undercover investigation. But maybe this was just your way of blunting an effort at blackmail." His gaze moved from her to Everett.

"Of course I wrote to Britt." Everett spoke too loudly. "It was only fair to let her know I felt I had to contact the authorities."

Kim gave a hoot of laughter. "That doesn't cut it, Everett. You wait more than a year and suddenly you have to alert the cops? More likely you were waiting for the estate to be settled. Besides, you aren't famous for tipping off people when you plan to gut them. How many guests have you sucker punched on your show, bringing up some unsavory piece of the past without warning?"

"Nobody puts a gun to their heads to come on my show." Everett smoothed his pompadour. "I've got the best numbers of anybody except for O'Reilly, and I'm gaining on him. Eat my dust, Kim."

"I hate those programs." Dana's round face flushed

and her voice was shaky, but she kept on, looking defiantly at her brother-in-law. "Grown people yelling at each other and talking right over each other. It's disgusting. And stupid. It teaches children the wrong things, that it's good to be a bully and being rude is cool."

Everett raised an eyebrow. "What exquisite principles you have, my dear. Now, let me see, how do you express them? Did you and Jay turn down the money you inherited from Jeremiah, which, sweetie, flowed right out of the ratings from shows like mine into Addison Media?"

Dana drew a sharp breath. Jay took a step toward Everett, hands doubled into fists. Lucinda edged away from Jay.

Craig reached out, grabbed his brother's arm. "We aren't here to debate the merits of television mores. Or," he said wryly, "the honorable—or dishonorable— intent of Everett's letter to Britt. Instead, although we didn't know it at the time, we are here to solve a murder."

"Clearly," Nick McRae said, "the hired man is guilty. Why else run away?"

Britt was no longer flushed. Instead, she looked pale and uneasy. "I know that's how it looks. But"—she shook her head abruptly—"it doesn't make sense. If Harry wanted to kill Jeremiah, he could have easily made his death look like an accident. They spent a lot of time out on the yacht. He could have pushed Jeremiah overboard and said he fell and no one could have proved otherwise. I can't see Harry setting up a trap. If I hadn't removed the wire, everyone would have known immediately that Jeremiah was murdered. Harry would have been right in the middle of a homicide investigation." She looked toward Max. "You think Harry skipped out because he was mixed up in drug running. Well, if he couldn't afford to be noticed by the police now, he couldn't afford it then."

Everyone looked toward her. Where there had been the beginning of relaxation, there was now a sense of uncertainty.

Gerald Gamble tugged at an earlobe. "Perhaps"—his voice was thoughtful, considering—"something arose that weekend which necessitated Jeremiah's death immediately. Perhaps Harry didn't have the luxury of waiting until Jeremiah was out on the yacht."

Craig frowned. "We don't know what happened that weekend. Certainly Harry's theft of the yacht puts him in a bad light. However, Britt's right to make her point. We don't *know*"—his emphasis on the verb was unmistakable—"that Harry Lyle is guilty."

"If it wasn't him," Millicent said sharply, "it must be someone here." She looked around the library.

Annie glanced at each in turn. Britt stared at the gashed and broken drawer. His face unreadable, Craig folded his arms. Isabel pressed fingertips against one temple. Jay pulled his wife to his side, curving a protective arm around her shoulders. Dana's lips trembled. Millicent suddenly appeared shrunken, no longer imperious. Nick looked wary. Kim Kennedy was alert, still as an animal scenting danger. Gerald Gamble stroked his chin. Lucinda cradled the casserole in her arms, her ruddy cheeks paling.

Everett Crenshaw was unabashed. "God, if we just

had a camera crew. Right here we've got the reality show of the century: Trapped on an island with a murderer. Who's the killer? Who"—his voice wavered in a ghostly wail—"will die next?"

"Shut up, Crenshaw." Craig's glare stopped Everett as effectively as a body block.

But Everett's words once spoken could not be erased from the consciousness of his listeners. Eyes flickered. Glances slid and darted.

Annie felt cold and knew the iciness that enveloped her welled up from the ill-assorted and now fearful group in the library.

Craig still stood with arms folded, the man in command. "Tomorrow when the charter boats arrive, we'll be able to contact the police. But we have more than twenty-four hours before we can expect to leave the island. Under the circumstances—"

Annie wondered if he meant the fact of Harry's departure or the possibility that the murderer was in the library at this moment, near enough to touch.

"—I want everyone to write a detailed description of that last weekend of my father's life." It was a demand, not a request. "Describe every encounter with my father, when it occurred, what was said. Whether Harry is guilty or not, this information will help the investigation." He looked at each person in turn, waiting until he received a nod in assent or a muttered agreement.

Annie understood that Craig expected acquiescence. Family members would not defy him. Gerald and Everett were Craig's employees. Kim was looking for a job. Millicent and her husband curried media support. Britt was the instigator of the entire investigation. Lucinda worked for Britt.

Everett was his usual combative self. "Okay, no cameras, so it's back to the written word. But it's still reality time. Come on, everybody, remember to tell all. That's what I intend to do. About each and every one of you. Isn't that right, Britt? The truth, the whole truth, and nothing but the truth." His malicious glance skated around the room. "You can bet Craig will read them before he turns them over to the cops. He can read mine first, then he'll know what to look for in the others."

Britt was crisp. "I don't think anyone needs pointers from you, Everett." She nodded toward Craig. "I'll be glad to take legal pads and pens to each cabin. There's time before lunch for everyone to write their recollections."

It was as if her words opened the front door. There was an immediate flurry of departure.

As everyone moved away, Craig called out, his voice loud and forceful. "For God's sake, if anyone saw anything that points to the murderer, now's the time to speak up."

Everett slouched past Annie. Only she heard his sardonic farewell, "Or forever hold your peace."

Max caught up with Everett at the foot of the stairs. "Got something to show you." He gestured to the side of the house.

When they were around the corner of the house, out of sight from the path through the garden and the other guests, Max confronted him. "You heard your boss?"

"Oh, yeah." Everett was sardonic. "The man wants a report. The man signs my checks. Don't worry. I'll—"

"I'm not talking about the reports." Max was brusque. "Craig asked anyone who knows the identity of the murderer to speak up—"

Everett's burst of laughter cut Max off. "How stupid do you think I am, Darling? Hell, I'm just having fun. Odds are Harry's guilty as hell. I just like to tease the animals. I figure the reports now will hew a lot closer to reality. Craig should give me a bonus. Maybe a gold star. The truth is nobody here"—the flick of his hand was dismissive—"has the guts. So you can peel yourself away. Take a break. I don't need a bodyguard."

"After they're rinsed, the bottles go in one box, the cans in another." Lucinda pushed back a black curl that had escaped from the red bandana looped over the top of her head and knotted at the back. "Course it was Harry's job to carry them out at the end of the day. Maybe your husband can see to that. The rest of it"—she pointed at a built-in trash compactor—"goes in there. I tell you, living on a island isn't easy. I sure appreciate your pitching in." She nodded at Annie. "I can't do all this by myself." Her face was still flushed and she darted about the kitchen in a controlled frenzy. "As for writing down what happened when Mr. Addison died"—she flicked a dismissive glance at the legal pad and pen lying on the counter near the blue ceramic flour canister—"that will have to wait until all these folks are gone and I've got a minute to myself."

Annie tossed a Styrofoam carton into the compactor. "If you'd like, I can write it down for you."

Lucinda splashed liquid soap into a huge skillet, turned on the water, and began to scrub. She shrugged plump shoulders. "I don't know anything everybody else doesn't know. I only saw Mr. Addison a couple of times that weekend. He was at it hammer and tongs with almost everybody. I felt sorry for that man. I remember him when he and Lorraine were happy. He looked gruff but he had a big booming laugh and he was always kind to everyone who worked for him. I hated the way he got twisted and bitter toward the end. That last weekend was awful, everybody sour and hateful. Britt treated him like a bad dog. She despised him for bringing that blond floozy here. His sons were mad because he divorced their mom. And Kim being here made them furious even though they didn't like Cissy either. But everything isn't always the way it looks on the surface. You see, he never got over losing Lorraine."

Annie looked at her in surprise. Hadn't Jeremiah divorced Lorraine to marry Cissy?

Lucinda glanced down at her left hand, wet and sudsy and ringless. "Seems like people never are smart enough to love the ones as loves them. I know all about that. I was married once." Steam rose from the sink. Lucinda paused to swipe her face with the back of her hand. "And I would have walked over coals from here to Jericho for that man and he went and fell in love with this skinny little woman who flounced around and giggled at everything he said. He left me flat. I'd turned down Joe, who thought I was a princess. By then, Joe was married and I don't hold with breaking up marriages. See, there was lots of love but none of it connected, so everybody ended up unhappy. That's how it was with Mr. Addison. When he found out—" She broke off, looking flustered. "Oh, maybe I shouldn't say anything about it. But that's what I mean when I say nothing's the way it seems to be."

"It can't do any harm now." Annie kept her tone casual.

The flap of the cat door popped up and the calico cat shouldered into the kitchen. She looked curiously at Annie, made a sharp mew.

Lucinda wiped her hands on a cloth, turned to open a cupboard. She pulled out a box of dry cat food, dribbled a half cup into a blue ceramic bowl, placed it on a gold mat. "Here you go, Muffin." Back at the sink, she gave Annie an uncertain glance. "I wished he would have told his sons what happened. I guess he had too much pride. He wouldn't want them to know that kind of thing about their mom. They loved her to pieces. She was a great mom, I'll sure give her that. She was always there for them, no matter what, especially Jay since his father was critical of him. Wanted him to be more a man, you know." She lifted the skillet, held it under the running water, shifted it to the counter. "After you dry it"—she jerked her head at the dish towels hanging from a rack—"you can put it on the shelf under the counter where the blender sits. Anyway, there was an artist Mr. Addison invited to the island. He kind of sponsored him. Gave him one of the cabins for the summer. His name was Todd Fairlee. Tall and thin, looked like a good wind would knock

him over. Wore his hair too long and had an earring
in one ear. I was surprised how he and Lorraine hit it
off. I don't suppose you ever knew her. She was a nice
enough woman, but plain as an old shoe. Still, there
was something about her, the way her eyes crinkled
when she laughed, the way she moved her hands when
she talked. She had a bright way of looking at you as
if you were the only person in the whole world. Anyway, he was here all that summer and one thing led to
another and pretty soon Lorraine went to Charleston
with him. Now, she didn't live with him. I guess she
didn't want her sons to know. But that's why Mr. Addison divorced her. I thought I'd hear Lorraine had
married him but I never did. I don't know what happened there. It was probably the same old story, she
was crazy for him but he wasn't for her. Just like Cissy
was crazy for Mr. Addison but I think he only married
her because his pride was so hurt. When she got sick,
I know he was sorry but it wasn't like she was the love
of his life. Then he got involved with that Kim. But he
didn't really care about her either. All he cared about
was Lorraine."

Annie finished drying the skillet, carried it to the
cabinet, taking care to avoid the cat, who had sprawled
in the center of the floor. "If he cared for her, why
didn't he help with the medical bills when she got
hurt?"

Lucinda scraped the sides of a casserole dish. "Mad.
Mad as a riled hornet. And sad as could be. That's
how it was ever since she left. That last weekend was
the worst of all, everybody out of sorts. Craig hardly
spoke a word to his wife, and his face was dark as a

thundercloud. I could have told him, marriages don't take that kind of strain. It wasn't his wife's fault he and Mr. Addison were spitting nails at each other. Jay looked like he'd like to kill—" Lucinda gasped. "I didn't mean that. Poor Jay. He's not the sort to fight people—he's a gentle soul—so it was harder for him than for a man used to quarrels. And there was Cissy lying sick in her bed with tears slipping down her face. I'm afraid she was up one night and saw Mr. Addison with that Kim."

Annie wondered if Britt had been aware of Cissy's knowledge. And, a darker, colder thought: If a heart-broken Cissy had been able to get up and about, could she have strung a wire on the stairs to trip her unfaithful husband? Yet where would she have found a wire? Wire likely was obtainable only from supplies in an outbuilding, and Cissy was surely too weak to make her way down the stairs and outside. Wire seemed another link to someone familiar with the island, someone like Harry Lyle. Of course, a guest might have brought wire, the murder already planned.

For an instant, a nebulous thought flickered in her mind. Setting a trap suggested an attacker who hadn't the courage to face down Jeremiah with a gun or knife. And hadn't there always been the possibility a fall might not be fatal? She pictured the stairway. Death might not have been utterly certain but it was very likely, given the steepness of the marble steps. The murderer could afford to take the chance because it was an anonymous attack. The murderer's luck held.

Annie realized Lucinda was talking fast.

". . . and there's no doubt that Kim's a brazen hussy."

Lucinda gave a disdainful sniff. "I heard her tell Britt
how she'd do some redecorating when she lived on
Golden Silk. She thought Mr. Addison would divorce
Cissy and marry her and she all but said as much to
Britt. She strolled away from Britt, arrogant as a peacock, but she forgot it's men as has the fancy feathers.
She got her comeuppance." Lucinda's tone was satisfied.
"Harry told me Mr. Addison said Kim was to be taken
off the island first thing Saturday morning. But it didn't
come to that because Mr. Addison was dead by then.
Oh, I don't think Golden Silk had ever seen as many
bitter folk. Mr. Addison had had 'em in his study one
by one. When they came out, they weren't so high stepping. That haughty Mrs. McRae was limp as a doll with
the stuffing seeped out and that fancy-pants Crenshaw's
hands were shaking and even Mr. Gamble was white
and grim as a man with a rope around his neck."

Annie murmured, "My goodness," and stacked a
second dry casserole dish on the counter. She would
find out in a moment where they went, but she didn't
want to interrupt the flow of Lucinda's reminis-
cences. It was quite possible that Harry Lyle might,
as Britt believed, be a criminal yet wholly innocent
of murder.

Ever impulsive, Annie exclaimed, "Did Harry have
a fight with Jeremiah, too?"

Lucinda filled a teakettle, set it on the stove. "Not
so's you'd know it. That night when Harry told me he
was supposed to take that woman off the island the
next morning, I asked him, I said, " 'Harry, what's got
Mr. Addison so crossways with these people?' Harry
said, 'Oh, he's not taking any guff off anybody. He

said as soon as everybody's gone, we'll go out on *The Yellow Kid* and drink some whisky and not shave and catch us the biggest blue marlin in the Atlantic.' "

Harry would scarcely advertise a disagreement with Jeremiah if he intended to arrange his death that very night. Still, if there was not an immediate, urgent reason for Harry to dispose of Jeremiah, he would soon have been out on the open ocean with Jeremiah. Just the two of them. Annie frowned. "When did you talk to Harry?"

"Late. We were cleaning up." The teakettle whistled. Lucinda bustled to the stove, picked it, carried it to the sink. She splashed boiling water onto the porcelain. "Now, I always thought there was something odd about Harry. I never met such a closemouthed man. I knew him for years and I couldn't tell you diddly-squat about where he came from or where he grew up and I never heard him talk about family or friends. He did his job and I did mine. There were things that bothered me. He roamed around late at night. And I'm pretty sure he was up to no good on shore. Once when we took *The Yellow Kid* in to Savannah and I had my grocery list, I started off, then sat down on a bench on the boardwalk because I was feeling sick that day. It was hot as a steam bath. In the nineties. Anyway, I was down by the dock and I saw Harry come off the boat. He was carrying a big blue duffel over his shoulder. He was a strong man and I could tell it was weighing him down. He didn't see me. He was walking along the boardwalk and there was a fellow waiting there, real dark, swarthy you know, and Harry came even with him and gave him just the littlest nod and then he

was past but the fellow started after Harry. I thought
that looked funny. I don't know why but I followed
them—"

Annie knew why. Curiosity. But as she listened, she
heard the quaver in Lucinda's voice.

"—and the dark man—I won't ever forget what he
looked like, greasy black hair and a mean face, thin as a
wire and a skull tattoo on one arm—moved past Harry.
He went along the harbor and sat down on a bench. He
had a newspaper under one arm. He opened it up and
acted like he was reading and after a little while Harry
strolled up. He leaned the duffel up against the bench
and then he walked to the railing and stood looking
out at the harbor. In a minute, the dark man got up.
He left the paper on the bench. He picked up that bag
and moved fast. Harry paid no attention. After a while,
he ambled over to the bench and sat down. He picked
up the paper. I couldn't quite see but I think there was
something in the paper, an envelope maybe. The way
Harry moved, I'd swear he slipped something into his
jacket. Now, you and I both know something fishy was
going on."

Annie was at the other sink, rinsing out bottles for
the recycling box. "You didn't tell anyone?"

Lucinda swiped a cloth across the counter. She
folded the cloth, hung it on a rack. "If you'd seen that
man—"

Annie heard fear and knew that Lucinda had recognized danger as clearly as if she'd seen the reddish
brown hourglass markings of a copperhead.

"—you'd understand. He was walking death. What
would I tell anybody? The man was gone. So was

the duffel. No, from that time on, I was real careful around Harry. Anything odd around here, I told myself it was none of my business. Though last week when I heard the gunshots, I don't see how it could have been Harry."

Startled, Annie swung to face Lucinda. "Gunshots?"

Max stepped into their bedroom. He glanced at the flung-back spread and a pillow that had toppled to the floor. He grinned. He envisioned Annie flying off the bed, late for a very important date. It was nice to know she'd hurried down to breakfast because of him. He headed for the table and the folders he'd tossed there upon arriving. Although it was very much on the order of locking the barn door after the horse's escape, he wanted to know more about Harry Lyle. He agreed with Everett. Harry was very likely the man they sought. Exploring Harry's cabin and meeting him, even if only briefly, had given Max a picture of his personality—a loner, a brawler, a fighter. He exuded toughness and that squared with Harry as a drug runner.

Max shuffled through the folders. Barb had printed in red HARRY LYLE on the blue folder. Max flipped it open. He stared in surprise. Barb's report was succinct:

This dude doesn't exist. Oh yeah, there's a SS# and regular payments into it, tax returns, an SC driver's license, but as far as I can figure out, the original Harold George Lyle's been in a cemetery in Dubuque, Iowa, since 1953. My guess is your dude needed a name and picked one up from the cemetery, applied for SS, got it and went his merry way. If nobody ever checked, no reason for the Feds to tumble to it. When you see him, ask how things are in Dubuque. Or maybe better not.

"Damn," Max swore aloud. If only he and Annie had read all the bios on their way to Golden Silk yesterday. He wouldn't go so far as to claim he would have exclaimed "Aha!" and immediately fingered Harry as the murderer. But he certainly would have looked Harry over with a critical eye.

Just to be thorough, he scanned the material on Lucinda Phillips, which was straightforward and held no surprises.

Whether or not Harry proved to be guilty of Jeremiah's murder, he was definitely going to be a person of interest to the police.

Max almost returned the folder to the stack, then shook his head. Britt should have this information—such as it was—to add to the collection intended for the police. He carried it with him. Maybe he'd catch her downstairs.

Annie turned off the water. She carried the bottles to the box, placed them inside. "What gunshots?"

Lucinda opened a cupboard, looked toward Annie. She was relaxed and cheerful. "I always have a cup of coffee this time of morning. Then I'll get started on the cabins. Want some coffee?"

Annie never met a coffee break she didn't enjoy, and Lucinda's coffee, a dark French roast, was strong enough to float a camel and delicious to boot. "I'd love some." When they settled at the table, Lucinda poured rich, thick cream into her coffee. Annie cradled her mug and asked again, "What gunshots?"

Lucinda turned sideways in her chair and welcomed Muffin into her lap. The cat made two turns and nestled against her. A little tuft of cat food clung to her pointed chin. She licked her lips. Lucinda stroked her as she drank the creamy coffee. "It was last Tuesday. That's the day Harry and I usually make a run to Savannah. Britt had already gone out in the motorboat. *Happy Days,* she calls it. When we don't have any guests, she takes a day off now and then, goes out by herself to fish. She left right after breakfast. Harry and I were set to leave at ten. I changed my mind about going. I had a new recipe I wanted to try and Harry said he'd pick up the grocery order. I'd put together the grocery list the day before and that made it easy for him." She drank coffee, looked bemused. "That Harry didn't miss a trick, did he? Ham radio gone. Computer gone. No way to raise an alarm till he's halfway to Mexico with a new name painted on *The Yellow Kid* and forged papers. Anyway, last week I was here in the kitchen, reading over my recipe, scallops and mushrooms in a sauce with cream and cognac and port. Perfect for winter. I had the windows open. I like fresh air and it wasn't very cold that day." She waved a hand at the bank of windows overlooking the clearing behind the house. "I heard a shot. Now, there's no mistaking the sound of a gun. I grew up around guns. My daddy had rifles and a shotgun and a forty-five. He taught all us kids how to shoot."

Annie stared at her in fascination, picturing the big,

comfortable-looking woman as a plump little girl, holding a gun in both hands, squeezing the trigger.

"The minute I heard that crack, I got up and went to the window. I heard it again. I wouldn't say it was a rifle. But bigger than a twenty-two." Lucinda's shrug was dismissive. "You can't hear a twenty-two any distance at all. But I shouldn't have heard a thing. I was supposed to be the only person on the island. I can tell you I felt spooky. Somebody with a gun and me here all alone." There was an echo of disquiet in her voice. "I went out on the steps. I almost yelled for Harry. I thought maybe he'd come back and was doing some target practice, though he'd never done a thing like that in all the years on the island. I opened my mouth. Then I stopped. I had a feeling least said soonest mended. I stood there and listened." She brushed the dry food from the cat's chin. "I never heard another thing. No more shots. Once I thought about going down to see if *The Yellow Kid* was back, but I decided against that. If Harry wanted to shoot off a gun and keep quiet about it, I wasn't going to bring it up. I went into the kitchen and set to work but I was glad when Britt came back in the afternoon."

Annie leaned forward. "What did Britt think about it?"

Lucinda downed the remainder of her coffee, pushed back her chair. The blue eyes gazing at Annie held remembered fear. "Now, if I'd told her, what would she have done? She'd have asked Harry. He'd have wanted to know what she was talking about and then she'd have told him I heard shots and then there I'd be in the middle of it. I don't know if you ever met Harry, but

I can tell you he's a man you wouldn't want to cross. Honey, I didn't say a word to her and I'd never have mentioned it now but he's gone. All I can say is, good riddance."

Max stood in the central hallway. The silence was broken only by the tick of the massive grandfather clock in the alcove beneath the stairway. The drawing room and dining room were unlighted. He turned, moved swiftly toward the library, the sound of his steps loud in the quiet. He opened the library door. The lights were off. He'd hoped Britt might be here, working on her report for Craig. Certainly the facts she'd admitted would be essential to any police investigation. Of course, she'd promised to take writing materials to each cabin and obviously hadn't returned yet. The best course would be to go down to the garden, wait by the fountain. He had no reason to remain in the library, yet he hesitated in the doorway, gazing about the room. The shattered drawer still hung askew from the battered frame. Nothing should be touched until the police fingerprinted it. Would Harry have bothered to wear gloves? Certainly he had no intention of being apprehended. Likely he had left no trace. In Max's estimation, Harry was not a novice at crime.

Max looked at the old-fashioned wooden file cabinet in one corner. Although surely as serviceable as any modern metal file, the wooden cabinet was unobtrusive in the genteel library setting. Probably Britt kept everything pertaining to Heron House and Golden Silk there. He wondered if there was a personnel file on Harry Lyle. Surely Britt had some information about her employee.

Max wasn't sure why he felt compelled to search for Harry's history. The police and their banks of computers would find what there was to discover. But he wasn't satisfied. He'd like some confirmation of the theory he'd spun from the presence of a locked trunk and Harry's flight. There could be no doubt of Harry's escape. But there was no proof of anything else. Maybe something would turn up in the reports now being written—concocted?—about that weekend, a pointer to the stealthy figure who had crept to the top of the staircase and set a trap to kill Jeremiah Addison. Max wondered if Craig Addison would permit Max and Annie to read those reports.

Max looked around the library one more time. As he did, he remembered Harry Lyle's well-stocked rifle case. Harry was already armed. Since he was leaving with the yacht and had the motorboat in tow, he didn't have to fear armed pursuit from anyone on the island. Why slip into the house and smash into the desk, taking the chance of rousing Britt and Annie?

Where was Britt? Surely she knew more about Harry. Max felt like a horse with a burr under its saddle. He wasn't going to be comfortable until he'd found out what there was to find.

In the main hallway, he looked toward the kitchen, changed his mind. He'd find Annie when he'd discharged his last duty, wrapped up this last loose end about Harry Lyle.

On the front piazza, the air was cool. The sky was a bright winter blue though woolly clouds mounded in the west. For now it was a beautiful day. Wisps of fog still wreathed the tops of the live oaks and pines. The painted wood floor was wet underfoot. He smiled, remembering a frost-slick porch on his grandmother's house and running with wild abandon to skid into the railing. What fun to be seven again. Instead, he walked carefully to the side piazza overlooking the garden. The fog was burning off though swirling patches still softened the banks of azaleas and camellias. The central path afforded a view of the fountain. Beyond the first slope, the garden was a patchwork of pines and shrubbery, creating secluded nooks.

He was halfway down the path to the fountain when he saw a flash of red. He'd not paid much attention at breakfast but he was almost sure Britt had worn a long-sleeved red sweater. Max picked up speed.

He reached the fountain. The water slipping over the granite ledges sparkled in the sun. He looked to his left. A trail curved around a clump of weeping willows. If he'd seen Britt, she must have taken this path. He might as well follow. He'd like a description of the light she'd thought she'd seen in the garden last night. As soon as he was done with Britt, he would find Annie, see if he could join in the housekeeping chores. When they finished, perhaps the reports would be done and he could offer to help Craig organize the material for the police.

The narrow dirt path curled around the willows and plunged into a stand of pines. Max's steps made no sound on the brown pine needles. A splash of sunlight marked the end of the trail. He was almost to the clearing when an angry voice brought him to a stop.

*   *   *

Low branches scraped the side of the golf cart. Ferns rippled against the sides. Annie steered cautiously. She stopped at the circle in the forest where individual paths branched off to cabins. She looked at a small map sketched by Lucinda. The paths, like spokes in a wheel, led to Cabins 1 through 8. Lucinda had also made an outer circle, indicating the cabins were linked one to another. So, Annie deduced, once she reached Cabin 1, she didn't need to return to the main path. She could take the path in the outer circle to Cabin 2. But if she were at Cabin 3 and wanted to go to Cabin 8, it would be quicker to return here and take the direct path to Cabin 8. She shook her head, beginning to have the feeling that always overcame her in math class when a problem began: If the boat goes upstream at 6 miles per hour but the current is 9 miles per hour and there are three occupants of the boat . . . Fortunately, Lucinda didn't expect miracles of her volunteer assistant. The housekeeper had departed the backyard in the other golf cart, also equipped with cleaning supplies and fresh towels and sheets, a few minutes before Annie, her goal Cabin 7, which, she blithely explained, could be reached more quickly by turning right from the main path at the intersection with the outer circle. Annie realized that if she'd not been geographically challenged, she could have shortened her trip to Cabin 1.

She nosed the cart onto the trail. Max's drug-smuggling theory had been corroborated by Lucinda's observation of the smoothly switched duffel bag between Harry and the dangerous-looking man in the Savannah harbor. Chalk one up for Max. From what Lucinda knew of Harry, it seemed very likely he wouldn't have hesitated to do away with anyone who threatened him. Jeremiah might have enjoyed Harry but he would have been furious if his beloved Golden Silk was used as a transit point for street drugs. Had a quarrel between Harry and Jeremiah culminated that weekend? Or had Harry chosen that weekend for murder because there were guests on the island? And more than a year after Jeremiah's death, what could have prompted the gunshots last week on the supposedly deserted island? Annie understood Lucinda's decision to remain silent. Obviously, she was afraid of Harry.

Lucinda's garrulousness in the kitchen this morning was a measure of her relief. Her revelations about the Addison family clearly indicated the depth of the strain between Jeremiah and his sons. It would be interesting to know how much or how little Craig and Jay revealed in their written summaries of their father's last weekend. Annie hoped they would never have to know about their mother's love affair. No good would come of that knowledge, though they might have a better—and kinder—understanding of their father.

She jammed on the brake. A white-tailed buck pawed the ground in front of her. He snorted, ducked his head to wave his antlers. Beyond him, a doe scrambled into the brush, disappeared. The buck snorted again, then plunged into the forest.

Annie's heart hammered. Although bucks began their search for does in November, obviously this male had not spent all his passion even though it was early January. She was thankful she had not loomed between the buck and the doe of his desire. Otherwise, she and the cart might have suffered from those flailing hooves.

She was grateful to reach the clearing unscathed. Light shone from the front windows. She glanced down at her map. *Isabel* was printed next to the cabin number. Annie felt more cheerful. Isabel seemed very nice. Annie was in no hurry to reach Cabin 2, which housed the McRaes.

She parked the cart by the steps, retrieved the tray with cleaning supplies, hoisted a broom over one shoulder. At the front door, she perched the tray against one hip, placed the broom on the porch, and knocked. When there was no answer, she knocked again and turned the knob, calling out, "Maid service."

She was halfway into the living room, noting that it was a twin of Everett's, when she saw Isabel, a white-faced figure of misery huddled in a basket chair near the fireplace. There was no blaze in the fireplace, only a few smoldering remnants. Despite the overhead light, the cabin seemed gloomy, weighted by Isabel's distress.

Isabel made no response. She scarcely seemed aware of Annie's presence. She stared blindly at the floor, her shoulders bowed, hands clasped.

"I'm sorry." Annie's exclamation was quick, unstudied. She started to back out the door, then stopped. She put down the cleaning supplies and hurried across the room to grip two cold and clammy hands in her own. "Isabel, what's wrong?"

Isabel's eyes filled with tears. "How could I have been so stupid? He'll never forgive me." It was a cry of utter hopelessness.

Annie knelt by the chair. She didn't know what had put Isabel in such an agony of spirit. But Annie understood making mistakes. Sometimes a mistake, no matter how we wish or pray, cannot be rectified. But sometimes a mistake can be rectified. Or forgiven. "Can you tell him"—Annie was sure Isabel spoke about Craig—"you're sorry?"

Isabel sniffed, pulled free a hand to wipe the tears from her cheeks. Imploring eyes looked mournfully at Annie. "You don't understand. How can I tell him I thought he was a murderer? How could I have believed such a dreadful thing?"

Annie kept her hands steady though she felt a jolt of surprise, followed quickly by comprehension. No wonder Isabel had fled after Jeremiah's death.

"I suppose you had reason." Annie's thoughts raced. If Isabel suspected Craig, there had to be something concrete, some occurrence that had given rise to her fear.

"I should have known better." Isabel wiped her face against her sleeve. "But Craig was furious that morning. He slammed out of the cabin, said he was going to catch his dad before he went out to jog and if he had to beat some sense into him over taking care of his mom, that's what he was going to do. When Jeremiah died, I was sure they'd struggled and Craig had shoved him. Oh, damn Britt, damn her! If I'd known about the wire, I'd have known it wasn't Craig. Craig would never sneak around and set a trap. Now it turns out it was that Harry creature. I never liked him. I always told Craig I was afraid of him. Craig laughed and said his dad thought the world of Harry. Oh, I wish I were dead! I've thrown away the man I love and I can never get him back." She turned to press her face against a pillow.

Annie squeezed her hands. "Let me get a wash-cloth." That would be a start. She'd try to help Isabel, calm her. She wasn't sure Isabel could make amends. Would Craig forgive his wife? Isabel would never know unless she asked.

"We've been waiting for you." Jay Addison's voice was loud and irritated.

"I'm sorry." Britt was breathless. "I came as soon as I could. I had to take the legal pads to the cabins. I left one at your cabin."

Max angled off the path. He brushed past ferns, stopped at the edge of the clearing. A rustic bridge spanned a cypress-rimmed pond. On the far side was a gazebo. A small area in front of the gazebo was paved with flagstones. A sundial was in the center. Screened by a saw palmetto, Max saw an odd tableau.

Britt stood near the sundial. She was flushed. Her breath came rapidly, unevenly. Jay waited near the ga-zebo, gaze demanding, arms folded. His wife raised a hand as if to restrain him, then let it fall. Dana gazed at her husband with a mixture of sadness and concern.

Jay's long hair curled on his collar. The hairstyle made him look young and vulnerable. His face twisted in anger. "The only reason I came to this stinking island was because you said you'd found something of my mother's. You told us you'd meet us here and you're damn long in coming."

Dana stepped forward, her expression placating. "Please, Britt, Jay's not himself. He's—"

Jay glared at her. "Shut up, Dana. I don't need any-body to make excuses for me."

Dana bit her lip. Her eyes glistened with quick tears.

Jay was oblivious to her distress. He turned to Britt. "All right, what have you got?" He gestured at the lagoon. "Why here?"

"You'll see." Her answer was clipped. She reached into the black canvas carryall that hung from her shoulder. She drew out a short strip of paper folded down to a quarter-inch strip. The paper looked old and yellowed. She handed it to Jay. "I had a baseboard replaced in the Meadowlark Room. The carpenter brought this to me. He'd found it pushed down in a gap behind the baseboard. He was laughing, thought it might have belonged to a kid playing hidden treasure. I understand why he thought so, but I don't think it was part of a game." She looked uncomfortable. "When I cleared out everything after Cissy died, there were lots of papers that belonged to your father. Some of them went back a long way. I wasn't snooping but I had to look things over to know where to send them." She glanced at Dana. "You'll remember I sent you several boxes last year."

"Pictures." Jay's tone was uneven. "Pictures of Mother with Craig and me."

Britt tried to sound matter-of-fact. "There were boxes filled helter-skelter with all kinds of pictures and notes and letters. Your dad must have swept up everything of your mother's and tossed it into boxes after she left. Pretty soon I was able to recognize your mother's handwriting. When I got this slip, I was sure she'd written it."

Jay stared at the little strip of paper with a puzzled frown. "Why would Mother hide a scrap of paper in her room?"

Dana and Britt exchanged a quick glance, as if the two of them had some knowledge that kept them silent.

Jay looked from one to the other. "What's wrong? I don't understand. Dammit, let me see it." He held out his hand.

Britt stepped forward. She placed the folded-up sheet in his hand. Her expression was a combination of sadness and pity.

Jay held the fragile strip for an instant, then slowly, using both hands, hands that trembled, unfolded the paper.

Dana's lips parted, but she made no sound.

Max had a sense of inevitability. Dana stared at the paper. He was sure that Dana wanted to grab it away from Jay. Instead, she bowed her head and listened as Jay read aloud, " 'My heart's treasure lies where time flies. The great blue heron watches as the sun's shadow moves. When the shadow is cast and noon is nigh, walk 2 north, 3 west.' " Jay rubbed his knuckles against his cheek. "It's Mother's writing." His voice was soft. He turned toward Dana. "What does it mean?" He was like a child awaiting direction.

Dana looked toward the sundial. "I expect," and there was false cheerfulness in her tone, "your mom was just enjoying the lovely lagoon. She spent a lot of time in the gazebo. That's all it is, Jay. She was writing about a place she loved."

Jay's brows drew down. "Why did she hide the scrap in the baseboard?" He stared down at the sundial. "The only reason to hide it would be if it was something she didn't want anyone to know about, something she didn't want Dad to see. That's it. Maybe she kept a journal and put things in it she was afraid for him to read."

Once again, Dana and Britt's glances held, locked, broke.

"I hated the way he treated her." His voice was feverish. "Dumped her out, like kicking an old dog out on a freeway. She had to go back to work and then she was hurt and he wouldn't do a thing for her, not a thing." He leaned down over the sundial, muttering, ". . . when the shadow is cast . . ." He followed an imaginary line to noon, walked ahead to the second flagstone, turned left, knelt by the third stone. Strong fingers grappled with the stone, tugged, pulled, lifted. "There's something here." He reached down, gripped an oilcloth-wrapped packet.

Dana watched, her face frozen. She looked helpless and hopeless, as if awaiting a dreadful moment she could do nothing to forestall.

Jay opened the packet. "Letters. A bunch of them. They're letters to Mother. They all say 'Lorraine' on the envelopes. I don't know the handwriting." Once again he looked toward Dana.

"Don't open them, Jay." Dana's voice was stern. "Whatever they are, whomever they're from, they belong to your mother, not to us. Leave them be."

"She hid them." Jay slowly rose. There was mud and pine straw on his trousers. " 'My heart's treasure . . .' " He hesitated, then opened the first letter, pulled out a sheet. " 'My darling Lorraine . . .' " He broke off. He slipped the sheet into the envelope, carefully replaced the letter in the packet. He thrust the packet at Dana, but he didn't look at her, didn't see the love and sadness and regret in her face. He blindly turned and blundered toward the path. Breaking into a run, he careened into the forest.

"Jay!" Dana's cry was high and frightened. She started after him. Max heard her gasping for breath as she ran past.

In the clearing, Britt walked slowly to the uplifted flagstone. She sighed and bent down to replace it over the shallow hole.

Max walked up to join her. "Love letters?"

She looked up, startled. "You overheard?"

Max nodded. "I saw you come this way. I wanted to show you"—he held up his folder—"what little I have about Harry and see if you've checked your records. When I got here, I overheard enough to know I didn't want to interrupt."

"I wish you had. I feel dreadful about Jay. He and Craig never knew about Lorraine's artist. Lucinda told me all about it. Lucinda didn't approve but she was sympathetic. She saw Lorraine as a fool for love." The flush she'd had when Max first reached the clearing had faded, leaving her pale. "He's—oh, damn, a grown man should be tougher. I guess his sweetness is what Dana adores and what his mother appreciated. And Jeremiah loathed. Now Jay's going to have to see his mother as a woman and not as his mother." Her thin face was pensive.

Max looked at her curiously. "You didn't have to tell him about that scrap of paper." The choice had been Britt's and she surely must have guessed why a married woman would resort to a secret hiding place.

She was obdurate. "I had to do it. Do you think Jay would have come to Golden Silk to honor his father?" Her laugh was derisive. "Do you know my number one suspect?"

Max remembered Annie's quick whisper before breakfast that Britt had a suspicion who might be guilty.

"Jay." Britt's voice was grim. "I thought it was Jay. I felt sad about that. Because he's a decent guy. He really is. And not tough enough. I knew he'd never have had the guts to face his father, but he might set a trap. He would consider it justified, a strike on behalf of his mother. Jay adores Lorraine and now he has to see her as an adulteress and he'll know his anger at his father wasn't justified. That will be terrible for him, but worst of all"—her voice was so faint Max scarcely heard—"what if he killed Jeremiah? What if he committed murder for the wrong reason? Oh God, I hope that's not what happened. Maybe I'm wrong. Maybe Harry did it after all." There was no conviction in her voice.

Max handed her his folder. "Harry doesn't exist."

Britt flipped it open, scanned. "I sent in social security contributions. There was never any reason to ask him anything personal. Come to think of it, Harry never mentioned a family, never said anything about growing up around here or anywhere. He talked about fishing and tides and weather and horses. He liked horse racing. And skeet shooting. That's how he met Jeremiah. I guess Harry was pretty good at keeping conversation directed away from himself. Well"—she slapped the folder shut, poked it into her carryall—"it's not our problem. The sheriff can handle it. And now"—she glanced at her watch—"I have to find Lucinda, help her service the cabins. Then we need to get lunch ready."

Max fell into step with Britt. He saw no point in telling her he was sure the interviews with the sheriff's office were going to be difficult. A murder reported more than a year late was going to trigger a grim response. "The sheriff's going to want all the help he can get. You've been all over the island this morning. Did you see anything—like digging or some kind of change—that might indicate Harry was getting something when you saw that light last night?"

She looked startled, then thoughtful. "I just made the round of the cabins. I didn't see anything different, but we can be on the lookout. We'll ask Lucinda, too."

"Annie's helping Lucinda." He smiled. "Let's find them and pitch in."

As they moved beneath the shadow of the interlocking tree branches, Max felt the damp January chill. A reader of Gothic thrillers might have attributed his sudden shiver to drama yet to unfold, like a storm heralded by faraway thunder and a darkening sky. Max was not a reader of Gothic novels. He walked faster and wished he had his jacket.

∽ *Eight* ∼

ANNIE SPRINKLED CLEANSER IN the shower. As she scoured, she sneezed twice and thought thankfully of the cleaning service that came weekly to the Darling household. She was grateful to be spared the daily task, though housework afforded great job satisfaction. A clean bathroom, a tidy bedroom, and a sparkling kitchen put a bright, shiny face on a home. She whistled as she scrubbed, pausing only long enough for an occasional sneeze. She wished it was as easy to wash sorrow and pain out of people's lives, but the stains of anger and distrust and despair often can't be eradicated. Had Isabel reached Craig's cabin yet? Annie had drawn a map for her and watched as Isabel, powder smoothed on her tear-streaked face, started out on her personal journey of hope.

Annie stood, turned on the shower, and watched the suds and bubbles swirl down the drain. Would Max forgive her if she'd suspected him of murder? Something deep inside recoiled. How could she possibly ever think Max capable of hurting anyone? A bleak question rose in her mind: What if someone threatened his mother? Or her? Max joked about Laurel's propensity for nonsense, her inability ever to be direct, her penchant for unexpected enthusiasms. But Max adored his mother. And though Max might fight like a tiger to protect Laurel or Annie or any creature in danger, he would never, ever slip through the night to rig a snare. Annie understood full well Isabel's certainty now of Craig's innocence.

Annie paused in the bathroom doorway, made one last check. Everything sparkled. She moved into the bedroom, broom and cleaning supplies in hand. As she worked, questions and assumptions and uncertainties swirled in her mind. It was easy to dismiss any possibility that she, Annie, could ever make Isabel's mistake. But perhaps Isabel shouldn't be faulted. She knew her husband better than anyone and she realized the depth of his fury with his father. She'd known how much Craig loved his mother, how angry he was and how anger can flare into violence. A struggle at the top of the stairs, a shove, a dreadful result—yes, she could love Craig and know his goodness and still envision such a moment. But she had immediately disclaimed any possibility of Craig setting a trap. Surely Craig would listen—

A rousing knock sounded at the door. "Lucinda?" Britt's call was brisk.

Annie scooted to the living room. She looked past Britt in the doorway and saw Max. A smile wreathed her face.

Max's lips curved in quick response. His eyes locked with hers.

Always when she saw him, whether in the deep of night or on a crisp winter day or from a moving car, coming or going, wherever, whenever, her heart lifted like a bird taking flight. *Oh, Max,* and she knew her eyes were telling him: *I love you, I love you, I love you.*

Britt glanced around the cabin. "Where's Isabel?" A frown. "I hoped she'd be working on her report, though when I saw her she was awfully upset."

Annie's face was grave. "Did you talk to her?"

Britt shook her head. "She got up, dashed into the bedroom. I could tell she'd been crying. I called out and said I'd leave the legal pad." She glanced at the coffee table and the legal pad lying there. "She hasn't even touched it." Britt glanced toward the bedroom. "Is she resting?"

Annie hesitated. She hated to reveal what she'd learned from Isabel, but there could be no quarter given in the search for a murderer. But there was one clear gain from Annie's encounter with Isabel: Annie was positive Isabel couldn't be guilty.

"She isn't here. She's gone to find Craig." Annie felt reluctant to speak. But truth couldn't hurt the innocent. "She wants to tell him she was wrong." Annie sighed. "She was afraid he and Jeremiah had quarreled and there might have been a struggle and Jeremiah could have fallen down the stairs. That's why she left Craig. The minute she knew about the wire, she was sure Craig was innocent. Now she's terrified he won't forgive her for suspecting him."

Max winced. "I wouldn't think he'd be pleased. On the other hand, there's something appealing about a wife seeing her husband as a hothead but not as a plotter. A struggle is one thing. An ambush is another. An ambush spells out a cold, determined assassin. When the murderer knelt on those stairs and stretched the wire, that was an exercise in arrogance."

Britt raised an eyebrow. Her gaze was sharp. " 'Arrogant' is a word easily applied to Craig."

Annie was surprised to find herself rushing to Craig's defense. "He takes charge." Her eyes smiled at Max. He took charge of his world, also. "I'll admit all I know about Craig is what I've seen this weekend, but he doesn't seem like a man who would put himself and what he wanted above everyone." That was what Max meant by arrogance, the overweening ego that placed itself and its desires above the life of another person. Yes, Annie could imagine Craig in an angry struggle, but she could not picture him crouched on the stairs in Heron House, stringing a deadly trap for his father. "Surely Craig will forgive Isabel."

Britt's voice was cool. "We'll hope so." Clearly Annie and Max's appraisal hadn't convinced her of Craig's innocence. Or perhaps of Isabel's either. "I guess we'll know when we see them at lunch." Another quick frown. "Are you here by yourself?" She looked at Annie. "Where's Lucinda?"

"We split up. She's starting with Cabin 7." Annie's nose wrinkled. She managed to squelch another sneeze. "I'm making the bed."

Britt flung out a hand. "Annie, you're wonderful to pitch in, but you've done enough. I'll find Lucinda and she and I can take care of everything now. You and Max can relax for a while, take a walk on the beach."

"No problem, Britt. Confidential Commissions' special sideline is dusting on demand." Max pushed up the sleeves of his sweater. "The three of us can straighten up this place in nothing flat. Then Annie and I will organize what we know for the sheriff." He strode toward the bedroom.

Britt yielded with a graceful smile. She grabbed the vacuum cleaner and bent to plug it in.

Annie caught up with Max. "We'll do the bedroom together."

They worked fast, smoothing the fitted sheet, pulling up the top sheet, tucking in. The vacuum cleaner roared in the living area. True to Max's prediction, the cabin was finished in less than fifteen minutes. Max insisted on carrying out the cleaning supplies and broom. Annie grabbed her windbreaker where she'd dropped it in the living room. Britt plopped the laundry bag in the back of the golf cart and slid behind the wheel. Warmed up by the housework, Annie tossed her jacket in back. Her cotton pullover was enough to keep her warm. She settled into the passenger seat.

Max clung to one side. "Who's next?" He was as casual as if subbing for a maid was as customary to him on a Saturday morning as teeing up to play golf.

Annie would have scrabbled for her map, but Britt answered quickly, "The McRaes are in Cabin 2."

Annie began to cool down as the cart trundled along the path. In the shadows beneath the canopy of trees, the air was damp and chill. Ferns brushed against Max. Annie was glad to turn over both the cart and the responsibility for cabin service to Britt. She didn't mind helping but she was sure that the next stop might have its challenges. Were Millicent and Nick writing their reports? Or was Nick asking Millicent pointed questions about Boca Raton?

"Oh dear." Britt sounded startled. The cart eased to a stop, its nose barely poked into the clearing around Cabin 2. She held up a hand for quiet. The outer path approached the side of the cabin. The living room windows looked out to the front and to each side. Millicent and Nick McRae were as clearly visible and distinct as if on a stage. Instead of a lifted curtain, the rattan shades were up. The window glass was the only barrier between the silent observers and the McRaes.

Nick appeared thin and defeated despite his expensive-looking clothes—a cashmere sweater the color of molten gold and faultlessly tailored tan wool slacks. There was no trace of his usual supercilious demeanor. Instead of dismissive arrogance, he exuded pain. He was a man stripped of every defense, his gaze naked with accusation and entreaty, despair and anguish.

Millicent's elegant sky blue sweater, so perfect for a January day, was in pathetic contrast to her haggard face. Her outstretched hands trembled. Her mouth was wide, an evident plea.

Annie reached out, gripped Max's wrist.

"Yeah." The single word contained pity and his understanding of Annie's reluctance to see an encounter that should be privy only to Millicent and Nick. "Come on, Britt. Let's—" He broke off as Nick turned away, strode to the front door, banged it open and thudded down the steps.

Millicent ran out onto the porch. "Nick, come back. Nick, he's lying. I swear he's lying. . . ."

Head down, Nick walked fast, taking the front path into the woods.

Millicent pressed her hands against her cheeks. There was the sound of her quick breaths, broken by sobs, and the diminishing crackle of underfoot twigs as Nick stormed away.

Annie wished she believed Millicent. Annie didn't claim to be a Lie-O-Meter, but in her heart she knew Millicent was lying. And so, she feared, did Nick.

Millicent took a step forward as if she would follow her husband, then, sobbing, shoulders shaking, she swung around and stepped into the cabin. The door closed.

"Let's go." Max was brusque.

The cart hummed to motion. Without a word, Britt steered behind the cabin, out of sight of the front windows. The cart reached the entrance to the outer ring path and they plunged back into the woods. A few yards deeper into the gloom, Britt looked at Annie and Max. "What was that all about?"

"That's Everett's dirty work." Annie's voice was laden with disgust.

Max and Britt looked at her blankly.

Annie realized abruptly that Britt hadn't heard the innuendos by Everett at breakfast and neither Max nor Britt was aware of the paper she'd filched from Everett's cabin the night before. Quickly, she described the situation at breakfast and relayed the contents of the paper she'd taken from the cabin, excepting, of course, his revelations about Britt's gambling debts.

Max looked amazed. And amused. "This morning

I swore up and down and sideways I hadn't taken the paper. And all the while you had scarpered with the goods."

Annie noted Max's use of the verb indigenous to long-ago British mysteries. At any other moment, she would have smiled. But she was too near the dreadful scene with the McRaes. "If only there were some way to shut Everett up. I feel sorry for Millicent." Unlikable, arrogant, stricken, sad Millicent.

"And Nick." Max's tone was sober. "If he's on his way to have it out with Everett, we'd better get there as soon as we can."

Annie was reaching for her map when Britt stopped the cart. "Everett's in the next cabin. We'll be there in just a minute. But first . . . I gather Everett rounded up something slimy about all of us."

Annie nodded. "Everett specializes in innuendo and scandal."

Britt's gaze was steely. "What did he say about me?"

Annie's mouth opened, closed.

Britt was determined. "Come on, Annie. Open up. I want to hear it."

Annie was uncomfortable. "All of the reports were accusatory and negative. He said that Cissy helped pay off some debts for you and that Jeremiah ordered her to stop."

Britt's burst of laughter was genuine. "You're the soul of tact, aren't you? Did he say they were gambling debts?"

Annie nodded, her cheeks pink.

"He got it right. I like to gamble. So"—and the

sparkle left her face—"I suppose if he got it right about me, he was right about Millicent McRae. But I don't understand"—her face squeezed in thought—"what precipitated that encounter at the cabin between Millicent and Nick. There wasn't anything direct said at breakfast, was there?"

Annie shook her head. "Not exactly. Everett smirked and dropped Bobby's name. Millicent was terrified Everett was going to say more. I tried to distract everybody."

"Something more must have happened." Britt tugged at a dark curl, looked thoughtful. "Breakfast was a long time ago. Why were Millicent and Nick fighting now? I wonder if Nick talked to Everett. What if Everett gave him all the facts, who the guy is and what happened and when?" She answered herself. "That's what must have happened." Abruptly she started the cart and it jolted forward. "Everett's caused enough trouble. Damn Harry for taking the boat. If *The Yellow Kid* were here, I guarantee you Everett Crenshaw would be off the island pronto. At the very least, I intend to give him a piece of—"

A sharp crack sounded.

"Get down," Max yelled. He crouched, blocking Annie and Britt from view.

"That was a gun." Britt's voice wavered. "Oh God, what now?"

Annie's throat felt tight. She bent forward to stare past Max. The forest was thick with undergrowth. No branches snapped underfoot. There was no sound of movement. If anyone wished to shoot at them, they were vulnerable. The live oaks rustled in the gentle breeze. The only sound was the whistle of their breaths and the ripple of leaves and the mournful coo of a dove.

"We're almost at Everett's cabin." Britt's voice was still shaky. "The clearing is just around that palmetto."

Max swung off the cart. "Stay here. I'll see." He was already moving up the trail, fast. He disappeared around the curve.

Annie jumped from the cart, hurried after him. The shot must have been very near, because woods have a muffling effect. She caught up with him, snagged a hand in the waistband of his trousers, held firm.

Max jerked to a stop, looked back at her. "Annie, dammit, that was a gun." He was impatient. "Stay with Britt. Let me look around."

"You," she hissed, "are not bulletproof. Anyway, I don't think anybody was trying to shoot us or we'd be shot. Why are we sneaking around? Let's make it clear we're coming. If somebody's taking target practice, they'll stop."

The cart trundled up behind them. "Have you found anyone?" Britt leaned to one side to look past them. "I don't understand this. There shouldn't be any guns on the island. You said Harry took his rifles. There was an automatic on the bridge of *The Yellow Kid,* but the boat's gone. Jeremiah's gun in the library was taken." Her face sharpened. "We thought Harry got it. What if we're wrong? What if someone else stole it?" She drew in a deep breath, looked up the path. "Why one shot? To scare us?"

Max nodded. "Maybe. But Annie's right. There's no reason for us to be quiet. If anybody wanted to shoot us, they've had every opportunity. Hello!" Max gave a stentorian bellow.

They waited, the three of them bent forward listening. The pine trees soughed. A crow cawed. A squirrel chut-chutted. No voice called out in response.

"Everett's cabin is just around the curve. If this is his idea of a joke"—Britt was grim—"he's going to regret ever having come to Golden Silk. Come on, let's see what he has to say." Annie took her seat. Max hung on to the side.

When the cart bounced into the clearing, Annie glanced swiftly around. It looked as it had yesterday, the looming pines choked with undergrowth, including lacy ferns and spiky saw palmettos, the live oaks graced with filigrees of Spanish moss, lovely and effervescent as a happy memory. Sunlight dappled the cabin this morning. The bamboo shades were down, blocking any view of the interior. The front door was ajar.

Britt parked the cart at the foot of the stairs. "Everett?" Her shout was brusque and her tone clear warning there was stormy weather ahead for Everett.

Max swung off the cart, started up the steps, his footsteps loud in the quiet. "Hey, Everett?"

Annie hurriedly slid out and followed Max. Britt was right behind her, muttering, "He's through treating people like dirt while he's on Golden Silk. . . ."

At the open door, Max lifted a fist to knock on the frame. He froze and stared into the living room. After an instant, he moved forward, swinging his hand behind him, once again signaling Annie to stop, but she was already in the doorway.

Everett lay on his back, arms outflung. Blood had welled from his chest, seeped onto the coconut matting. His face was slack and grayish, the famous pompadour incongruently sleek and arched, unblemished by death.

"Oh God." Britt's moan wavered in the stillness. "That's what we heard. Oh my God, Everett's hurt. We've got to help him." She tried to push past Max.

He grabbed her arm. "Steady. We can't touch anything."

Britt tried to pull away. "Maybe we can stop the bleeding."

"He's dead, Britt." Max's voice was harsh. "The damn fool."

Annie knew Max's anger was directed at himself as well as at Everett. He had opposed Britt's initial plan. He'd feared what might happen if a murderer was provoked. Everett's body was proof that Max was right. Proof, too, that Harry Lyle might be guilty of all manner of crimes, including theft and smuggling, but he was not guilty of Jeremiah's murder or Everett's. Harry had fled because he couldn't afford to be part of a police investigation. Max was probably right in figuring that Harry was a drug runner. It was likely there had been a shipment in that trunk.

Max was stricken. "I should have stuck to Everett like a burr. But he convinced me he was just fooling this morning. I should have known Everett was playing his own game. After Craig told everyone to write a report, Everett taunted the murderer. Everett's report—" Max broke off, walked across the room, skirting Everett's body.

Max stopped beside the coffee table. He bent down though he made no effort to touch the legal pad lying askew on the blue ceramic tile. "Britt, were the legal pads new, never used before?"

"Yes. For God's sake, what difference does that make?" She was trembling.

"Some pages are gone. Torn out." Max straightened, turned. His gaze moved from the sofa to Everett's body. "It looks like Everett was sitting here writing and someone arrived. When Everett got up and walked toward the door, he was shot. After he fell, the murderer ran over here and ripped off the sheets."

Annie looked out into the clearing. "We must have just missed seeing the murderer." They had been so near when the gun was fired.

Max jammed his hands in his pockets. "We should have known there was danger when that gun was stolen. Dammit, I should have known."

Britt tugged at the collar of her turtleneck. "I never thought Harry took Jeremiah's gun. He wouldn't make that kind of mess breaking into the desk. But no one knew the gun was there except for me and Annie."

Annie remembered watching Britt place the gun in the drawer last night and lock the drawer. She spoke quickly, urgently. "Someone saw you put the gun away."

Britt looked at her strangely. "You were the only person there."

"Through the windows." Annie remembered clearly. "Last night you saw a light in the garden and went out to see. When you came back, we walked into the library. The blinds weren't shut. Somebody followed you up to the house and looked inside and saw us. And the gun." Annie shivered, imagining a watchful figure observing their every move.

"I was so careful." Britt's tone was brittle. "I locked the damn thing up but if I hadn't taken it out with me, he"—she jerked her head toward the body—"might still be alive."

Max was quick to offer solace. "Don't beat yourself up, Britt. Sure, the murderer saw the gun, decided to get it. But there are knives and rocks and ropes. Once the murderer decided Everett was a threat, his death was inevitable. One way or another."

"I guess so." Britt shuddered. "This is all my fault. You warned me when I came to see you. You told me it was dangerous to confront a killer. All I thought about was saving myself. That's dreadful, isn't it? Me. The great me. That's all I thought about . . ." She buried her face in her hands. Her shoulders shook.

Annie moved close, slipped her arm around those quivering shoulders. "You had nothing to do with Everett's decision to bait the murderer. Maybe he was after money. Maybe"—she tried to be charitable—"he thought he could flush out the killer, break a big story. None of that is your fault."

Britt's hands fell away from her tear-streaked face. She made no answer, shook her head.

Annie knew Britt was grappling with horrendous guilt, refusing to shift any blame to Everett.

"Come on, Britt." Max's tone was peremptory. "There will be time enough to second-guess everything we've done. And," he said wearily, "there's plenty of blame to go around. But now we have to deal with what's happened. Our first job is to secure the crime scene." Max's face creased in thought. "When did we hear that shot?"

"Five minutes ago? Ten?" Annie was uncertain. It seemed a long time ago that they'd heard that chilling crack.

"Almost ten, I'd say. That puts Everett's death at"—he glanced at his watch—"about ten-thirty. All right, let's get started. We have to make a record for the police."

Britt spoke jerkily. "Make a record . . . How can you talk like that? He's lying there in his blood." She clasped shaking hands together, held them tightly but could not stop the trembling. "Do you realize there's no way we can call anybody, get help? We're stuck on this island until the charters show up at five tomorrow."

"I know." Max was calm. "It's up to us to handle everything." He stepped in front of her, blocking her view of the dead man. "Do you have a camera?"

"A camera?" Her voice rose. "What good is that?"

"I'll take a series of pictures of the crime scene." He was brisk. "Since the police can't get here until late tomorrow, that will ensure they know precisely how everything appeared today."

Annie nodded approval at Max. He was trying to divert Britt from her distress and doing a good job of it. He was absolutely right about the importance of making a record. Photos and sketches and diagrams were the only means of assuring an accurate representation of the cabin at this moment.

"This is important, Britt." He gestured toward the door. "If you'll get a camera and bring down another tablet and a tape measure and some gallon-size plastic bags, Annie and I will get started."

Britt's rapid breathing slowed. She still looked upset, but she was trying to be calm. "All right. If you think that's what we should do, I'll get what you need." She turned toward the door, moving fast, clearly eager to leave behind the cabin and its lifeless occupant.

Max called out, "Don't tell anyone what's happened. Let's keep this to ourselves until we finish here."

Britt looked back, her face creasing in a troubled frown. "Shouldn't everyone know so they can be on guard?"

Annie was puzzled. "Why would anyone else be in danger?"

Britt jammed fingers through tangled black curls. "I don't know. I never thought Everett was in danger. It seems to me as long as a murderer is roaming around with a gun, we should warn everyone."

Max looked swiftly around the room.

Annie looked, too. Britt had been more observant than they despite her distress. There was no trace of a weapon in the living room. It seemed unlikely the murderer would have left the weapon in either the kitchen or bedroom, though they would check. Possibly the murderer had dropped the gun outside, perhaps flung it deep into the woods. They would search. If not . . .

Max moved close to the body. He knelt, looked beneath a nearby chair. When he got up, he looked worried. "You're right, the gun isn't here." He massaged one cheek. "If the murderer still has the gun and intends to use it, we can't round up everyone in time to prevent another shooting."

Britt looked stricken. "That's horrible."

"But true." Max was grim. "The best thing we can do is get a good record ready for the sheriff. That won't take long. By then everyone will have had time to finish their reports. I'd like to get those before anyone knows about Everett. Let's keep his murder quiet until then."

"All right." She was clearly reluctant. "I guess that's the right thing to do. I won't say a word to anyone. I'll get the things and be back as quickly as I can." She turned and hurried down the stairs. The cart rumbled into motion, headed into the forest.

Max paced slowly around the perimeter of the room, scanning the floor.

Annie understood his need to get started. The sooner they finished their investigation, the sooner everyone could be called together, informed about Everett and alerted to the possibility of danger. But they were losing any opportunity to observe the suspects before they were informed about this new crime. What was everyone doing now? In her heart, Annie believed a murderer alone surely must show in face or actions some trace of the violent deed. If someone could slip unobserved close to each cabin, look for signs of stress. Or triumph. Or cruelty. If someone . . .

Britt was on her way to get materials from the house. Max was gathering information. She took a step toward him. "You don't need me here. I'll make a circuit of the cabins, see what everyone's doing." She glanced at her watch. It was a quarter to eleven. If she hurried, she'd catch everyone before they started up to the house for lunch.

She was turning toward the door when he strode across the room, caught her hand. "No." He held her hand in a tight, warm, determined grasp.

She looked into blue eyes dark with fear. For her.

"Hey, I'll be okay." She felt cold inside, but she didn't want him to know. None of them were safe until the murderer was caught. "I don't threaten anyone."

"I suppose that's true." His tone was grudging. "But you're so damn transparent. Right this minute, you look like the ship's going down and you don't have a life preserver. Anybody can look at you and figure out something's up."

Annie gave his hand a squeeze, pulled free. She lifted her hands to her face, closed her eyes, concentrated. When her hands dropped, she was on stage. She gave him a saucy look. "Excuse me. Who was an off-Broadway actress?" It was a relief to remember happy days when her only concern had been whether that handsome blond guy named Max would call her for a date.

He didn't answer. There was the shadow of a smile in his eyes, but his face was still worried.

She qualified her claim. "Okay, off-off-Broadway. If anyone sees me, I'll have on a happy face. I'll be a cheerful bird on the wing, hunting for Britt. Nobody will have any idea of"—she spread her hands—"this."

Finally, slowly, he nodded. "Okay. But first, go up to the house. Get my gun out of the gym bag. Somebody's killed twice. Be damn sure you look cheerful.

Whatever you do, don't take any chances. Come back here as soon as you finish."

The house had the feel of emptiness. Annie closed the front door behind her, listened for a moment. She almost called out for Britt in case she was still here, then quickly clamped her lips shut. She had a distinct feeling she'd better not tell Britt she was getting Max's gun. Annie thought it quite likely she'd try to commandeer the gun. Britt liked to be in charge. And Britt should be safe enough. She was likely on her way back to the cabin now with the camera. Then she'd be with Max.

As Annie crossed the central hallway, the clock chimed the hour. Annie was suddenly sure she was alone in the house. She started up the stairs, paused midway. The thought of night on the island, marooned with an armed murderer, made her stomach lurch. At least they'd be armed, too. Maybe they'd find out enough today—somehow, someway—to trap the murderer.

She made no effort to be quiet, hurrying down the hallway to their room. The door was open. She frowned. She'd certainly shut it behind her when she'd raced up to grab her windbreaker before setting out on her cleaning mission. She stopped in the doorway, stared.

Their suitcases were upended, clothes flung every which way. The sheets had been pulled from the bed, dumped into a heap.

Annie ran across the room, seeking their stack of folders and the legal pad upon which she'd made notes,

and the scrap of paper she'd taken from Everett's green
leather folder.

The tabletop was bare.

She whirled, heart pounding. Could Max have rear-
ranged their papers, moved them? It took only a frantic
moment to cross the room, open drawers, lift up the
scattered clothes, stoop to look under the bed. The papers
were gone and with them the information they'd amassed
about Jeremiah and his guests that last weekend. Annie
hesitated, then began to straighten. There was no point
in worrying about fingerprints. This thief certainly
wouldn't have left any identifying mark. She scarcely
noted what she was doing as she picked up their clothes,
returned them to the drawers. Instead, she felt a flicker
of satisfaction. The ransacker, unwittingly, had left the
most important marker possible. The theft was proof,
if any had been needed, that Everett had died because
he possessed some special knowledge about Jeremiah's
murder. Everett's report of the weekend had been taken
from his cabin. The linkage was clear.

She restored the linens to the bed. As she turned, she
noted Max's gym bag upside down in a corner near the
fireplace. She frowned, hurried to it. Max wanted her
to carry the gun when she went to the cabins. She'd
left her windbreaker in the cleaning cart so there was
no place to tuck a gun, hide it from view. She'd have
to figure out a way to carry the gun. Maybe she'd take
the gym bag with her. She didn't like guns. She didn't
like the greasy feel of their metal or their rock-heavy
weight. Most of all, she didn't like the knowledge that
she had the means to kill. To hold a gun steady, aim it
at a living creature, press the trigger—

She reached for the bag. The moment she lifted it, she knew. The bag was much too light. She turned it over. It was unzipped. She plunged a hand inside, felt clothes, but no metal. She pulled out Max's clothes and his shaving kit.

Max's gun was gone.

Max frowned at the legal pad that lay askew on the coffee table. Would it be better to leave it lying there until the sheriff's men arrived? Maybe not. In fact, he couldn't trust anyone except Annie and Britt. Everyone else had to be suspect until and unless one of them could prove an alibi for the moment the shot sounded. The only way to secure this cabin would be to set himself or Annie or Britt as a sentinel. Sure, they could trade off guard times, but he had no intention of leaving any one of them at risk alone here. If he tried to protect the crime scene by himself, exhaustion inevitably would suck him down into drowsiness. That would leave Annie to fend for herself.

His mouth quirked. Annie, of course, would not see that as a problem. Her capability was exceeded only by her confidence. The smile slipped away. Yes, she was capable and confident and brave and he'd be damned if he'd risk her safety.

His original impulse was right. He'd capture all the elements of the crime scene, sketch them, photograph them, describe them in infinite detail. Moreover, he would take custody of any evidence that could be filched. He'd need a plastic bag for the legal pad—

"Put your hands up." The voice from the doorway

behind him was deep, harsh, and strained. "I've got you covered."

Max felt as though his back was a bull's-eye, concentric red and blue circles with a white spot at the center. Slowly, stiffly, he raised his arms. The only sound from the open doorway was the scrape of a shoe.

Max started to turn. He wanted to see his captor.

"Don't move." The words grated like steel pulled on concrete.

Max stopped. His shoulders ached. He tried to relax his muscles but his body had tightened against the possibility of a gunshot.

Shoes thudded against the matting. A hand roughly knocked against Max's sides and back, then the steps receded. "Where's the gun? What did you do with it?"

"What gun?" Max felt a flicker of hope as the words danced in his mind.

"Don't take me for a damn fool." The voice rose in anger. "You shot Everett. If you'd stabbed him, you'd have blood all over you. So come on, where's the gun?"

Max's shoulders stopped aching. He took a deep breath. "Let's start over. I didn't shoot Everett and I can prove it. The gun was gone when we got here. Now I'm going to turn around and we'll straighten this out." Max eased around slowly, still feeling that his vulnerable back was a target the size of a billboard.

Gerald Gamble was backing away, his angular face pasty, sweat beading his upper lip despite the cool day. One hand was shoved deep into the pocket of his jacket, a bulge protruding toward Max. "How do I know you didn't kill him? I don't know a damn thing about you. You claim to be a private detective—"

Max almost interrupted but it wasn't a moment to explain the fine points of Confidential Commissions. And the more Gerald talked, the less frightened he would be.

"—but you could be anybody. Here you are, and there's Everett"—Gerald jerked his head toward the still form—"dead as hell."

Max stood at ease, hands loose. He kept his voice pleasant, reassuring. "In a few minutes Britt will be back with a camera so I can take photographs for the sheriff. Then I'm going to sketch the crime scene. Someone shot Everett around ten-thirty. I was with my wife and Britt when we heard the shot. By the time we got to the cabin, no one was here. And, as you see"— Max waved his hand—"there's no gun visible."

Gerald took a deep breath. He pulled his hand out of the jacket pocket. It was empty.

Max watched him with narrowed eyes. Gerald had been bluffing. But was the gun the only bluff? If he was Everett's murderer, returning to search the cabin, what better way to profess innocence than to accuse Max of the crime?

Max took a step toward him. "What did you want from Everett?"

Annie paused at the head of the stairs. The house lay still and empty below her, quiet as a graveyard. Annie wished Britt were there. Obviously she'd already retrieved the camera and a fresh legal pad and was on her way back to the cabin. There were so many paths, they easily could have missed each other. Annie felt a hunger for human companionship. She didn't like the stillness of this house or its dark, brooding quality. Her eyes slid sideways, sought the wall, and the telltale prick that spoke of murder. She took a breath and plunged down the hard steps.

A door banged.

Annie jolted to a stop, peered down into the gloom. She almost called out for Britt. The impulse withered in the chilly quiet. She eased down the steps, every sense alert. Had someone entered the house or left it? The sound had come from the back of the house.

In the central hallway she hesitated, then moved toward the door to the kitchen. Slowly she opened it. The light was off. There was a smell of baking. Lucinda must have put something—a cake?—into the oven before she left to clean the cabins. Annie crossed the tiled floor, grateful she wore sneakers that made no sound. Even so, the calico cat on the windowsill turned her head to watch Annie with wary amber eyes.

Annie reached the back door. She opened it and saw Kim Kennedy striding into the garden, disappearing behind a bank of azaleas. A leather shoulder bag slapped against her side.

Annie started down the steps, stopped, whirled, returned to the kitchen. She pounded across the floor to the counter where a butcher's block held an assortment of knives. Annie chose a knife with a seven-inch blade. She held it uncertainly, her eyes scanning the room. Ah. She darted to the stove, picked up a pink pot holder. She wrapped it around the blade. She thought for a moment, then slid the knife into a baggy side pocket of her sweater. Part of the pot holder protruded but she wasn't worried about fashion at this moment. Once outside, she walked purposefully but cautiously toward the garden.

Gerald didn't respond to Max's question. He hunched his shoulders and stared at the floor, his vulture-sharp face bloodless and grim. "You said he was shot around ten-thirty?"

"That's right. Where were you?" Max had the sense that Gerald was scrambling to think, trying to make a decision.

Gerald's tone was vague. "I don't know. I'd gone for a walk." His hooded eyes avoided Max's gaze.

Max walked toward him. "Where?"

Gerald frowned. "This is a goddam mess, isn't it?"

Max's tone was wry. "I guess you could call murder a mess. That puts it as well as anything."

Gerald dropped his hand, flexed his fingers. "I thought the whole thing about Jeremiah being murdered was a hoax. I didn't believe a word Britt said. Or Everett." His glance at the corpse was dismissive. "The man was a snake. Unscrupulous. Untrustworthy. I thought he and Britt had planned the whole weekend, maybe as a way to scam money out of the family. I wouldn't put any scheme past either of them. But now he's dead. That has to mean Jeremiah was murdered and Everett knew something that led to the killer. The damn fool must have tried blackmail. So it's dangerous to keep quiet, isn't it?"

"Deadly dangerous." Max looked at him curiously.

A tic jerked at Gerald's thin mouth. His eyes were

wide and staring. Abruptly, he looked over his shoulder. Turning, he took two strides, closed the front door, and once again faced Max. "That last afternoon, Millicent threatened Jeremiah. I heard her. She said, 'I'll see you dead first.' Jeremiah laughed. He was ruthless, you know. And he hated women who cheated on their husbands. He told her he was going to run a full-page editorial the week before the election, tell the world about her young lover, then quote her pious blathers about home and family. She tried to bluster, told him he was wrong, that the story wasn't true. He cited dates and hotel room numbers. He pulled out a folder and said he had pictures of her with her lover. I was in the hallway by the library. I heard every word. I saw her face when she came out. If she'd had a gun with her, Jeremiah would have died then. He died the next morning. She set the trap. She killed him."

Annie paused at the fountain, puzzled. If Kim were en route to her cabin, she should have curved around the fountain and taken the path into the forest. Instead, there were ferns quivering only a few feet away, ferns that lapped over a path that led—if Annie remembered correctly—to a lagoon and gazebo. Why would Kim go in that direction? Annie hesitated, unable to decide. Of course, she'd taken a moment in the kitchen to find a knife and her progress through the garden had been slow and cautious. Finally, with a shrug, she took the main path into the woods and headed for Kim's cabin.

Annie wished she had the skill of James Fenimore Cooper's forest-savvy Hawkeye. Instead of moving with grace and stealth, her every step snapped another twig. She reached the edge of the clearing around Kim's cabin, heart beating, alert for any signs of ambush. If Kim had stolen the gun from Max's bag, pursuit might be foolish. Or fatal.

Annie took a deep breath, crossed the clearing. She climbed the steps, knocked on the door. "Kim?"

There was no answer and no movement inside.

Annie hesitated, then opened the door, poked her head inside. The cabin was clearly empty. So much for following Kim and finding out what she'd been doing in the house.

Annie closed the door, hurried down the steps. She was ready to take the outer path, her goal Everett's cabin, when she heard the crackling sound of someone approaching. Annie stepped behind a pine and waited.

Kim strode into the clearing from the diagonal path. She looked pleased with herself, a slight smile touching her round face. She didn't look right or left, marching straight to the steps, one hand clamped on the strap to her shoulder bag.

Annie stared at the bag, intent as a cormorant spotting menhaden. If Kim was the thief, the gun was in her purse. There was no bulge in her black zippered sweater, and her black slacks fit sleekly. Her steps rattled on the stairs.

Annie knew this was the moment to catch Kim. She would have no opportunity to hide the gun. Annie frowned. Kim might possibly have hidden the gun in the forest or near the lagoon.

Kim was at the door, reaching out to turn the knob.

Annie took a deep breath. So her roles had been

off-Broadway. She'd been good. Not good enough to pursue an acting career, but good. She plunged into the clearing. "Kim—hey, Kim!" Voice bright. Big smile.

"Maybe." Max looked thoughtfully at the longtime Addison Media employee. His accusation could be true. Millicent McRae's anguish at her husband's knowledge of her unfaithfulness was a memory Max would be long in forgetting. This morning he and Annie and Britt had seen more of Millicent's heart and soul than strangers should. For now, he had to remember that searing moment. Of them all, Millicent might have the most compelling motive. Max didn't doubt she would do anything to protect her marriage. She had committed adultery. Whatever her motive, lust or loneliness or infatuation, clearly she loved Nick. But Millicent surely had not been the only person overwrought by Jeremiah's threats. Max recalled Everett's totting up of motives on the sheet of paper Annie took from the cabin.

"You overheard Millicent and Jeremiah." Max's tone was pleasant. "Then you went in to see him. Right? He was pretty nasty about you and Craig." It wasn't a question.

Angry splotches flared in Gerald's cheeks. He doubled his fists, took a step forward.

Max waited, his own hands curling tight. He was twenty pounds heavier, twenty-five years younger. But if Gamble wanted a fight, he could have one.

Gerald whirled, stalked to the door, his steps pounding.

Max hurried after him. "Hold up, man. Keep quiet about Everett. Don't tell anyone . . ."

Gerald was halfway across the clearing. He didn't look back.

"Damn." Max jammed his fingers in his hair. He'd lost control of the encounter, though obviously there was no way he could have made Gerald remain at the cabin. The likelihood was good that he was on his way to find Craig. As Gerald strode into the forest, he heard Britt call out, "Gerald. Where are you doing here?" She sounded surprised. And wary.

Max thudded down the stairs, ran to the path. Gerald was facing the golf cart.

Britt saw Max. The relief on her face indicated the depth of her uneasiness in unexpectedly confronting Gerald. Max approved of her caution. None of them could afford to forget that one familiar face masked a clever and ruthless killer.

"Gerald." Max was conciliatory. "I'd appreciate some help at the cabin. I sent Britt to find a camera. It's important we put together a record so the sheriff will know there's been no tampering with the crime scene. Will you take the pictures for me? That will free Britt to make the circuit of the cabins and pick up the statements for Craig."

Clearly Gerald wanted to leave. But he was a responsible man and he had worked for Jeremiah Addison for many years. "All right." His tone was grudging. "I can do that."

Britt looked relieved. Max knew she wouldn't have complained but obviously she preferred not to be in the cabin with Everett's body. She gave Gerald a grateful look. "Thank you."

"And, Gerald, if you have your report handy, Britt can take it."

Gerald gave a bark of laughter. "You want those statements in hand before anyone knows about Everett. No creative touching up, right?" He answered himself. "That's fair enough. God knows this has to be dealt with. Someone"—his eyes looked haunted—"is dangerous as hell." He reached into an inner pocket, pulled out several folded sheets, handed them to Britt.

Britt took the sheets. "I'll take good care of them. I won't let any of the reports out of my sight."

Max checked his watch. Eleven-twenty. "Ask everyone to meet at the house at noon. Tell them I have some information for them." He bent to retrieve the legal pad, measuring tape, and plastic bags from the passenger seat of the cart. He handed the camera to Gerald.

Britt nodded. "I'll hurry. That will give me time to get back to the house and write up my report."

As the cart chugged away, Max called out. "Britt, keep an eye out for Annie." He was deliberately vague. "She was going to take a look around the cabins. I thought she'd be back by now."

He'd not liked the idea of Annie making the circuit of the cabins even though she might learn something of value. As he followed Gerald up the stairs into Everett's cabin, Max reassured himself. Annie was safe enough. After all, she had the gun.

∿ Nine ∿

"I was hoping I'd catch you." Annie was as cheery as a real estate agent pushing a million-dollar house. She darted across the clearing and up the stairs before Kim could open the door.

Kim half turned toward Annie, her expression startled. There was no trace of concern. "Catch me?"

Annie contrived to trip on the top step, propel herself forward, arms windmilling. As she collided with Kim, Annie reached out, apparently grabbing for support. Her hand clutched the strap of the purse, pulling it loose. Annie tumbled to one side and the purse was dumped upside down, its contents bouncing onto the porch. "Oh golly, I'm sorry. The porch is slick. Ouch, I banged my knee." Annie sat awkwardly, massaging her left knee. Her right hand was within inches of the knife in her sweater pocket.

"My camera," Kim wailed, and she was on her hands and knees reaching for a sleek silver digital camera. She grabbed it, checked for damage.

"I'm so sorry. I hope it's okay. Here, I'll help pick everything up." Annie scrambled closer, grabbed the purse. The minute she lifted the black Coach bag, her thudding heart slowed. The leather purse was heavy but not heavy enough to hold a gun. With an apologetic smile, Annie opened it wide and started retrieving the spilled contents. She dropped in a change purse, billfold, compact, address book, three pens. Kim absently picked up some items, but she was still inspecting her camera.

It only took a moment, then Kim, fluid and graceful, came to her feet. She reached down, helped Annie up. Kim slipped the purse strap over one shoulder. Her attention was still focused on the camera. She turned toward Annie, lifted it, pushed the button. There was a bright flash. "It's okay. Come on in."

Annie, still apologizing, followed her into the cabin. ". . . these shoes skid on wet wood. I'm awfully sorry . . ." As she chattered, she wondered where Kim had been. And why. Annie settled on the sofa and looked at the coffee table. For an instant, there was a chilling memory of Everett's identical coffee table and the legal pad with missing sheets. Kim's legal pad, obviously new and untouched, was pristine. Nothing had been written on it and no sheets torn away.

Kim saw her gaze. "Oh, yeah. I've got to get that done." She dropped her purse casually on the floor, but she still held the camera. She lifted it, aimed with the ease of long practice, swiftly took three more pictures of Annie. "How long have you been working for Britt?"

Annie was startled.

Kim leaned forward. "Are you and your husband partners or do you handle secretarial stuff?"

Annie realized with a flash of surprise that she was

being interviewed. "Partners." Her response was automatic and true though perhaps not in the sense meant by Kim.

Kim's smile was admiring. "Running a detective agency must be fascinating. I doubt too many clients walk through the door and ask you to find a murderer. Tell me how you felt when Britt hired you."

Annie was intrigued. Kim's smile invited confidences. Her gaze was warm. She was laying on the charm, hoping for an exclusive about the gathering on Golden Silk. "That's a good angle for a story," Annie replied. She could play the admiration game, too. "Is that what you've been working on this morning instead of your report?"

Kim's smile fled. Obviously, she preferred to ask questions rather than answer them. "What do you mean?"

"I saw you near the house a little while ago." Annie's hand hovered near the concealed knife. "I wondered what you were doing there." Stealing Max's gun? Grabbing our papers?

Kim looked satisfied. "Nothing that would interest you. I'm looking for a ticket back to the big time. I'm going to scoop the hell out of Everett."

Annie challenged her. "If you've found out anything to help solve Jeremiah's murder, Craig Addison will insist you reveal it." Not to mention the police.

Kim shook her head. "I don't have anything new. If I did, I'd take it right to Craig. That would get me hired." She gave a little shrug. "Unless he's the one that pushed dear old Dad down the stairs."

She claimed to be working on a story. . . . Annie

glanced at the silver camera Kim had placed on the coffee table. "Were you taking pictures?"

Now Kim didn't look quite so pleasant, her eyes cold and determined. "What I do is none of your business. And damn sure none of Everett's business."

Annie stared into glittering blue eyes. Kim was either innocent of Everett's murder or an arrogant killer spreading a smokescreen. "I won't be telling Everett anything. You can count on it. Anyway you're obviously leagues ahead of him." Being alive was a definite advantage.

Kim gloried in Annie's admiring tone. "You bet I am. He's not a real reporter. While he's lying around this morning—"

Annie recalled that still form and grayish face and perfect pompadour and blood.

"—I was working. The world will know all about it when I sell the story."

"Look," Annie said, "if you'll tell me what you were doing"—Kim was out of her cabin during the critical moment when Everett was shot. If she was innocent of Everett's murder, where had she been? Had she seen anyone?—"I'll give you an exclusive on being hired by Britt. I won't breathe a word to Everett about what you've discovered."

Kim brushed back a golden curl, her face thoughtful. Slowly she nodded. "All right." Her gaze was avid. "You first."

Annie wished for the inventiveness of Agatha Christie's Tuppence Beresford in *N or M*. Tuppence was never at a loss for easy prattle. Further, Annie had to come up with something interesting enough for Kim to consider a trade of information worth her while. Annie scooted to the edge of the chair, opened her eyes wide. "When Britt explained the situation, I had the most extraordinary feeling. I wouldn't claim to be psychic—"

There was a flicker of disdain in Kim's eyes, but her encouraging smile never wavered. She wrote fast as Annie spoke.

"—but I felt distinctly cold. An unearthly coldness. It was as though I'd stepped onto a glacier. I knew then that something dreadful was going to happen if Britt reunited everyone on the island." Annie imagined Kim's breathy tones in a voice-over: Private Investigator Annie Darling shared her innermost foreboding and her conviction that the deadly specter of Death awaited all who traveled to Golden Silk. "Max insisted she contact the sheriff instead. She refused. In fact, she was on her way out of the office when he stopped her. When he realized she was determined to proceed, he agreed for us to come. He was afraid the murderer might attack her. Britt insisted on going forward even though she understood the danger. My own feeling at the time"—Annie lifted a hand to her throat, an artistic gesture—"was one of deep foreboding." Annie dropped her voice. "I felt even worse the next morning when we were on our way to Golden Silk." There was sincerity in her tone. "I sensed impending doom. I was touched by emanations of evil. I truly believe Golden Silk harbors death." Annie doubted even Tuppence could have topped this performance.

Kim finished her notes with a flourish. "Okay. That's

good." Another sharp look. "You won't give this to Everett?"

Annie's pleasure in playacting seeped away. "No. I won't tell Everett. Where did you go this morning?"

Kim looked as satisfied as a cat in the sun. "I had the run of the island. Everyone was tucked in a cabin, writing about that weekend. I got pix of the boathouse and Harry's cabin and the smashed desk in the library. Everett's not a real reporter." Her disdain was evident. "All he knows are scripts. When we get off this island, I'll have the story and the pix and he can eat his heart out."

Every word could be true. Perhaps Kim had done as she claimed, hoping for an exclusive. If so, she hadn't been near the cabins at the critical time. There might be proof of that. "May I see the pictures?" Some digital cameras record not only the date but the time the picture was taken.

"You'll see them when the story runs." Kim slipped the camera into her pocket. "Now, why did you want to catch me?"

The better to eat you, my dear . . . Annie managed another bright smile. "I think you are the very best person to help us trap Jeremiah's murderer."

This time flattery didn't charm. Kim's cold blue eyes regarded Annie thoughtfully. "Why me?"

"Well," Annie said, settling into the cushions with the air of a woman ready for a just-between-us-girls chat, "as I understand it, wedding bells were going to ring." Annie made no mention of Cissy. What was an invalid wife when discussing the course of true love?

Kim rocked back against the sofa, locking her fingers around one knee. "It was a little early for an announcement." Her voice was bland. "But yes, that was our plan."

"You were almost the only person on the island who wasn't angry with Jeremiah." Annie looked at her eagerly. "You must have been in his confidence. Did he plan something that one of them simply wouldn't tolerate? Or was he afraid of one of them?"

For an instant, Kim looked discomfited, her expression defensive.

Annie was as sure as though Jeremiah stood in the room with them, his face sardonic and a trifle cruel, that Kim had romanticized her relationship with him. She hadn't been in his confidence. She was a pretty girl and he enjoyed pretty girls, and that was the extent of his interest.

Kim's smile was feminine and secretive, but her eyes still looked cold. "We had better things to do than waste our time talking about people he despised. Craig irritated him because he was always trying to take over. Jeremiah said he didn't trust Craig's instincts. Jeremiah was disappointed in Jay. He thought Jay was weak and indecisive. Jeremiah loathed Britt, called her a bloodsucking leech. But he was never afraid of anybody." She loosed her hands, reached for the legal pad. "I'd better get this done."

Annie knew better than to press for more. Kim didn't want to talk further about Jeremiah's last weekend and reveal how much or how little she knew of his plans.

Annie sighed and stood up. "I have to go up to the house. I promised I'd help with lunch. I hate to go by myself. It's spooky there. I keep imagining noises. Once I thought it sounded like someone falling down stairs." She shivered. "I think I'll look around for Britt. Did you see her or anyone while you were out?" Annie hoped Kim would think this an inconsequential question, a nervous woman seeking company.

"Only Dana." Kim's tone was dismissive.

Annie smiled. "Oh, she's nice. Where was she? Maybe I can find her." Dana should have been in her cabin, she and Jay, working on the reports.

Kim gestured vaguely toward the forest. "I doubt she's still there. I was on my way back here and I saw her skulking along the path that goes to the lagoon. She kept looking over her shoulder. She scuttled. Like a crab. I thought that was odd. I followed her."

Annie figured the timing in her mind. This explained Kim's excursion on that path and why she had arrived at the cabin after Annie.

"Just about the time I got to the lagoon, there was a big splash. She was standing on the bank. I almost asked her what she'd thrown away. But there was something about the way she stood there . . ." Kim's voice trailed away. "She had her back to me. She never knew I saw her. I got a couple of pictures just in case. She's such a silly woman. Who knows what she was doing? I doubt it mattered. Probably something to do with her wimp of a husband."

Annie pictured Dana's slender form standing stiffly at the edge of the lagoon. What had she thrown that was large enough, heavy enough to make a splash? Not the packet of letters. They would have slapped into the water, slipped quietly down.

A gun would splash.

Two guns were missing, the one that had killed Everett and the one Max had brought to the island. Was one of them resting on the bottom of the lagoon?

Max used the ice tongs from the kitchen to lift the legal pad from Everett's coffee table, slid it carefully into the gallon-sized plastic bag. He slipped a second bag over the exposed end. Britt's fingerprints, of course, would be on the pad. It was unlikely the murderer was foolish enough to leave any trace, but the pad had to be checked. All that remained was for Britt to provide a secure place to keep the evidence until the sheriff arrived.

Gerald was waiting by the front door. He held up the small camera. "I've got shots from every angle, including close-ups of Everett. I'll do a panorama and we'll be done."

"Right." Max walked out onto the porch. He added a final note to a sheet with detailed descriptions of the approximate time the shot was heard, the arrival of himself and Annie and Britt at the cabin, the contents of the room, the appearance of the victim. This information added to the array of photographs should assure the sheriff on his arrival that the scene was unchanged. Any deviation would be starkly apparent.

Gerald was framed in the doorway. A series of clicks marked his final photographs. He lowered the camera, but he made no move to join Max.

Max had a clear view of his profile.

Face somber, Gerald stared into the living room. "I met Everett's mother once. He was getting an Emmy and she came to the awards. Somehow she and I ended up talking at the cocktail party. She got out of an abusive marriage. Everett was about twelve. They were dirt-poor. On food stamps. She worked three jobs at one point. Sometimes they didn't have enough to eat. She said Everett got a job as soon as he could. She looked kind of wistful. She told me sometimes she worried that he cared so much for things. She said, 'Mr. Gamble, it's not good for him to want to be so rich. I know he hated being poor, it made him feel like he didn't count. He swore I'd never have to go hungry when he could work. But now'—and she'd touched her sleeve, it was a silk dress—'he wants me to be fine. I keep telling him that he doesn't need to buy me fancy clothes. And I worry that he sounds mean on his program. He says he's just being aggressive. But quarrelsome words can come back to haunt you.' "

Gamble turned toward Max and stepped out onto the porch. "Aggressive." His tone was musing. "Everett always thought he could batter anybody down. I guess he met his match."

Max was thoughtful. "Do you believe he tried blackmail?"

"I think it was his specialty." Gerald's voice was bitter.

Max watched him closely. "Do you know of an instance when Everett used knowledge to get money?"

Gerald was derisive. "Figure it out for yourself. That's obviously why he sent the letter to Britt. I expect it surprised the hell out of him when she invited all of us back to the island. He must have gone into high gear, scraping around to find out who was on Jer-

emiah's blacklist. He was good at finding out secrets."
There was grudging respect in his voice. "Who knows
what kind of information he dredged up? My guess is
he tried a ploy—maybe more than one—but he riled
the wrong snake." He glanced down at the camera.
"Now he's a still life for the sheriff." A sour twist of his
mouth was the only indication of his pun. "His mother
was right to worry." Gerald thrust the camera at Max.
"I guess you're in charge."

He guessed he was. He hoped he'd thought of everything. "All right. We're done here." He reached out,
closed the door. He wished he could as easily close
away the indelible memory of the body sprawled on
the floor. "Let's go up to the house." He looked soberly
at Gerald. "You've been a big help. I hope you'll keep
on helping. Don't tell anyone"—he meant Craig and
knew Gerald understood that full well—"what's happened until we've got everyone together."

Gerald's stare was bleak. Abruptly, he shrugged.
"I'll play along. I didn't kill him. Or Jeremiah. I know
Craig's innocent. Handle it however you want to."

Max led the way down the steps. It was time to
share the grim news of murder.

Clouds bunched overhead, blotting out the pale January sun. Annie shivered though it wasn't cold, merely
cool and damp. If she were walking vigorously toward
the beach on Broward's Rock, looking forward to
building a blazing fire from driftwood, picnic hamper
in hand, Max at her side, she wouldn't feel the chill at
all or, if she did, she'd welcome the changing season.
Here on Golden Silk, knowing that the next face she

saw might be that of a murderer, she found the gray
sky and darkening woods and isolation forbidding.

She was, in fact, scared. She hesitated before
leaving the clearing around Kim's cabin, reluctant
to plunge into the forest. She steadied her breaths,
drew air deep into her lungs. As always, her solution to fear or worry or sadness was action. Everything was better when she was busy. Resolutely,
she pulled the crumpled sheet from her pocket. It
seemed a long time ago that a bustling Lucinda drew
this map of the cabins.

This morning her first stop had been Cabin 1, where
she'd found the distraught Isabel. After Max and Britt
joined her, they'd walked to Cabin 2, where they'd
watched the unsettling domestic drama between Millicent and Nick McRae. On their way to Everett's cabin,
number 3, they had heard the shot.

Annie studied Lucinda's map, visualizing the cabins
on a clock face:

Cabin 1—Isabel Addison (ten o'clock)

Cabin 2—Millicent and Nick McRae (eleven o'clock)

Cabin 3—Everett Crenshaw (one o'clock)

Cabin 4—Jay and Dana Addison (two o'clock)

Cabin 5—Kim Kennedy (four o'clock)

Cabin 6—Gerald Gamble (five o'clock)

Cabin 7—Craig Addison (seven o'clock)

Cabin 8—Unoccupied (eight o'clock)

If she stayed on the perimeter path, depending upon
her direction, she would reach either Cabin 4 or Cabin
6. With a quick nod, she headed for Jay and Dana's

cabin. She couldn't find it in her heart to be afraid of Dana. The path curved into the dimness. A tangle of Spanish moss brushed against one cheek, the touch as cool and light on her skin as the skitter of a spider. She forced herself to walk faster. The sooner she got to the cabin, the sooner she would know if Dana had returned from her visit to the lagoon. If she was there . . . Annie doubted there was a tactful way of asking whether Dana had tossed a gun into the water.

A branch snapped behind her. There was a crackle of movement.

Annie froze. She whirled, hand at her pocket, ready to clutch the knife. A knife was no defense against a gun . . . why would anyone shoot her . . . why hadn't she stayed with Kim . . . or gone back to the house . . . maybe if she yelled . . . no one was near . . . she'd never felt so alone and vulnerable . . .

At almost the same instant she recognized the hum of a golf cart. The maneuverable vehicle zoomed around a live oak and quivered to a stop a scant foot away.

"Annie!" Britt's voice lifted in relief.

"Britt. Oh golly, I'm glad to see you." Annie was embarrassed because she was having trouble breathing calmly.

"Me too." Britt's eyes were wide and strained. "I heard someone walking and all of a sudden I had this terrible feeling that I was going to come around the curve and something horrible would be there." Britt too was struggling with her breath. "I'm sorry to be such a fool but I can't find a soul anywhere. Nobody. It's like a magic wand was waved and poof! I can't find anyone. The idea of being on the island all by myself terrified me."

Annie certainly understood.

A gusty breeze rattled palmetto fronds. Britt's eyes darted around as if looking for danger. "Max asked me to pick up the reports. Gerald was with Max so I got Gerald's report, then I went to the McRaes'. Nobody was there. I went on to Isabel's cabin. Empty. It got darker and darker in the woods. . . ." She took a deep breath. "I wanted to go back to the house and go up to my room and stay there until tomorrow. I told myself it wouldn't take long to check the rest of the cabins. Then Craig wasn't in his cabin." Her voice wavered.

Annie imagined the untenanted cabins, silent and sinister in the cloudy gloom, and Britt's growing sense of isolation.

Britt shivered. "The only thing that kept me from running away was Lucinda. She was coming out of Gerald's cabin." Britt gave an unconvincing laugh. "She said I was as white as a mausoleum." With a little of her old verve, Britt said lightly, "I told her it was my Garbo look, the latest fashion among those marooned on an island. I asked Lucinda to go up to the house and start lunch. She can do the rest of the cabins this afternoon." Britt was once again somber and strained. "I watched her cart chug away and it took all my control not to hurry right after her, but I'd promised to get the reports. Not," she said wryly, "that I was having much luck to that point. Kim was in her cabin. I've never liked her, and she must have thought I was a nut I was so excited to see her. She's still working on her report. Anyway"—Britt patted the seat beside her—"jump in.

We'll check on Dana and Jay, then we'd better get up to the house and help Lucinda." Her glance at Annie was uncertain. "That is, if you don't mind pitching in again."

"I'd love to." Annie would have peeled a bucket of onions to gain the cheerful companionship of the kitchen.

No longer alone, Annie found the cart's rustling progress cheerful as it brushed against ferns, crackled over small branches. She was relaxed until they reached the clearing for Cabin 4. The front door was ajar, eerily reminiscent of Everett's cabin. She frowned as the cart stopped at the base of the stairs.

"Oh my God, it doesn't look like anybody's here either. Where is everybody?" Britt's voice was thin. "It's just like Everett. Look!" A wavering finger pointed at the partially open front door. The blinds were closed, blocking any view of the interior. The silence was made even more somber by the occasional *chut-chut* of scampering squirrels, a raucous cry from a blue jay, the imperious caw of two unseen crows.

Britt made no move to get out of the cart.

"I guess . . ." Annie struggled for composure. ". . . we should check inside."

They shared a long look.

"Okay." Britt swung out of the cart.

Annie took a deep breath. She felt better once she had her feet on the ground. She started up the wooden steps, grateful to hear Britt behind her. She stopped on the porch. "Jay? Dana?"

Britt moved past her, poked her head inside. "Anybody home?" She stepped inside. Light flooded out onto the porch. Annie quickly followed. Her eyes darted first to the living room. Two unused legal pads lay on the coffee table. Annie wondered if she would ever again see a legal pad without thinking of Everett.

It took only a moment for them to be sure the cabin was empty, Britt checking the bedroom, Annie hurrying into the small kitchen.

Annie's relief almost made her light-headed. "Maybe Dana's still at the lagoon."

Britt stared at her. "That was right after breakfast. And she didn't stay. She ran after Jay."

"I meant later. About twenty minutes ago." Quickly, Annie explained how Kim had followed Dana. ". . . and Dana threw something into the lagoon. Something heavy. It made a big splash. A gun would make a big splash. There wasn't a gun in Everett's cabin. Do you suppose Dana got the gun and threw it away?" But who had Max's gun?

"Dana?" Disbelief lifted Britt's voice.

Annie understood her reaction. It was hard to imagine mild-mannered, gentle Dana touching a gun, much less firing it. But she was sure Kim had told the truth about what she'd seen and heard. "Kim said Dana threw something heavy enough to cause a splash. She took a picture."

Britt's face furrowed. "Annie, this could be important." She glanced at her watch. "Max should be at the house by now. We need to tell him. Maybe that's where everybody is. Come on. Let's hurry."

Max looked around the drawing room. The guests were getting restive. Despite the gleaming twin chandeliers, the room was cheerless, the crimson drapes a dark reminder of blood, the mantel oddly bare after the removal of the statuesque silver candlesticks by Kim, the cool gray walls an echo of the bleak sky, where thick clouds bunched to hide the sun. His plan had seemed excellent: Preserve the evidence, collect the assorted essays, gather the survivors, announce Everett's murder. He'd taken it for granted that everyone would do as Craig had requested, write about the last weekend with Jeremiah and bring the reports to the house at lunchtime. Instead, he had only three responses. Gerald had turned over his sheets at Everett's cabin. Craig had, after a thoughtful moment, relinquished his legal pad when he arrived at the house. The final offering came from Kim, whose buoyant step and unbridled energy underscored her confidence that the stars were aligned in her favor. No one else had responded. Worse than that, Jay and Dana Addison hadn't shown up. Where were they and what could they be doing? The clock had already chimed the noon hour. Max glanced toward the front Palladian window. Annie stood there, looking outside. She'd taken up her post, saying worriedly, "Surely they'll come soon." But Jay and Dana hadn't arrived. Was one of them—or both—prowling the island with a gun? Annie's discovery that his gun had been taken, combined with the absence of a weapon at Everett's cabin, meant they were marooned with an armed murderer. If Kim's story was true, one gun might be at the bottom of the gazebo lagoon. Or it might not. . . .

Gerald cleared his throat. His hooded eyes swept the room. "Jay and Dana should be here." His dour gaze challenged Max. "Considering what's happened, we'd better find them." One hand picked at the golden tassel on a cushion.

Craig was staring at Gerald, his eyes questioning. He looked like a man sensing imminent danger.

Britt sped an anxious look at Max. Dark smudges beneath her eyes stood out against a waxen pallor. She sat hunched in a corner chair as if surrounded by frightful specters.

Max stood with his face furrowed into a tight frown. Gerald was right. It was time to speak. Past time. Max had no illusion that he was in control of events. Everything at this point seemed to be careening into chaos—Everett dead, Jay and Dana missing, a gun or guns on the loose, nothing to hint at the identity of the murderer. He surveyed the sullen, somber group.

Lucinda Phillips waited in the doorway, restive, clearly impatient to return to her kitchen. Today the kerchief banding her dark hair was bright yellow. Matching buttercups spangled a dainty apron that emphasized her bulk. She frowned, her blue eyes darting from face to face, as if seeking reassurance and finding none.

Millicent was as withdrawn and forlorn as a troubled figure in a Goya painting, the luster of her blond hair and sleek richness of her cashmere sweater a wrenching counterpoint to the dullness of her gaze and the raddled splotchiness of her face.

Nick stood on the opposite side of the room from Millicent. He might have been a thousand miles distant, with his lined face empty, blank eyes staring at the floor. He looked old and shrunken, arrogance shed like a too large coat.

Kim had the air of a cat at a mouse hole—patient, alert, expectant. Hungry.

Isabel watched Craig like a child uncertain of acceptance, hope and fear warring in her lovely face. Yet her entire demeanor was different. There was an easiness in her posture that spoke of a heavy burden lifted.

Max took a step forward. "I had hoped for everyone to be present. But I can't delay any longer. I am sorry to have to tell you that Everett Crenshaw was shot and killed this morning." Max quickly looked at every face in turn, swift as a blackjack dealer gathering cards.

Gerald, too, was scanning the room, seeking, as Max sought, some telltale sign.

Craig's face twisted in a sudden scowl. He looked like a man tabulating figures and the sums didn't add up.

Lucinda's mouth gaped. She pressed her fingers against her round cheeks, breathed harshly.

Millicent gave a shrill cry. She pushed up from her chair, moved unsteadily toward her husband, her hands outstretched.

Nick hesitated, then opened his arms. She huddled against him, her head on his shoulder. He looked down, his expression uncertain, anguish clear in the set of his mouth, the hunch of his shoulders.

After a shocked gasp, Kim pulled a notebook from a pocket, began to write.

Isabel came to her feet. "Someone shot Everett? When?" Her lustrous dark hair framed a face stiff with shock.

"At ten-thirty," Annie answered. "Max and Britt and I were on our way to his cabin. We heard a shot. We ran and"—she managed to keep her voice steady but remembered horror was in her eyes—"found Everett. He was lying on the living room floor of his cabin. He was dead. We didn't find the gun."

"Did you see anyone?" Craig looked at her, then shook his head as if realizing the answer.

"No one." Annie shivered. If they had reached the cabin and seen the murderer . . . How many bullets were in that gun?

Kim pushed up from the small gilt chair. She glared at Annie. "Cat tie your tongue this morning? You didn't bother to mention a little matter of murder when I told you I saw Dana at the lagoon and she'd obviously thrown something heavy into the water." Kim glanced at her shocked audience. "That's right, sweet little Miss Dana, mama of the year." She paused, rummaged in another pocket, lifted out her digital camera. "FYI, I always use the optional setting to display time and date." She pushed a button, watched the liquid crystal display, her face absorbed and intent. "There she is. Eleven-oh-three. Dana at the lagoon. She'd just thrown something into the water that made a big splash. Come on, we've got to see if we can find it."

Craig held up his hand. "If the gun's in the bottom of the lagoon, it can stay there a little longer. We'll hope it's there. It's ugly enough without thinking someone on the island has a gun."

"Someone has a gun. Maybe two guns." Max's tone was grim. "I brought a gun to the island. It was in our room. Somebody stole it this morning. Just as someone stole Jeremiah's gun from the library last night.

More than likely, Jeremiah's gun was used to shoot Everett."

"God, two guns." Gerald folded his lanky arms. "I'd say you messed up big-time, Darling. If you were fool enough to bring a gun to the island, you should have kept it on you."

Annie's eyes flashed. "He brought the gun in case we figured out who killed Jeremiah. There was no way to know Everett was going to be shot this morning."

Millicent twisted to look wildly around the room. Her reflection in the ormolu framed mirror was a flash of jerky movement. "Everett shot . . . We're trapped on this hideous island with a murderer." Frantic with fear, she glared at Britt, spat out the words. "Are you satisfied now? Do you see what you've done? You brought us here knowing someone killed Jeremiah. Now none of us are safe. What are we going to do?" She didn't wait for an answer. Crimson nails gripped her husband's arm. "Nick, I'm sorry. I wish to God you'd stayed home. If only I hadn't asked you to come. Oh God, Nick, I love you." Her cry, naked and vulnerable, pierced the stricken silence.

Nick McRae's haughty, supercilious face softened. His lips quivered. "It's all right, Millie. We'll be all right. I'll take care of you." He took her hand, drew her close, pressed his cheek against her head. It might have been absurd, the wail of love from an unfaithful wife, the protestation of protection from her elderly husband. It wasn't. There was a passion of caring, however imperfect, in her cry and in his declaration.

Max observed them thoughtfully. What would either

be willing to do to maintain their relationship? Lie? That was a given. Steal? He didn't doubt it. Murder?

"Everybody loves a lover, but let's cut to the chase." Kim's voice was tight and clipped. Her sharp blue eyes swept the room. "Where was everybody at ten-thirty?" Once again she scanned the shots in her camera. "Here it is. At 10:28 A.M., I took a picture of the interior of Harry Lyle's cabin, a close-up of the dusty square where a trunk once stood." She glanced at Craig, her expression challenging. "Readers will love speculating about the contents of that missing trunk. Thank God I've got hustle. The time's here for all to see."

Max strolled to her, held out his hand. He looked at the display. The time was just as Kim claimed.

Craig strode toward them. He glanced at the camera. "Okay, fine. Kim's in the clear. And"—he nodded at Max—"you and your wife and Britt are alibied. All right, is there anyone else who can prove where they were at ten-thirty?"

Lucinda snapped, "I was cleaning up cabins. Where were you?"

Everyone looked at Craig.

He shrugged. "I'd finished the report. I decided to take a walk on the beach. I didn't see anyone else."

Isabel looked at Craig forlornly. "I was looking for you. When I didn't find you, I went back to my cabin." She glanced at Annie. "You were gone. Then I went up to the house. I didn't find Craig there, so I went down to the dock."

Millicent's eyes were haunted. She smoothed back a golden strand of hair. "I . . ." She looked toward her husband. "Nick and I went for a stroll."

"Nice day for it. All that sunshine." Kim's tone was dry.

Nick patted his wife's shoulder. "I don't think that's when we were out." His voice was tired. "I'd gone for a walk. I'm afraid I was alone at ten-thirty."

Millicent flushed. "I saw you. In the garden. I'm sure it was around ten-thirty."

Gerald was the last to speak. "I wasn't paying any attention to the time. I took the path to the main trail, then angled up to Everett's cabin."

Abruptly the room was quiet.

Gerald spoke briskly. "It must have been soon after ten-thirty when I got there. I found Max"—he jerked his head toward him—"standing guard over the corpse."

Craig nodded. "That accounts for everyone but Jay and Dana. They were likely together. Dana's never far from Jay." His face furrowed with worry. "We need to find them. They don't know what's happened. We know there's at least one gun on the loose. We need to warn them—"

"Warn them!" Millicent's voice quivered. "That's crazy. Why aren't they here? I'll tell you why. Your brother shot that odious man. And his wife got rid of the gun. They're the ones we need to be afraid of. Everett must have known something that proved Jay strung that wire on the stairs." Her hand tightened on her husband's arm. "We're not stepping a foot out of this house until Jay's found and locked up."

Craig ignored her. He jabbed a hand toward Britt. "Do you have a bullhorn? Something we can use to call for Jay and Dana? Or a tape recorder? I can make a tape and turn the volume up all the way. Isn't there a tape recorder in the library?"

"Tape recorder?" Britt concentrated, her face pulled into a frown. Then she nodded. "I think it's in the cupboard nearest the file cabinet."

Craig looked toward Gerald. "Get it."

Gerald looked glad to be occupied. He moved fast toward the hall.

Craig looked around the drawing room. "We'll grid the island, search in parties of two."

Isabel crossed the room, her face determined. "I'll go with you, Craig."

He looked down at her and slowly he smiled, his frown replaced by tenderness. "Thanks, honey. But I don't have an alibi."

Her lips trembled. "I don't either. But I know you're innocent."

His fingers brushed her cheek. "I want you to go with Annie."

"No." Isabel gave a firm, decided head shake. "I'm going with you."

Hurried footsteps sounded in the central hall. Gerald looked anxious as he came into the drawing room. "I didn't see a tape recorder anywhere. Not in any of the cabinets. Or shelves."

"I'll find it," Britt said impatiently. She dashed into the hall.

Gerald turned and followed her. "I looked where you said . . ."

Max lifted a hand. "Wait a minute, Craig. What are you suggesting?"

Craig stood with his shoulders forward, legs apart.

"We're going to search the island. It won't take long. We have to find Jay and Dana."

Lucinda moved heavily toward Craig, her plump face set in a stubborn frown. "I don't plan to go outside as long as people are running around with guns. Anyway, everybody's got to eat. I've got the platters ready—"

Britt and Gerald returned. Gerald held a ship's bell mounted on a walnut base.

Britt looked puzzled. "I couldn't find the tape recorder. We can use the bell." She pointed to a side table. Gerald eased it down. Britt pulled the cord. The deep clang reverberated in the room.

Millicent covered her ears.

Kim gave a hoot of laughter. "Ring the bell till the cows come home? For God's sake, why would Jay or Dana come if they heard a bell rung?"

"It's easier than trying to call out for them." Gerald said. "And everybody knows a ringing bell's a signal."

Craig squinted at the bell. "It's better than nothing. I'll carry it." He walked to the table, picked it up.

Isabel clapped her hands together. "Gerald's right. They'll know something's happened if they hear the bell clanging."

Kim looked sardonic. "We aren't playing all's-out-come-in-free. People who run away usually have something to hide." She lifted the camera, took a picture of Craig. "That's a great shot. The bell has a high shine."

Craig scowled at her.

Kim's smile challenged him. "Remember the Addison motto: All the News, All the Time."

Lucinda looked toward Britt. "I don't hunt for murderers. I'm a cook. If it's all the same to you, I'll be getting back to my kitchen. If people are wanting to eat, I've got most everything out on the buffet. I'll get the rest of it now."

Britt gestured toward the dining room. "Lunch is ready. Let's eat before we search. After all, everyone is here except Jay and Dana."

The implication was clear. Either the murderer was among them, which meant Jay and Dana were safe for the moment . . .

Or Jay and Dana had no reason for fear.

∴ *Ten* ∾

THE WIND PICKED UP, sending a fine mist from the tumbling waterfall. Britt pulled a scarf from her pocket, slipped it over her head. The breeze stirred Craig's thick blond curls, ruffled Max's hair. Kim buttoned her sweater. Isabel flipped an end of her plaid shawl over one shoulder. Gerald rubbed chilled hands together, his hooded eyes focused on Craig.

Annie stepped back a few feet from the fountain and wished she'd taken time to retrieve her windbreaker from the cleaning cart. She hadn't given the jacket a thought when she and Britt trundled back to the house before lunch, intent upon telling Max about Dana and the splash at the lagoon.

Annie wrapped her arms across her front. The gloom that had permeated their rushed lunch still clung to the chilled and grim group gathered around Craig Addison. They were all here except for Lucinda and the McRaes. Millicent had threatened hysterics when Nick offered to join the search. So he had stayed at the house, soothing Millicent and carrying dishes to the kitchen for Lucinda.

The small band of searchers huddled together, lis-

tening to Craig. Every face was wary, eyes darkened
by fear. Heavy gray clouds hung low. The wind rattled
the palmettos and the waxy leaves of the magnolias.
Craig spoke loudly to be heard above the ever present
murmur of the cascading water in the fountain. Beyond
lay the woods. The path to the left led to the lagoon,
where a gun might be settled in the bottom muck. The
path to the right plunged into the woods and ultimately
led to the cabins. The garden stretched behind them in
winter dullness except for brilliant patches of pansies,
purple and gold, yellow and white. Their brightness
was cheerless as splotches of makeup on the cheeks of
an old woman.

". . . that way everyone is paired with someone who
could not have killed Everett." Craig cradled the bell
under one arm.

"Oh goody." Kim's carrying voice was sarcastic.
"Just me and a possible murderer. Do we get to pick
our companion in crime?" Her gaze raked the group.
"Me, I'm not stirring a foot with anyone but Isabel. If
she's a killer, I'll re-enroll in Psych 101."

Isabel stood straight and tall. "I'm going with Craig."

Gerald gave a bark of cold laughter. "Anybody vot-
ing for me?"

Annie wondered if he realized he looked the part
of First Murderer better than anyone, with his hooded
eyes, saturnine face, and bitter mouth.

Britt clapped her hands above the discordant voices.
"Wait a minute! Hold up, everybody. Let's stay together. We can cover the island in less than an hour. I
don't see any need to hurry. There's no reason to think
anything's happened to either Dana or Jay. With"—she

counted—"seven of us we can spread out and be sure we don't miss anything. That way, no one has to be concerned about their safety."

Kim didn't mind stating the obvious. "Unless somebody starts taking potshots at us with one of the missing guns."

Craig made an impatient movement. The bell under his arm gave a muffled clang. "That implies Jay or Dana has a gun."

Kim's gaze was defiant. "Somebody has at least one. Maybe there's a gun in the lagoon. Maybe not. If not, there are two guns somewhere on the island. That makes the rest of us sitting ducks. I don't like the odds."

Max shot her a quick glance. "Unless you know something that will lead to the murderer, you should be perfectly safe. Everett threatened somebody. That's why his report was taken. That's why he was shot."

There was a general murmur.

Still shivering, Annie stepped forward. "That's why the murderer took all the information we'd gathered as well as Max's gun this morning. So, if anyone knows anything about how Jeremiah died or who shot Everett, now's the time to speak up."

Palmetto fronds rattled. A flying V of mallards honked overhead. Pines soughed in the wind.

No one spoke. Each face was shuttered as a closed and barricaded house.

"All right then." Max turned toward Britt. "It's your island. Where should we start?"

Annie occasionally lagged behind the group to jog in

place. The exercise pumped her blood, warming her. By the time they'd backtracked through the garden to check the secluded harbor and the shed bereft of the ham radio—Annie looked longingly at the table and the ripped-out wires—and the employee cabins, she was no longer chilled. Craig kept up a steady peal from the bell, a dirgelike sound that thrummed at Annie's nerves.

There was little conversation, though Kim kept up a running commentary as she shot pictures. ". . . I can see a spin-off exploring how many people slide through life under assumed names like Harry. Hundreds of people disappear every year. Nobody ever sees them again. How many of them pick up new identities?" She was the last one out of Harry's cabin, banging the door behind her, a lonely final sound.

At the lagoon, Kim pointed toward the middle. ". . . right about there's where something landed."

Craig rang the bell again and again.

Annie once again felt icy. The lagoon appeared dark and somber and cold, a fitting resting place for a weapon of death.

The bell clanged.

Kim looked eagerly at Britt. "Have you got a rowboat and some rakes? If nobody else is game, I'll give it a try . . ."

"Not now." Craig was impatient. "Whatever's there can wait until we find Jay and Dana. Come on, everybody." He gestured and they followed. Craig walked fast and still the bell tolled.

Kim was the only one talking when they once again reached the fountain and curved around it to enter the woods. But Kim fell silent when the seven reached the center of the forest path where narrow trails angled off to each cabin. Though it was midafternoon, the winter sun had slipped below the treetops. The light was dim and the faces in shadow.

"Which way, Craig?" Gerald looked uneasy.

Kim tapped the top of the arrow pointing to Cabin 3. "That's where he is? Everett?" She still held her camera, but she made no move to go up the trail.

Gerald's smile was cruel. "Where's our intrepid reporter? Are you going to miss a photo op?"

"Jay and Dana might be there." Britt's breath was uneven. "No one would look for them in Everett's cabin."

Craig was angry. "That's absurd. If they are in a cabin, they'll be in their own. They aren't hiding from us." He lifted the bell, pulled the cord, and the clapper clanged against the rim, *whang, whang, whang,* the deep ring loud enough to hurt Annie's ears.

There was a crackle of sound in the forest. High and frantic, a woman's voice cried out, "Who's there?"

Dana burst into the clearing. She'd come from the path that twisted out of sight toward the beach. The damp air had frizzed her hair into fine coils. Despite the roundness of her face, she looked gaunt, eyes huge, cheek muscles slack, mouth trembling. Smudges marked her face. Pieces of vegetation were snagged on her white sweater. Dirt streaked her yellow wool slacks. Mud clumped thickly on her boaters. She stopped, looked swiftly around the clearing, and began to cry.

Isabel darted to Dana, took her hands. "What's happened to you?"

Sobbing, Dana struggled to speak. Her voice was hoarse. "I heard the bell. I couldn't imagine what it meant but when I came and saw a crowd, I thought maybe Jay was with you. But he isn't." It was a wail. "Oh, Isabel, I can't find Jay. I can't find him anywhere. I've been all over the island, looked everywhere. I've called and called. I'm so frightened."

"Here." Isabel pulled a packet of tissues from her pocket, handed it to Dana. "Use these and take a deep breath. We'll help you look for Jay." Her voice was low and kind and soothing. "When did you last see him?"

Craig looked at his sister-in-law, his face grim.

Annie felt certain he feared Dana's answer.

Dana scrubbed at her face, gulped air. She seemed unaware of the intensity of her listeners. "This morning at the lagoon."

Britt supplied the time. "It must have been just after nine-thirty. Jay ran away."

"Has anyone seen him since?" Craig asked.

No one spoke. Quick glances flickered around the dusky clearing. Jay had been somewhere in the forest, no one knew where, when the gunshot sounded at ten-thirty.

Dana ignored Britt. Words tumbled out. "He was upset. He ran away. I tried to follow him but he was so much faster and then I was in the forest and I couldn't hear him anywhere. I don't know how long I searched. I went up and down the trails. Finally I went back to our cabin. I thought he'd come there." She shuddered, then spoke fast. "Oh, Isabel, I should never have let him come back to the island, but I didn't know he'd find out about his mother and . . ." She trailed off, slid a hesitant glance toward Craig.

Britt spoke out, her voice harsh. "All right. Go ahead and tell them. Everyone will blame me if he's gone off the rails. But maybe it's time he grew up, realized his mother wasn't the saint he thought she was. Maybe it's time he understood that Jeremiah, to give the devil his due, had plenty of reason to kick Lorraine out."

Craig strode toward her, scowling. "What are you talking about?"

Isabel called out, "Craig . . ." Her face held knowledge and sadness.

Annie understood. No matter what Isabel had known or how she'd known about Lorraine and her lover, this was not something she would tell her husband.

Britt stood her ground, eyes flashing, hands on her hips. "Did you know Jay wrote me, asking for your mother's correspondence and all of her things? I boxed up everything and sent it to him. Later I did some sprucing up. The carpenter found a slip of paper that she'd tucked behind a baseboard in her bedroom. I recognized her handwriting. She'd written directions to a hiding place. It wasn't up to me to dig up what she'd hidden." Her tone was defensive. "I'd promised Jay he could have everything. So I wrote him about that piece of paper. Then when he found the letters, he didn't want them."

"Letters?" Craig looked at Isabel and Dana.

Dana brushed back a tangle of frizzed hair. "I've got them." Her voice was dull. "Jay ran away. I haven't seen him since we found them. But he knew when he looked at the first one."

Craig's stare demanded an answer.

Dana pressed shaking hands to her cheeks. She stood mute, her face stricken.

Craig swung toward Isabel. "Tell me."

Isabel was suddenly angry. She looked at Britt. "You caused this. You tell him."

"A love affair." Britt's tone was brittle. "Your mother and Todd Fairlee. You remember him? The artist. She'd saved his letters to her, buried them beneath a brick near the sundial. She ran off to Savannah with him. That's why your father divorced her."

Shock grooved deep lines around Craig's mouth.

Isabel stepped close, took one big hand in hers.

Gerald cleared his throat. His weary face looked sad. "Let it go, Craig."

If Craig heard, he made no sign. He looked somberly at Dana. "You haven't seen Jay since then?" Craig's voice was uninflected, but his eyes were worried.

Annie figured the hours since that moment near the sundial. It had been a long time. Time enough for Everett to die. Time enough for a gun to be stolen. Time enough for Dana to throw something into the lagoon.

Tears trickled down Dana's cheeks. "I've looked everywhere."

Kim moved closer, her camera once again raised. "You didn't spend all your time searching, did you? I saw you at the lagoon around eleven-thirty. You threw something into the water. It must have been heavy the way it splashed, heavy as a gun." The camera clicked.

Kim lowered it. "Did you know the gun used to shoot Everett is missing?"

Dana took one step back, two. "Everett . . ." Panic squeezed her features. "Everett's dead?"

Kim flung out her question. "Didn't you know? I think you did. Tell us about the gun, Dana. Where did it come from? Did it have a smell, like firecrackers?"

Dana's head jerked up. "I don't know what you're talking about." Abruptly, she whirled, fled toward the trail leading to Cabin 4.

Kim took another step after her, her expression keen as a hound's sighting a tiring fox.

Craig's voice was steely. "Leave her alone."

Kim hesitated, shrugged, stopped. She started to speak, looked at Craig and remained silent. Her expression, suspicious, accusing, determined, spoke for her.

"I'll take care of Dana." Isabel moved swiftly toward the trail.

"Everybody else go back to the house." Craig was brusque. "I'll see about Jay. I may know where he's gone." Craig thrust the bell at Max, strode toward the seaside path.

Max moved quickly. He handed the bell to Gerald. "I'll go after Craig. In case he needs help. Tell everyone to stay together at the house until we get back." He looked toward Annie, a look that urged caution, then hurried after Craig.

Annie watched him disappear into the dimness and hated the hollow feeling that engulfed her. *Oh, Max, be careful, watch out, don't trust anyone. . . .*

Kim stared at the trail. She took an impatient breath, glared at Britt. "It isn't *his* island."

Britt's lips curled in a wry smile. "I know. But maybe we should leave Craig to deal with this. They were boys here. Craig may know someplace Jay could have gone."

Gerald was definite. "Craig can handle Jay. Now I suggest we go up to the house as Craig instructed."

"Do as you please. Not me." Kim whirled toward Britt. "We need to know where we stand. If you've got a rowboat, let's search the lagoon."

Max followed Craig's progress from the crackle and snap ahead of him. Craig was moving fast, breaking twigs, popping acorns, but the noise of his progress was less and less distinct. Max broke into a slow jog. He reached a fork and hesitated, head bent to listen. He wasn't sure but he thought Craig had turned to the northeast.

This trail was scarcely more than a faint path that curved and curled among huge pines. Saw palmettos poked out stiff fronds. Ferns scalloped the base of trees. Undergrowth was thick enough to provide sanctuary for foxes and cotton rats and even wild boars. Max wondered if a tawny yellow Carolina cougar lay on a limb, golden eyes watching him pass.

Max heard the ocean before he saw it. The roar was thunderous as the trees thinned. He stopped in the shadow of a pine, eyes widening at the dramatic seascape. Rust-colored bluffs jutted fifteen feet above roiled water. Waves crashed against the headland. Currents swirled from the incoming tide to run in great swaths around the base of the bluffs, picking up silt to mound the tidal pools with foam.

Driftwood poked from churning surf. Occasionally a huge log boomed against an old seawall. On the far bluff sagged remnants of a once proud house, only a few columns of brick remaining. The cloud-darkened day was turning into the deep gray of a late winter afternoon.

Craig was a darker shadow in the dim light. He moved swiftly toward the top of a near bluff, disappeared around a bent pine that hung near oblivion, victim of stormy surf and the ever encroaching sea.

Max broke into a run, careful of his footing when he neared the edge of the bluffs. Waves crashed against the rust-red headland.

"A few more feet to your left." Kim gestured with one hand. She held her camera in the other.

"Maybe she should be paddling the damn thing." Gerald's voice was as sour as his face. But he lifted the sleek paddle and swiped with dexterity, maneuvering the small yellow inflatable raft past a floating mass of lily pads and nearer the center of the pond. A half dozen Florida gallinules, distinctive with their red shield faces and yellow bills, clucked in alarm and flapped skyward.

Annie was poised at the raft's front end, Britt at the back. Annie balanced two rakes on the rim and looked down into water murky as a mud puddle, trying not to imagine the tangle of aquatic weeds.

Kim studied the display screen in her camera. "That big pine was just behind her. Come this way . . . another few feet . . . there."

Gerald was sweating despite the dank chill that lay

over the lagoon and the waft of icy coolness rising from the water. He steadied the oars, keeping the rocking craft as near immobile as possible. "I don't see any point to this. We should leave it for the sheriff. So what if we find a gun?"

Annie cautiously slid one rake down into the water.

"Then we know what we have to do." Britt's tone was bleak.

Gerald twisted to look at her but the raft dipped. He grunted and eased his weight nearer the middle of the seat. "Okay. We find a gun and do what? Save it for the cops?"

Britt shivered. "If Dana threw a gun into the lagoon, where did she get it? How did she get it? She has to tell us. She can't keep running away. If she won't answer, that tells us anyway. She's protecting Jay. If we bring up the gun, we'll know Jay shot Everett, and if they find him, we can protect ourselves."

The words hung in Annie's mind, clear as letters spewed from a skywriting plane, but they soon lost their substance, became wavy and indistinct. Britt was assuming too much. Even if a gun was retrieved, only a ballistics test could prove it to be the murder weapon. There was also the question of Max's gun. Of course, Max would know his own gun. . . . Annie leaned forward.

The raft sagged down. Water slapped over the front, sousing her elbows and knees. She felt the shock of the frigid water. Cold . . . Damn, she was cold. . . .

"Ooops. I'll lean!" Britt moved quickly, counterbalancing Annie. The raft rose.

Annie eased upright, but the rake dangled straight

down. "Thanks, Britt." She emphatically didn't want to pitch into this mucky water. "Okay, watch me. When I go forward, you go back. . . ."

It was a stressful ballet, Annie bending over the side, the rake pointed toward the bottom, Britt watching Annie's every move and adjusting her position. Gerald poked the paddles into the water, using short swift strokes to keep the raft almost stationary. Kim kibitzed. ". . . take your time . . . don't jerk . . . be fluid, smooth . . ."

The rake tangled in the roots of lily pads. Carefully, Annie tugged it free, moved a few inches, again started the descent. This time the rake was almost at its full length, her fingers within an inch of the water, when she felt a jolt. "I've hit bottom." She pulled the rake toward her, then pushed out. A thunk. Now it was time for the second rake. Her arms ached, her back twisted in a strain, but finally she had both tools on either side of the hard object. "I've got something."

"The gun?" Kim squealed in delight. She raised the camera.

Sweat slid down Annie's back. Her hands were moist. She certainly didn't need her jacket now. The rakes cradled her find. She slipped her fingers down the handles, a few inches at a time. The water bubbled and tumbled as the prongs came clear.

Annie blew out a spurt of exasperation. She grabbed the remnant of plantation brick in one hand and flung it across the water. The raft wobbled.

"Steady," Gerald warned.

Three more times she pulled the prongs of one rake back and forth along the mucky bottom. Once she yanked up part of a broken picnic hamper. Another time it took patient jiggling to free the rake from some large obstruction, likely a sunken log. Moving a few inches to her left, she again began the laborious movement of the rake. She had pulled it almost to the boat, ready to admit defeat and relieve the strain on her shoulders and back, when she felt the prongs thud against something that moved. Something not too big and not too small . . . Grimly, her muscles hot with misery, she swung the second rake down. She was getting better. This time, the two rakes came together smoothly, their prongs interlocking.

"I'll get this up." Annie knew this was her last effort. If anyone else wanted to dangle over the edge of the raft, they could be her guest. Maybe Kim would let go of that damn camera for a minute and see how it felt . . .

The pressed-together prongs broke above the surface. A riffle of water fell away. Annie willed her hands not to shake. If she dropped a rake, tilted them . . . The harsh blue black of the gun was dark as spilled ink. Max's gun was silver and shiny as a nickel. Dimly she heard Kim's shout, felt the jerk of the boat as Gerald craned to see.

"Oh my God." Britt's voice was thin and strained. "Jeremiah's gun."

Annie didn't need Britt to make the identification. Annie remembered only too well seeing this gun in the drawer of the library desk.

Annie edged the rakes and gun into the raft, eased them to the floor, felt the cold splash of dripping water on her legs and feet. She'd been so hot. Now the trickles of sweat were cold against her back. She was chilled to the bone, her wet slacks icy against her skin. She nudged the gun with the toe of her shoe. It would take forensic comparisons to prove this was the murder weapon. Annie didn't doubt that it was. The timing sorted itself in her mind. This gun was stolen last night. Max's gun wasn't taken until this morning, very likely after Everett already lay dead in his cabin. No, the gun Britt had carried last night was the gun that killed Everett.

Gerald pointed. "That's Jeremiah's gun. It was stolen. How could Dana have had it?"

That was the question Dana must now answer.

Spume misted over Max from the waves crashing against the bluff. He held to a drooping pine bough as he skirted the edge of the bluff. He concentrated on the path. Past the tree, the point jutted into the water. The path stopped. He felt a moment's uncertainty. Where was Craig? There was no more path, only the crumbling bluff and tilted boulders and beleaguered pines soon to fall. He looked out at the water. His eyes widened. The boy's heart that had thrilled to tales of Blackbeard and Long John Silver admired the rusting hulk of a cargo ship that had foundered in a storm. Years of pounding waves had torn much of the ship away, but the remains of the stern, including a tilted funnel, were wedged among boulders. A swaying catwalk, somewhat frayed but still serviceable, was anchored to iron rods driven down into the mudflat. The rods must have gone deep enough to strike rock or they would long ago have washed away. The project surely had been costly, but the result must have thrilled two little boys. The derelict ship certainly wasn't a safe place to play but when a man owns an island, he can set the rules. Perhaps Jeremiah wanted his sons to taste danger and understand that adventure comes at a price.

The bluff had worn away enough in recent years that it would take a good two-foot jump to reach the catwalk. Max balanced and sprang. The wooden planks were slick from the spray. He skidded and caught at one of the rods, held until the bridge stopped swaying. The water beneath him roiled in a frenzy of currents. Max moved quickly though he kept a hand on the rod. He reached the wreck and dropped lightly onto the slick deck, skidding to a stop. He walked swiftly toward the funnel. There was no need for stealth. The hiss and roar of the water masked his approach. At the funnel, he began to skirt it, stopped when he heard Craig's voice.

"It doesn't change who Mother was." Craig spoke quietly.

Max pressed against the rusting funnel. He slid forward until he could see the brothers. Craig faced Jay. Craig's burly body looked solid, immovable, determined. Jay sat on the deck, slumped against the remnants of the wheelhouse. His shaggy brown hair was damp, lay limp on his shoulders. Even his mustache drooped. The muscles in his face were slack, his eyes pools of misery. Every so often a long shudder rippled through his lanky frame.

Craig moved closer, knelt, and put a gentle hand on Jay's shoulder. "Think about you and Judy."

Jay's head jerked up. Abruptly he gripped his brother's arm, his hand vise tight. "What the hell does she have to do with this?"

"Nothing. Everything." Craig didn't falter. "Love makes people do crazy things. You. Even though you'd never leave Dana. Mom. Yet no matter what you do, you're Jay and Mom is Mom. Dana forgave you. Maybe 'forgiveness' isn't the right word for Mom. Don't be angry with her. People do the best they can."

"And Dad . . ." Jay's voice wavered. "I hated him for the way he treated Mom after she was hurt. He wouldn't do a thing and he knew we didn't have the money to take care of her. Every time I thought about him and all his money and Dana having to go back to work, I got madder and madder. You know how he was. He never let us have an extra cent. Yeah, he had all the money in the world but none of it for Mom. Or for us. Especially not for me. At least you pleased him by working in the business. He didn't want me there." Years of bitterness curdled his voice. "But I couldn't understand how he could treat Mom that way after she was hurt and helpless. Those bills about ruined me. Dana and I were damn broke. Now I guess I see what happened. He was mad at Mom. Even so, he shouldn't have thrown her out. But if she was cheating on him . . . Oh God, I don't know what's right, but now it's too late. I'm stuck with the way it ended. Do you know I was glad when he died? I thought you . . . but now I know better."

Craig rocked back on his heels, stared at Jay. "What do you mean by that?"

Jay clawed at his mustache. "I was out early that

morning. I was going to try and catch him when he jogged. That's the only thing I ever did that he admired. I could outrun him. He hated that. I was going to—oh, it was stupid—I know he wouldn't have changed anything, but I was going to jog and meet up with him and tell him how bad everything was and how if he'd just pay the nursing-home bill—but he didn't come. I saw you heading toward the house. I guess it's kind of crazy, but I thought you'd gone to see him and maybe he'd swiped at you and you hit back and he'd gone down the stairs. I knew damn well he never fell down a flight of stairs. Not Dad. Then when Isabel walked out on you, I thought that proved it."

Craig looked stunned. "You think that's why Isabel left?" He came to his feet, paced back and forth.

"Oh, sure." Jay was confident. "I ran into her occasionally and she looked like a ghost. I thought she couldn't bring herself to go to the cops but she wasn't going to stay around and soak up the luxury."

Craig's face was an odd mixture of astonishment, anger, and relief. "Oh my God . . ." He stopped and gave a bark of choked laughter. "How about that? My wife and my brother think I'm a murderer."

"Not now." Jay's expression was earnest. "The minute Everett spilled it about Britt untying that wire, I knew it wasn't you. You might have got mad and punched him. You wouldn't sneak around and rig a trap."

Max nodded. That was what Isabel had said to Annie: Craig wouldn't set a trap.

Jay hurried on. "Last night I was watching Isabel when Everett described the stairs. She looked like she'd just broken the bank at Monte Carlo."

"I might have shoved Dad but I wouldn't have tripped him!" Craig's tone was wondering. "I ought to be glad neither of you tabs me as a premeditated murderer, but it kind of knocks me back that my wife and my brother suspected me and never said a word."

Jay tugged on his mustache. He looked shamefaced. "I guess we were both nuts."

Craig shoved a hand through his thick curls. His lips twisted in a wry grin. "Hell, Jay. I can't be mad. See, I thought you'd pushed Dad."

"Me?" Jay's amazement lifted his voice.

At that moment, if he'd been asked to report to the sheriff, Max would have wagered Confidential Commissions that neither brother had killed Jeremiah and surely that absolved them of Everett's death as well.

Jay came to his feet, moving stiffly. He took two quick steps and gave his brother a bear hug, let him go, and managed an unsteady laugh. "I feel better than I have ever since Dad died. It's like I've been carrying the damn world on my back and now the weight's gone. The cops'll find Harry. He's got to be the one. You know how Dad would have felt about Golden Silk being used as a way station for drugs."

Craig rubbed the back of his neck as if comfort eluded him.

Jay's ebullience drained away. "What's wrong?" He leaned toward his brother, his gaze intent.

"Harry." Craig said the name as if recalling a long-ago acquaintance. "Yeah. That's what we all thought at breakfast." He stared at his brother, his expression somber. "Everybody but Britt, as I recall. Turns out her instinct was right. Listen, Jay, we've got big trouble. Somebody shot Everett this morning—"

Jay stood stone still. He listened as Craig described murder on an island with only a handful of suspects.

"—so they found him dead around ten-thirty. It had to be murder because there wasn't a gun anywhere."

"I was here." Doves in a nearby live oak made their mournful cry, low and somber as funeral bells. Jay gestured toward the tree. "But these are my only witnesses." His eyes narrowed. "The gun's gone? My God, that means everybody's in danger. Where's Dana? I've got to find Dana." He turned, plunged across the sloping deck.

Max slipped behind the other side of the funnel as Jay dashed past him toward the rope bridge, Craig close behind. "Jay, wait. For God's sake, Jay, let me tell you . . ."

Annie wanted to stand between Dana, a huddled mass of misery in the basket chair with its gay red cushions so clearly designed for a happy holiday, and the demanding questioners, intent as a flock of piranhas gouging flesh from a drowning creature. Britt had led the charge to Jay and Dana's cabin after the gun was found.

Dana's eyes, reddened by crying, were dry now, dry but filled with panic. She stared at the coffee table and its grisly burden, the blue-black automatic in a clear plastic bag. Her hands were in a tight grip, the fingers blanched from pressure.

Britt paced up and down, eyes flashing with anger

and determination, patches of red in her narrow cheeks, dark hair becomingly tousled by the wind. She might have been a DA confronting the accused, but there was a driving, personal urgency behind her attack. ". . . got to know! Don't you see, Dana? We're scared. All of us. Scared to death. We've got to know who's behind this. We can't keep on looking at every face and thinking, 'Are you the one? Are you going to kill me?' "

Isabel's fingers twined in the fringe of her shawl. She darted worried glances from Dana to the gun. "I don't know what's going on, but Dana's too upset to talk to anyone right now."

Gerald cleared his throat. "Isabel's right. There's no point in badgering her. I'd say she's in shock."

Kim's round face softened in sympathy, but her blue eyes were cold and merciless. "Come on, Dana. Tell us what happened. We'll take care of you. Did Everett threaten you? Were you frightened? Did the gun go off by accident?"

Dana licked dry lips. Her voice was faint, the words scarcely audible. "I didn't know about Everett. I swear I didn't."

Annie's instinct to protect a helpless creature was overborne by the icy realization that Dana had to explain where she got the gun. She claimed she didn't know Everett had been shot. If not, why had she thrown the gun into the lagoon? Was she protecting herself? Or her husband?

"Of course you didn't." Kim's voice was kindly, encouraging, inviting, her eyes probing. "It seems pretty clear Jay gave you the gun and—"

"No," Dana wailed. "Leave me alone." She pushed

up and stood unsteadily, eyes wild. "Why don't you help me find Jay? I've got to find him. I'm going to go out and look for him."

The door burst open, slammed back against the wall.

Dana's face lighted. "Jay." It was almost a scream. That she'd never expected to see him again was utterly clear in the wobbling, frantic cry. That she was distraught, frightened, and sick with fear was equally apparent.

Jay was across the sisal matting in two long strides, scowling furiously, arms outstretched.

The room now seemed jammed with people, Dana clutching the back of the basket chair for support, a wary Britt a scant foot from her, Isabel sitting stiffly on the sofa, Gerald an aloof presence near the fireplace, a watchful Annie near the breakfast bar.

Jay demanded, "What's wrong? By God, if anybody's bothering you, I'll take care of them." He grabbed her in a tight embrace. She held to him, sobbing. His furious gaze moved from face to face. "What the hell's going on here?"

Craig stood in the doorway, looked toward Isabel. She pointed to the coffee table. Craig saw the gun, drew in a deep breath.

Britt was only a few feet from Jay and Dana. She held her head high, returned his glare. "Dana threw that gun into the lagoon. She's got to tell us where she found it. Or whether she's the one who stole it last night from the library."

"That's absurd," Jay retorted. "Dana wouldn't touch a gun. She hates guns."

"She touched one." Kim spoke with authority. She pointed at the table. "There it is. We just fished it out of the lagoon and I saw her toss it in. She damn sure touched it."

Jay looked down at his wife. Slowly his face changed. Assurance was replaced by puzzlement. "Dana?"

She looked up at him, mute as a scolded child. Once again tears slid down her cheeks.

"Come on, honey. It's all right. You can tell me. I'll take care of it." They might have been alone in that crowded room, just the two of them, love and strength running between them shining as a crystal arch.

Annie blinked back tears. Kim leaned forward, camera up. The flash blinked. Britt folded her arms, her face skeptical.

Dana shuddered. "I found that gun. It was lying in the pine straw near the front steps of our cabin. I'd been out hunting for you. I was so frightened when you ran away. I went all over the woods and down to the beach and then up to the house. I couldn't find you anywhere." Her voice quivered. "I thought maybe you might have gone back to the cabin. That's when I found the gun. I thought it was probably the gun somebody stole from the library. I didn't know why it was near our cabin, but it frightened me." For an instant, horror looked out from her eyes. "I wanted to get rid of it." Her voice was stronger. "I took it up to the lagoon and threw it away."

"You found it near our steps?" Jay's face hardened. "That means somebody dumped it on us after they shot Everett."

"Oh, really?" Britt looked pugnacious, jaw jutting,

hands on her hips. "That's a good story, Jay, but hard to believe. That would have been a big risk to take. For all the murderer knew, you and Dana were in your cabin, working on your reports. How could the murderer have known you were gone and it was safe to bring the gun and leave it?"

Jay shrugged. "I'm not in the confidence of the murderer, so I don't know how it happened." His tone was sarcastic, his dislike of Britt evident. "That's up to the police to figure out. Anyway, you people get out of here. My wife's upset and needs to rest."

Gerald held up a hand. He sounded uncomfortable but determined. "We'd better all stick together, Jay."

"One for all and all for one? I don't think so, Gerald. The less I see"—he glanced at Britt—"of the woman who caused this, the better I'll feel."

"Damn you!" Britt's voice was deep and husky, quivering with anger. "I didn't cause a damn thing. I didn't kill your father. Or Everett. But the same can't be said of you. Or your wife. Or your brother. Or—"

Face twisting in fury, Jay moved toward her, a hand upraised.

Craig and Max rushed to Jay, grabbed his arms. Craig talked fast. "Ease up, buddy. Calm down. Now Dana's crying again—"

Gradually, the tension eased out of Jay, his scowl replaced by concern.

Annie wondered about Jay's temper. Was his fury the answer to Jeremiah's plunge down the stairs, the splintered desk drawer, Everett's murder?

Britt wasn't cowed. "You may not like what I'm saying, but you can't kill the messenger, Jay. Or maybe that's just what you'd like to do. I can tell you I don't want to die. The only way I can feel safe—or anyone on the island can feel safe—is for you to be in plain sight of all of us until help comes."

Gerald moved between Britt and Jay. He clapped a hand on the younger Addison's shoulder. "Ignore her. The point isn't you, Jay. Yeah, it's a problem that Dana found the gun here. But it could be just like you said, the killer came by here, dumped it to incriminate you or Dana. In any event, everyone who can't prove where they were when Everett was shot is a suspect. That's me. You. Dana. Craig. Isabel. The McRaes. Lucinda. I've been thinking about it. The answer is for all of us to stick together until the boats get here tomorrow and we can get in touch with the sheriff. So you and Dana better come up to Heron House with us."

They were all present in the drawing room to lock away the gun retrieved from the lagoon. Britt had emptied a tackle box. It sat on the coffee table in front of the sofa. She placed the plastic bag in the box, added the reports written by Kim, Gerald, and Craig. "If everyone had stayed in their cabins and written their reports . . ."

Annie understood her thought. If no one had wandered, Jay and Dana would have been together, as well as Millicent and Nick. As it was, no one could claim to have been with anyone at the time the shot sounded except Annie and Max and Britt. Kim had been alone but her presence away from Everett's cabin was confirmed by the digital camera.

" 'If wishes were horses . . .' " Gerald quoted softly.

Lucinda stepped forward. The cook's cheeks had

lost their ruddy color. She swallowed jerkily. "Here's a padlock. Found it in my catch-all drawer."

Britt took the lock, slipped it in the hasp. She removed the small key, snapped the lock shut. The click was distinct. "That's done."

There was no easing of tension in the elegant, somber room.

Lucinda's gaze skittered around the room, wary, searching, fearful. "Somebody here . . ." Her voice trailed away.

Late afternoon twilight pressed against the windows. Despite the glitter of the twin chandeliers and crackle of the fire, apprehension filled the room.

Standing near a Palladian window, Annie felt as if darkness surrounded her. She gripped the pull cord of the velvet drape so hard her palm ached. She shut out the encroaching night, but she couldn't shut out the fear that lay against them all, heavy as a funeral pall.

There was no avoiding the truth. Someone in this room—someone who stood within a few feet of her— had killed twice. The list of suspects was terrifyingly brief. She looked at them in turn, knowing as her gaze locked with each for an instant, she was meeting the eyes of a killer. Who was it? Who could it be?

Lucinda pleated the hem of her apron, moved restlessly, a step forward, a step back, her gaze flickering around the room.

Annie knew Lucinda's apparent uneasiness could be the wily pretense of a murderess. Annie remembered their far-ranging chatter that morning in the kitchen. Lucinda herself had made it clear she knew how to shoot a gun. Her talk of shots fired on the island when she had thought herself to be alone didn't seem to fit into the puzzle. Was that an invention for some obscure reason of her own? If it was, what could have been the purpose?

Gerald stood with shoulders hunched, hands jammed into trouser pockets. His searching gaze touched Annie, moved to Millicent McRae. His hooded eyes were hard and suspicious.

Annie wondered if this was a pose. If Gerald had twice murdered, of course it would be to his benefit to appear suspicious of someone. Or did he suspect Millicent because she was perhaps the most volatile person there and clearly willing to do whatever was required to protect the marriage she had violated?

Millicent's air of elegance was frayed like a once fine tapestry exposed to harsh sunlight and pelting rain. Staring at her husband, she looked gaunt, haggard, and haunted.

Nick seemed oblivious. He slumped in a wing chair, eyes blank, sunk in thoughts that pulled life and vigor from his face.

Annie shivered. Perhaps that was how a murderer would feel, exhausted, drained. Damned?

Dana sat on the satin upholstered love seat within the protective curve of Jay's arm. Despite her scream of joy at her husband's reappearance, she looked miserable and frightened. Her lips trembled and her eyes were huge.

Annie was chilled by Dana's obvious fear. Dana was afraid for Jay, that was clear. She might *claim* to have thrown away the gun because she found it abhorrent, but Annie had no doubt that Dana was desperately afraid her husband had killed Everett.

Jay's gaze was defiant. He knew he was the chief suspect. His anger was matched only by the fear that was apparent in the occasional tic of one eyelid, the shakiness of his hands.

Jay's bitterness at his father's treatment of Lorraine could have resulted in that strand of wire at the stair top. Murder once committed made a second murder if threatened a swift response. But nowhere in Jay's shifting glance did Annie read the shock he must surely feel if he had killed his father only to discover that all his father's actions were understandable. Not, perhaps, excusable, but certainly understandable.

Craig stood protectively by Isabel, holding her hand firmly. Though his face was somber, drawn in heavy lines of fatigue and uncertainty, there was a glow in his eyes when he looked at his wife.

Annie saw that glow. If it was genuine, surely Craig was innocent.

Isabel was still pale but she, too, had an air of peace. She might have been a swimmer who had battled deadly currents to finally reach, exhausted and pummeled, the safety of the shore.

Annie felt pummeled, too, buffeted by the emotions that swirled around her. She'd looked in every eye and nowhere did she find guilt. Yet behind one of these faces, familiar faces now, touched by pain and sorrow and fear, a quick, desperate, malevolent intelligence had planned murder.

Who?

There was a clatter on the hardwood floor.

Britt jerked forward, bent down to pick up the key that had fallen from her hand. "Sorry." Her voice broke the brooding silence.

Annie knew that Britt, too, felt the huge strain of being in this room, knowing a predator was within reach. Annie felt overwhelmed by a sense of imminent danger. She found it hard to breathe.

Millicent gave a little scream. "I can't bear it. One of you . . . but we don't know which one . . . oh God, Nick, we've got to do something. One of them has a gun. We may all be dead—"

There was a thunderous rapping at the front door.

Everyone in the drawing room jerked to look toward the hallway. Each face reflected astonishment and shock and bewilderment. And fear.

Annie's hand went to her throat. A knock at the door . . . but there was no one else on the island . . . no one else . . .

The knock sounded again, heavy, desperate, demanding.

∴ *Eleven* ∾

THE HEAVY FRONT DOOR crashed open.

Everyone looked toward the hall. They stood frozen, waiting. Annie knew each of them had the same sense of bewilderment laced with fear. There was no one else on the island. Not another living soul. Everyone was in the drawing room.

Who or what was coming toward them?

A hoarse voice shouted, "Britt? Britt, where are you?" Running steps thudded on the wooden floor.

Max moved fast toward the hall, face wary and alert, shoulders hunched, ready for battle. Craig, too, was striding across the room, hands curled into fists. Before they reached the arch, a lanky man in a worn suede jacket, age-paled jeans, and deck shoes skidded to a stop just inside the drawing room. He was a little over six feet in height with brown hair, dark eyes, and a resolute, intelligent face. When he saw Britt, a mélange of expressions slipped across his face—acute relief, startled awareness of an audience, embarrassment as he realized everyone was looking toward him in amazement.

"Loomis." Britt's voice was deep in her throat,

almost a whisper. There was a look of disbelief in her eyes, and something more. Distress? She reached out both hands toward him. Suddenly tears brimmed, slipped down pale cheeks.

He was across the room in an instant, drawing her into his arms. "What's wrong? I knew there was something wrong when I couldn't raise you. I kept trying your call letters all day and there was nothing. It was like you and the island had disappeared into the Sound. Hour after hour, nothing. I had to come."

Craig strode toward him. "Can you radio to shore?"

Millicent plunged across the room, her voice high and shrill. "Do you have a boat? I insist that my husband and I be taken off this island at once. I am Representative McRae . . ."

A half dozen voices rose. ". . . save us from being killed . . . there's a gun somewhere . . . got to get help . . ."

Britt pushed away from Loomis, swiped a hand at wet cheeks. "Quiet, everyone. Let me tell him. Loomis, we're in terrible trouble. Thank God you've come. There's been a murder. Harry stole the yacht. He took the radio, everything. That's why you couldn't contact me. We've been stranded. You can call for help." She took a deep breath. "Everyone, this is Loomis Mitchell. . . ."

Loomis Mitchell led the way down the dock, his head bent as he listened to Britt. Max held Annie's elbow as they walked. The only light was a single 500-watt bulb near the end of the pier. It shed a golden radiance on the cabin cruiser tied there, but the greater portion of the pier was in darkness. The boat, perhaps a twenty-eight-footer, rose and fell in the swells. "Nice." Max's tone was admiring. When they reached the ladder, Max gave her elbow a squeeze, then followed Loomis down the steps.

The breeze off the water was cold. None of them had stopped for coats. Once again Annie wished she'd taken time to retrieve her jacket. Everyone was there. Annie wondered if they'd all come because of the sense of safety provided by staying together or because of their hunger to be connected to the mainland, even at a remove. They could hear Max and Loomis on the boat. They clustered near the ladder, Jay and Dana together, Isabel holding tight to Craig's arm, Millicent and Nick on the outskirts, present but aloof, Britt with a hand on a piling, leaning forward to catch every word, Gerald a dark, elusive, listening shadow, Lucinda watching with folded arms, Kim peppering Britt with questions—"What does Mitchell do? Where does he live? Talk about saved by the bell. Do you credit him with ESP?" Britt snapped, "Shh. I can't hear him."

Annie shivered, but it was worth the chill to listen and know without doubt or question that this dreadful episode was nearing an end. It was almost as good as a bridge to the mainland to hear Loomis Mitchell's clear, precise voice and know he was being heard by the Coast Guard, which would contact the sheriff.

". . . Loomis Mitchell contacting you from Golden Silk to report a murder." Loomis gave the latitude and longitude of the island and the known circumstances of Everett's death. He paused. "No, sir, this was the first time it was possible to make a report. The island was cut off from communication until I arrived. The radio was stolen as well as a yacht, leaving the group marooned here. . . . Yes, sir. . . . So we can expect help this evening. Within two hours at the outside . . ."

The logs crackled cheerfully in the bedroom fireplace. Max pulled the table a little closer to the fire, welcoming the waft of heat. Lucinda must have found time to start the blaze. Surely it was she who had done so and not Britt. The last he'd seen of Britt after a quick and unceremonious buffet dinner, she was walking arm in arm toward the library with Loomis. He wondered how Loomis would react to her admission that she had engineered the gathering on Golden Silk, hoping to solve a murder. Would it change his feelings for Britt to know she'd connived to keep Jeremiah's murder a secret?

That was between the two of them.

The dancing flames were cheerful, though their warmth did nothing to ease Max's weary sense of failure. He'd been hired to catch a murderer and he'd failed. Worse than that failure was the hard truth that Everett Crenshaw was dead.

Max pushed back his chair, walked to the fireplace, stretched a hand to clamp the mantel. He stared into the flames, remembering Everett's quick intelligence, his capacity for digging up unpalatable facts, and, most of all, his taunts. At the time, the jabs had seemed part and parcel of Everett's arrogance and penchant for stirring up trouble. This time he'd triggered a swift and deadly response from Jeremiah's murderer.

"Damn." Max pushed away from the mantel, moved

back to the table. Seated, he picked up a pen. It was
too late now to regret the fact he'd dismissed Everett's
gibes as nothing more than a performance. Everett's
sardonic voice sounded in his mind: *The truth, the
whole truth, and nothing but the truth.* One of those
listening had heard a threat. And dealt with it.

The Meissen clock on the mantel struck seven. In
something less than an hour they could expect deliver-
ance. Or, if not immediate departure from the island,
certainly they could expect to be protected. There
would be armed deputies to station in the house and to
patrol the circuit of the cabins. Rest might not be easy
this final night on the island, but it should be secure.

Max pulled the legal pad close. The murderer had
taken not only Max's gun this morning but also all of
the information he'd accrued about the guests. That
didn't matter. Even though he couldn't hand over that
background information to the authorities, he could
present a record of everything that had happened this
weekend. First he'd make a cogent summary and then
he'd pluck out critical facts for ready reference. He
began to write.

Lucinda hummed "Do, Lord" with cheer and gusto as
she poured boiling water from a steam kettle to scald
the sink. Occasionally, she paused to clap damp hands
in rhythm and sing a verse in a surprisingly sweet con-
tralto. She placed the empty kettle on the drainboard,
lifted a cloth to give a final swipe to the gleaming
tiles.

Annie paused in wrapping a platter of ham-and-
cheese sandwiches with pink plastic to observe Lu-

cinda in amazement. Ever since the cook had been
assured that the Coast Guard was en route, her entire
demeanor had changed. She'd whistled through the
preparations for the buffet supper, and when Annie
came in to help with cleaning up, Lucinda's conversation was punctuated by praise of the Coast Guard: "My
cousin Maude's son is on a ship out of Norfolk. Plenty
of good they do and very little attention paid." "The
Coast Guard will put everything right, we can count
on that." "They can use a metal detector and find that
missing gun."

Annie finished tucking the plastic wrap. She doubted
either the Coast Guard or the sheriff's office, which-
ever took charge, would have any luck finding Max's
gun. The island was small but the possibilities of con-
cealment were almost endless. But soon—she glanced
at the ceramic clock over the sink—the missing gun
would no longer matter. Even now, with help on the
way, everyone was staying in the house. The murderer
wouldn't have any opportunity to retrieve the gun.
Likely it had been hidden near a cabin or perhaps near
the central fountain, close to a landmark but covered
with dirt or leaves. Perhaps a mound of pine cones
marked the spot, meaningless to everyone but the
murderer. Almost certainly it was hidden far from the
house.

Annie took comfort in that thought. She wasn't as
ebullient as Lucinda but her spirits were improving rapidly. She carried the sandwich platter to the refrigerator,
slid it onto a center shelf. Two other platters were there.
Lucinda had insisted that sandwiches be ready to offer to

their rescuers for a late supper, and she had just brewed the thirty-cup percolator of coffee.

Annie took a look around the kitchen. Everything was done. She untied her borrowed apron.

Lucinda followed her glance. "Everything's tidy and I appreciate your help. Would you like a cup of coffee?"

Annie smiled. "Not now, thanks." She moved toward the kitchen door. "I'm going upstairs for a while." She hoped working on a report for the sheriff had helped ease Max's feeling of failure. No, they hadn't solved the crime, but it wasn't fair for him to feel guilty about Everett's death. It was Everett who had decided to keep to himself damning facts. Not Britt. Not Max. Not Annie.

She pushed through the swinging door into the dining room.

Kim looked up from a table near the far window, her round face excited. "Hey, Annie, can I count on you and Max being down at the dock when the cavalry arrives?"

Annie shot her a startled glance. "Yes. I imagine everyone will go down. Why?"

Kim had the grace to appear uncomfortable. She pushed back a strand of blond hair. The faint flicker of embarrassment was superseded by a rush of enthusiasm. "Think about it. 'Marooned Murder Suspects Greet Rescuers.' God, what a story. I'm going to get the pix of a lifetime. You'll definitely be there?"

"I wouldn't miss it for the world." Annie's tone was dry, but she knew her sarcasm went right over Kim's ambitious blond head.

Kim bent again to her legal pad, the blood-red nails on one hand thrumming against the tabletop.

Annie reached the hallway. Millicent and Nick had pulled chairs from the dining room to the front of the hall, near one of the side windows. Their heads were close together. Millicent's voice was a murmur. Though they were only a half dozen feet away, they were unaware of Annie, immersed in their private world. Millicent's hand was tucked in his. Millicent hadn't quite regained her impermeable confidence, but she no longer looked haunted or frightened. Nick's face was weary but at peace.

Perhaps the clearest reflection of the easing of tensions since Loomis's arrival was the soft and soothing sound of "Clair de Lune," the notes glorious and perfect as butterflies drifting in summer sunlight. Annie looked through the archway into the drawing room. Gerald's fingers moved with graceful precision over the keyboard of the rosewood piano tucked in a far corner. In profile, his lined and drooping face was serene. He no longer looked villainous to Annie. He was a tired, middle-aged man finding solace in music. Occasionally he glanced toward an alcove where Craig and Isabel sat. Gerald's faint smile was a benediction.

Craig leaned toward Isabel, his expression reassuring. And loving. The piano, though soft, overrode his voice. Isabel's smile was tremulous but joyful. They were absorbed in each other, shutting out their surroundings. There was no hint in his face of the tough, combative employer quick to issue orders and demand compliance. Isabel's misery of the morning was gone.

In the other alcove, Dana rested her head on Jay's

shoulder. They sat close together on the love seat. Jay patted her shoulder, the kind of pat offered for reassurance, a pat that meant *Don't worry, everything's going to be all right, I'm here.* Occasionally he made a quiet comment. Dana still looked uneasy, but there was no trace of her earlier panic. She lifted her arm, looked at her watch.

Annie too checked her watch. It wouldn't be long now. Their rescuers should arrive in a little over thirty minutes. Oh yes, she was sure that everyone in the house would crowd onto the dock. Only then would they feel safe.

How would the murderer feel? Fearful? Triumphant? Tense? Surely that huge burden, a burden that could never be shed, weighed upon the murderer. There should be some indication of guilt in one of the faces she had just seen. But she'd observed nothing.

The elegant notes of "Clair de Lune" followed her into the hallway and up the stairs. She avoided the step where Jeremiah had fallen. Soon she would be free of Golden Silk. She would not have to go up and down those stairs, feeling each time that she was close to evil. As she hurried toward their room, it was almost as if she were shaking away the sticky, clinging strands of a monstrous web.

She moved quickly, her footsteps muted by the oriental runner. She reached their room, opened the door, paused on the threshold.

Max sat at the writing table, his back to her. He was intent on the pad in front of him, his hand moving in swift, determined strokes.

Annie slipped inside, closed the door softly behind

her. Dear Max. She loved the way his thick blond hair swirled to a point on the nape of his neck. She loved the strong set of his shoulders. If only there were some way she could help him find the truth . . .

"Max." There was magic in saying the name of someone you love. There was a special resonance when you felt the name on your tongue and in your heart. She said, "Max," and it was a remembrance and promise and vow.

He looked around. The tight lines in his face eased. His blue eyes smiled even before his mouth curved. "Almost through." He gestured toward the opposite chair. "Come see what you think."

Annie settled in the chair nearest the fire, welcoming the sweep of warmth. Lucinda kept her kitchen cold, probably because she was heavy and moved about so vigorously. It had also been cold in the dining room and the drawing room. The flames dancing in the bedroom fireplace banished the remainder of Annie's chill from their trek onto the pier. She picked up the sheets with Max's bold, slanting script and began to read.

For a few minutes, there was no sound but the scratching of his pen and the rustle of the pages as she read. She finished and looked up to meet his inquiring gaze.

"Have I forgotten anything?" He was somber.

Annie wanted to grip his shoulders and tell him he wasn't responsible for anything that had happened. It was Britt who had called everyone to Golden Silk. Max had warned against her plan, but she'd made it clear she intended to proceed with or without him.

Who was to know what difference his presence and Annie's had made on the island? It was quite possible that Max's immediate response to Everett's murder, his careful collection of evidence, and now his painstaking re-creation of the day's events might yet play a big role in solving both the new crime and the old.

He had done the best he could. But this wasn't the moment to try to free him from the burden of Everett's death.

Annie tapped the sheets into a neat pile. "It's all here. Everything."

"And here's this." He handed her another sheet.

Annie took it, read quickly:

CRITICAL FACTS AT A GLANCE

1. Britt Barlow admits removing a wire strung across the top of the stairs that caused Jeremiah Addison's fatal fall last year.
2. Everett Crenshaw saw Britt remove the wire.
3. He sent Britt a letter suggesting he felt compelled to notify the police.
4. In response, Britt invited Crenshaw and everyone else who was present when Jeremiah died to return to Golden Silk this weekend.
5. Britt hired Max Darling of Confidential Commissions to assist her in her efforts to discover who set the trap for Jeremiah.
6. Crenshaw revealed the true purpose of the gathering at dinner last night.
7. Several times both after dinner and at breakfast this morning Crenshaw suggested he was privy to more information than he had

publicly revealed. It seems clear he knew the identity of Jeremiah's murderer and intended to use that information to his own advantage, but the murderer silenced him.

8. The shot that killed Everett Crenshaw was heard at approximately 10:30 a.m. by Britt Barlow, Annie Darling, and Max Darling.

9. Claimed location of weekend guests and employees at 10:30 a.m.:

Isabel Addison (Cabin 1)—En route to Cabin 7.

Millicent McRae (Cabin 2)—On path from her cabin to central pathway. (See attached drawing. Envision cabins on a clock face, Cabin 1 at 10 a.m. An outer path links the cabins in a circle. Individual paths, like spokes in a wheel, lead to the main path that bisects the circle.)

Nick McRae (Cabin 2)—On central pathway walking toward the beach.

Dana Addison (Cabin 4)—Searching for husband, cannot pinpoint location.

Jay Addison (Cabin 4)—At the northeast end of the island on the remains of a wrecked freighter.

Kim Kennedy (Cabin 5)—Taking a photograph in the living room of Harry Lyle's quarters. The timing device in the digital camera proves her presence there at the time Crenshaw was shot.

Gerald Gamble (Cabin 6)—In his cabin, completing his report on the weekend Jeremiah Addison died.

Craig Addison (Cabin 7)—Walking on the beach.

Lucinda Phillips—Cleaning Cabin 7 or en route to Cabin 6.

Harry Lyle—Disappeared from the island Friday

night, taking the yacht The Yellow *Kid and the ham radio.*

10. A semiautomatic handgun, a Smith and Wesson .45 caliber, retrieved from bottom of lagoon. Dana Addison said she found the gun near the steps of their cabin (4) and threw it into the lagoon because the gun frightened her. She insists she had no knowledge of Crenshaw's death. Britt Barlow identified the gun as one that was stolen on Friday night from a locked desk drawer in the library.

11. Jay Addison stated he never saw Crenshaw after breakfast and knew nothing about the gun's presence at their cabin.

12. There was no trace in Crenshaw's cabin of the report he had been asked to write along with others about the weekend that Jeremiah Addison died. Serrated edges indicate pages had been removed from the legal pad found on the coffee table. (Britt Barlow had earlier delivered new legal pads to each cabin.) Moreover, material Everett had gathered about those present on the island was also missing.

13. A handgun (Colt .45, Lightweight Commander model, silver finish) was stolen from the room of Max Darling sometime between breakfast Saturday and Mrs. Darling's return to the room at approximately 10:45 a.m. Information gathered by Darling prior to arrival on the island was also taken. Neither the gun nor the papers have been found.

Annie placed the fact sheet on top of Max's summary. She gave him a rueful smile. "Everything's there, but nothing points to the identity of the killer. It could be anyone."

"Not quite. We're in the clear and so are Britt and Kim," he said briskly. "That leaves Craig, Isabel, Jay, Dana, Millicent, Nick, Gerald, and Lucinda. Which one? We have to think about who they are as well as why each one wanted Jeremiah dead. Obviously Everett was killed because he threatened the murderer. We can't forget it all goes back to Jeremiah. Let's take Craig. His father ostensibly intended to groom him to take over the business. That obviously hadn't gone well. In fact, Jeremiah had publicly humiliated him. When you add this to the way Jeremiah treated his exwife, you had plenty of motive for Craig."

Annie knew this was true and that these facts were why Craig's wife had suspected a struggle between father and son. She also knew what had happened since Everett's revelation about the wire at the top of the stairs. "Not Craig." Annie spoke with certainty. "No one knows him better than Isabel. She says there's no way Craig would set a trap."

Max slowly nodded. "That's exactly what Jay said. I heard Jay and Craig talking. Each one had suspected the other. But"—he looked skeptical—"if either one's guilty, he wouldn't admit it."

"Jay had the strongest motive." Annie knew that was true. "He's emotional enough to lose control of himself and kill somebody. But that's not what happened. Stringing a wire takes planning."

Max leaned forward, his face eager. "So did shooting

Everett. The gun was taken from the library sometime during the night on Friday. That means both Jeremiah's and Everett's murders were planned."

"I'd say Millicent McRae is a super planner." Or was. Annie wondered if the artful politician would ever completely recover from the trauma of this weekend. "Next to Jay, I think she was the most emotionally bruised by Jeremiah. She'd do anything to try and save her marriage."

"And how badly did Nick McRae want to avoid public disclosure of his wife's affair?" Max pulled the legal pad close, wrote swiftly.

Annie watched. "If you're listing them in order of likelihood, I'd put Isabel and Dana last. Isabel thought Craig was guilty all year. If she'd killed Jeremiah, she wouldn't have left Craig."

Max shrugged. "Unless she couldn't deal with her guilt after it was done. As for Dana, she resented the way Jeremiah treated Jay and she was very bitter over their financial strain from taking care of Lorraine."

Annie sighed. "Okay. I guess they have to stay on the list, but I'd put them at the bottom."

"Along with Lucinda. There's never been any suggestion she had any reason to kill Jeremiah. That leaves Gerald. Jeremiah implied he was gay. Gerald was furious with him." Max finished writing, then read aloud, "Suspects in order of probability on the basis of motive and personality and opportunity: Jay Addison, Millicent McRae, Nick McRae, Craig Addison, Gerald Gamble, Dana Addison, Isabel Addison, Lucinda Phillips."

Annie heard the names and had a quick picture of

each in her mind as she'd seen them downstairs—Lucinda's voice lifted in thankful song, Millicent and Nick obviously reconciled and thinking only of each other, Craig and Isabel subdued but radiating hope and peace, Jay clearly reassuring Dana, which suggested he expected suspicion but wasn't afraid, Dana uneasy but gaining confidence, Gerald immersed in the elegant, uplifting music.

"I don't believe it!" She was emphatic. "Max, I just saw them and there's no doubt they're all relieved. They're glad the Coast Guard is coming. All of them. I know it doesn't make sense, but I can't imagine a single one of them being the murderer."

Max spread out his hands palms up. "We have to deal with facts, Annie."

She wanted to disagree, but he was right. One of them. It had to be one of them . . .

The clock chimed the three-quarter hour. Max gathered up the papers, stood. His face was weary and troubled.

Annie pushed back her chair, rushed around the table, gave him a swift, hard hug. "Don't blame yourself," she said softly. "You did your best."

He rested his face against the top of her head. "Not good enough, honey." He took a deep breath, stepped back. "Anyway, we've got plenty to give to the sheriff." He frowned. "I want to be extra careful"—he jerked his head toward the tackle box sitting on the bed—"with the gun." He glanced toward their suitcase and the carryall that had held his gun. The carryall lay where Annie had dropped it that morning when she turned it upside down to be certain it was empty. "I doubt there are any finger-prints—"

Annie was sure the murderer had worn gloves. She felt a sudden chill. Only a few hours ago the murderer had entered their room, moved with purposeful steps, and taken not only Max's information about the suspects but the gun that should have served as their protection. Annie imagined a swift-moving figure, but there was no form and no face, only menace and danger. She pressed her lips together. There was no need now to be afraid. Help was on the way.

"—but there might be. I'll use a washcloth and put it in—" He paused, looked around the room. His face brightened. "—one of our pillowcases. I want to be sure all this stuff reaches the sheriff." He glanced toward the dark windows, night pressing against them. "I don't expect an ambush between here and the dock, but it won't hurt to ask Loomis to help out. Between the two of us, everything should be safe enough."

Annie grinned. "Do I get just a hint that you don't find me qualified for guard duty?"

Max grinned back. "You are not, thank God, six feet tall with muscles."

Annie wasn't offended. Besides, she didn't want to touch the tackle box. That brought her way too close to a murder weapon. "He's down in the library with Britt. I'll get him."

Annie again felt invisible when she reached the central hallway. She'd not been upstairs long but everyone remained where she'd last seen them, Kim bent over her work at the farthest table in the dining room, Millicent and Nick in their chairs near the front door, the Addison brothers and their wives occupying twin alcoves in the drawing room, Gerald at the piano, now playing Cole Porter's "Night and Day." Lucinda was likely still in the kitchen, completing preparations to serve their rescuers.

Annie felt amazingly carefree. She turned and walked toward the library. Heron House no longer held any threat or danger. Rescue was now certain. As soon as the Coast Guard launch arrived, Max's responsibility ended. Of course, she and Max would be called upon to report what they knew and everything they had observed, but they would no longer be responsible for anyone's safety. Max's summary contained every fact and supposition that could possibly aid in the investigation.

She was smiling when she reached the library door. As she lifted her hand to knock, the door moved inward a trace.

Loomis Mitchell's voice was very near. He had to be standing on the opposite side of the door, his hand on the knob. He'd opened the door that fraction.

Annie stepped back a pace, but she couldn't help hearing.

"Why didn't you call me when you got that letter?" Loomis sounded bewildered, forlorn. "For God's sake, Britt, how could you keep something like that from me? When I think of the things I've told you . . . I thought we'd come to an understanding. Maybe we hadn't put it in words, but I thought you and I would face things together, the good and the bad. But I guess not."

"Loomis." Britt's voice wavered. "Oh God, Loomis, I didn't want you to know. Can't you understand? I didn't want you to know what I'd done. But when I got that letter, I had to do something. Everett wanted money, of course." Her tone was bitter. "It was such a smarmy letter, saying he'd been thinking about everything and he felt that he had to get in touch with the police, tell them what he'd seen. I had to respond, but I didn't want to involve you. I hoped I could see it through, figure out what had happened to Jeremiah, make it where you and I could be together and there wouldn't be anything that could come between us. If I'd paid him off, there would never have been an end to it."

"Paid him?" Loomis was shocked.

"Oh, it was blackmail, pure and simple," she said grimly. "I wasn't going to be blackmailed."

"You should have called me." The hurt was clear.

"I couldn't." A chair scraped. Steps sounded. "I was ashamed." Now her voice was near.

There was a long, strained pause. Loomis said suddenly, "Oh hell, Britt, I understand how it happened. Cissy was sick. You didn't want the place overrun with police. You bought her peace. I'd have done the same thing myself. And obviously you had to respond when you got that letter. But I don't think I'll ever understand why you did it without me. You should have known I'd have helped. If nothing else, I could have kept you from putting together this crazy scheme. I'd have insisted we go to the police, put everything out in the open. Instead, here you are with another death. Why didn't this detective you hired make it plain what kind of danger was involved?"

Annie bristled. She lifted her hand to rap on the door.

Britt was subdued. "He warned me. Actually, he turned me down, wouldn't take the job. When I made it clear I intended to go ahead, that's when he agreed to come."

The grandfather clock in the hallway, only a few feet from Annie, began to chime seven o'clock. Time was running out. Annie heard steps on the stairs. Max was on his way down. And she hadn't spoken yet to Loomis. She knocked.

The door swung in. Loomis and Britt stood only a foot or so apart, but there was the sense of a wide gulf. Loomis's face was long and somber. He looked as if he was thinking hard and the thoughts were unpleasant. Britt clasped her hands tightly together. Her face looked sharp and pinched. There was an angry spark in her eyes.

Annie wondered briefly if Britt would ever be able to assuage Loomis's feeling of exclusion. Perhaps nothing tests love as much as what a lover doesn't share. Complete love, complete honesty? Perhaps Britt would someday persuade him that love seeks always to protect its object. Maybe she would succeed. Maybe not. But now . . . "Loomis, Max would appreciate help in keeping watch over the evidence. He wants to take the tackle box and some other things down to the dock."

Loomis seemed to welcome her arrival. He moved past her. "Sure. I'll be glad to help."

Max reached the hallway and saw them. He stopped at the foot of the stairs, holding the tackle box, a filled pillowcase resting on top, papers in a folder beneath his arm. "Thanks, Loomis. If you'll take the pillowcase and folder, I'd appreciate it. I want to have everything on the dock when they get here."

Annie loved Max's voice, its resonance and tone. He was always easy to hear. In fact, he was loud. His words boomed in the hallway and carried into the dining room and drawing room.

Millicent looked up eagerly. "Has the boat arrived?" She came to her feet and Nick rose too.

Max was upbeat. "It's due any time now."

Nick moved stiffly to the coat tree, pulled down two coats. He turned back toward Millicent. She came forward, slipped into her coat.

Kim was across the dining room in a flash, shrugging into a quilted jacket. She carried a camera in one hand, a flashlight in the other. The swinging door banged from the kitchen and Lucinda called out, "Wait up, everybody. I'm coming too. I'll get my coat," and the door swung shut.

The piano stopped. Gerald strolled forward. "Are we all going down to be a welcoming committee?" He picked up a leather coat from a mahogany bench.

Dana tugged on Jay's hand. "Let's go too. Maybe they'll take us back to the mainland now."

Craig took Isabel's arm. "I should be there. Come on, I don't want you to stay here by yourself."

In the midst of the flurry, Loomis reached Max. Loomis took the pillowcase and folder. Carrying the tackle box under his arm, Max strode to the front door. "Come one, come all."

Annie started forward, then stopped as the misty

cool air swept inside. She heard the rattle of magnolia leaves. The wind was up. It would be even colder now than it had been earlier on the pier. Annie turned, headed for the back door.

Britt was standing in the doorway to the library. "Where are you going?"

"I need to get my jacket." Annie pointed toward the door. "The carts are out there, aren't they?" That's where Britt had parked when she and Annie hurried up before lunch to tell Max about the splash when Dana threw something into the lagoon. "I left my jacket in the cart. It won't take a minute to get it."

Britt stepped into the hall. "There are extra coats in the hall closet. Wait, I'll get one for you."

Annie was already at the door. She said, "No, really, that's okay," then opened the door, started down the steps. They were moist and slick in the damp air. Light spilled from the open doorway and from the windows of the kitchen. Two carts were parked side by side perhaps twenty feet from the back steps. Annie hurried across the uneven ground. It was cold enough that she shivered. But in just a moment, she'd be warm. She stopped behind the carts, uncertain which one she'd used earlier that day.

Footsteps sounded behind her. She glanced back. "Oh, you didn't have to come. I'll catch up with everyone." She took two quick steps to the farther cart. Her jacket was bunched up in the back beneath a laundry bag. She leaned forward, grabbed the jacket, pulled. The duffel shifted but the jacket was still held fast by something heavy. She used both hands, tugged again. A dark shape moved, tilted, and fell out of the cart, landing with a dull smack on the ground. "I'm sorry. I hope I haven't broken anything." She pulled on her jacket, then bent and picked up the object. She lifted it into the light from the kitchen window. Was it a radio? Oh, a portable radio . . . There was a whirring sound. She must have pushed some button when she touched it. She stared at the bottom row of buttons, remembered a portable radio she'd once had, a radio and tape player and tape recorder . . .

Abruptly, the machine was yanked out of her hands. There was swift movement, a click, the sound stopped.

A tape recorder. That was odd. Earlier Britt had told Craig there was a tape recorder in the library when Craig wanted to record a message to help in their search for Jay. Gerald had gone to get it, but the tape recorder wasn't to be found. Britt had gone and looked, too, and she hadn't found it either. Instead Craig had carried the mounted ship's bell with him, ringing it over and over again. Now Annie had found the tape recorder in one of the cleaning carts.

Annie turned. The words she'd started to say died in her throat.

A scant foot away, Britt stared at Annie, her face implacable, a pale oval of concentrated hatred and fury. Tucked under one arm was the tape recorder, silent now. Britt held a shiny silver gun—Max's missing gun—in her right hand. She held it steady, the barrel pointed at Annie's heart. She moved closer to the cart and slipped the tape recorder beneath the laundry bag without taking her eyes away from Annie.

Annie felt as if a giant's fist had fastened on her

heart. It was utterly quiet in the backyard. There was no one near. No one at all. She saw death in Britt's cold stare. One squeeze of Britt's finger and a shot would explode. Annie would fall as Everett had fallen, flesh and blood spewing, life wrenched away.

Britt's arm began to straighten. Any instant now . . .

Annie forced the words from a throat tightened by terror. "They'll hear the shot." Her voice was thin but sharp. She said it again. And again. Dear God, how much time had passed? It seemed an eon ago that she'd clattered down the steps of the back stairs, intent upon warmth. Actually only a minute or two had passed. The others would be just a little way down the front walk en route to the dock. They would hear a shot, oh yes, my God, they would hear! "They'll hear the shot!" Her voice was loud, taking strength from the only fact that could save her. "Everyone's together." Now the words stampeded, loud, harsh, certain, rushing over each other, pelting Britt, David's stones against Goliath. "You'll be the only one who could have done it. They'll know you're the one."

The pointed gun remained steady. Burning eyes watched Annie. Lips moved soundlessly.

"They'll know it's you." Annie wagered her life on a flickering hope of delay. "You can't shoot me."

There was a squeak as the back door opened. Lucinda stood on the porch, bulky in a red quilted jacket. "I thought I saw you two come out here. That's a good idea to take a cart. I'll do that too. It's too dark to be walking anywhere and besides I'm tired and ready to ride."

Britt moved fast. She came around the back of the second cart, stood next to Annie, pressed the gun to her back. Her voice was low. "Not a word from you. If you make any sound, I'll kill you both. Get into the cart. The passenger side."

Annie walked slowly and stiffly, slid into the right side of the cart. Her throat ached. She wanted to cry out, but Britt meant every word. She was a killer. Did it matter to her that there was scarcely a chance now for her to escape? Would she kill in anger at her failure? Annie had no doubt that she would kill again without qualm or hesitation if provoked.

Lucinda, talking a mile a minute, reached the other cart. She plopped into the seat. The cart hummed into motion. ". . . sure going to be glad to see the Coast Guard. I don't know when I've spent a worse time than this. Look into a face and all you see is a smile but one face is a lie. . . ."

Britt eased into the cart. She used her left hand with the key and the wheel. The right hand with the gun was turned toward Annie. "Put your hands in your pockets. Keep them there." The first cart chugged out of the backyard. Lucinda was perhaps ten feet ahead of them. "I've only got one chance. There aren't enough bullets to kill everyone. And Loomis . . ." Just for an instant there was pain in her voice, a deep and abiding agony. Then once again, clipped quick words. "I've got to get away. I'll take Loomis's boat. Don't try any heroics. If you do anything to warn them, I'll shoot Max first. That's a promise. I keep promises."

Annie pressed against the side of the cart. She'd

known fear. Now horror flooded her. Max. Oh God, could she keep him safe? She'd be quiet. Of course she would. Whatever it took, that was what she'd do. Blood thrummed in her ears. Britt meant every word. She spoke in the low voice that Annie had once thought attractive, a husky, memorable voice. The words were at such a hideous variance from the cultivated tone. Annie knew the only way to keep Max and the others safe was to placate Britt. Could she possibly get past the overweening ego of a killer and convince Britt that her situation was hopeless? "They'll know it's you." They would know that Britt was the murderer. Everett had seen her remove the wire that killed her sister's husband. He'd assumed she was the murderer. He was right. Britt had said she'd heard Jeremiah fall. And when she had come to the stairs, she had looked down to see if he was dead. But if he'd survived the fall, she would have hurried down the steps to finish her task. As it was, the hard marble had killed him. She'd waited. When no one had come, she had removed all traces of murder.

"Everett saw you. You set the trap. You killed Jeremiah." And Britt's dying sister outlived Jeremiah to provide Britt with a magnificent inheritance and the money to pay debts that had to be paid. "We thought Everett was shot when you were with us. He was already dead, wasn't he?"

"Damn you." Britt's voice quivered with rage. "Everything worked perfectly. Until you went to the cart tonight."

The wind whipped the live oak branches that arched overhead. The dark tunnel to the dock was cold and black. Annie couldn't see the gun, but she knew it was aimed at her. Every second took them nearer to the others. And to Max.

Annie's jacket had snagged on the tape recorder, the telltale tape recorder. "You rigged that shot." Annie remembered the single loud report as they trundled along the path to Everett's cabin, how shocked they'd been and frightened, their instinctive duck for cover. She and Max were both participants and audience for a performance carefully crafted by Britt. "That's why Lucinda heard gunshots when no one was on the island. You were practicing, taping each shot, then running the recorder, seeing how to get the loudest sound. That means you were going to kill Everett right from the start. You planned everything before you invited anyone back to the island. You intended to kill Everett before you ever came to see Max."

"Oh, yes." There was arrogant pride in Britt's answer. "It was easy. I persuaded Everett I was innocent and I was going to let him in on a great murder hunt, a surefire boost to his ratings. Everything was planned. I asked him to accuse me after dinner. I told him he'd make the real murderer nervous and we'd get some action going. We did, didn't we?" The cart was nearing the end of the live oak avenue. "Everything went like clockwork. I made a great tape of the gunshot. Last night—that's when you saw me in the garden—I put the player in a tree near the cabin and left it with the volume turned up. I timed it to turn on at ten-thirty this morning. I got us there just the right moment. That's why I stopped the cart in the path and talked. I figured everything perfectly. I got Craig to ask everyone to write a report on Jeremiah. That gave me a reason to go to each cabin with a legal pad. That's when I shot Everett. I used a silencer, so no one heard that shot. It would have worked except for *you*," she concluded bitterly.

Annie knew that the woman beside her wanted to shoot, wanted it with every warped fiber of her being. Somehow Annie forced out words though her throat was tight and her chest ached and she felt the cold, dank breath of death. "A silencer. That was clever. Is that why you took the gun away after you shot him? Because it had the silencer on it?"

"Of course. Besides, I wanted to put the gun where it would do me the most good. I took the silencer off and ran to Jay and Dana's cabin and left the gun. I knew they were waiting for me at the lagoon. Don't you see? Everything worked together. I dropped the silencer in the fountain pool on my way to the lagoon. There was nothing to connect me to Everett's death except the tape recorder. I picked it up when Max sent me around to get the reports. I didn't have a chance to get rid of it after that. I was going to do it tonight. There shouldn't have been any hurry. Why would anyone look in the back of the cleaning cart?" A pause, then the gritted, angry curse: "Damn you."

The tape recorder with its damning echo of a gunshot destroyed her alibi. She could not afford to have it found. At her leisure, she would have been able to erase the tape. But Britt had never been alone after she and Annie met at Jay and Dana's cabin.

Annie saw how everything had happened. She didn't

understand why. "Why did you shoot him? If you'd persuaded him you were innocent, he wasn't a threat."

Britt's laughter was quick. And cold. "He wasn't a threat. I could handle him without any trouble. But the sheriff might not have been so gullible. He might have been very interested in the wire and my removal of it. My only hope was to help catch the 'murderer' or somehow prove I couldn't be guilty." Her ripple of laughter was pleased and satisfied. "That's what I did. If Everett died and everyone was convinced he died because he knew the identity of the murderer, and if I had an alibi for the moment of his death, I was safe. And I would have been. Except for you."

They reached the end of the tunnel. The ground sloped away, a gravel walk leading to the pier. The cart slowed, stopped. Britt turned toward Annie. It was too dark to see her face, but Annie knew Britt watched her every move. "We'll get out at the dock. We'll walk together. No one will pay any attention. You're not to call out. If you do, I'll shoot him, then you." The cart lurched ahead.

Annie didn't need to ask whom Britt meant. If only Max remained absorbed in looking for the Coast Guard cutter. There might be safety in numbers; they would all be there, clustered at the end of the dock. And death would walk toward them.

Annie was only dimly aware of the cart's rattling onto the pier. She was terribly attuned to the taut, dangerous woman so near her, the anger that drove her, the merciless self-absorption that would see Annie's life end without a quiver of remorse. The cart stopped.

Annie felt a harsh poke against her side. She stepped out onto the pier. She tried not to tremble.

Max leaned against a railing at the end, looking out to the Sound. "I think I see running lights. Look to the west." Max's voice was clear and strong. Annie drew the sound deep into her heart. These might be the last words she ever heard from him. Dear Max. Light of her life. They had laughed in the sunshine, always the two of them together. Together they could meet any challenge. . . .

Dark figures moved toward Max, everyone intent upon glimpsing the arriving ship.

"Hurry." The word was tight and harsh. Annie felt Britt's terrible urgency in another sharp jab of the gun. "Not a word, not a sound . . ."

Annie and Britt walked together, their steps a sharp clatter against the wood. Annie had eyes only for Max. *Goodbye. God love you, keep you safe, guide your steps, salve your sorrow.* She was beyond tears. There was nothing now but the ache of finality, the sweetness of memory, the emptiness of farewell. He was so near and yet he was now forever beyond her touch and call. They were almost to the end of the pier, nearing the ladder down to Loomis's boat, when Max abruptly turned.

Annie knew some instinct touched him, some primal fear.

Max jerked around, shouted, "Annie?" He started toward them.

Annie's cry was harsh. "Max, no! Stop!" She drew herself together, felt her muscles straining, ready to fling herself in front of the gun. But the gun was pressed against the back of her head now.

"Don't move, anyone. I'll shoot her." Britt's high, thin voice was almost unrecognizable.

Millicent screamed. Nick moved to shield her. Jay pushed Dana behind him. Craig stepped in front of Isabel. Gerald hunched in a fighting posture. "Oh my God," Lucinda wailed.

Annie heard Britt's short quick breaths but the pressure of the barrel was rock steady.

"Britt . . . Oh my God, what are you saying?" Loomis took a step forward, held out a seeking hand. He stood near the single light at the end of the pier. His face was stricken, drawn in anguish and horror and disbelief.

Britt choked back a sob. "Loomis, please. Don't look at me like that."

"Britt." He took another step. He looked sick and shaken.

"She killed them." Lucinda's voice was high and shrill.

"Britt, say it's not true." Loomis's voice was faint.

Britt shuddered but still the gun pressed against Annie. "Loomis, I didn't have any choice. I did what I had to do. For Cissy. I had to get rid of Jeremiah. He was going to send me away. Cissy needed me. She was dying and he was going to throw me out. I hated him. He was selfish and mean and cruel. Then Everett tried to blackmail me. I couldn't let him do that."

Loomis took one step, another. "I don't believe it. Not you. Oh, Britt." It was a cry of loss.

"I've got to get away." She sounded feverish. "Everything would have worked except for her." She jabbed the gun against Annie's head.

Annie's head jolted forward. Could she turn, grab the gun before . . . No. Britt would shoot.

"I've got to get away," Britt said frantically. "I'm going to take your boat. You understand, don't you?"

The pressure of the gun eased. Annie felt dizzy and sick.

Britt poked Annie in the back. "This way. To the ladder."

In a grotesque sideways lockstep, Annie and Britt moved toward the ladder. When they reached it, Britt held the gun steady on Annie. "Listen to me, everyone. Stay where you are. She's going down the ladder first, then me. If anyone comes after us, I shoot her, then the first person I see. All right, Annie."

Annie looked at Max. This was goodbye. Britt would keep her alive only long enough to get away from Golden Silk. No longer. She saw the anguish in his face.

So did Britt.

"One step and she's dead." The words were sharp as ice slivers.

Max stood frozen, face twisted in horror, hands outstretched.

"Hurry." Britt's order was brusque, imperative.

Annie reached the edge of the dock, swung around to back down the ladder.

The only sounds were the slap of water against the pilings and Britt's ragged breaths. Then came the click of shoes on the dock.

"Britt, don't do this. Please." Loomis walked toward her.

Annie stopped, hands tight on the ladder. She was

nearest Britt. She saw a dead-white face leached of life and hope.

"Give me the gun. End this now, Britt." The words drifted light as winter leaves before a January breeze.

"There are lights!" It was a scream from Lucinda. "Out there. They're coming. The Coast Guard."

Annie saw every vestige of pride and anger collapse into nothingness. Britt said, "Loomis," a farewell to love and life.

She raised the gun to her head and fired.

∴ *Twelve* ∴

As INGRID WEBB LOCKED the front door of Death on Demand, signaling the official end of the author event, Emma Clyde's cold blue eyes appraised the stack of books remaining at one side of the table near the fireplace. "I expected to sell out." Her tone was frosty. She sat in regal splendor in the high-backed signing chair, colorful in an aquamarine velour caftan, her short silver hair spiky as an irritated porcupine's, her square-jawed face demanding.

Annie restrained herself from strangling the island's most successful—and impossible—mystery writer. They'd sold 186 copies of *The Plight of the Panicked Panther*. That was amazing for an early February signing. Moreover, had they sold out—God forbid—Emma would have been at her throat for not ordering enough copies! Annie felt her cheeks burn.

Laurel Roethke clapped her hands. "Family, friends, Islanders, mystery aficionados, we gather here today . . ." She paused, tipped her head in thought, her golden hair softly swirling.

Annie shifted her glare to Laurel, immediately began to smile. Max's mother might be spacey as a moon launch, but she was also the soul of tact, and she was now hastening to fling herself, metaphorically speaking, between an enraged bookseller and an intractable author. Dear Laurel.

Laurel's glance was suddenly sober. ". . . to celebrate not only the launch of Emma's wonderful new book, surely one of the most brilliantly plotted mysteries ever—" Her tone was reverential.

Emma shifted in the throne chair, rather like a peacock adjusting spectacular plumage, a satisfied smile warming her glacial features.

"—but to give thanks for the remarkable escape of our own dear—and very brave—Annie from near death." Laurel's blue eyes softened with tears.

Annie drew a sharp breath. She'd not expected to survive. . . .

Emma's eyes glittered. She sat forward, pointed a stubby, commanding finger. "All I know is what I heard on TV. Tell us."

Voices rose with eager questions.

Annie looked around the coffee area, safe in her own wonderful, adored bookstore. She looked into faces filled with concern and love. Everyone was here, home from their travels. Ingrid straightened a stack of Emma's books. Pudge held Sylvia's hand tight in his. Rachel and Cole, tanned from their days on the beach, sipped hot chocolate. Henny gripped the head of the walking stick she'd brought home from England.

And Max, of course. She looked at him, her eyes aglow. She and Max here at Death on Demand, against all odds. They too were home from a journey, a frightful sojourn that had almost cost her life. She remembered her eagerness to escape the tedium of winter and how pleased she'd been to go to Golden Silk. "It all started when Britt Barlow came to see Max. . . ."

Annie talked fast and sometimes Max told his part. Then, her throat tight with remembered horror, she said, "And she was pointing the gun at me and I knew if I got on the boat I was doomed."

"Oooooh!" Rachel clapped her hands over her mouth. Her eyes were huge in a gamine face. "Annie, how awful!"

Cole nudged her with the toe of his sneaker. "Oh, come on, Rachel." Her new stepbrother and bosom buddy and most vociferous champion if there were a need wasn't big on histrionics. "Annie's fine. I mean, look, she's right there in front of the fire." He gestured at Annie standing near the mantel.

Annie reached out a hand. She couldn't describe those final moments, the pressure of the gun, the muted cry that Britt gave as she backed away from Loomis's seeking hand, the terrible fear that pulsed on that cold, windy pier.

Max came quickly, slipped his arm around her shoulders. "We owe everything to Loomis Mitchell." He bent his head, pressed his cheek against Annie's hair.

There had been a moment of stricken shock after Britt turned the gun on herself, then screams and cries and the sadness of watching Loomis kneel beside the dying Britt. Annie couldn't remember much of what followed, but she would never forget Max's shout and how he stormed across the dock and how tight he held her. As if he'd never let her go.

Emma's gruff voice was pontifical. "As Marigold

said in *The Curse of the Crimson Calliope:* Even the
wiliest of foes cannot guard against the uncaring winds
of mischance."

Annie forced her hands to remain lax. It wouldn't
do for a bookseller to maim a bestselling author. But
Annie simply writhed with loathing when Emma began
to quote her obnoxious (to Annie) protagonist Marigold Rembrandt.

There was a short silence. Emma, of course, accepted the quiet as homage to Marigold's wisdom.
They all knew who had created Marigold. . . .

Once again Laurel's effervescence transformed the
moment. "Dear Marigold. She is an inspiration to all of
us. Just like our dear Annie. A salute to Annie!"

Cheers rose. Applause was brisk.

Emma, perhaps satisfied that Marigold and she had
been duly admired, was only a trifle grudging in her
accolade. "Of course Annie played a role in the resolution. Thanks to Annie, retribution has been exacted.
Annie"—an imperious nod—"I salute you. Though I
must say you and Max were babes in the woods. The
next time"—sardonic blue eyes touched Max—"a
beautiful damsel approaches Confidential Commissions with a tale of murder observed and a claim of
innocence, I recommend a hearty dose of skepticism."

Max stood his ground, though his ears reddened. "I
suppose you would have figured it out from the start."

Emma pushed up from the chair and the velour caftan rippled and swirled, majestic as a queen's cloak. "I
doubt I would have fallen for her story hook, line, and
sinker." Emma's eyes widened. There was an electric
pause. *"Hook, Line and Sinker.* A great title!"

Annie knew they were present at the beginning of Emma Clyde's next novel.

A huge smile wreathed the author's square face. She beamed at Annie in high good humor, disappointment over the paltry—to her—sales dismissed. Emma gazed around the gathering. "This has been most instructive."

Annie felt only a tiny quiver of irritation at realizing her deadly peril had served to fan Emma's creative juices. Emma was Emma.

"And"—Emma nodded toward the watercolors above the fireplace—"I commend you for your taste."

Annie looked up with pride. "No one's figured out the January titles. I've decided to leave them up for another month."

"No need," Emma said crisply. She identified them in turn. "*Chronicle of a Death Foretold* by Gabriel García Márquez, *Little Indiscretions* by Carmen Posadas, *The No. 1 Ladies Detective Agency* by Alexander McCall Smith, *The Sirens Sang of Murder* by Sarah Caudwell, and *Death in Zanzibar* by M. M. Kaye."

On that note of triumph, the redoubtable author swept toward the front door.

Annie took a deep breath and joined in the chorus of admiring farewells. After all, Emma was Emma! But Annie made a vow to herself. She'd be damned if she'd hold a signing for *Hook, Line and Sinker* at Death on Demand!

Can't wait to see what's next for Annie and Max?

Turn the page for a sneak peek at the next Death on Demand Mystery,

DEAD DAYS OF SUMMER

**All it took to change Annie's life was a quick phone call from her husband.
Now a woman is dead, Max is missing, and it's up to Annie to convince the world her husband didn't commit the perfect crime before he become the next victim. . . .**

∾ *One* ∾

THE MOON BROKE FREE from the low-lying bank of clouds, revealing the white crests of breaking surf. Pinpoints of light sparkled at water's edge, the luminescent glow of tiny zooplankton. Humid summer air lay over land and sea heavy as a funeral pall. Waves boomed and water surged around the pilings of the fishing pier. Footsteps echoed as a shadowy figure walked alone to the end of the pier, reached out to grip the railing. The grasp was tight, unrelenting.

Anger burned, scalding and uncontrolled. The thought came, words vivid as scarlet neon: She had to die.

Resolution provided release. Taut muscles eased. The hands fell away.

She had to die.

Vanessa Taylor surveyed the dimly lit restaurant with satisfaction. Not a woman she saw could match her for beauty. Vanessa felt exultant. Everything she wanted was within her grasp. She looked across the table at her companion. Her richly red lips curved in a cat-in-the-cream smile.

He reached into the pocket of his blazer, pulled out a photograph, handed it to her. His eyes were intent, though he managed a smile. "Think you can handle it?"

She glanced at the photograph. "Of course. And once it's done, we'll be together. Everything will be wonderful." She lifted her wineglass. "To us."

He raised his glass, dark head bent forward.

Vanessa drank every drop and laughed aloud.

The burst of laughter turned the head of a nearby diner, a tired single-mom real estate agent out for an evening with a chattering group of friends. She rubbed an aching temple. God, to be young again, to be happy and confident, to be triumphant. Not to be worried about the slowdown in house sales and the ugly whispers that real estate might be the next bubble to burst. Not to be frantic about her son Mike and his thirteen-year-old girlfriend who wore her blouses too tight and her shorts too short. Not to be fearful that her mom was making less and less sense. Not to be tired to her bones, yet wake up in the night scared and anxious, sleepless until dawn. Too beaten down for envy, she stared at Vanessa, admiring the raven-black hair that curled in soft ringlets, the bold forceful features, the voluptuous body in the low-cut crimson dress.

The older woman sighed. If she ever had a dress like that, it would hang from her thin shoulders, making her look like a bony hag. Her face bleak, she watched as Vanessa dropped a snapshot into a small silver purse. The man with her watched attentively. He wasn't smiling. He looked intense and determined.

The observer wondered what that look meant. Was

he crazy about the girl who laughed with such delight? Probably. The single woman's face drooped. Nobody had looked across a table at her for more years than she wanted to remember. She felt a hot rush of tears, dipped her face until her hair swung forward. She was tired, so tired. She wished bitterly that she and the dark-haired woman in the beautiful red dress could change places. Just for one night.

Heather Whitman ignored the knock on her bedroom door. It came again, soft, inquiring, yet subdued. Heather pulled the pillow over her ears. But it was silent except for the rev of a motor in the drive in front of the house, the throaty purr of Jon's car. It must be close to noon. Her stepfather always took his own sweet time but he had no need to hurry to his office. Not since he'd married Mother. Of course, Mother always lauded him to the sky, said how lucky the island was to have a man of his caliber on the island, implying that he was so successful. Successful at marrying a really rich woman, that was for sure. Damn Jon. She didn't like him. He was always snide about Kyle. How many times had Jon brought up the flagpole flap? For God's sake, it was years ago when they were seniors in high school. Heather pushed away other moments when Kyle's daring and defiance landed him in trouble. And now . . . Could she overlook this last wild escapade? Oh damn, damn, damn.

Thoroughly awake, Heather rolled from the bed. She stopped at the vanity, yanked up a brush to pull at her tousled dark hair. She didn't look at her face. She was likely pale as a ghost with huge smudges beneath her eyes. Whenever she got upset, she looked like a wraith, all gray and silver, insubstantial as a ghost. She flung down the brush, walked to the French window. She pulled it wide, looked out at the familiar sweep of the gardens, brilliant with roses and hibiscus and bougainvillea. The wedding was supposed to be there at the gazebo. I, Heather, take thee, Kyle . . .

Was there going to be a wedding?

Lillian Whitman Dodd paused at the top of the steps, looked down the hall toward Heather's room. Perhaps she should go back, knock again. Clearly, Heather was upset. Lillian was surprised at her sudden feeling of dismay. That was odd. She should be overjoyed if this marriage didn't happen. She'd never tried to hide her dismay at the engagement. She'd hoped Heather would outgrow Kyle, but she had never looked at another boy, not from the first moment she met him. Admittedly Kyle was appealing with an impish charm and dark good looks, but he was a disaster waiting to happen. So why now did Lillian feel sadness for her daughter? Perhaps because passionate love is rare and when it happens it is worth fighting for. Just as she'd been determined to marry Jon despite Heather's opposition. Lillian had been certain Jon was the right man for her from the moment they'd met. He'd done such a fabulous job on the promotions for the Art League. He had such an eye for color and the charm of a successful public relations executive. How lucky she was that he'd chosen the island to start his own business. He'd spent so many years in much larger venues. Jon was enormously empathetic. He knew how troubled she was about Heather. It was too bad Heather disliked him. She needed a man's counsel. Not for the first time Lillian regretted Heather's romanticized memories of her father. Howard Whitman, wealthy, cultivated, charming . . . Lillian stood stiff and still at the top of the stairs. As always when she remembered Howard, she felt a curl of ice in her soul. How could she have been so wrong . . .

Maybelle Whittle carried her tray of cleaning supplies with an edge resting on one hip. She walked slowly across the room. Summer nights were good nights for the h'ants. That's what Dr. Fox said. Maybelle's mouth opened. She gulped in air. She always had trouble breathing when she thought of the wizened old man who lived in a dark tumbledown shack at the end of a twisty gray road on the other side of the island. Dr. Fox talked in a low voice as whispery as a cougar rustling through the forest about people who went against what was right and who treated people bad. Dr. Fox could make a root bag and those folks would do what you wanted. If they wouldn't do good, you could fix them where they'd never trouble you again. Her mind shied away from what he meant. That kind of talk could lead you into hell, that was what Aunt Esther said. But Maybelle knew there was truth in the old man's voice, no matter what her aunt said. Maybelle sighed. She'd better hurry or Aunt Esther would be scolding her for taking too long to see about the cottages. At least this one was empty and all it took was a lick and a promise. Maybelle opened the door, then stood still. Vanessa Taylor was going inside her cottage. A man stood on her porch, staring after her. Vanessa had closed the door so she didn't see his face convulse with rage. He stared at the shut door, his face ugly as sin, then turned on his heel, hurried down the steps.

Maybelle didn't stir. She couldn't move for the life of her. The memory of those glaring eyes and twisted lips were seared into her mind. She'd never thought white folks had the power, but sure as the tides rose and fell she knew what she'd seen. She'd seen the Evil Eye.

City Hall on Broward's Rock was a modest one-story building south of the police station. Justine Prior, the mayor's secretary, was the last person out of the office. She pulled the door shut, waggled the knob to be sure the lock caught. Not that they had to worry too much about crime. After all, the police were right next door. Justine glanced toward the station. Billy Cameron, the acting chief, and his wife Mavis, who served as secretary, dispatcher and all-around helper, were hurrying down the front steps of the station. Seemed like Billy and Mavis were always in a hurry, on their way to a ball game, a meeting, a church group, or dinner with friends. They were laughing.

Justine almost called out, then clamped her lips tight. Much as she loved Billy and Mavis, it would be worth her job if she tipped them off. What good would it do? Que sera sera.

Max Darling ambled along the boardwalk. The gentle breeze off the harbor ruffled his thick blond hair. His blue eyes held a reflection of laughter. He looked toward Annie, winked.

Annie Darling shot her husband an affectionate and just slightly impatient glance. Okay, okay. There really wasn't any hurry this gorgeous August afternoon. There was the easy hum of activity from the harbor where yachts and sailboats rode in the pea-green water. A sail was unfurled on a ketch-rig, an outboard choked and sputtered, sunburned guests lined the rails of a boat returning from a morning of deep-sea fishing. Along the boardwalk customers thronged the shops, buying everything necessary for a happy holiday, beachwear, Low Country baskets, jewelry, trinkets, and, of course, books. God was in his heaven and all was right with the world on the little South Carolina sea island of Broward's Rock.

The island was at its busiest during the dog days of August, teeming with tourists who needed beach books. The temperature was in the mid-nineties and the air squishy as melting asphalt. What was more cooling than relaxing in a beach chair beneath an umbrella with a wonderful mystery and a jug of iced tea? As proprietor of Death on Demand, the best mystery bookstore east of Atlanta, Annie was happy to oblige both with books and tea or coffee to go.

Annie was in a hurry to get back to the store. In fact, she'd been reluctant to take time for lunch though Max would certainly have been startled had she turned down an invitation to Parotti's Bar and Grill, her favorite restaurant in all the world. There were, of course, books to unpack and customers to welcome. Deliberately, she shied away from the real reason for her rush. This was no time for Max to pick up on her thoughts. She slowed to a saunter. Surely she could pretend to be as relaxed as Max. Sure she could. No problema. She'd play it cool and no way would Max realize she was in an itching, tearing, urgent hurry to get back to the store. She walked even slower.

Max slipped his arm around her shoulders, gave a squeeze. "Okay, what's the deal?"

Annie felt a moment of panic. Was all her hard work for naught? Had Max found out?

He lifted his hand, brushed her cheek gently with his knuckles. "Come on, Annie. If you were a microwave, you'd be pinging. A greyhound at the post couldn't be more ready to race. What gives? Is it the boxes you need to unpack? New books by Ridley Pearson, Lindsey Davis, Sharon Kahn, Rochelle Krich, right?"

She felt such a rush of tenderness she almost cried. Damn. How perfect could a husband be? So okay, Max could be dilatory and too laid-back and he and the notion of hard work had never meshed, but he was so attuned to her moods that her best effort to be casual didn't fool him for a minute. Of course, he assumed she was eager to get to Death on Demand because of the slew of boxes that had arrived late Friday. And he cared enough about her and her world that he'd even noted the names of the authors on the unopened boxes.

"Hey, I'll give you a hand." He jerked his head toward the dark windows of his office. "My place is slower than a funeral dirge. I told Barb to take the week off. She's gone shopping in Atlanta."

Annie stopped, planted her heels on the board-walk. Max at Death on Demand! Oh no. Not today of all days. "Max—" She gazed out at the bustling harbor, seeking inspiration. Almost all the slips were taken. Yachts plied the Inland Waterway in August, and Broward's Rock was a favorite stop. Slip 13 was empty. That was where island mystery author Emma Clyde moored Marigold's Pleasure, named in honor of her spinster detective Marigold Rembrandt. Empty. No one there . . . "—Honey," she beamed at him, "that would be great but you really shouldn't leave your office empty. Why, all kinds of people may need help."

She swept her hand at the front window where gold letters announced: Confidential Commissions. Max was quick to insist that he wasn't a private detective. The Sovereign State of South Carolina has specific and demanding requirements for private detective agencies. Max, however, was eager to solve problems, whatever they might be. No law against that.

Max's expression was quizzical.

Before he could pursue his suspicion, surely still nebulous, that Annie was trying to ditch him, she reached back to her acting days—and yes, she'd been off Broadway once with an improvisation troupe that, to put it kindly, never quite jelled—and launched a diversion. "Max, I was talking to your mom just the other day"—All right, it was two years ago but in Laurel Darling Roethke's madcap world, a year was a moment, a day simply a breath.—"and she said she'd had the strongest sense that you were fated to save someone"—Annie almost said *from a fate worse than,* then decided Max would believe many things about his mother but triteness wasn't one of them.—"from the most unexpected circumstances. What if today's the day!"

He intoned in a resonant voice reminiscent of The

Shadow. "Who knows what fate holds in store for us?"
Laurel had given him a collection of the radio serial for
Christmas. "Okay, I'll be at my duty station."

Max was still smiling as he stepped into the long,
narrow—and deadly quiet—front office. Barb's computer was shrouded with a plastic cover and there
were no delicious smells. Truth to tell, Confidential
Commissions was rarely overwhelmed with assign-
ments despite the tasteful ad that ran every day in the
personals column of the *Island Gazette:* Troubled,
puzzled, curious? Contact Confidential Commissions.
321-HELP

Max squinted thoughtfully. Maybe they needed to
jazz up the ad. Something like: You got troubles? Call
Max. He's The Man.

Anyway, for the moment, he had nothing on his
agenda. Not even a lost dog. And it was awfully quiet
without Barb. Barb wore her bouffant hair Texas style,
kept up a running chatter, and, to while away the time,
cooked up a variety of delectable messes, as she called
them. He missed the chatter and the food. Last week
Barb had baked brown sugar ice box cookies that sent
Annie into transports of joy, recalling them as a special
treat from her childhood.

He wandered slowly into his interior office, flipped
on the lights. Well, there was always his putter and
the indoor green Annie had given him. He sauntered
toward his desk, a massive Italian Renaissance table
that had likely once graced the dining hall of a refectory. He reached for the putter, conveniently stowed
in a stoneware receptable patterned after an elephant's

foot. Too bad he didn't have a case. It always pleased
Annie when he was busy. Well, maybe something
would happen this afternoon. He would hope for the
best. Maybe a good-looking girl would rush to him for
help, waving a treasure map she'd found in Grandma's
trunk. Blackbeard's gold . . . That would be fun . . .

The bell jangled at the front door.

Annie paused at the front window of Death on Demand. Should she change the display? Instead of
new releases, these were all collectibles that caught
the essence of past days as memorably as long-ago
photographs by Arthur Telfer or Charles J. Belden or
Chansonetta Emmons. The books lay faceup, some
scuffed and faded, but treasures still: *The Scarlet Pim-
pernel* by Countess Emma Orczy, *The Mystery of Dr.
Fu-Manchu* by Sax Rohmer, *The Moonstone* by Wilkie
Collins, *Suicide Excepted* by Cyril Hare, and *Blue
Fire* by Phyllis A. Whitney. Oh hey, she loved these
books, let them enjoy another moment in the sun. The
Countess's famous book was published in 1905. It was
fun to consider that a book published in 2005 by Janet
Evanovich or Faye Kellerman might grace a bookstore
window in 2105.

Besides, she didn't have time to think about a new
display. Not this week or next. She opened the door
and plunged inside. She didn't stop to admire her do-
main as was her usual custom, the table featuring New
Arrivals, Edgar, the stuffed black raven on his pedestal,
bookshelves slanting away from the central corridor,
hundreds of wonderful titles from Susan Wittig Albert
to Margaret Yorke, and the sofas and armchairs wait-

ing to cosset readers. Agatha, the elegant black cat who ruled the store, curled atop a red cushion. She languidly lifted her head, watched Annie with somnolent golden eyes. Hmm, Ingrid must have fed her a succulent lunch.

Annie detoured a few steps, stroked a sleepy Agatha, then bolted to the central cash desk, flung out her hands. "Ingrid, any word on the jazz band?"

Ingrid's iron-gray hair frizzed even without humidity. Bright blue ink smudged her green smock near the bookstore logo, a silver dagger with a red tip. She gestured with her pen. "It's a no-go. The band's van crashed into a seawall down in the Keys and they can't get here, not even by Saturday a week. Leader said probably they wouldn't get out of the Keys until some Saturday next year. He said they'll be playing in Key Largo until they are old men with long beards. But—" she spoke above Annie's wail "—not to worry. I've already talked to Ben—" Ben Parotti, owner of Parotti's Bar and Grill as well as the ferry and a good deal of island real estate "—and he said his wife's nephew who's a deejay in Savannah had a cancellation by the Jaycees for that Saturday and he's got a thousand—well, maybe a hundred—CDS with songs from the Twenties and he'll handle everything."

Annie leaned against the counter in relief. "Oh golly, Ingrid, that's great. I mean, I'd rather have a band. They had bands in the Twenties, no CDs, but with only eleven days to go I guess I'd better settle for—"

The telephone rang. Ingrid scooped up the receiver. "Death on Demand, the finest mystery bookstore east of—Oh hi, Laurel. Annie?" Ingrid shot a questioning look at her boss.

Annie hesitated. But Max's mother had antenna that rivaled a praying mantis and she probably knew—Annie determinedly refused to ponder her mother-in-law's uncanny gift for ascertaining Annie's thoughts, whereabouts and attitudes—that Annie was standing within a foot of the phone. Annie took the receiver. "Laurel, hi." Her tone was so effusive Laurel would know she'd debated not answering. Oh well . . .

"My dear, I felt compelled to call." The husky voice gamboled. Those who doubt that voices gambol had never listened to Laurel Darling Roethke. Laurel delivered every utterance with such elan that a listener could not be blamed for expecting, at the very least, a pronouncement of cosmic importance.

"Yes?" Annie said expectantly, then she shook her head, her sandy hair—newly cut in an old-fashioned bob—quivering, chagrined that she'd once again bought into Laurel's effervescence. When would she learn? The truth was, Laurel could dazzle with a grocery list. Annie's glance moved to the shelf with classic mysteries and Phoebe Atwood Taylor's *Out of Order,* in which Cape Cod sleuth Asey Mayo struggles with Aunt Eugenia's grocery order. Order . . . Oh Lord, had she ordered enough white wine? Wine wasn't on the menu at Parotti's.

Laurel's throaty murmur rivaled Bacall. "I am agog with delight . . ."

Annie considered the state of being agog. Agogment? Agogged?

". . . and I know you will agree. Here is the question:

What Ohio newspaper publisher became president on his 55th birthday?"

Annie was not agogged. "President of what?"

The pause was brief. Then a kindly sigh. "I see. Well, perhaps I shall continue in my quest although one would think that Warren Harding might immediately come to mind."

Annie was silent.

"But then again, perhaps not." Laurel's tone was forgiving. "We do want our partygoers to feel clever, don't we?" Laurel was brisk. "Ah well, I shall persevere. You may count on me, my dear. I will have a question prepared for each table and midway through the evening, we shall ask the guests to canvass their table, agree on an answer and—a trill of delight—a spokesperson from each table shall come to the microphone and announce the answer and then we shall vote on the best question and answer and the prize—" her voice rang clear as a Sunday morning bell "—will be a drive with Max in the Stutz Bearcat. I've announced it on the website."

"Website?" Annie had a sudden sense of strangling, a not-unfamiliar sensation when dealing with her always unpredictable, madcap mother-in-law. "What website?"

A burst of cheery laughter. "The party website. Of course, everyone is sworn not to reveal its existence to Max. We want his surprise party to be a surprise, don't we? Ta, ta."

The connection ended as Annie gaped at the phone.

Ingrid's lips quivered. "I gather she's been busy."

"Website. Stuzt Bearcat. Oh, good grief!" Annie

leaned across the counter and fumbled for a folder. She spilled out the contents and picked up a computer-generated invitation. Around the border of the thick white cardboard, a tiny couple in Twenties garb danced the Charleston. Foil bright blue letters announced:

MAX DOESN'T HAVE A CLUE
COME ALL FRIENDS TRUE BLUE
CELEBRATE HIS BIRTHDAY
AND DANCE THE CHARLESTON, TOO!
Parotti's Bar & Grill 7 p.m. until ???? Saturday, August 28
Dance the night away in a reprise of the Roaring '20s
Prizes for Best Costume, Best Dancers

Annie flipped over the invitation. On the back was a magnificent picture of Max in, admittedly, a bright yellow Stutz Bearcat. "Ingrid," Annie's tone was close to a wail. "What am I going to do? That car doesn't exist." She'd taken a picture of Max in his new red Jag and transposed him via the magic of a computer into a photograph of a vintage car. "If Laurel's promised the grand winner a ride with Max in a Stutz Bearcat, what am I going to do? I don't have time to deal with this."

Ingrid was kindly but firm. "If she's promised a Stutz Bearcat on the party website . . ."

"Okay, okay, but Stuzt Bearcats don't grow on trees. I'll try to find one, but first," Annie waggled the invitation, "I need to see about the table prizes and make sure everything's all set. Let's see," she reached for a notebook, flipped it open, "the deep-sea fishing trip is a go. Edith Cummings will give a private class at the library in how to search the web." Annie grinned. The island's canny research librarian was quite capable of teaching even a rank beginner how to find out obscure facts, such as the best wildlife viewing season in the Bering Sea (summer), urgent advice to a snake bite victim (remain still) and the four presidents who won the electoral college but not the popular vote (John Quincy Adams, Rutherford B. Hayes, Benjamin Harrison and George W. Bush). "I've ordered a signed Sammy Sosa baseball card from a store in Savannah. It should arrive tomorrow. There are a few things I haven't pinned down." She glanced down the list. Still to be gathered up were a bushel of Vidalia onions and a certificate from the photography studio. Emma Clyde had promised an outing on her yacht. Other confirmed prizes included a spa day, lawn design consultation, a Gullah dictionary, a basket-weaving lesson, a ghost walk in Charleston, a hot air balloon ride, a New Year's Day oyster roast for twenty-five, and an autographed copy of *South Carolina A History* by Dr. Walter Edgar, the Palmetto state's premier historian.

The bell jangled at the front door. The door opened to a chattering horde of middle-aged women. Annie slid her papers back into the folder. Customers took precedence. "I'll man the coffee bar."

Get cozy with

CAROLYN HART's

award-winning DEATH ON DEMAND mysteries

"Nobody does it better than Hart."
Cleveland Plain Dealer

SUGARPLUM DEAD
0-380-80719-X/$6.99 US/$9.99 Can

At the Death on Demand mystery bookstore,
owner Annie Darling's yuletide preparations have to
be put on hold thanks to several rather inconvenient
distractions—including murder, as she has to prove
the innocence of her own deadbeat Dad.

WHITE ELEPHANT DEAD
0-380-79325-3/$6.99 US/$9.99 Can

Annie's dear friend (and best customer) Henny
Brawley stands accused of murdering a Women's Club
volunteer-cum-blackmailer. And only Annie and her
husband Max can prove the hapless Henny innocent.

YANKEE DOODLE DEAD
0-380-79326-1/$6.99 US/$9.99 Can

Annie and Max watch their Fourth of July holiday
explode not only with fun and fireworks, but with
murder as well, as retired Brigadier General Charlton
"Bud" Hatch is shot dead before Annie's eyes.